THE UNFORESEEN

ALSO BY CLAIRE ACKROYD

The Surfacing

THE UNFORESEEN

CLAIRE ACKROYD

This is a work of fiction. Names, characters, organizations, places, events, and incidents are either products of the author's imagination or used fictitiously. Any resemblance to actual persons, living or dead, or actual events is purely coincidental.

Published by Lake Union Publishing, Seattle

www.apub.com

EU Product Safety contact:
Amazon Media EU S.à r.l.
38, avenue John F. Kennedy, L-1855 Luxembourg
amazonpublishing-gpsr@amazon.com

ISBN-13: 9781662525896
eISBN: 9781662525889

Cover design by Will Speed
Cover image: © Sundra © Bowonpat Sakaew © Irina Zdyrko
© Erik Svoboda / Shutterstock

Printed in the United States of America

FRIDAY

LARA

To see the future is a terrible thing. And I should know.

I've been told countless times that I don't possess any foresight, that I'll drive myself mad if I read too much into my dreams. But they're more than just dreams; they come to me so vividly that it's as if I'm living a second life within my sleep, one from which I can only return with a pounding heart and sense of sick inevitability. The scenes I've witnessed hovering at the front of my brain for days, or even weeks – ghost-like and inescapable.

Tomorrow will be Saturday – the start of the family festivities – and the dream-images are more indelible than ever. Mum isn't turning fifty until Wednesday, but she's rented the cottage in the Peak District for a week. 'It's not every day you reach half a century,' she keeps saying, as if a half-century possesses some sort of magic which can make everything okay. But it can't: extinguishing fifty candles won't buy shoes for Poppy's ever-growing feet, nor make the dreams go away. And it certainly won't make our family whole again.

I look at my watch and see it's just gone 9 a.m. Which means it's nearly time for my sister, Hannah, to go to the airport. It's surreal to think of her in Singapore, climbing into a taxi with her luggage while I'm seven hours behind in the UK, at a till in Lewisham, watching a woman peruse toothbrushes. Incongruous that, in an hour or so, Poppy will eat her morning snack at preschool while

Hannah stands in line at Changi Airport. And stranger still that tonight, when I'm lying in bed watching the minutes crawl forward, listening to the rise and fall of Poppy's breath and hoping for undisturbed sleep, Hannah will be flying back in time towards me.

If only we could both travel further. Back to when we were children, sharing a bunk bed and playing make-believe. Back when we ran wild in the garden, climbing trees and finding secret passages through the rhododendron bushes. Before I got sick and underwent all those hours of treatment. Before I had wires in my arms and drugs that made me nauseous, no longer able to play. Before my transplant, and the rift that formed between us. Before Dad's death, and France, and all of it.

A middle-aged man walks up to the counter with two cans of deodorant and a meal deal and for a moment I think it's him, Dad, somehow raised from the dead. But this man has a narrow face, slim shoulders, and no gut to speak of. Plus he's buying a chicken salad sandwich, and Dad never ate salad.

'Do you have any bags?' the man who isn't Dad asks me now.

'They're twenty pence each,' I say, pulling one from under the counter.

'I'll leave it then.' He makes a shooing gesture at the bag, like it's a wasp trying to land on his (still packaged) sandwich.

'Okay.' I return the bag and scan his items. 'That will be £10.29, please.'

'£10.29!' He shakes his head. 'Do you remember when you could get an entire weekly shop for under a tenner?'

'Not really.' I buy as inexpensively as possible – large bags of supermarket own-brand pasta, cheap cuts of chicken, bags of misshapen carrots – but it still hurts my bank balance, every time. Thank goodness Poppy is out of nappies.

He looks at me for a couple of seconds and then laughs. 'No, I don't suppose you do. You're far too young. Still footloose and fancy-free!'

'I wouldn't say that.' I think of the way my breath catches whenever Poppy hurts herself, and how my chest aches when her tiny hand nestles in mine. Of the fear which is so tightly enmeshed in my love for her that I can't tell where one ends and the other begins, or whether they are essentially the same emotion. Whether the cost of loving someone is to fear for their safety.

The man taps his card on the reader and smiles. 'I know what you young people are like. My daughter must be a similar age to you.'

My daughter, my daughter, my daughter. I give him my best customer-service smile as I think of the day Poppy was born: a wrinkled curl of red flesh with gummy eyes and a searching mouth. And of the day I left France, with Poppy strapped to my front and a small rucksack strapped to my back. Like all the straps in the world might stop me from breaking apart. 'Would you like a receipt with that?'

'No thank you.' He balances his deodorants and meal deal in a heap in his arms. 'You have a good day, then.'

'You too.'

If it's true about our emotions – if fear is indeed yin to love's yang – then I must still care deeply for my sister, despite everything. Because recently, instead of having my usual dreams where I'm buried alive, I've been dreaming about Hannah. I've seen her with veined, bulging eyes, her face like a grotesque Halloween mask. I've seen her falling backwards, her body limp and unresisting. I've seen her running frantically, as if fleeing something monstrous.

But last night's dream was the most terrifying of all. Hannah was lying on a slab of stone, limbs flung wide and eyes blank. The light around her strangely orange, casting an amber glow across her cheeks. She was wearing jeans and a white shirt, the latter unbuttoned at the neck.

And she was drenched in blood.

HANNAH

Returning to Colder Climes

So this is it: I'm finally going back to the UK! As regular readers of this blog know, I've been away for several months, first travelling in Southeast Asia and now teaching in Singapore. It's been such an amazing experience, but I'm excited to return, even if it's only a flying visit. It will be great to catch up with my family again, plus we get to celebrate all week (hello champagne), because my mum is turning fifty.

I'm writing this quickly from the airport, before heading to my gate. Everything feels rushed today: I did most of my packing last night, but there were still some bits I had to add this morning, including my **Mellow Morning Mist** (a gentle spray which helps revive my skin when it's looking grey and tired) and my **Eyetrix Concealer** (soooo good at covering up dark undereye circles). I used **Linton's vacuum-pack**

bags and **Cool Dean's packing cubes** to help fit everything in my case and keep it organised.

My OH, Chris, treated me to an amazing breakfast of poached eggs with smoked salmon, plus some thick Greek yogurt with granola and blueberries, coffee and freshly squeezed orange juice. It was super tasty . . . I'm really going to miss Chris while I'm away, and not just because of his five-star breakfasts! We're going to stay in touch using the **Connect app** (99p for the first month, then £10 for a year's subscription), which has a neat premise: once a day, without warning (although you can set some time constraints – useful when on different sides of the globe!) the app alerts you to photograph whatever you're doing at that precise moment (one photo from your phone's front camera, and one from its rear). And then you get just TWO minutes to take and share your photos, so no time for staging or filters! Which sounds great fun, if a little scary (I don't think Chris has ever seen me without mascara – ha ha). Plus the set-up is clever, in that you don't get to see the other person's photos unless you share yours. Anyway, I'll let you know how it goes. I might even post some of my photos on here, but only if they're not too terrible . . .

My advanced students were really sweet today, asking me about my week away. Their English is so good that I sometimes wonder if they actually need lessons, but they claim they're useful. I guess English is a hard language to learn; it's only since starting teaching that I've realised how many weird quirks it has. Like why, when we talk about 'going over' someone's work, do we mean to review it, not walk over it? And why do we have so many different pronunciations for the letters 'ough'?

Anyway, I doubt you're reading this for an English lesson (!), so let me tell you a bit more about my trip. We're going to be staying in **Grove Cottage**: a pretty-looking three-bedroom bungalow in the Peak District, which sits just below **Curbar Edge**. For those who don't know, the Peak District was the first national park to be established in the UK, and is an area of outstanding natural beauty, with many long, rocky ridges (known locally as 'edges'). Curbar Edge, Froggatt Edge and Baslow Edge run across the national park for about four miles in total, with gorgeous views out across the surrounding countryside. It's a special place for us as a family because we used to go there every summer when I was a child. I remember lots of long walks, when the only way my parents could keep my little legs going was by bribing me with chocolate (now I'm an adult, I'm planning to keep my energy levels up by eating protein-rich **Goodness bars** instead). I can't wait to see the Peak District in the middle of autumn; after my trip to New England a couple of years ago (see **here** for a write-up of that trip, along with some suggested New England itineraries), I've become a fan of leaf peeping, and I think the Peak District will be perfect for some autumn walks. So long as we don't have too much rain!

It's going to be a full house: as well as me, my mum, my sister and my gorgeous niece, Mum's oldest friend is coming to stay, along with her son and his girlfriend. On Mum's birthday, we're all going out for a fancy meal at **The Shot**, which sounds incredible: they specialise in game (think venison, rabbit and pheasant, not Monopoly) which is sourced within a 30-mile radius, so full marks on the sustainability front. Plus they have a super-cute children's menu, with a signature dish called 'Sweeter Rabbit', where you get rabbit, sweet potato fries, and veg in the shape of a rabbit's face. Sounds amazing – I will have to order it even if my niece doesn't!

I was hoping to have time to look round Singapore airport before my flight, but sadly I've left it too late. It's regularly voted as the best airport in the world – it has a giant waterfall which cascades from the ceiling, a butterfly garden and a tropical vivarium. Plus a four-storey slide (!) and every shop and eatery a person could ever want. I'll have to make sure to look round it very soon – perhaps on my return to Singapore next weekend? Although that depends on how jet-lagged I'm feeling . . .

Anyway, that's it for now – thanks for reading, and see you on the other side!

I upload the post and sit back, nibbling at my nails before remembering I'm trying to keep them nice. I'm checked in for my flight and up to date with my blog, so there's nothing more to do. For now, anyway. I try to post at least once a day, twice if possible, and also keep a close eye on my analytics: the visits and bounce rate; the page views and time spent on each page. I'm being even more diligent than usual at the moment because – *stop nibbling!* – I've received some interest in my blog from a women's magazine. They're reviewing it with a mind to possibly taking me on as a regular columnist, which gets me all quivery with excitement every time I think about it. A potential breakthrough at last! Although I try not to think about it too often, in case it makes my posts seem forced. 'Authentic, relatable lifestyles is what we're after,' the editor has told me. 'Travel and relationships, food and activities, aimed at today's modern woman.'

The Peak District should offer a lot on this front. Beautiful photographs of the countryside, plus recommendations on things to do and places to see. I've already got our meal at The Shot lined up, as well as a 'tart crawl', which will involve visiting nine bakeries/coffee shops in Bakewell, to sample different versions of the town's famous tart. But I'll need to balance out my foodie content with some more active pursuits: walks to famous or undiscovered beauty spots, a trip to one of the underground caverns, cycling along the Peak District's scenic trails. I have fond memories of riding the Monsal Trail when we were young, Lara pedalling furiously on her little red bike while I sat on the back of Dad's large blue one, loving the feel of the wind in my hair and the sight of my sister beside me. Sometimes I made my best bug face at her – eyes crossed, cheeks bulging – until she started to laugh and wobble.

Jackie and her son Max are an integral part of these memories too. Jackie has been Mum's best friend since forever – we lived near them, growing up, and took many joint holidays to the Peak District. But while Mum and Jackie would cycle slowly along the trails, chatting and stopping to look at interesting flowers, Dad and us three children – me, Lara and Max – wanted to cover as much ground as possible. Max used to try to look cool by taking his hands off the handlebars, but never for long; he was always more of a people-pleaser than a rebel. Grinning, with shining eyes and dimpled cheeks; brushing his hair from his eyes and explaining that he didn't have enough gears on his bike to go as fast as the rest of us. A fact I reminded him of many years later, at a sixth-former's house party, making him laugh. The two of us were pressed close on a kitchen bench, close enough that I could see the pale tips of his eyelashes; close enough that if I'd leaned over I could have brushed my lips against his neck. Close enough that the night was full of promise until Lara rang and he went elsewhere.

My phone beeps from inside my handbag; surely it can't be the Connect app already? More likely it's Chris himself, telling me I've left something behind. Reaching into my bag, I mentally run through the scene in my bedroom this morning: the clothes on the bed, the shoes on the floor, the toiletries on the sideboard. Chris said it looked like I was going away for year, not a week, but I managed to get everything in my case (with only a little help) and don't think I forgot anything.

But it's neither Chris nor the app. It's my sister. Which must be a mistake, because I initiate every single conversation we have. She's only rung me once over the last five years, and even that was an accidental pocket dial. I answer tentatively. 'Hello?'

'Hannah!'

'Hi. Is everything all right?'

'Yes,' she says. 'I mean, not really. Sort of.'

'What's happened?'

There's a long pause, and my pulse accelerates. 'You're scaring me,' I say. 'Is it Poppy? Has something happened to her?'

'No, Poppy's fine.'

'Thank God.'

'She's at preschool today.'

'Right.' I wait for my sister to say something more, and prompt her again when she doesn't. 'So, what's happened?'

'I . . . it's . . . it sounds silly but . . . I've been dreaming about you. And . . . I'm worried.'

Any fear I had instantly turns to frustration – my sister clearly shouldn't have lowered her medication. She's only recently managed to reduce her nightmares and panic attacks, to get herself on an even keel; so it's insane that she's throwing it all up in the air again by cutting back on the pills. And for what? For some vague notion that she needs to *feel more* in life?

'You don't need to worry about me,' I say, trying to keep the frustration out of my voice.

'But the dreams seem so real,' she replies. 'I'm sure they're telling me something.'

They're telling you to up your dose, I want to say, but manage to hold my tongue. Mum has stressed the importance of 'being there' for Lara this week, 'Because if she's ever going to wean herself off the meds, a week with her family is the best time to do it. We can look after Poppy and take your sister on long, vigorous walks; make her nutritious, filling meals. Do everything we can to support her.'

That's all we've ever bloody done, I wanted to say, but held my tongue then too. I didn't think Mum would appreciate my bitter tone and, if I'm honest, it isn't strictly true. I failed Lara horribly, and everyone knows it.

'You can't see the future,' I reassure my sister now.

'I know you don't think so,' she replies, her words tumbling out in a rush. 'But I feel there's a reason I'm having these dreams.'

'It's because of your past.' I do my best to inject sympathy into my voice. 'The leukaemia and the transplant. Dad's death.' *And whatever happened in France after. Whatever led you to disappear, break all contact for months, and reappear with a baby.* But I don't say this last bit. I'm getting good at not saying things.

'It's just . . . what if there's an important reason the dreams are coming to me now?'

'I'm at the airport,' I say, changing the subject. 'So I should probably go if I want to make it to Mum's celebrations on time.'

'But that's what I mean. The timing, what with Mum's celebrations and everything . . .'

There's a familiar feeling of deflation: a slow, inevitable puncture at the base of my lungs. 'Mum's been looking forward to this for weeks. Months, even.' It's not an exaggeration – Mum has been making packing lists and researching possible days out since June at least. I know this because she sent me a spreadsheet with colour-coded activities according to their suitability for different weathers. And another in which she'd planned our meals for the week, which had to be entirely revised a month ago when Max's girlfriend, Cassie, stopped eating gluten.

'I know,' says Lara. 'But even so. I do wonder.'

'What?'

'If you should come.'

For God's sake. I get up from my chair and walk towards the departures board, wondering why my sister always has to make things so difficult. Why there always has to be drama when she's involved. And why, when things aren't easy, she can't just get on with them regardless, like the rest of us. If I had it my way, Max wouldn't be coming to the cottage at all, but it's Mum's special week, not mine, so I'm just going to suck it up; pretend I never had a teenage crush on him, and that he never had a crush on Lara. (Not that 'crush' is an adequate word, in either case, but the point still stands.) 'I have to go,' I say again. 'It's not long until my flight.'

'No!'

'What do you mean, "no"?'

'It's just . . .' There's panic in her voice now. 'I saw you on a *rock*. You were injured. And the Peak District is full of rocks.'

'Well, I promise to be very careful around rocks.' My gate number has been posted. Number nine, nearly a twenty-minute walk away.

'You were covered in blood!'

'Lara—'

'You could stay in Singapore,' she says. 'Stay where it's safe. It's such a long way for you to come that everyone would understand if you couldn't make it.'

'I've already bought my ticket. I'm at the *airport*—'

'I know, but I'm worried—'

'You don't need to worry.' I can hear the annoyance in my own voice and try to dial it back, like that family therapist taught us years ago. *When talking to an anxious person, always speak calmly and without judgement.* Although she also told us to validate their feelings, and that's a step too far. 'Look, it's been nice speaking to you, but I do actually have to go.'

There's a long pause, during which I can feel her tightly coiled presence on the other end of the line. 'Lara?'

Nothing.

'Lara?' I say again.

'Yes.' Her voice has become clipped, abrupt. 'You have to go. I get it.'

'But I'm really looking forward to seeing you and Poppy.'

She doesn't reply.

'Okay then,' I say, shrugging my shoulders even though she can't see. 'Take care.'

When she still doesn't reply, I hang up. Walking towards my gate, I feel a knot of annoyance pulling tight.

And, alongside the knot, a niggling sensation I recognise as apprehension. Not because I give any credence to my sister's far-fetched theories.

But because she does.

SATURDAY

LARA

As I drive, I can't help but reflect on my many failures. Even with a nursery rhyme playing at high volume, even with Poppy asking about snacks, my worst mistakes push their way to the front of my brain and sit there, stubborn and unyielding, forcing me to examine their ugly outlines while changing lanes on the M1.

First: the way I refused to spend any time with Mum and Hannah after Dad died. It seems unforgivable now but, back then, I couldn't bear the idea of another second in the family home, surrounded by Dad's possessions and drowning in Mum's grief. I'd spent most of my childhood smothered by her protectiveness and needed to escape, to get away and live. To live: ha! I had no idea then that living isn't about big, showy activities – travelling the globe and racing down mountains – but is actually about the small everyday things that most people take for granted. The freedom to make decisions independently. To not exist under a shadow or, worse, *as* a shadow. To raise a child on your own terms.

Which brings me on to my second failure: accidentally getting pregnant. A failure which requires no self-interrogation, just self-flagellation. Stupid, stupid, stupid. Contraception exists for a reason, and it isn't to sit in a bedside drawer while insemination takes place in the snow outside.

Third: the man I accidentally became pregnant by. I don't want to dwell on that one.

Fourth: my inability to be a good sister. Because I'm worried some terrible fate will befall Hannah in the Peak District, but I've failed to convince *her*. And now she's on her way to the UK, and there's nothing I can do about it.

'Mummy, my tummy feels bad.'

I glance in the rear-view mirror and see Poppy's face is paler than usual.

'I'm sorry, sweetheart.' My voice sounds wooden, like I haven't used it in years. 'Do you think you're going to be sick?'

'I don't know.'

Looking at her again, I wonder whether we should stop at the services, get her a drink. Or whether we should stop altogether – turn around and head home. Because something about this trip feels seriously off.

Except my doctor warned me that I might experience ups and downs as I reduced my medication. That I should allow time for my body to regulate; to adjust to its new normal. And it's not as if my dreams have ever meant anything concrete in the past. Perhaps Hannah is right that this new anxiety is just old trauma resurfacing. And, if so, perhaps that's even a good thing. Because if I want to live – to *truly* live – at some point I need to stop shoving difficult memories and feelings aside.

And face them.

HANNAH

As I slow the hire car to a stop, I'm surprised that Grove Cottage looks smaller than it did on the website: a compact bungalow built of light grey stone, with casement windows and ivy creeping up one side. But the views are much the same; it's set back at the end of a long drive surrounded by golden-brown trees, with the cliffs of Curbar Edge rising behind. Climbing out of the car to gather my belongings, the front door opens and Mum appears, arms wide for a hug. Ever since Dad died, I can't get over how much older she looks: her hair is white and wispy, her face deeply lined. Almost as if he brushed her with Death on his way out.

'Hannah! So good to see you!'

'You too.' As we hug one another, I bury my face into her shoulder and breathe in her sweet jasmine scent. A smell which hasn't changed over the years, and which takes me back to earlier, happier times. As I inhale again, she starts telling me about the house: how the main reception room is beautiful, but the sofa bed isn't yet made up. 'There's bedding in the cupboard, but I'm afraid we're going to have to clear away the bed each day – I hope you don't mind?'

'That's fine,' I say, drawing back at last.

'I'm sorry you haven't got your own room,' she goes on. 'But I couldn't very well make Max and Cassie sleep on the sofa bed, or your sister and Poppy . . .'

'It's fine,' I say again. 'Honestly.'

'Well, if you're sure? Some of the others are already here, by the way. They're just freshening up; Max and Cassie beat you by about half an hour. I'm so pleased the cottage owners let us have an early check-in. Cup of tea?'

'That sounds amazing. The one I had at the services earlier was awful.' I was so jet-lagged on the drive up that I stopped twice, first for coffee, and then for tea. After being presented with a cup of grey, grainy liquid, I regretted not having bought coffee again.

'It always is.' She leads me inside, explaining how the food order is coming in a few hours, but the house owners left a welcome pack with teabags, milk and cake. 'All the essentials! Although the cake isn't gluten-free, so poor Cassie can't have any.' We take off our shoes and walk down a carpeted corridor into a vast open-plan room. The view through the windows is spectacular: a garden full of crimson and russet trees backs on to a hillside of wild, golden bracken, which heads up steeply to the foot of a long escarpment of rock. Climbers are just visible, spots of brightness against the dark stone. Above them, clouds scud through a sullen grey sky.

As I'm taking in the spectacle, there's a commotion behind me and I turn to see Jackie rushing into the room, her full figure swathed in a silky gold-and-cream-striped kaftan. 'I thought I heard you!' I receive my second hug in as many minutes, enveloped in a cloud of heady perfume. 'How is our Singapore nomad?'

'Very well, thanks. How are you?'

She holds me out at arm's length. 'Yes, you look it. Your skin is dewy—'

'I think that might be plane scum—'

'Nonsense.' She goes on to tell me that humid climates are good for some complexions and to ask Mum whether she's ever used retinol, and then the two of them are lost in one of their incomprehensible exchanges: something about a girl who had bad acne and used to put toothpaste on her spots. They've known each other for so many years – first meeting at school, and subsequently spending most of their lives living near each other, or at least talking every other day – that they've developed their own conversational shorthand. Certainly, they don't bother with anything as mundane as context, instead launching straight from the girl with spots to something about a golden retriever, and then on to a time when our tent collapsed on an ill-fated trip to the seaside, and the anti-whaling protest they attended in their twenties.

I'm saved by the arrival of Max and Cassie. Although 'saved' isn't quite the right word, as the sight of Max makes my stomach contract. A sensation I hoped I'd left in the past: it seems so *teenage* to be experiencing butterflies again. I'm twenty-four, for God's sake, with a proper job and a boyfriend and a not entirely unsuccessful online presence.

'Hannah.' He kisses me on both cheeks and I'm acutely aware of the fact I haven't showered since flying halfway across the world.

'Good to see you,' I say, keeping my tone light and trying to block out the background chatter from Mum and Jackie to focus upon him. His boyish good looks have morphed seamlessly into a handsome older form. Slight lines around his eyes give him a knowing, sexy expression, while a shadow of stubble brings definition to his jaw.

'You too. It's been too long! And this is Cassie.' He gestures to his girlfriend, who is standing beside us with one hand upon his shoulder. She's more attractive than I'd prefer: all long, glossy hair and long, glossy legs, the latter shown off by a short skater skirt. Her make-up is impeccable too: a touch of eyeliner, a slick of lip gloss. In fact, she looks even better than she did when I drunkenly snooped her social media profiles – which is rare, and infuriating.

'Lovely to meet you,' I say.

'You too.' She smiles, and I'm relieved to see her teeth are crooked at the bottom. 'How was your journey?'

We engage in small talk until Mum brings over a cup of tea. And then there's gentle chaos as she offers everyone else drinks, Max accompanies her into the kitchen to try to figure out the coffee machine, and Jackie leads me to a sofa. I collapse into its cushions, cup hot and soothing between my hands, while Jackie and Cassie sit on the sofa opposite.

The room we're in is L-shaped, with the living area leading into the dining area, and the kitchen round the corner. The decor is stylish, which will be good for my blog: there are two sleek sofas and a couple of armchairs, plus a large copper floor lamp and a floor-to-ceiling bookshelf with books arranged by colour. The dining area is dominated by a heavy-looking stone table surrounded by mismatched designer chairs. The kitchen, meanwhile, is shiny, with marbled worktops and cream cabinets.

Jackie has started telling Cassie about the time Max and I performed naked handstands on the lawn, after covering ourselves in face paint. She's laughing uproariously while Cassie smiles politely, making little noises of acknowledgement. I wonder how many of these stories she's had to sit through since she and Max got together, because there's certainly no shortage of them, nor of Jackie's desire to relay them. Growing up, we lived in the same street, which meant the three of us – Lara, Max and me – spent hours together before Lara's illness: playing board games, making dens; all that old-fashioned stuff. An idyllic-sounding childhood, if you ignore the fact Jackie and her husband argued constantly and viciously, to the point where Max came over to ours primarily to get away from them. In the early years, at least; later, when Jackie was divorced and their home more peaceful, he kept coming, perhaps out of habit, or just because he liked our company. He was bang in the middle of me and Lara, age-wise, and always trying to impress her: jumping off our garden shed to show how daring he was, and once eating a woodlouse because she bet him he wouldn't. Yet with me he seemed a lot more relaxed, able to let loose and have fun. When the two of us were alone, we drew silly faces in chalk on the patio, or dressed up as knights and chased each other around the garden on pretend horses.

And, yes, did naked handstands.

'Do you remember that, Hannah?' Jackie asks me now. 'How you decided to cover your entire bodies in face paint?'

'I do.' I nod. 'We wanted to be tigers, only we didn't have any orange paint, or black, so we—'

'Used yellow and green instead! Like cobs of sweetcorn!' Jackie is laughing so much she's almost crying.

'I should point out that we were about four years old at the time.' I address this to Cassie, who is still smiling politely.

'Max had just started school,' Jackie says. 'I remember because I couldn't get all the face paint off, and had to apologise to his teacher. I did try though, for *hours*, with everything I could get my hands on. Baby lotion, olive oil, a scrubbing brush: you name it!'

'Sounds painful,' says Cassie.

'Not this again, Mum.' Max has appeared with a cup of coffee, which he hands to Cassie. 'No one wants to hear about me covering myself in face paint.' His voice is chiding but gentle, and I try not to notice how his shirtsleeves have been rolled up above his elbows, revealing his forearms. Strong forearms, which seem to belong to an entirely different person to the one who played with me in the garden all those years ago.

'But they *do* want to hear about the naked handstands,' I say, before blushing and wishing I'd kept quiet.

Max laughs. 'Of course. Who wouldn't?'

Your girlfriend, I think, as I look at Cassie again. She is sitting forward at the edge of the sofa, legs crossed at the ankles, lips pursed as she sips her coffee. 'How did you two meet?' I ask, to change the subject, even though I already know because Mum likes to keep me up to date on everything relating to Jackie.

'At work,' says Max, at the exact same moment Cassie says, 'Through Le Petit Jardin.' Her French accent is very breathy.

'Le Petit Jardin's the restaurant we work at,' Max clarifies, unnecessarily. He nods at Cassie. 'Go on: you tell.'

There is nothing much to tell (as far as I can tell): she works front of house at the restaurant and he joined as a chef, and that's it. But Cassie starts talking in detail about their early moments together: the celeriac soup Max made at the restaurant that first night, which was too salty; the uncomfortable shoes she was wearing; the cat they adopted together after just a few weeks. She is animated as she talks, waving one manicured hand about and nodding at Max who smiles back. He's one of those people who has always enjoyed being part of a couple; who, since the age of fifteen, has gone straight from one relationship to another with barely a fallow period. I like to think this means the women in question aren't particularly special to him.

Except he's been with Cassie for nearly two years. Longer than any of the others. I watch him watching her, and try to see if there's anything different in his gaze. Whether he looks at her the way he used to look at Lara, back when we were teenagers: his eyes focused with a deep intensity, lips pressed together almost in pain. But, right now, his face seems neutral, relaxed. 'What's it like working together?' I say, to keep the conversation going.

'People always ask that.' Cassie puts her coffee down on the glass table. 'I think they think it must be a nightmare – to work with your other half in a restaurant.'

'And is it?'

Max laughs, saying, 'No!' as Cassie says, 'No, not at all. It's very convenient, because it means I know where Max is at all times.'

Now I laugh, assuming it's a joke, before realising Cassie is raising her eyebrows, and perhaps isn't the sort of person who would joke about acting like a stalker. Who perhaps isn't the sort of person who would make a joke at all.

But then, if she isn't joking, isn't what she said kind of creepy?

'How about you, Hannah?' Jackie asks.

'How about me what?'

'I hear you have a boyfriend these days.'

I'm not keen on the way she says 'these days', as if there's something unusual about my having a partner, but at least Max gets to hear that I'm coupled up. That someone wants me. 'Yes. Chris.'

'And he does something exciting, doesn't he?'

'He's a photojournalist.'

'Is a photojournalist the same as a regular journalist?' Cassie asks, at the same time as Max asks, 'Who for?' I wonder if the two of them make a habit of talking over one another. As I explain that he's freelance, Mum and Jackie start talking about the surprise spa trip they've planned for Lara later in the week, before re-joining our conversation on photojournalism and diverting it to the time a boy in their sixth form took photos down his trousers. Soon they're laughing so hard I can barely make out what they're saying. Max remains standing, jiggling one foot as if he's got too much energy, while Cassie stares at her coffee cup, or maybe at her hands, which are wrapped around it. She has pretty nails: long and shapely, painted pearly white. Definitely front-of-house nails. After a while she looks up, and Max catches her eye, like it's some kind of signal, and the two of them leave the room, saying they've more unpacking to do, which I hope is not a euphemism.

I get up too, because I'm going to fall asleep if I stay on the sofa. As I head back into the hallway, I hear the crunch of gravel. Another car is pulling into the drive. Opening the door, I stand on the front step, watching as the car comes to a halt under the awning of a horse chestnut tree. As the driver's door opens, a woman steps out and spins round on the spot, all pale skin and long, slender limbs. Delicate features and dark, feathered hair. An anxious, fragile beauty.

My sister has arrived.

LARA

We've finally made it, after several hours of driving and lots of complaining from Poppy, and initial impressions of the cottage are better than I expected. It's secluded enough that people can't peer in, but close enough to other houses that we won't be entirely isolated. On the downside, all its windows are at ground level and the rear of the property is more exposed than I'd prefer, backing straight on to open land – although my mind is eased by the nature of the terrain, the fact it rises so steeply behind the house and is swathed in deep bracken, both difficult and noisy to walk through.

There are already four cars parked in the driveway, which seems too many for seven guests. The first person I see is Hannah, standing on the front step, her dark blonde hair in a plait across one shoulder. She doesn't look happy to see me; just calls my name and stays where she is, biting at her nails. Mum and Jackie appear behind her. When I release Poppy from her car seat, her car sickness is instantly forgotten and she races across the gravel. 'Granny!'

Mum lifts Poppy off the ground, hugs her close. Next Jackie swoops in, encircling my daughter's body in a tight embrace. And then it's my sister's turn – all three women squealing with delight and affection at the small girl in their midst. I open the boot and start removing our bags. I can carry most of them at once if I get the configuration right: large rucksack on my back, small rucksack on my front, suitcase and kit bag in either hand. I'm just getting myself organised when I hear Mum calling. 'Hello! Let me help with those!' Moving away from the car with bags in position, I see her walking towards me, waving wildly as if I might not have noticed she's there.

'Hi Mum.'

'Lara!' She tries to hug me, but my luggage is in the way and we awkwardly bump each other. 'It's so good to see you! Let me take one of those bags.'

I try to explain that I don't need any help, but she insists, and I'm struck by the familiar, unpleasant sensation of not having enough space when she's around. Of barely being able to breathe. But I force myself to relax and hand the kit bag over. Because I'm beginning to understand that all those past restrictions she placed on me – the not going out, the home schooling, the constant monitoring – came from a place of love. From the fierce, almost feral protectiveness that a mother has for her child.

And God knows, I've learned this the hard way.

'I'll take it.' This comes from Hannah, who has appeared alongside us. Singapore clearly suits her: she has colour in her cheeks and a light smattering of freckles across her nose. She leans over to give me a quick kiss while simultaneously lifting the kit bag from Mum and taking the small rucksack from my front. 'Is everything okay?'

'Everything's fine.'

'It's just . . . your call . . . when I was at the airport . . .'

'What call?' Mum sounds worried.

'Everything's *fine*,' I repeat. I'd rather she didn't know about my recent nightmares. 'We're all here, and . . .' I trail off.

'Yes,' Mum agrees. 'Isn't it wonderful? That we're all here together. Apart from your dad, of course, but I like to think he's with us in spirit.'

I breathe in deeply. I still find it difficult to think about Dad, not just because I miss him (that dull ache has never eased, no matter how much time has passed) but because of what came next. Disappearing off to a ski resort in France mere days after his funeral; trying to outrun the pain by hurtling down mountains and drinking myself into oblivion. So desperate to escape my grief that I didn't stop to consider what might replace it.

'Conklas, Mummy!' shouts Poppy suddenly, running off to the side of the drive.

'What? Oh, con*kers*,' I correct her, as she crouches beneath a horse chestnut tree, picking through its offerings. I must remember the positives of being here. Mum is thrilled we've come, and Poppy will have much more space than usual; she'll be able to burn off her energy breathing in fresh air, not fumes, and climbing trees and rocks instead of rusting playground equipment. I sometimes wonder if she ever remembers living in the Alps, the jagged peaks shining white against an impossibly blue sky. The air so cold it scoured our lungs and reddened our cheeks.

But of course she won't remember; she was still a baby when we left. An entirely different person. I watch as she attempts to pile several conkers in her hands, drops them, and tries again. Mum moves to help her but I ask her to stay back, let Poppy do it herself. I want my daughter to grow up to be resilient and resourceful. Confident in her own abilities.

All the things I wasn't.

Jackie gives me a huge hug hello and we stand together, watching, as Poppy returns triumphantly, holding four conkers. 'Would you like a conkla, Granny?' she asks.

'Con*ker*,' I say, as Mum replies, 'Yes please,' and takes one. 'Ooh, this is lovely. Very brown and shiny. Thank you so much.'

'You're welcome, Granny. Would you like one, Mummy?'

'Maybe later – I'm carrying a suitcase right now.'

'I can carry it,' Mum offers.

'I'm *fine*,' I say, moving away from her. 'Really.'

'Okay.' She stands back, eyes downcast, and I feel immediately guilty.

'Perhaps you could show us where we'll be sleeping?'

'Yes.' She perks up again, holding her conker aloft as she walks ahead of us. 'Come on, Popsicle!'

We follow her into a dimly lit hallway and I can't help inspecting the security set-up. There's a lock box with a code by the front door – not ideal, as it relies on everyone remembering to scramble the numbers – but at least there's a door chain which can be pulled across from inside. 'You'll be in the master suite,' Mum explains.

'Surely you and Jackie should take that?'

'No, we want you to have it. It's the only room with a bath, so you'll need it for Poppy. And it's furthest from the living room, so you'll have more peace and quiet.'

I open my mouth to protest, before thinking better of it. This is Mum's special week, and if this is the bedroom arrangement she wants, I'm not going to argue.

'What's in here?' Poppy pushes open one of the doors we're passing, to reveal twin beds, set up against a pale purple wall, and a large window looking out to Curbar Edge beyond.

'That's where I'm sleeping, along with your Auntie Jackie,' says Mum.

'Is Auntie Jackie actually my auntie?'

'No,' Mum explains. 'But the word "auntie" can be used as a term of endearment.'

'What does end-e-ment mean?'

'Endearment.' As another explanation unfolds, Poppy pushes open the next door along, only for us to be confronted by Cassie holding a bundle of clothes, and Max, topless, just behind her. I mumble an apology while shutting the door.

Seconds later, it reopens and Max comes out, now wearing a shirt. 'Lara,' he says, kissing my cheek. 'Great to see you!'

'You too.' And I'm not just saying it to be polite. Being around Max always makes me feel calmer – safe without being stifled. Because all my life he's been there for me, in the best possible way. 'I'm so glad you're here this week.'

His face flushes. 'Me too.'

'How are you?'

'Well, thanks.' His voice is a little stilted. 'How about you? Poppy!' He reaches to give her a hug but she darts past him down the corridor.

'Sorry. She's a little overexcited.'

'No worries. Here, let me take your case.'

My arm feels light when released from its burden, and my head starts feeling light too, voices whirling around me. Poppy's high-pitched chirruping and now another voice, Home Counties plummy, saying how lovely it is to see me again. Cassie. As I walk to the room at the far end of the corridor, there's more small talk: yes, it's great to see her again too; no, our journey here wasn't bad; yes, she's still working at the restaurant.

And then we enter the master bedroom and all talk turns to its size, and the furnishings. It's an enormous space, bigger than the other two bedrooms put together, with a ludicrously large bed festooned with pillows and a quilted bedspread, and a smaller bed to one side. There's also a bank of fitted wardrobes, a wall-mounted TV above a chest of drawers, an en-suite bathroom, and a vast window looking out to Curbar Edge, framed by thick, floor-length navy curtains. After some admiring of the view, the others leave us to settle in, Mum shouting something about the kettle as she goes.

And then it's just me and Poppy, alone in the giant room. Poppy runs back and forth, screeching with excitement, before throwing herself on to the bed and messing up the quilt. I head to the window and look out at the cliffs, which seem ominously sheer from this angle, rearing up into the grey sky. And ominously dark too: the exact same colour as the slab of stone in my dreams about Hannah. My heart starts pounding. Is it possible that something terrible is going to happen right here? That my sister is going to fall from the very cliffs I can see from my bedroom window?

Poppy lets out a squeal, and I realise I'm being ridiculous. 'There's a staircase!'

'What?' She's playing with the curtains and I come to stand beside her, assuming this is some game, or reference to the cliffs outside, but no, there is actually a staircase, hidden behind the right-hand curtain. A spiral staircase, with wooden steps and a curved metal banister. Poppy scrambles up, using both hands and feet, and I follow behind, warning her to be careful. But she is too excited to slow down and, upon reaching the top, lets out another squeal. 'It's a secret den!'

I wouldn't agree with her assessment – I'd say it's a dusty attic, not a den, with limited head height where the roof slopes down – but I understand what she means. It has an untouched, hidden quality to it, like no one's been here for years. The furniture is sparse and old-fashioned: there's a small wooden dresser, a narrow wooden desk with a hard-backed chair, and a bookshelf filled with yellowing children's books. Books written in the forties and fifties, about ballet and boarding school; a far cry from the colourful rhyming books Poppy likes to read. Light comes from a small round window above the desk, and there's an old lamp in one corner, although it's not plugged in; its cord trails to one side, blue and dusty. And there's a different smell up here: one of warm wood and decay, instead of the clean, floral smell elsewhere in the house.

'Can I bring my toys up?'

'Maybe in a bit.' I undertake a quick risk assessment, hating myself for it: solid flooring (albeit wooden, which means possible splinters), low ceiling (not an issue for Poppy) and steep stairs (definitely the most dangerous aspect). 'Did we bring your slippers?'

'The ones with the flamingos?' She pronounces it 'flammy-goes'.

'Flam-*in*-gos. Yes. You don't have any others, do you?'

'No.' She trails a finger through the dust on the table, and there's an unwelcome twisting in my gut. Perhaps it's just because the ceiling is so low, and the window so small. 'Let's go and find Granny,' I say.

She's reluctant at first, but I coax her to the staircase with the promise of a snack.

'Can I come back here after?' she asks, as I hurry her along.

'Maybe in a bit.' My voice sounds higher than usual, and I make an effort to lower it as we descend the steps. 'After we've unpacked. Make sure you look where you're going.'

We wander back through the house to find Mum pouring tea in a vast open-plan room, and something about the place pulls me up short again. As with the attic, it's fine from a practical perspective – Mum's already Poppy-proofed the dining table with an oilcloth and corner guards, and has fitted protectors in the plug sockets, so there's nothing obviously dangerous – but the aura of the place is off. And this time it's definitely nothing to do with low ceilings; the proportions of the room are absurdly generous.

'Lara? Are you okay?' Mum pulls out a chair for me and it's not a moment too soon, because my vision is narrowing and I think I might faint. I sit, hunched over, head almost touching the floor until the dizziness passes and my full sight returns. Then, slowly, I sit up, see the concerned faces around me. Mum is hovering by my shoulder, and Jackie is just beyond her, fetching a glass of water. Cassie is with Hannah and Poppy by the window, while Max is a couple of feet away, staring in my direction, unblinking.

And a horrible certainty washes over me. Grove Cottage might be set in a beautiful location. But something terrible is going to happen here.

HANNAH

My sister is already creating drama. A few moments ago, she was gasping and flailing like a fish exposed to air, but now she's sitting up again, breathing entirely normally, looking round the room and telling everyone not to worry. *It's a bit bloody late for that*, I want to say, as Mum stares at her with wide, terrified eyes, and Jackie scurries to the kitchen to fetch water and cake. Worst of all, Max runs to her side, gazing at her with an exquisite concern and tenderness as he asks if he can do anything to help.

'No, thank you,' my sister says, and then she starts to apologise for the disturbance, but in a profuse, exaggerated manner which keeps her right at the centre of proceedings, with everyone insisting she has no reason to be sorry; that they just hope she's all right. She says she was feeling a little faint, which prompts a raft of suggested remedies: Jackie insists she eat some cake, in case her blood sugar is low, while Mum wonders if she'd benefit from a nap. And I want to be sympathetic but the fact remains I've just travelled halfway across the world and nobody's worrying about how tired I am, or fetching me cake, or watching me with concerned tenderness. And, moreover, even if I wanted a nap, I couldn't have one, because my bed is still in sofa form, surrounded by people fussing over my sister.

Plus ça bloody *change*.

It's not that I don't care about Lara; I just find her presence exhausting. When she's around, everything is always so complicated and fraught with emotion. Everyone treading on eggshells in case they upset her, or worsen her mental state. Everyone willing to forgive the way she ran off after Dad's death, leaving me alone with Mum and forcing me to postpone my place at university. And everyone so grateful to accept her back a year later, despite her disappearing act and the baby she reappeared with; so quick to accept that she was no longer in touch with Poppy's father, and didn't want to discuss the reasons why.

And the most galling thing? Mum said it was Poppy who got her through the worst of those dark times; that the presence of a new, and unexpected, granddaughter after her husband's death felt like some sort of benediction, like the circle of life writ large. Like maybe he was looking down on us and trying to make our lives better. Whereas I know for a fact that if I'd been the one who had broken contact and then turned up with a baby, there would have been no benediction about it – simply hell to pay. I'd have been chastised for my carelessness in getting pregnant so young, reprimanded for keeping it secret. I'd have been told to be less selfish, more responsible. To be, in short, more like my sister. Because that's been the catchphrase of my life: if, as a child, I fell over and cried, my grandparents told me to take a leaf from Lara's book and not make such a fuss. If I talked in lessons, my teachers said they expected more from Lara's sister. And if I got a good mark in a test, my parents' praise was nothing compared to the compliments lavished on Lara, because she had had 'so many obstacles to overcome'. As if not having any obstacles can't be an obstacle in itself.

Max is helping Lara to her feet now, weaving a strong arm through her slender one as they head towards the double doors that lead outside. I look at his hands – at the way he rests one of them gently under her elbow. Ever her knight in shining armour. Jackie rushes to open the doors. 'A bit of fresh air will be just the thing,' she says, watching with approval as Max and Lara stroll into the garden. I turn to see if Poppy wants to go out too, and notice Cassie staring in Max's direction, her arms folded tightly across her chest. Poppy, meanwhile, has found something of interest on the bookshelf. Coming closer, I see it's a book about insects, and ask if she'd like to read it.

'Yes please, Auntie Hannah!'

I sit on the sofa and she clambers on to my knee, cuddles in close, all warm skin and milky scent. Whatever my grievances with Lara, at least none of them relate to her daughter. Poppy is the most remarkable source of warmth and curiosity, love and energy. The main downside to living in Singapore is not getting to see her. And Lara doesn't 'do' electronic devices, which means most of my relationship with my niece is old-school, conducted through phone calls and letters. And presents; I'm always sending Poppy presents, even though I can tell it irritates Lara. She thinks I'm spoiling her, but when I come across a gorgeous little dress, or pair of miniature sunglasses, it's hard to resist. I've brought her some Singaporean rice crackers this week, and a cute pyjama set with tigers. Plus a toy doctor's kit, because Lara doesn't think snacks and clothes are aspirational. Which of course they aren't, but that's not really the point of gifts, is it?

I start to read, talking Poppy through the constituent parts of an insect: the head, thorax and abdomen. She listens intently for a few seconds, before flicking ahead through the pages until she finds one she likes. 'What are these?'

'Termites,' I say.

'Why are there so many of them?'

'Because they live in great big groups, so they can all work together to do things. Like building these huge nests, can you see?'

'But people don't do that—'

'No, people have houses rather than nests—'

'It's just me and Mummy in our house—'

'That's right—'

'I don't have a daddy.'

I've no idea what to say to this. Whether to tell her that everyone has a daddy, but she just doesn't see hers, or whether to go along with the conceit that she sprang from Lara's loins without assistance. I cast around the room for help, but the others are in the garden.

Lara has never explained what happened. All she's said is that Poppy was the result of a one-night stand with a snowboarder called Gareth. A man whom she's never seen since, and for whom she has no contact details. Which is possible, I suppose, but doesn't quite ring true. Because Lara, with her dark-lashed eyes and angular cheekbones, is so bloody beautiful that I can't believe any man would up and leave her. And also because, even if he did genuinely disappear after that night, I'm sure she could find him if she tried. If she *really* tried, instead of letting her pride and stubbornness get in the way. Even the most reluctant of fathers are normally involved in some way in their children's lives: through holidays or weekend visits, or financial support at the very least. But with Lara it's like a void; like the father of her child never even existed. And if I ask her about Gareth, she clams up or grows angry, saying she never pries into my personal life, and would appreciate it if I could afford her the same respect.

Yet aren't sisters supposed to know about each other's personal lives? Isn't that a key part of being siblings: to understand and support one another, through whatever life throws at you?

But I suppose that came to an end when we were teenagers. When I overheard her saying those awful, hurtful things about me.

And the worst part of it all?

Every word was true.

LARA

After my dizzy spell, the rest of the morning passes quickly. The supermarket delivery arrives with a ridiculous quantity of food – crates and crates of the stuff. There's a whole chicken and several packs of mince, four kilos of potatoes, five loaves of bread, twenty-four bottles of wine, and that's just for starters; as I unpack a crate of tins – baked beans, kidney beans, tuna, lentils – I wonder aloud if there's been some sort of mistake, but Mum assures me there hasn't. 'We've six adults here, plus Poppy, for a week. And Cassie's gluten-free.'

I don't point out that being gluten-free doesn't mean eating everything else. Instead, I nod and go along with it, even though there's not enough space in the kitchen to put all the shopping away. Once the cupboards are full, Jackie makes a pile of sundries in the living room, by the bookshelf. But when the chilled items fail to fit in the fridge, Mum decides we should eat some of them immediately.

And thus we sit down to an early lunch of quiche, salad and other fancy foodstuffs. I try not to think about how much the Nocellara olives and Italian bresaola must have cost, opting instead for the plainer items: carrots, cucumber and a couple of breadsticks. Poppy deposits a piece of chewed quiche on to the side of my plate.

My sister, meanwhile, appears to be curating her food rather than eating it. She cuts three slices of quiche before deeming one worthy to be her centrepiece, and then starts arranging salad around it.

'Are you creating an artwork, Hannah?' Jackie asks.

It's a good question; if Poppy did the same, I'd tell her off for playing with her food.

'Oh, sorry!' Hannah laughs. 'I forget other people aren't used to this. I'm just preparing a photo for my blog.'

'Of your lunch?'

'Yes.'

'Why do people want to see your lunch?'

Another good question.

'Mum.' Max shakes his head. 'Have you never been on the internet? People want to see *everything*.'

'But why?' Jackie looks genuinely perplexed. 'What's interesting about someone else's lunch? Unless they're eating, I don't know, a polar bear or something?'

'No one eats polar bears,' says Cassie. 'That would be terribly cruel.'

Jackie frowns. 'I know, I just meant it as an example.'

'It's a lifestyle thing,' my sister says, moving a leaf a little to the left. 'People are interested in how other people live: where they go, what they wear, what they eat, all that sort of stuff.'

'I'm not,' Jackie replies, reaching for the taramasalata.

'I don't think you're the target market, Mum,' says Max.

'It gives people inspiration for their own lives,' Cassie says, joining in. 'Seeing how others live theirs.'

'How depressing,' Jackie responds. 'Can't people think for themselves?'

Hannah arranges a strand of vine tomatoes across the side of her plate. 'My blog isn't really like that. I want people to feel they're part of something relatable.'

It's an ironic choice of words, given I'm *actually* related to her but can't identify at all with her online sharing. Because my life is mine, and not for the consumption of others. A tenet which becomes all the more important when you've lost sight of yourself in the past.

Plus, on a more prosaic note: vine tomatoes are hardly relatable. And tomato and broccoli gluten-free quiche certainly isn't.

'Well, I think it's a nice hobby to have.' Mum is speaking in her official tone now, the one she uses when she wants to shut a conversation down. 'So, this afternoon . . .' she begins.

But Hannah isn't prepared to move on. 'I wouldn't call it a hobby. I've grown my followers by twenty-seven per cent this year.'

'That's impressive,' says Max, earning him a glare from Cassie and a grateful smile from my sister.

'Thank you. And, what's more, I'm starting to get some potential . . . um . . . professional interest in it. I mean, it's early days, and it might not come to anything, but still . . .'

Max just nods this time.

'I'm really hoping that . . . you know . . . that this might be it. The moment the blog takes off.'

Mum wrinkles her nose. 'What do you mean by that?'

'You know. Like, maybe, I could do it as a job.'

'Oh.' There is a long silence. When Mum speaks again, her voice has an edge to it. 'But I thought you were enjoying the teaching?'

'I am.'

'And the teacher training took a while, didn't it? Cost a fair bit?'

'What's that got to do with anything?'

'There's no need to get defensive. All I'm saying is . . . you've made an *investment.* So doesn't it make sense to stick with the teaching? For a while, at least?'

'I *am* sticking with it!' Hannah drizzles some dressing across her salad, her hand tight around the bottle. 'I just think it would be amazing . . . you know . . .'

'No, I don't; you'll have to explain—'

My sister sets the bottle down too hard, spattering dressing across the oilcloth. 'I'm just saying I think it would be amazing to make enough from my blog that I don't *need* to teach anymore.'

'But what would you do instead?'

'Travel more—'

'But you're already travelling?'

'Yes, but . . .' Hannah looks down at her plate. 'You're missing the point.'

'Then tell me what the point is.'

I'm not going to get involved, but I agree with Mum on this. She prints and sends several of Hannah's blog posts to me, and I read them just to see what my sister is up to, but I can't believe they're of interest to the wider public. The ones I've read seem to be a mishmash of travelogue, confessional and advertising: an unhappy triumvirate which means no single element is executed well.

'I just want to be able to do my own thing.' She removes a salad leaf from her plate. 'To be successful on my own terms, to be able to pick and choose what I do on a daily basis—'

'But that's not how the real world works,' Mum says. 'Work is called "work" for a reason; people can't just pick and choose—'

'Fine – okay!' my sister breaks in. 'You've made your point.'

'There's no need to be upset—'

'I'm not upset.' But another long silence follows.

'Speaking of travel,' Jackie says, and nobody objects that we weren't, not really, 'do you remember, Helen, when we went on that interrailing trip, and talked our way into that hotel in Rome?'

'How could I forget?' Mum shakes her head a little, as if to dispel the bad atmosphere. 'I think they thought we were hook—' She breaks off, looking at Poppy, before giving an apologetic smile in my direction. 'Ladies of the night.'

'We *were* ladies of the night.' Jackie chuckles. 'Just not that sort. More women who stayed up all night to avoid the cost of a hotel room.'

As they start reminiscing on time spent in bus stations and twenty-four-hour supermarkets, I bite into a carrot, wondering if I'll ever be able to look back on my past in such a breezy manner. It's not that I've never had fun; it's just that so much of my childhood was stolen by leukaemia, and the difficulties that followed. Lying in a series of hospital beds when other children were out playing, and then, when I was finally well enough to return home, missing out on so many of the traditional teenage milestones. Watching music festivals on TV while my friends were there in person, or hobbling round the garden while they were off on a hike. Taking a cocktail of medicinal drugs while my peers drank actual cocktails and enjoyed drugs of the recreational variety. Not going on dates, or to parties; not sharing cigarettes or stealing kisses in the moonlight.

There's a loud beep, and I jump, before realising it's just Hannah's phone. Muttering something, she runs off into the garden, and I wonder what's so urgent that she has to leave like that. Or whether she's just flouncing off in a mood.

'Can I go into the garden too?' Poppy asks, twisting round on her chair.

'No,' I say. 'We're eating lunch.'

'But Auntie Hannah's gone.'

'I'm sure Auntie Hannah has her reasons for needing to go outside. But we're eating.'

'I'm not hungry.'

'You can go out soon, little one.' I look back to the window, to the sight of my sister pacing back and forth under the trees, framed by the cliffs. She seems agitated, looking down at her phone, then behind her, as if expecting a killer to come creeping through the bracken. Or perhaps that's just my own fears coming through – it's hard to forget those monstrous dreams of Hannah with veined, bulging eyes, with blood upon her shirt. My pulse accelerates as I continue to watch her, but then she stops still and smiles – a wide, open-mouthed smile, like she's never been happier – and lifts her phone to her face. And I realise: she's not worried at all.

She's taking a bloody selfie.

HANNAH

There's a pressure behind my eyes and a sourness at the back of my throat – telltale signs I'm about to cry. But I won't let Mum get to me, I won't. I'll shrug off the fact she's dismissive of my ambitions, that she didn't ask questions about the professional interest I mentioned. Because I *can* make a success of myself, either with or without my family's support. In fact, maybe success will be all the sweeter if no one expects it; if I'm able to casually drop into conversation that I've secured a magazine column and regular pay cheques for my supposed 'hobby'.

And I can't be crying in the photos I send to Chris. I have just two minutes to take them, so I blink and pat at the skin around my eyes, while also trying to find a good backdrop. The trees are the obvious choice, with Curbar Edge behind. Searching in my pockets for make-up, I find a red lipstick which I smear across my lips, before positioning myself in front of the trees. I pinch my cheeks to get some colour into them, and shoot.

The results are a shock. The rear camera image is halfway decent – it shows the picnic table near the house, with a canopy of leaves above – but the front image makes my face look fat, with sunken, creepy eyes, and blood-red lips, like a vampire. The dark line of the cliffs adds to the gothic vibes.

I delete it straightaway.

Only thirty seconds remain, so I need to think smarter. I can't send Chris a photo of me looking like I've sucked on another man's veins, so the lipstick will have to go. Or . . .

Seizing a pale yellow leaf from the ground, I draw it to my mouth and kiss it, leaving a faint imprint of my lips behind. Then I take a close-up photo of the leaf, with the cliffs blurred in the background, keeping my face well out of shot.

Much better. I send it through the Connect app, along with the accompanying photo from my rear camera (an image of a beech tree, with pleasing contrast between the copper leaves and grey sky). As soon as I've pressed send, Chris's photos become available to me. The first depicts a pair of boxer shorts on his bed, captioned, *Everything feels empty without you*, while the second is of the plain white ceiling above. I smile, feeling better knowing that at least one person appreciates me. And better still when he sends a follow-up message saying, *Thanks for the kiss. I miss you x*

I miss you too, I write back.

Are you free for a call?

I peer into the kitchen, where everyone is starting to clear the table. I'm conscious that there's lots to do: that I should help tidy up, and also update my blog; it's been well over twenty-four hours since my last post. But I'm equally aware that it's already evening in Singapore. *Not right now*, I reply. *But I could ring in an hour or so?*

He replies with a thumbs up and a kissing emoji, and I'm just debating which emoji to send back when I hear a voice.

'What are you doing, Auntie Hannah?'

I look up to see Poppy coming towards me, barefoot, eating raspberries as she half walks, half jumps through the grass.

'I'm just sharing some photos with Chris.'

'Is Chris your boyfriend?'

'That's right.'

'Mummy doesn't have a boyfriend.'

'No.' Although it occurs to me that, even if Lara did, she wouldn't tell me. We don't have that sort of relationship. Not anymore.

'Can I see your photos?'

'Of course.' I sit on the picnic bench and she perches on my knee, giggling when I show her the picture of Chris's boxers. 'Why's he sent you a photo of his pants?'

As I try to explain about the app, Poppy sucks on her fingers, which are stained pink from the raspberries. 'Can I see more?' she asks, reaching for my phone and I swiftly move it further away.

'Yes, but let me show you.' I scroll through my recent snaps, checking they're suitable for a four-year-old's viewing. No nudity, no smoking, no gratuitous alcohol consumption. I opt for the photos of me at Singapore Zoo, because they're child-friendly and I think she'll like the orangutans.

'Poppy – my God!' screeches through the air and Lara comes running towards us at speed. I glance round to check there's nothing behind us – no rapidly spreading fire or giant spiders – but see only trees and bracken.

'What's wrong?'

'Have you taken any photos of her?'

'What?' My sister's question doesn't align with the panic in her voice; with the way she's standing in front of us, breath heaving. 'No.' I get to my feet. 'I was just showing her my photos. Are you all right?'

She doesn't look relieved. 'Don't take any photos of her. And definitely don't *share* any photos of her.'

'I would never share any photos of her without checking with you first. You don't need to wor—'

'But don't even take any!'

'Okay, but why—'

'I mean it, Hannah!'

'Okay!' I raise my hands in the air. 'What's going on?'

She stares at me. 'Nothing's *going on.* I just don't want you to take any photos of my daughter, that's all.' She turns to Poppy. 'Time to go inside.'

Poppy giggles. 'I saw his pants! In the photo.'

My sister's expression grows venomous. '*Whose* pants?'

'Auntie Hannah's boyfriend.'

'It's just his pants!' I say quickly. 'He's not in them, or anything!' That sounds worse. 'I mean . . .'

'Get up,' Lara says to Poppy, her voice strained.

'But Mummy—'

'*Now.*'

Poppy stands up. 'But Mummy—'

'No. It's not appropriate for someone your age to be looking at a smartphone—'

'We were only looking at photos,' I say, frustrated by my sister's overreaction. 'Nothing else. And the pants thing was just silly, nothing inappropriate.'

Lara ignores me. She takes Poppy by the arm. 'We're going inside.'

'But I want to see—'

'What part of "no" do you not understand?!' She clutches Poppy's arm tighter. 'It's about time you did what you're told, instead of arguing back.'

Poppy's lip begins to quiver. 'It's not fair!'

'What isn't fair, exactly?' Lara's voice is icy. 'That I'm trying to protect you? That I don't want you exposed to all the horrors of social media: the unrealistic body imagery, the filters and artifice, the vacuous narcissism and navel-gazing?'

It's clear that this diatribe is aimed at me, not Poppy. *Well, fuck you, Lara,* I want to say in return. *What gives you the right to look down on me; to be so critical of my life choices when you've hardly made the best ones? When all I'm trying to do is make something of myself, while you got knocked up in your twenties by a total fucking stranger?*

But I don't say any of this. Instead, I watch as they head back inside, Poppy crying as my sister drags her along.

And then I head in the opposite direction, out of the garden into the bracken, where I slump down against a rock and let my own tears fall.

Settling In

I've arrived! So far the weather here in the UK has been pretty grey but the Peak District is every bit as beautiful as I remember. Our home for the week, **Grove Cottage***, is surrounded by trees with gorgeous autumn foliage, just as I'd hoped – there has already been some conker collecting, but no conker fights (yet!). The cottage is a clever blend of old and new, with period features such as beams and farmhouse doors, but also a modern, open-plan extension for the main living/entertainment/cooking space, with large glass windows that look out directly to* **Curbar Edge***. A view I could stare at for hours. I'm actually on my own at the moment because the others have gone for a walk there. I would have loved to go with them but decided to have a nap instead, as I didn't sleep much on the flight and am feeling rather jet-lagged. Which is a shame, but it's important to look after my health, and those amazing views will still be there tomorrow. Maybe with some added sunshine, if we're lucky . . .*

Talking of health, my lunch earlier was both tasty and packed with nutrients: I had a slice of tomato and broccoli gluten-free quiche, with vine tomatoes, radicchio and a drizzle of aioli. And I'm hoping to have a kale and watercress smoothie later, provided I can find a blender. Plus I've got my trusty **Globetrotter tablets** *with me, which contain a blend of vitamins for general health, melatonin to regulate my sleep, ginger for energy, and curcumin to maintain good gut function.*

I'll be on the sofa bed for my nap, but I've got my **Satin eye mask** *and travel ear plugs to help me reset, along with some* **Breathe lavender oil** *– just a couple of drops on the pillow is all that's needed to enter a much deeper state of relaxation, so it's great when travelling.*

That's it for now – wish me sweet dreams!

LARA

Curbar Edge seems more hazardous than I remember. There are rocks everywhere, each presenting its own unique danger: some lie embedded in the dirt, waiting to turn an ankle, while others sit at the side of the path, inviting exploration yet harbouring unstable surfaces. And then there are the cliffs themselves, which look smooth from down at Grove Cottage but which, up close, reveal themselves as a mosaic of rocky pillars, riven with cracks where the ground drops away.

I watch Poppy skipping down the path, leaping over obstacles, and resist the urge to rein her in. To tell her to be careful. It's probably my reduced medication making me wary; I never worried about Curbar Edge before. I used to feel so free up here as a young child, jumping from rock to rock as if I were flying. Dad sometimes dangled me by my ankles so the ground was beneath my nose: a magical, upside-down world with a ceiling of grass and a floor made of sky. And I want that so badly for Poppy too – that sense of being able to touch the sky, of soaring.

But you have to perform safety checks before you can fly. Hannah probably thinks I overreacted earlier, in the garden, but there's a reason I only own an old Nokia and keep away from modern devices more generally – because everything is interconnected, and I don't want to leave a digital footprint. Not after receiving that message two years ago. It's becoming increasingly difficult to stay offline: banks and councils conduct most of their business digitally these days, and even dishwasher and fridge manufacturers are getting in on the act, selling white goods with 'smart' features that are actually the opposite. But I'm doing my best: going to post offices that let me complete forms in person, and travelling across London to visit the few bank branches that remain open. Sending letters, not emails, and navigating with paper maps. Reading Mum's printouts of my sister's blog, instead of reading it online. Never shopping on websites, and using cash where I can.

What's weird is that my recent nightmares should be about Hannah. Before I started taking my meds, I only ever had bad dreams about me and Poppy, and I can't tell whether my newfound fears for my sister stem from my own troubles, or whether it's something to do with the two of us being back together in the same country, confronted by our difficult relationship. Although perhaps it's naive to think that the two things can be separated; after all, when I was at my lowest point and needed Hannah the most, she didn't help me. Did she really resent me so much? Or was she just indifferent to my suffering?

Whatever the truth, I'll never stop loving her. Which is why I did that slightly mad thing, just before we came on this walk. I might not understand my dreams, but I'll do everything I can to guard against them being realised.

We've only recently left the cars but are already spread out along the path. Max and Cassie are at the front, holding hands and setting a brisk pace, while Mum remains near the road, doing some sketching. Poppy, meanwhile, is a short distance ahead of me, and Jackie a similar distance behind. As Poppy stops to scramble on some rocks, and I stop to watch, Jackie rustles up alongside, wearing a large waterproof poncho even though it's not raining.

We stand in silence for a few seconds, as my daughter tries to find a foothold. Then Jackie turns to me. 'Can I ask you a question?'

I feel myself tense, but nod in agreement.

'Do you think Cassie's a good partner for Max?'

My body relaxes; this is not about Gareth, or Poppy. Or my sister, for that matter. I look ahead to where Max and Cassie are walking, hand in hand, and shrug. 'I'm hardly an expert.'

But Jackie won't let it go that easily. 'You must have a view on what they're like together. You know Max better than almost anybody.'

This certainly used to be true. Back when I was a teenager, recovering from my transplant, Max and I spent hours together. He talked to me when I was bored, and sat in silence when I was tired – reading or doing his homework at my desk while I rested – and all that time in each other's company made us close; gave us an easy understanding and intimacy. He used to tell me about his hopes for the future: how he wanted a big family, lots of dogs, and old-fashioned holidays at the seaside. Crabbing with a line off the harbour wall, rock pooling, donkey rides at the beach. How he wanted a partner to share it all with: the highs and the lows, the long chats and sandy sandwiches. The accumulation of a shared history.

And I told him how I wanted to be free.

I remember a time when we were all on holiday together in Norfolk: Dad and Mum, me and Hannah, Jackie and Max. We were staying in a house on the coast, the sea air and expansive views deemed good for my recovery. Yet in reality they were a sweet sort of torture: being able to see the sea but never touch it; watching walkers on the beach and imagining the feel of my feet, sinking into damp sand, water pooling around my toes. I begged my parents to let me go down to the shore but Mum forbade it, saying it wasn't safe; that the coastal path was too steep and rocky, and I might bruise myself. That the risk of infection was too high. And I accepted this, day after day, until one afternoon, propped up in bed by the window, I burst into tears, furious at the world for being so beautiful when I was broken. Max asked what was wrong, and when I explained, he looked thoughtful for a few seconds. Then he said he was heading out and wouldn't be long.

Half an hour later, he returned, and I could hear him clattering about in the en-suite bathroom before he appeared by my bed, beaming. 'Up you get.'

'I can't go anywhere.' I rubbed at my face. 'Mum will have a fit.'

'You're not going anywhere,' he replied, still smiling. 'Or, at least, not anywhere your Mum will notice.'

'I can't sneak out—'

'You're not sneaking out. Come on!' He supported me to my feet and across the carpet. 'Now, shut your eyes.'

I gave him a look. 'Really?'

'Yes. You said you wanted to live more freely, and all I'm asking is—'

'Fine. But only because it's you.' I shut my eyes and let him lead me in small, shuffling steps. Almost immediately we came to a halt.

'Okay. You can look now.'

I opened my eyes to see we were in the en-suite bathroom. At first glance, there was nothing of note: the frosted glass window and small vase of dried flowers were exactly as they'd always been; the sink too, with its blue-and-white splashback tiles and scalloped mirror above. But then I saw the bath. All around its rim were seashells, pebbles and seaweed, and a pile of dark sand lay at its base.

'If you can't go to the beach, I thought maybe the beach could come to you,' Max said.

'You're insane,' I replied, but there were tears in my eyes as I said it. And more tears as he helped me into the bath, still wearing my pyjamas, hems rolled up around my knees. I stood upon the blissfully cold, grainy sand and wriggled my toes into it until I came to the hard enamel of the bath below.

'That's not everything,' he said, and I laughed as he produced a bucket and spade and the two of us built a tiny, lopsided castle. 'It's the worst sandcastle ever,' I said, so we tried again, but the second attempt was no better, and we laughed even harder. We made two more before accepting defeat. Max helped me rinse my hands and feet, after which I sat on the closed lid of the toilet, letting my skin dry naturally as he cleaned up. Watching him scoop sand from the bath into a series of buckets and bowls, I tried to thank him – to say how much I appreciated what he had done, and how much his friendship meant to me – but I could see, from an increasing redness in his cheeks and a new tension in his shoulders, that I was making him uncomfortable. And so I stopped gushing and asked him to tell me something he'd never told anyone before.

For a few seconds he was silent, so I prompted him again. And then, while picking up a piece of seaweed and looking away to the frosted window, he told me he hated his dad. That he couldn't bear the phoney holiday he took with him each summer, where his dad played at fatherhood, cramming their week with games of football and darts that left no time for talking, or just being in each other's presence. 'He never mentions the fact that we won't see each other for the rest of the year, or that he and Mum can't be in the same room for more than five minutes without screaming,' said Max. 'He just pretends that everything is fine; that we're a normal family and all is well. And I don't even *like* darts.'

So, yes, Max and I used to know each other better than anyone else. But I'm not sure it's true anymore. Not since I went to France and our lives diverged so completely.

I watch Poppy navigate her way on to a small boulder, and think how much my life has changed since then. How I swapped one lack of freedom for another.

'Max and Cassie seem compatible enough,' I say to Jackie now.

'What do you mean, *enough*?'

'Just that they seem fine together.'

'Define "fine".'

'Look, you're really asking the wrong person here. Particularly as I've hardly spoken to Cassie.' It's true: I've only met Cassie a couple of times, when she and Max have come to my flat in London, and even then they've never stayed for more than half an hour. Just long enough to drop off Jackie's deliveries and have a cup of tea.

'Exactly.'

'What?' I'm distracted when, suddenly, Poppy jumps down, and my heart lurches as she falls forward on to her hands. But a split second later she's back on her feet, running off along the path. Jackie and I follow. 'I'm not sure I understand what you're saying.'

She nods at me. 'You don't know Cassie.'

I look ahead to where Max and Cassie are walking. They stop and turn their faces to the sky. 'That's what I said.'

'And that's my point.' Jackie looks out across the valley. '*No one* seems to know Cassie.'

'What? You must do—'

'No.' Jackie gives a little shake of her head. 'She and Max have been together for a couple of years, but I still barely know her at all. I've met her on several occasions, and she's always been very polite and perfectly pleasant, but . . . I've no idea what she's interested in, or what she's passionate about; I don't even know if she *has* passions.'

'But surely you don't need to know that?' I can't understand why Jackie is getting so agitated about this, and wonder if it's a result of being the single mother of a single child. Of her attention being so focused upon one individual for so long that it's hard to accept another person in their life. And whether I will struggle with the same issue in twenty years' time. It seems too distant to contemplate. 'Surely all that matters is Max being happy.'

'But that's the thing.' She fiddles with the pocket on her poncho. 'I don't know if he is.'

'He seems happy.'

'Does he?'

'Yes.' But even as I'm saying it, I'm doubting myself. Because what do I know about Max's happiness? I know he is a kind, loyal friend, who was hurt horribly by his parents' divorce, and who once dreamed of creating a family of his own. But whether that's still the case, and whether Cassie is the person to fulfil that dream, I have no idea.

'Maybe you're right,' says Jackie. 'Maybe I'm just worrying because . . . well, I suppose I'm a little surprised that Max and Cassie are here in the first place.'

'On Curbar Edge?'

'No, here, in the Peak District. They've never wanted to come on holiday with me before.' There's a note of hurt in her voice.

'Perhaps they've just been busy, with the restaurant and everything,' I say, hoping to comfort her.

'They're still busy with that. Which makes me wonder whether they're here for a specific purpose . . . to make an announcement about their future, maybe . . .'

'You think they're going to get engaged?'

'Maybe, or maybe I'm just second-guessing,' she sighs. 'It'd just be good to know that there's something there, if there's a chance they'll settle down for the long run. Something real and substantive – love and passion.'

I watch Poppy digging in the dirt with a stick, and think back to the early days with Gareth. How intense it was; how, just a few weeks into our relationship, I moved out of my dorm and into his chalet. 'Passion isn't necessarily a good thing.'

Jackie glances at me. 'You're thinking of *him*, aren't you? Poppy's dad.'

I nod.

'Look, I don't know the details of what happened,' she says. 'All Max has told me is that he was a nasty piece of work—'

'That's one way of putting it—'

'And I don't need to know. But don't you think you should tell your mum?'

Almost dutifully, I look behind us, to where Mum is sitting on a rock with her sketchbook. She's gazing out at the view: at the dark clumps of heather and spindly bracken, the tufted grass and dry sandy earth. I can just about make out the movement of her arm, pulling pencil across paper, her face fixed with concentration. The idea of telling her what happened is impossible.

'It's been five years since your dad's death,' Jackie says, as if reading my thoughts. 'She's a lot stronger than she was.'

But am I? I turn back to see Poppy abandon her stick and run to catch up with Max and Cassie. She says something and all three of them return the way they've come, pausing at a dip in the path.

'Listen, Lara.' Jackie reaches out to my arm. 'I've known plenty of worthless men in my time. Not least my ex-husband. And what I've learned is you have to find a way to talk about what happened. With a therapist maybe, if not your mum?'

I shake my head. Jackie is kind and well-meaning, but she doesn't get it.

'Meditation, then? Or, better still, a new man? A better man. Although not a better: they're unreliable and tend to lose money.' She laughs at her own joke.

I don't say anything. Dating anyone again seems preposterous; I've lost trust in my own judgement. Besides, I'm too busy with work and parenthood; with the tireless task of keeping my family healthy and safe.

Poppy looks up as I draw closer. 'The bird's fallen over,' she says.

Before I can ask which bird, or explain that birds don't fall over in the first place, I see a heap of black feathers in the dip by her feet. It looks dead, its beak protruding from a crumpled body, but as I examine it more closely it starts to make a stuttering, choking noise. A *chuk-chuk-chuk*, over and over.

'It's a blackbird,' says Max. 'But it doesn't seem very well.'

'Can we make it better?' asks Poppy.

'I don't think so.' As if to prove his point, the bird attempts to get to its feet, but collapses almost immediately. The *chuk-chuk* gets louder. 'Perhaps we should put it out of its misery.'

'What do you mean?'

Max gives me a long, searching look. Then he turns to Poppy. 'Why don't you and your mum walk on ahead? While I try to make the bird feel better?'

'What are you going to do?' she asks curiously.

'Come on, Poppy,' I say. 'How about we have a race to that big boulder over there? Ready . . . steady . . .'

She is already off. I run behind her, making a point of staying close, but not actually overtaking. When we are at a suitable distance from the others, I pause and turn.

I'm just in time to see Max raise a rock above his head and bring it down upon the bird's body. His blow is strong and decisive, creating a thud as it makes contact with the feathered mass.

And then all is quiet.

HANNAH

Upon waking, I am groggy and confused. It takes me a few seconds to remember where I am: on a sofa bed in the Peak District. The sky is light, albeit grey, which means it's daytime, but for a moment I think it's morning, until I remember I went for my nap after lunch. The house is quiet and I have no concept of how much time has passed; whether I've been asleep for minutes or hours. I lean over to the glass table and pick up my phone. Just gone 4 p.m., UK time, so I've been asleep for forty minutes. And still nothing from the magazine editor. It's been over three months since she was last in contact, which I can't believe is a good sign (although I suppose I'm unlikely to hear anything on a weekend). After the others left for their walk earlier, I lay down and rang Chris, but we only spoke briefly because my eyes began to shut of their own accord. The last thing I remember is him saying he missed me, and I think I might have mumbled it back, but then I was gone, fully gone, into a slumber without thoughts or dreams.

Now, as I rise from my 'bed' for the week, my thoughts come crashing back. Lara's fury, for a start. Her response to me showing photos to Poppy was completely disproportionate, even for a person who hates social media and smartphones. It wasn't as if I was giving Poppy her own phone, for God's sake, or letting her watch porn. I can only hope my sister isn't going to be too strict with Poppy as she grows up, that she allows her to do the same fun things as her friends. It would be awful for history to repeat itself – for Lara's daughter to be as socially isolated as she was.

But, more immediately, I'm concerned for Lara. The strange dreams, the phone call to me at the airport, the outburst in the garden – these don't add up to a picture of good health. As I go to my suitcase to pick out some clothes, I wonder if I should discuss Lara's mental state with Mum. She's always said we can talk to her about anything, and yet, when I've raised certain subjects with her in the past, Mum's become upset and defensive. Like the time when, aged fourteen, I said it sometimes felt like Lara got all the attention, and Mum burst into tears, saying I had to understand she'd thought Lara was going to die. When I pointed out Lara no longer had leukaemia, she cried even harder, saying she was still at risk, and continued to cry until eventually Dad told me I should go upstairs. And since his death it's been even worse – like when, a year ago, I told Mum that Lara never spoke to me anymore, and she wept so profusely she gave herself a nosebleed.

So talking to Mum about Lara's mental health doesn't seem like the best idea. Particularly this week, when we're supposed to be celebrating – not upsetting – her. Maybe speaking to Jackie would be a better option. Or maybe even Max. It was Max, after all, who eventually brought my sister back from France, although he's still tight-lipped about what happened. Unfailingly loyal to Lara and her desire for secrecy, even when it isn't necessarily in her best interest.

Thinking of Max, I can't decide what to wear. I want to look good but not like I'm trying too hard. Which means my figure-hugging orange dress is a no, as is my V-neck black top, because the V is very deep and reveals a lot of cleavage. But then my polka dot dress isn't warm enough and my jersey dress is too warm.

And then I remember my white shirt. It's not particularly exciting, but it's sexy in a subtle way – it makes my skin look brighter, and I can undo enough buttons to provide just a hint of cleavage. I'll wear it with my jeans and style my hair into loose waves; apply a bit of blusher and my volumising mascara. I'm aware that neither Max nor I are single, but that's not really the point; this is less about seduction and more about asserting myself as an adult female, able to hold my own alongside my sister. No longer simply the little kid in fancy dress or doing naked handstands on the lawn.

Except I can't find the shirt. I remember laying it near the top of my luggage, along with my orange dress, but while the dress is still here, the shirt is not. It's possible it moved in transit, or when I was getting my pyjamas out earlier, so I rummage down lower in my case, picking through socks and jeans from one packing cube, and jumpers and magazines from another. But still no shirt.

I glance around the living room, wondering if I dropped it in my half-asleep state earlier, or whether someone else moved it – my case has been lying open all morning. But the only other clothes I can see are the ones I wore on the plane, which are piled next to the tinned lentils. I take one last look through the case before admitting defeat.

Collecting my washbag from the floor, I make my way to the bathroom. The water from the shower feels good: falling in hot sheets around me, stripping away my exhaustion. As I soap my hair, and watch the suds trail down my body, I think about Chris, but my mental image of his face morphs into Max's features, and I find myself imagining what it might be like if Max were with me instead: our hands upon one another, slippery and warm; our bodies pressed together against the glass screen. Me murmuring that I've always wanted this, and him saying the same; that it is actually me, not Lara, that he desires.

I've forgotten my conditioner. Leaving the shower still running, I step out and give my hair a cursory squeeze, before wrapping a towel around my body and going to the living room, trying not to drip too much as I locate my conditioner and head back to the bathroom again. My towel slips as I walk, so I rearrange it across my chest, secure it one-handed with a tuck. I'm humming as I turn the corner to the hall.

And then I see someone, standing by the front door, and a bolt of cold rushes through me.

'It's me! It's only me.'

Pulling my towel tighter, it takes a couple of seconds to realise who has spoken. Max, subject of my shower fantasies, is standing on the doormat, his hair sticking a little to his scalp.

'I'm sorry,' he says. 'I didn't mean to shock you.'

'No, sorry, I . . .' My words are muddled. 'I didn't hear you all come back. The shower . . .' I gesture towards the bathroom, where the sound of running water is audible.

'It's only me who's come back,' he says, and I'm suddenly conscious that we're alone, and I'm naked. That perhaps he saw me rearranging my towel. I look down to check it's still covering my chest, and up again in time to notice his gaze has slipped to the same area. Heat rushes to my cheeks. 'I forgot my conditioner,' I say, waving the bottle around as if that explains everything.

'The others are still walking,' he replies.

'Yes. Walking.'

'But I've come back early to start the cooking.'

'The cooking.' I sound like a simpleton.

'For your mum's dinner.'

'Yes.' I stop myself from parroting his words for a third time. 'I should . . .' I say, walking towards the bathroom. Which means walking towards *him*.

'Right.' Now it's his turn to look flustered. He stands back against the door, but as I pass his presence has a proximity which belies the physics of the act. His clothes are tinged with sweat, with the scent of him, and my body chafes against my towel as I walk. I think I feel him watching as I go to the bathroom, but I don't dare to turn around.

As I lock the bathroom door and return to the heat of the shower, I think about him out there, and replay our conversation in my head. There are so many better things I could have said: how kind it is of him to cook for us all, how much I'm looking forward to it, does he need any help in the kitchen? Or how was his trip to Curbar Edge? But instead I just stood there like a moron, waving a bottle of conditioner and flashing too much skin.

And I can't even find my white shirt for tonight, to make myself look halfway decent. Although perhaps it no longer matters. Because my objective with the shirt was to change Max's perception of me; to make him think of me as a woman, not a child.

And I'm pretty certain I've achieved that already.

LARA

Dinner is an over-elaborate affair: lots of tiny courses, brought out one after the other in quick succession, providing just a mouthful of food each time. Max is the chef, bustling around in the kitchen with multiple pans, while Cassie is both sous chef and waitress, balancing dishes on her arm and providing verbose explanations of what we're about to eat. 'Here we have haricot beans with a tomato compote and mustard reduction, accompanied by shards of sourdough – deconstructed baked beans on toast!' or, 'This is a fillet of John Dory, with a hazelnut gratin and seaweed foam.' Fancy, fussy food, which isn't to my taste, and definitely isn't to Poppy's: after several *yuk*s, and lots of scowling and pushing her food around, I concede defeat and make her a ham sandwich.

But everyone else seems to love what they're eating. The meal is Max and Cassie's birthday present for Mum, and she's effusive in her praise for it, oohing and aahing and declaring it the best food she's ever tasted. Jackie watches on serenely, taking pleasure in Mum's pleasure, and pride in her son's skill. Hannah, meanwhile, takes photos: of her food, the 'tablescape' (her word), and of Max at work in the kitchen. So many photos of Max at work in the kitchen . . . chopping carrots with his chef's knife, whisking egg whites in a copper bowl, plating up tiny fripperies and spooning on thimblefuls of sauce. She takes some photos of Mum and Jackie too, but is sensible enough not to turn the camera on me or Poppy.

When Cassie brings out bowls of orecchiette with vodka, the conversation turns to alcohol and cocktails. My sister says Singapore has some of the best cocktail bars in Asia, if not the world.

'It's not just Singapore slings at five-star hotels?' Max says.

'God, no,' says Hannah. 'There are some incredible bars that are essentially reinventing cocktails, or at least putting a fresh spin on the classics. Using herbs and spices, Asian fruits—'

'I don't think I've ever had a Singapore sling,' says Cassie, while Max simultaneously asks what fruits they use.

'All sorts. Dragon fruit and mangosteen, lychee, rambutan . . .'

'Sounds incredible,' says Max, while Cassie asks what rambutan is, and Hannah tries to explain.

'It looks kind of like a hairy strawberry, but tastes more like a lychee—'

'Do you have a favourite cocktail?' Max asks.

'It's hard to say. But the signature cocktail at the Kaleidoscope Bar is pretty incredible. It—'

'The Kaleidoscope Bar!' Mum breaks in. 'Isn't that where you had your first date with Chris?'

Hannah blushes. 'It's where we first met. But it wasn't a *date*; I was there with some friends.'

'So how did you meet him?' asks Jackie, leaning forward and smiling. 'Was it love at first sight across the bar?'

I don't know much about Hannah's latest boyfriend; only what Mum's told me over the phone. But I want to tell her what I *do* know: that first appearances can be deceptive. That men are good at putting on a front.

Now she blushes more deeply; looks across at Max and then at her hands. 'I'm not sure about that. He came over to our table because he knew one of the people I was there with.'

'And?' prompts Jackie.

'And what?'

'What happened next? How did the two of you end up together?'

'Mum,' says Max, in a gently reprimanding way.

Hannah shrugs. 'I don't remember exactly—'

'You don't *remember*!'

'I mean, I remember in broad terms, but we'd both had a bit to drink, so it's kind of hazy. I remember chatting to him, and liking him; thinking he was easy to talk to—'

'As well as devilishly handsome, no doubt?' Jackie gives Mum a nudge and the two of them giggle like schoolgirls.

'Um.' My sister runs her fork across her plate. She seems uncomfortable, but I might be misreading the situation – I'm not sure I know her moods anymore. 'He was nice to look at—'

'*Nice*? That's a damning compliment—'

'I just mean that it felt relaxed with him from the beginning; almost familiar—'

'Familiar? That's even worse!'

'Is it?' Hannah gives a strained laugh. 'I don't know what I should be saying. I just know that I liked him.'

'That's sweet,' says Cassie.

'Have you got any pictures of him?' Jackie asks.

'Yes, but not any good ones.' Hannah pulls her phone from her pocket.

'Oh, Jacks, don't encourage her to get her phone out!'

Hannah turns towards Mum, her chin trembling, before turning away again. 'Here you are,' she says, handing the phone to Jackie. 'It was a fancy dress party.'

Jackie peers down at the screen, before deciding she needs her glasses. After the glasses have been located and cleaned, she looks for a second time, and promptly lets out a squeal of laughter. 'Oh, he looks *fun*!' The phone is duly handed round the table, and the sentiment reiterated, until it comes to me.

The photo in question has been taken indoors, in front of an alcohol-laden sideboard. My sister is wearing a black jumpsuit and a cat mask replete with whiskers, while the man next to her is wearing a blue Lycra all-in-one, with a shiny red mask and cape, and giant red underpants. I'm not surprised the others find it funny, but comedy pants aren't enough to make me trust him.

I pass the phone back silently and, as Jackie goes on to quiz Hannah about her and Chris's living arrangements in Singapore, I think about the first time I met Gareth. How, unlike my sister, I remember every last detail. The pinkness of the sky and the way the snow was falling in fat, deliberate flakes. How Gareth was standing by a wooden table at the piste-side restaurant in a bright yellow fleece, talking into a phone with a snowboard under one arm, and how he turned to look at me as I approached: eyes shining, mouth teasing. His beard flecked with snow and his goggles pushed back into his hair, which was nearly shoulder-length and so blond it was almost white. Devilishly handsome, for sure. I heard him say 'Bye Liv' as he hung up, his voice assertive, British, with a slight Essex twang. And then he smiled at me. 'Hello you.' Like he'd been expecting my arrival. 'Can I get you a drink?'

We drank *vin chaud*, hot and velvety upon my tongue, and talked about the runs we'd done that day: Aigle and Forêts, Arpettes and Grand Couloir. Each name somehow suggestive of sexual acts. His physical assurance was captivating: the way he moved, so confident in his own body; his limbs strong and capable. The way he smiled, with a tiny curl of his lips; his eyes on mine knowingly, as if the two of us shared a secret hidden to the rest of the world. The way he leaned towards me as the evening progressed, such that our very skin strained to make contact. I could feel the heat of him even before we kissed, and for hours after too, when I was lying in my dorm bed, lips branded by his touch.

Devilishly handsome, yes.

But the detail's in the devil.

HANNAH

I'm sure Max is acting differently around me tonight. Nothing dramatic or obvious, but a new layer of *something*: of intrigue, or awkwardness maybe, or a combination of the two. When he talks to me, it's as if he's pushing to sound normal; making an effort to modulate his tone and the spacing of his words. And although it's possible I'm imagining it, I can't be imagining the way his eyes linger on me over our espresso martinis. Or, if 'linger' is too strong a word, at least 'loiter', like the briefest of pauses before jumping off a diving board. Thoughts of our earlier encounter perhaps fresh in his mind. Him just back from his walk, and me in only a towel, staring at each other across the hall.

And he's such a talented chef. All those tiny courses, like miniature culinary artworks, almost too beautiful to eat. Clearly a man who is good with his hands (*stop it, Hannah*). Although I could have done without the conversation over the orecchiette about how I met Chris. All that talk of handsomeness and chemistry made me painfully aware of Max watching me with his brown, steady eyes, and thinking about Chris made me feel guilty for having such an awareness. And for the way I talked about our first encounter at the Kaleidoscope Bar, like it wasn't anything special. Because there definitely was – *is* – chemistry between me and Chris; it's just that meeting him didn't involve a lightning bolt, or anything crazed and passionate. Instead, being around him has always felt easy and fun. We haven't been together long, just a couple of months, but I like the fact he isn't ashamed to engage in life's pleasures – after many cocktails, we went back to his flat together that very first night. There was a brief period of embarrassment the next morning when we woke up next to one another, naked and hungover. But then he started to run his hands over me, and any discomfort quickly vanished.

It turns out that espresso martinis are also effective at banishing discomfort. I'm on to my third now, after several glasses of wine with dinner, and the combination of coffee and vodka is exactly what the doctor ordered: the coffee combating the jet lag, and the vodka loosening the tension in my shoulders. Taking another mouthful of creamy foam, I wonder if perhaps I've been worrying too much about my family of late. Mum hasn't found the last five years easy but, watching her at this very moment – drinking brandy and laughing at something Jackie has said – it seems perhaps she's turned a corner. And as for Lara: well, she's got a long way to go, but she's here, isn't she, along with the gorgeous Poppy. And then there's Max and Jackie, two constants in our lives, a part of our family in all but name. Looking round at them, I feel a swell of warmth and belonging. A glow of affection that even Cassie's presence can't dispel.

My sister gets to her feet, and for a moment I think she's going to make a speech, finally tell us about her past, but instead she runs her hand through Poppy's hair. 'Time for bed, Popsicle.' If only she'd loosen up a little, stop holding everything inside. Even before Dad's death she was like this: contained and precise, sensible beyond her years. Her illness meant she never went out and got wasted, never enjoyed any late-night escapades. And so when I *did*, and sought a confidante at home, she was never interested. I tried a few times – perching on the end of her bed in the early hours of the morning, telling her about the club my friends and I had sneaked into, or the bearded man I'd kissed by the DJ booth – but she always dismissed me, saying she was too tired for my stories. Making me feel somehow sordid and silly for what I'd done.

I'd like to challenge her about the incident in the garden earlier, and to explain that my blog isn't a manifestation of narcissism, as she seems to think, but rather a way to find meaning. I'd also like to know what she wants, long-term: if she's keen to find a partner, or if she'd prefer to focus on herself and Poppy. I can't believe she'll want to work at the pharmacy forever, not when she used to want to be a marine biologist, studying kelp forests and the diverse life forms within them. When she was at her most sick, Dad bought her a subscription to the National Geographic channel, and she spent hours watching documentaries about the oceans, her room awash with pale blue light. Sometimes she'd be up all night watching them – she might have been too tired for my stories, but she wasn't too tired for the sharks, snails, and bright serpent stars with their curling, reaching arms.

Poppy is getting up from the table, her colouring book clamped to one side as she says her goodnights. My sister stands behind her, effortlessly beautiful with her dark hair tied in a messy bun, and a plain blue T-shirt showing off the curve of her neck. I don't think she's even wearing any make-up. 'Are you off to bed too?' Jackie asks.

Lara nods.

'I was going to serve some petits fours in a moment,' Max says, pushing back his chair.

'Oh God, I couldn't eat another thing,' my sister replies, clutching her stomach with a rueful smile, and I want to shake her, because can't she see the slight slump in his shoulders, the disappointment in his eyes? Or perhaps I want to shake *him*, because why does he still seek her approval after all these years?

Why does he still worship her when she ran away from him – from *us* – only to have another man's child? I'm so sick of everything revolving around Lara because she is pretty and needy.

There was a period, just before her A levels, when she briefly became the muse for a guitarist. He was a teacher's son, dispatched to our house to deliver textbooks and papers for Lara (who was mostly studying from home at the time). Struck by her looks and sad story, he started composing songs for her, or at least inspired by her: sprawling, tragic ballads about beauty and solitude, which he would perform on our couch, his eyes upturned to the ceiling or shut altogether.

Around the same time, Max compiled a flash drive of music for Lara. 'A random mix of upbeat songs, to counteract all that sentimental guitar shite,' he said, although his explanation didn't fool me for a second. Because the songs he picked weren't in any way random. They were songs from our parents' old CDs, which we'd warbled along to on car journeys together. Songs Lara and Max had listened to after her transplant, during long, sultry afternoons by the coast. Songs that would make my sister laugh and reminisce; that would make her think of him, or at least occasions spent together. Plus some weird song about having sand under your feet, which always made Lara smile.

The guitarist disappeared soon enough, when it became clear my sister wasn't all that interested in him or his music. But the 'mix of upbeat songs' lives on in a drawer, in my flat in Singapore. Lara abandoned it when she left home, but I took it, cleaned it, and proceeded to play it on repeat, wallowing in its thwarted romance. Full of conviction that Max and I were soulmates, shaped by the sting of rejection, and that one day he would see this. That one day he'd realise he'd been in love with *the wrong sister*.

It was fanciful teenage nonsense, of course, but that doesn't mean its effects don't resonate. And watching him now, eyes upon

Lara, I wonder whether the grooves scored in a teenage heart can ever be fully ironed out.

'Night night, Auntie Hannah.' Poppy comes towards me and I pull her on to my lap for an embrace. 'Goodnight,' I say. 'Sleep tight.'

'And don't let the bed bugs bite!' she says, drawing back from me and smiling.

'That's right,' I say. 'You're a poet and you don't know it!'

'Come on, Poppy,' says Lara. She hurries her through her remaining goodnights, and takes her hand. 'Night, everyone.'

'Goodnight!' Mum, Jackie and I chorus. But Max doesn't say anything; just watches my sister's back as she leaves the room.

And Cassie doesn't say anything either. Instead, she watches Max watching, her face impassive. Then she goes to fetch the petits fours.

LARA

It is with considerable relief that I leave the dining room, take Poppy down the corridor, run her a shallow bath, and sit by the tub as she splashes around. Afterwards, the two of us cuddle in bed to read some books. I can see her eyes closing, but when I suggest she moves across to the bed by the window she says she's scared and wants to sleep in the big bed with me, and I give in easily. Probably too easily – I know the parenting advice says you shouldn't co-sleep with your children, but I don't have the energy to argue. Besides, there's something deeply soothing about lying beside her small body, feeling her warm breath on my cheek and knowing she's right *there*; that she's alive and safe.

It all started so well with her father. Gareth wasn't just good-looking; he was also good at listening, and that's what I needed most back then – a sounding board for my emotions. Talking about Dad's heart attack was still too raw, but I vented my feelings obliquely, by ranting about the lack of preventative health care in the UK while Gareth nodded thoughtfully and asked gentle questions. He also let me sound off about my frustrations with my upbringing: how my illness had consumed so much of my family's energy and time, and how guilty I felt about it. Like there was now this enormous pressure on me to do something worthwhile with my life, to make up for all their sacrifices.

He listened and listened, and then he helped me to break free. To liberate my mind by pushing myself on the pistes: going faster, longer, harder. To forget about my health concerns by drinking *vin chaud* and shots of *génépi* in the evenings, once my hotel shift was over, and to think bigger by lying in the snow with him, holding hands while gazing at the huge, dark sky.

In terms of physical intimacy, he held back at first, saying he didn't want to take advantage when I'd been recently bereaved. But the more we kissed and held hands, and the more he was all kind and sensitive about it, the more I wanted more. And so one night, after we'd left the bar, I asked him to walk me back to his place instead of my hotel dorm.

'I'm not sure.' He ran his fingers through his long hair. 'I mean, don't get me wrong – I want to, obviously, but are you sure that's what you want, when—'

I stopped him from talking by showing him exactly what I wanted.

And then the floodgates opened.

SUNDAY

HANNAH

I can't sleep. It wasn't a problem earlier, after dinner, despite my afternoon nap, but now, at 3 a.m., my disrupted circadian rhythm is making itself known. And the wine and espresso martinis probably aren't helping. My eyes twitch when I shut them, and my brain races: thinking of Max, Chris, Max again. Of Lara shouting at me and Poppy in the garden. Of the way Max watched her as she left for bed. Of the editor, who still hasn't emailed. I feel hot and uncomfortable, hemmed in by my own skin. Too much food and alcohol swilling around in my stomach.

I open my eyes and survey my surroundings, which look otherworldly in the dark. The ceiling with its pendant light like a UFO. The tall lamp in the corner with a huge, bulbous shade – a hovering moon. The glass table, which has been shifted from the centre of the room to make way for my bed, and which crouches by the bookshelf like a smooth alien creature. I stretch my arms, drink some water, take my time in swallowing.

There's a noise in the hallway. Footsteps. And then a creak as the door opens and someone comes in. I sit up. 'Hello?'

No response, but I can see a shape moving through the darkness. 'Hello?' I venture again, more loudly.

The figure stops at the kitchen entrance. 'Hello,' it – *he* – says. Max.

Heat rushes to my skin and I make a mental assessment of what I'm wearing: a silky pyjama top on my upper half, and knickers down below. Just knickers; I'll have to keep my legs under the covers.

'Sorry,' he says. 'I didn't mean to wake you.'

'You didn't.'

Silence.

'I can't sleep,' I explain, wondering what state my hair is in. 'Jet lag.'

'Ah.' He moves into the kitchen and, although I can't see his features, I can tell he's looking in my direction. 'I can't sleep either. Not jet lag though.'

'What, then? Just general restlessness?'

'Hunger.'

I laugh. 'After a ten-course meal?'

He laughs too. 'I know. It's ridiculous. But, in my defence, I didn't get to eat quite as much as everyone else, because I was cooking.'

'Fair enough. It was very impressive, by the way.' There's a pause. 'Your food.' I cringe at the fact I felt the need to specify this.

'Thank you.'

'There's lots of bread, if you fancy it? Or cereal. Or crisps, or biscuits.' I bite down on my lower lip to stop myself from talking.

'I wouldn't want to disturb you.'

'You wouldn't. You won't. I'd be glad of the company.'

'Are you sure?'

'Definitely.'

'Okay then. Do you mind if I switch on a light?'

'Not at all.'

'Thanks.' He fumbles towards the switch and the kitchen is abruptly illuminated, leading him to raise an arm to block out the glare. I, however, am still in relative darkness on the sofa bed, and can see him without having to squint. On his bottom half he's wearing navy pyjamas, but his top half is naked, and I can't help but study his bare chest, which isn't super-muscled but is hard in the way of someone who runs or cycles a lot. Does he run or cycle a lot? He used to ride his bike almost every day, back when we were teenagers, but then so did I, because that was the only way to get around. His torso is covered in hair: thick and dark on his chest, and thinner, sparser, on his abdomen, forming a line which leads under his waistband—

For God's sake, Hannah. Stop ogling the man while he's too dazzled to see. He looks at me now and I make a point of looking back, but only at his face, taking care to keep my gaze above his shoulders.

'Do you want something?' he asks.

'Excuse me?'

'Some food? If I make some?'

'Oh, what? No. Thank you.' Is he going to cook right now? I watch him peering into cupboards, and note how different he is from Chris in a physical sense: shorter, darker, hairier. Less graceful in his movements.

He fetches a bowl and pours granola into it, followed by milk, which makes me smile, because it's such a contrast from what he prepared last night. He stays standing as he starts to eat, looking at me sideways and then down at his bowl again. Chewing long and slow, before taking a second spoonful. The crunch of his mastication is the only sound in the room, and I know I need to say something, that I can't just listen to him masticate. (*Stop thinking about mastication.*) But my mind is weirdly blank, or perhaps the opposite: so full of competing thoughts that there's no space left for conversation.

'Do you think Lara's okay?' My question comes out of nowhere, and I want to take it back but already Max has stopped eating, his spoon hovering halfway between bowl and mouth.

'What do you mean?'

I shrug. 'It's just . . . I don't know . . . I worry . . .' My fingernails rise to my lips and I pull them away.

Max returns his spoon to the bowl. 'She's been through a lot.'

'Maybe.'

His eyebrows arch. 'Maybe?'

'I mean, yes, I'm sure she has. It's just she doesn't really tell me anything anymore.' My voice has taken on an unpleasant whining tone and I try to lift it, to smile through my words. 'But you and she are close, aren't you, and I just wondered, if you knew anything . . .'

'What kind of thing?'

'Just . . .' I fiddle with one of the buttons on my pyjama top. 'How she is. How she *really* is.'

He frowns. 'I think you'd have to ask her that. But she's got a good set-up in London, with Poppy, hasn't she? What with having a park on their doorstep, and the pharmacy and childminder just round the corner.'

'Right.' There's a clenching in my stomach, like I've swallowed something hard, and I can't tell whether I'm jealous of *Lara*, for having Max to visit, or *him*, for being invited. 'You sound like you know it well.'

'I wouldn't say "well". But Cassie and I don't live too far away, and Mum often wants me to drop stuff off for Poppy—'

'What kind of stuff?'

'Children's clothes. Car seats and things. You know.'

But I don't, not really, and maybe that's part of the problem: that everyone seems to inhabit a more adult world than I do. And it's not that I want to be a parent just yet, or know about children's car seats for that matter; I simply want to be viewed as an equal. To not have Lara's teenage words forever ringing in my brain. *Hannah is useless*. 'That's kind of your mum,' I say.

'Yeah.' He pokes at the bowl with his spoon. 'I guess she knows how hard it can be. Raising a child on your own.'

And now the jealousy gives way to compassion as I think about Max, growing up without his dad. The only time he saw him was for a week in the summer holidays, when his dad would race up our street in an open-top sports car, which young Max thought was just about the coolest thing ever. He would run out to the car with his bag and jump in, his dad not even bothering to turn off the engine, and they'd disappear to some swanky resort where his dad paid other people to look after him. Then, when Max was older, his dad still turned up in an open-top sports car, only Max no longer thought it was cool, or ran out to him; instead, he sulked inside until his dad yelled at him to 'get in the bloody car', at which point he'd stomp out and make a point of slamming the car door, and we'd hear his dad shouting at him all the way down the road.

'Of course,' I say gently now. And then, 'Do you ever see your dad these days?'

Max's face hardens. 'No.'

'I'm sorry.'

He pokes the bowl more vigorously. 'Yeah, well, good riddance. Not all of us are lucky enough to have kind fathers.'

And there it is: the pain of loss, creeping up my ribcage, spreading across my chest. A pain I once thought I'd defeated but which I've since learned lurks in the very depths of my body – in the fibres of my muscles, the subcutaneous tissue of my skin – and can come to the surface without warning. The chronic condition of grief.

'I'm sorry,' Max says. 'I didn't mean—'

'I know,' I say.

'Your dad was a wonderful man. More of a dad to me than my own, if I'm honest.'

I nod, thinking of young Max on his BMX. Of Dad showing him how to mend a puncture. Of the two of them trimming the hedge: Dad wielding the chainsaw, and Max holding the ladder. Of Max helping to carry Dad's coffin, his back ramrod-straight as he walked down the aisle of the church.

'I should go to bed,' Max says, and I nod again. 'Shall I switch the light off?'

When I say yes, he snaps it off immediately, and the darkness feels absolute. I can just about make out the sound of his breath, the brush of his fingers along the wall.

And then I'm alone once more.

LARA

As soon as I fall asleep, I dream about Hannah again. There's the slab of rock and the orange light, just like before; her twisted body in the blood-soaked white shirt. But there's something else too; something just beyond my understanding. I try to find a different way in – to grasp whatever it is that lies so close.

And then I wake up.

It takes a few seconds to orient myself: to see I'm in the master bedroom at Grove Cottage, with its bank of wardrobes and strange spiral staircase in the corner; with its curtains pulled tight to shut out the long, dark window and the cliffs beyond. Poppy is stretched diagonally across the bed, taking up more room than seems possible for one so small, and I wrap my arms around her, soak up her warmth and feel her heartbeat through her thin nightie. She murmurs something in her sleep and I stroke her cheek, lowering my lips to her forehead. Whoever said love and hate are two sides of the same coin had it wrong, because it's love and fear, for sure, and they're directly proportional to one another. Particularly in the middle of the night, in that dark gap between winding down and beginning anew, when a person is most truly and bone-shatteringly alone. The greater the love, the greater the fear, and when the love is all-consuming, the fear is too: a yawning crevasse of possibility which feels like it might immobilise me forever. As a child, I remember learning how, when threatened, female rabbits sometimes eat their young, and thinking it was preposterous, pointless, stupid. Whereas now, lying here with Poppy in my arms, I can almost understand it. Because if she didn't exist, I wouldn't worry about needing to protect her.

I must remember there is good in the world. I only have to think of Dad; of the way he always prioritised my health and happiness. Like when we found out I needed a stem cell transplant, and he instantly put himself forward for tests. And the practical optimism he displayed when we learned he wasn't a match, telling me there were other family members we could try, and a whole register of donors beyond that. The small acts he undertook to make my life bearable while we were waiting: helping me with my maths, even when Mum thought I was too sick to study, and putting up silly posters in my room. And the sacrifices he and Mum made. They'd always talked about moving to upstate New York, about living in the Adirondack Mountains where the whole family could hike and kayak and ski, but that was clearly a non-starter once I needed constant medical care.

And now Dad's dead and they'll never get to go.

I stroke one hand along Poppy's forearm, the soft, unblemished flesh a rebuke to the world's hard edges. And vow, for the millionth time, to do whatever it takes to keep her safe.

But protecting my sister is a different matter altogether. Unlike Poppy, I have no mandate over Hannah's actions, nor any ability to influence her. Quite the opposite, in fact. I think about standing in that hospital corridor, the phone clutched to my ear, being told Hannah was coming very shortly. 'Tell her I need her right now,' I had said. 'Tell her it's urgent. Tell her I'm in trouble.'

'I'll tell her,' the voice on the other end had said, and yet still my sister didn't come.

A man's footsteps came instead.

HANNAH

I'm woken by the sound of whispering voices: one far away, quiet, and one much closer, not really quiet at all, more of a stage whisper. 'Auntie Hannah!' When I open my eyes, Poppy's face is the first thing I see: big eyes and rounded cheeks, wispy blonde hair falling across her forehead. She's leaning against my bed, one hand on the mattress. 'Auntie Hannah!' she says again, breaking into a smile.

'Good morning.' Light is seeping through the blinds but it's a gentle, nebulous light instead of the shine of morning proper. 'What time is it?'

'Seven o'clock. Mummy says I'm allowed to get up at seven.'

I resist the urge to check my phone or pull the duvet over my head. 'Do you want to jump in?'

'Sorry.' This is Lara's voice, from across the room. 'She wasn't supposed to disturb you.'

'She's not disturbing me. Come on, Pops!'

Poppy jumps on to the bed, snuggling down under the duvet beside me. 'Ooh, your feet are cold!' I protest, and she giggles, pressing them against my thighs.

'You weren't supposed to wake Auntie Hannah,' Lara says. 'Remember? I told you we were just going to tiptoe in and get some cereal.'

This makes me think of Max, standing by the worktop last night. Chewing and gazing, chewing and gazing; the world reduced to the simplest of wants.

'But she was already awake!' Poppy protests, warm breath against my neck.

'I'm not sure she was—'

'No, I was,' I lie. 'Or, at least, I was only dozing. Do you know what the plan is for today?'

'Will you read me *Hoarse Horse* again?' Poppy scurries out of the bed and grabs her book from the table.

Lara pulls her dressing gown cord tight, busying herself with bowls and spoons. 'A trip to Chatsworth, I think.'

'Auntie Hannah.' Poppy taps my arm. 'Will you read me *Hoarse Horse* again? Please?'

'Chatsworth sounds good.' My sister is even thinner than I'd realised yesterday, her dressing gown accentuating the tininess of her waist. 'And yes' – I turn to Poppy – 'I'll read it again. But only if you'll do the "neighs" and "nays"?'

'Yes!'

'You don't have to read to her,' Lara says.

'I want to.'

She shrugs. 'If you're sure.'

I pull the blinds open and settle back on to the pillows. Poppy wiggles herself into my armpit and puts her thumb in her mouth, sucks away contentedly as I start to read. The book is sufficiently simple that it doesn't require my full attention, so I let my eyes wander between its pages and my sister as I recite the repetitive rhymes; see Lara fetch a carton of milk as I orate the woes of a horse with a bad throat. See her take a loaf of bread from the bread bin, before wandering over to the double doors. Looking out at the view as the horse tries gargling, chewing clover, taking honey from a beehive (bad idea) and visiting a horse whisperer, before eventually accepting it just needs to rest.

As I close the book's cover, I ask Lara what she's looking at. She doesn't reply. 'Lara?' I say again, more gently. 'Are you okay?'

'Hmm?' She turns towards me, her eyes glazed. 'Yes, I'm fine. I was just looking at the sky.'

I twist round. 'It's beautiful, isn't it,' I say. 'Such a lovely orange colour—'

'Orange?' My sister snaps to attention almost violently. 'You think it looks *orange*?'

'Well, orangey pink,' I say, unsettled by her reaction. Wondering if she's worried about some sort of folklore, like a red sky in the morning being a shepherd's warning. 'Why—'

'It doesn't matter.' She shakes her head. 'Forget I said anything. Poppy, it's time for breakfast.'

'Will you read *Hoarse Horse* again?' Poppy asks me.

'Er . . . I think your mum would like you to have something to eat.'

'Just one more time?'

'Poppy!' Lara's tone is sharp. 'I've asked you once, and shouldn't have to ask you again. Come and get breakfast. Now.'

With a sulk in her shoulders, Poppy gets out of the sofa bed and trudges to the table. There's some negotiation over which cereal she's going to have, but as soon as she's eating, her mood improves. 'Auntie Hannah, will you make a birthday cake for Granny with me?'

'Um . . . I'm not particularly great at baking but . . . I don't see why not,' I say, as Lara simultaneously tells us Jackie has already made one.

'But we could make another?' says Poppy.

'I don't think Granny needs two cakes.'

'How about cupcakes?' I suggest.

Poppy is happy with this idea but my sister frowns. 'Let's not promise anything—'

'I'm not promising,' I say. 'But cupcakes seem like a good compromise: they're easier to make than a big cake, and we can have fun icing them, maybe add some Halloween decorations—'

'Yes, yes!' Poppy is off her chair now, dancing across the sisal mat. 'Can we get sprinkles, in lots of different colours?'

I nod. 'If we can find them. And as long as your mum says it's okay—'

Poppy makes a whooping sound, then looks at Lara. 'Can I have some bread and jam now?'

'Yes. Go and fetch the jam from the fridge. The strawberry one.' As Poppy runs off, Lara turns to me. 'Please don't promise anything to Poppy unless you're definitely going to follow through on it.'

I feel a pang of hurt, deep inside my abdomen. 'What's that supposed to mean?'

'Just what I said—'

'But I *am* going to follow through on it—'

'Poppy's had enough disappointment in her life—'

'I'm promising cupcakes, Lara! Not a trip to the moon—'

'I thought you weren't promising anything—'

'You know what I mean.'

'Sure.' Lara turns away to close the cereal packet.

'For goodness' sake!' The hurt has turned to anger, a flicker of white heat in my chest. 'It'd be nice if you had the tiniest bit of faith in me. If you hadn't decided I'm totally *useless*.'

If she picks up on the emphasised word, she doesn't let on. Instead she watches Poppy, who is searching through the shelves of the fridge. Picking through vegetables and pots of yogurt, apparently unable to see the jar sitting directly in front of her. 'The jam's *there*!' Lara says eventually, her voice full of exasperation, and I feel like telling her that maybe she should reflect on her own behaviour, instead of criticising mine. That at least I'm *flexible*, open to change and opportunity, instead of being constantly uptight.

'There, Poppy! On the shelf in front of you!' She marches to the fridge and picks up the jar herself, before marching back to the table. Watching her, I'm too tired to be angry anymore. My muscles feel heavy, my eyes even heavier. I let them shut.

'Do you want to use my bed?'

I open my eyes again to see Lara watching me, her expression softer. 'No, I'm fine.' I say, and then, as an afterthought, 'But thanks.'

She dumps a teaspoon of jam on to the buttered bread. 'You should,' she says quietly. 'You look done in.'

I'm about to protest when I realise that, actually, I could really use some more sleep. And that it would be a relief to shut myself away from everyone else for a couple of hours: from Mum and Jackie, who will no doubt appear for breakfast soon, talking loudly; from Max, whom I'm in no fit state to see, and Cassie, who probably eats something annoyingly virtuous in the mornings, like rolled oats with chia seeds; and from Poppy and my sister, who are both – for very different reasons – exhausting. 'Maybe I will go . . .'

She nods.

I pick up my phone and stumble along the corridor to the master bedroom. There's a weird spiral staircase in the corner that I didn't notice yesterday – I take a quick look up it and find a dusty attic at its top, with a couple of Poppy's toys strewn across the floor. Returning to the bedroom below, the bed looks huge and inviting and I smile when I see Moo Moo, Lara's old and rather worn cuddly cow, tucked under the duvet. I move Moo Moo to the gap between the pillows and, within seconds of lying down beside his balding black-and-white belly, I'm falling asleep.

LARA

It takes me a while to compose myself after Hannah has left. I lean against one of the dining chairs, watching as Poppy munches on her jam-soaked bread, turning our conversation over in my mind.

She said the sky looked orange.

I look out through the double doors. There is no longer any discernible orange – the colours of sunrise have given way to a hazy blue – and yet this isn't enough to reassure me. I know dreams don't translate directly into reality, but nor do they spring from a void – they come from lived experience and fears. Which means an orange sky might not be a disaster, but it's hardly auspicious.

I clutch the chair harder. Is the entirety of the week going to be like this? An endless series of observations – of the colour of the sky, my sister's whereabouts, her clothing – accompanied by endless spikes of adrenaline, and subsequent attempts to steer us to a safer trajectory? Attempts which might be entirely futile or pointless but which I'll have to undertake, just in case . . .

'Good morning.'

I turn to see Max and Cassie entering the kitchen – he in a thick navy dressing gown and she in a silky kimono.

'Good morning,' I reply.

As they set about frying bacon for breakfast, Jackie and Mum appear, and soon the kitchen is full of noise and chatter.

'Mummy?' Poppy presses her nose against the glass of the double doors. 'Will you come and play in the leaves with me?'

'I've got to clear up—' I begin, but Mum cuts across me.

'We'll do that,' she says. 'You head out; you look like you could do with a break.'

I'm about to object, to point out I'm fine and Poppy and I need to get dressed, but manage to stop myself. Mum's only being nice, and actually, who cares what Poppy and I are wearing? I've got so used to being responsible, to worrying about every last detail of our lives, that perhaps I've forgotten how to have fun.

So, instead of declining, I thank Mum and open up the double doors. 'Let's go, little one!' And, for the next ten minutes, my daughter and I throw leaves at one another, and ignore the rest of the world.

HANNAH

There's a pinging sound, which is coming from real life, not my dream. Pulling myself awake, I see the light is pouring through the open curtains. I turn to my phone. Just gone nine; I've been asleep for nearly two hours. And the messages are from Chris, not the editor (but then, it is Sunday). He's asking if I'm up, if I'd like to speak.

I check my appearance. My skin has more colour than it did yesterday and my eyes look better too – no longer quite so sunken. I'd like to put on some mascara, but it's in my case in the living room, so I have to make do with running a hand through my hair. Then I call.

He answers straightaway, only the top of his face in shot. His blue eyes and sandy brown fringe. 'Afternoon, gorgeous,' he says. 'No, I mean morning. For you.'

'Good morning.'

'Are you on your own?' His tone is flirtatious.

'Yes.'

'Good – that means I don't have to behave.' He moves the phone so I can see his full face. 'Are you still in bed?'

'I'm afraid so. Sorry.'

'No, I *like* it.' His voice becomes conspiratorial. 'I like finishing work for the day and seeing you still in bed.'

'Really?'

'Yes. I like thinking what I'd do to you if I were there.'

I laugh. 'And what would you do?'

He starts to list the acts, in order of increasing filthiness. It's fun to watch his lips as he speaks, knowing they're the protagonist of many of the acts mentioned. And a relief, too, that he's distracting me from thinking about the editor or Max.

'And what would you like to do to me?' he asks.

I falter. It's not that I don't like having sex with him; I just feel stupid talking about it.

I'm saved by a beep from my phone. Chris laughs. 'I wouldn't have paid for that bloody app if I'd known it would interrupt us when we're already in the middle of . . . *connecting.*'

I laugh too. 'Is that what we're calling it?'

'It's what the app's called—'

'Yes, but . . . shall we hang up and do our photos anyway? Then we can call back and discuss them.'

'Okay.' He grins. 'See you shortly.'

Hanging up, I cast around for inspiration. There's nothing interesting or comical in here; what I really want is some sort of euphemistic item: an aubergine, perhaps, or a marrow. There's a hairbrush on the chest of drawers and I wonder if I could do something suggestive with it, but I'm not keen to promote spanking. Could moisturiser stand in for some sort of lube? Or would it just look like moisturiser?

I'm running out of time. In desperation, I pull up my pyjama top and take a photo of my breasts. The result is less pert than I'd prefer so I prop up my breasts with a pillow and try again, being careful to keep the pillow and Moo Moo out of shot. Much better.

I press send. Seconds later, his images come through too: a pack of condoms from the front camera, and a torn-open wrapper from the rear.

I didn't even think about my rear camera. Looking now, I see it's captured the spiral staircase to the attic. Perhaps I can pass that off as something.

Chris's number comes up on the screen and, when I answer, his smile is so wide it threatens to crack his face in two. 'Your best photo yet,' he declares.

'You liked it?'

'Of course I liked it. Such gorgeous curves, which made me want to climb on—'

'To *connect*—' I correct him.

'To connect,' he agrees. 'And unusual too. I've never seen a spiral staircase in a bedroom before—'

'Oi!' I shout at the phone, and he laughs. 'Just kidding,' he says. 'Your tits were obviously better than the stairs. I'll be taking that image to bed with me tonight.' He winks. 'Quite literally.'

'Disgraceful,' I joke.

'Although, in all seriousness' – his forehead creases, but he's still smiling – 'I really have never seen a spiral staircase in a bedroom before.'

I laugh. 'Me neither. It's kind of weird. Although cool, I guess, in a quirky sort of way. I'm in my sister's room.'

'Your *sister*'s room?' He adopts an expression of mock horror. 'Are you honestly telling me you sent lewd photos of yourself—'

'Lewd?'

'*Lewd* photos of yourself . . .' he repeats, 'from your sister's bed?'

'I'm afraid so. But it's better than taking them from *my* bed, given I'm basically sleeping in the kitchen, and everyone's having breakfast—'

He tips his head back and laughs. 'So have you taken any photos on your trip which are suitable for public consumption?'

'Yes. I haven't just been taking pictures of my chest.'

'How disappointing.' He laughs again. 'No, but seriously, I'd like to see your other photos too. You've hardly put any on your blog so far.'

I'm touched, and a little surprised, by his interest. 'I didn't know you read my blog.'

'I don't always,' he admits. 'But, given you're away, it's nice to hear what you're up to.'

'Awww. You're a softie really—'

'I wouldn't go that far—'

'Well, you'll be pleased to know I intend to write a longer update tonight. There wasn't much time yesterday.'

'Great.' He smiles. 'I'll look forward to it.'

'Don't get your hopes up too much—'

'All right. But weird spiral staircases and beds in the kitchen aside, do you like it, where you're staying?'

I nod. 'I'd prefer my own room, but the cottage itself is nice.' I'm about to offer him a tour when I notice some movement from outside. With my phone still in my hand, I get out of bed and walk to the window. Just beyond it, only a few metres away, is Max. He's standing under a tree with his back to the house, talking to someone. They seem to be having an earnest conversation, leaning towards one another and whispering. Are he and my sister enjoying a bit of alone time?

The thought creates a flare of jealousy, followed closely by relief, and then confusion, when he steps to the side and I see who the other person is. She nods at him and puts a finger to her lips, before turning and walking away.

Not my sister, or Cassie.

Mum.

LARA

Poppy is only four years old but I've already seen enough playgrounds to last a lifetime. Slides, swings, seesaws, climbing frames; I've seen them all, in various guises and permutations, and normally from an uncomfortable angle: hunched over to stop Poppy tumbling backwards, or stretched up to stop her falling down. And although Chatsworth Adventure Playground is a superior example – with tunnels and bridges, elevated rope walkways and water play – I still find myself in a variety of contorted positions, wishing to be elsewhere. Not wanting to be crouched in sandy water while Poppy tries to spin the waterwheel, nor trying to balance the two of us on a swaying bridge as she inches across, before being confronted by a tube slide which I'm worried I'll get stuck inside. But at least she's safe.

And so is Hannah. I can see her from the bridge, sitting on a wooden bench, looking at her phone. Wearing a blue gilet with a striped top underneath; no white shirt in sight. No rocks either, other than a couple in the water play area, which are much smaller than those from my dreams.

Mum, Jackie and Cassie have gone to Chatsworth House, and Max stayed behind at the cottage, so it's just the three of us in the playground: Poppy, Hannah and me. Plus a whole load of people I don't know: young mums chatting as their children run around hollering and whooping; dads dragging unwilling children across high walkways; grandparents being unfeasibly patient while toddlers scream in their faces. But when I am halfway down the tube slide – Poppy on my lap and my hands clawing at the metal to get us down faster – an awful thought occurs to me: what if a stranger is going to hurt Hannah?

My heart starts to race and, by the time we reach the bottom of the slide, I've convinced myself she's in imminent danger. I tell Poppy we need to go and see Auntie Hannah immediately, that we need to hurry, and when she asks why, I tell her there's no time to explain. I start to run, pulling her with me, away from the slides and across the small bridge to the benches.

But Hannah's no longer there.

I can feel panic rising as I shout her name, as I push past a mother handing out snacks, as I scan the area uselessly for a blue gilet.

'Lara! What's wrong?'

It's her – oh thank God, it's her – standing a few metres away, beside a small stream.

'I just . . .' I begin. 'I thought something had happened to you.'

'No, I'm all good.' She smiles, but it's only a half-smile. 'Not unless you count the fact a bird took a crap on me. Or, at least, on the bench right next to me; I'm hoping none of it got on my clothes.'

I can't bring myself to smile back.

'I'm fine, Lara!' she says. 'Great, in fact, bird excrement aside. How are *you* doing?'

'Oh, I'm okay.'

'Are you sure?' She drops her voice, reaches for my hand. Her fingers clutch mine and for a moment it's like we're young children again, sitting on the top bunk, swapping secrets. Able to tell each other everything.

But then I think of standing in that hospital corridor, waiting for her to come to the phone, and I pull my hand away. 'Yes.'

'Okay.' She sighs, after which there is a long silence, filled only by the chatter and squeal of children. When she speaks again, her tone is business-like. 'Do you know why Max hasn't come out with us today?'

It's an odd question – who cares why Max decided to stay behind? Or maybe I've just forgotten the art of pointless conversation. 'I imagine he's not all that interested in stately homes or adventure playgrounds.'

'Probably not,' she agrees. 'But the thing is, I saw him talking with Mum earlier . . .' She breaks off, and I'm left wondering if this is some sort of joke. But she doesn't laugh.

'So?' I say.

'So it was kind of secretive, and weird.'

'In what way?'

'It was out in the garden, just the two of them, and it looked like they were whispering—'

'Perhaps they're having an affair?' I don't know why I say this but, seeing Hannah's eyes widen, I regret it immediately. 'Do you think so?' she asks.

'No, of course not.' I press my hands to the back of my neck. 'He was probably just seeking her advice on something.'

'Like what?'

'I honestly have no idea. Why do people keep asking me about Max?'

Hannah looks sharply at me. 'Who else has been asking you about him?'

I've got my foot in my bloody mouth today. 'Oh, no one.' I attempt to wave her interest away.

'Was it Cassie?'

'No – Jackie.'

'What was she asking?'

'Just what I think of Max and Cassie as a couple.' I try to keep my voice flat so as not to invite any further questions, but Hannah instantly asks why. I shrug. 'She thinks they might be about to get engaged.'

'Engaged?' All the colour drains from my sister's face. 'Engaged?' she repeats. 'Max and Cassie?'

I shrug for a second time. 'Jackie was only speculating.'

'But she thinks it's possible?'

'Look, I really don't know.' I fold my arms across my chest. 'But it's not like it matters either way, so long as Mum has a good week and Poppy—' I turn to the right, to where my daughter was standing, but she's no longer there. My stomach drops. 'Where's Poppy?'

Hannah turns too, ninety degrees at first, and then in a full circle. 'She was here a second ago.'

'Poppy!' I scan all around quickly, looking for a glimmer of red or green. There's a boy in a red hat, and an elderly woman in a green raincoat, but no Poppy. 'She was wearing her coat with the apples on it,' I say, my heart starting to thud. 'Poppy? Pops! POPPY!'

I run, erratically, from left to right and left again, across bridges, under walkways, looking up through gaps in the wood, grabbing the net around the trampoline and thrusting my face to it to get a better view of the children within, peering up into the branches of the trees, and behind their trunks; splashing through the water play area in case she's hidden by the wheel or, God forbid, is lying face down in the water. All the while I'm shouting her name, more and more frantically, and people are turning in my direction, so many faces, all looking, staring, but none of them is her; none of them belongs to my sweet, precious daughter.

And then my vision narrows to a single, agonising point of realisation.

Poppy isn't here.

HANNAH

She can't have gone far. She was standing by us just a couple of minutes ago. There's no need to panic. I head in the opposite direction to my sister, along the tree line, walking briskly. I ask an old lady on a bench if she's seen a girl with blonde hair and a coat with apples on it, but she shakes her head, so I ask the family on the next bench along, but it's a no from them too. I can hear Lara screaming Poppy's name and turn to see her running around the playground in a frenzy, and wonder if I should go to her, try to calm her, but decide the only thing that will help is finding her daughter. She can't be far away. As I continue to search, I think of how much Poppy loves playing hide-and-seek, and wonder if she's hiding now; if she's standing behind one of the trees, giggling. I weave my way through the trees to see, and as I peer behind one tree after another, I get to thinking about Max and Cassie. Surely they're not going to get engaged? They're only in their mid-twenties, and haven't been together that long.

But now isn't the time to be dwelling on such matters. 'Poppy!' I call out. 'Poppy, if you're hiding, you've done really well, because we can't find you! You've won! Poppy?' I pause, waiting for her little body to come wriggling out of some hidey-hole, a grin plastered across her face. And when it doesn't, I feel the first twinge of actual fear.

I pick up the pace, running around the perimeter of the playground and asking everyone I pass if they've seen a girl matching Poppy's description. I try to keep my voice calm, to keep my mind calm, to ignore the churn within, because it won't help anyone if I succumb to hysteria too. And, besides, she can't have gone far. A few people join the search, which prompts a couple of others to get involved, and one of them tells me there's a meeting point for lost children at the far side of the playground, by the first aid station, so I head there, and on the way I pass my sister climbing up a slide and screaming, so I grab her arm. At first she tries to push me away, shouting, 'I've lost Poppy! It's happening – Gillian, oh my God. The message . . .' but I hold on and shush her as she screams and flails and then suddenly it's like all the fight goes out of her, because her body slumps in defeat. I help her down the slide like she's a child herself, lead her over to the first aid station where I explain to a woman in a high-vis jacket what's happened and she speaks into a walkie-talkie while my sister sits, coiled, in a chair. Another member of staff tells my sister everything is going to be fine; that children frequently get separated from their parents, and there's good procedures in place to find them, and it's only then, when other adults are taking charge of the situation, that I think about what my sister just said. *It's happening – Gillian . . . The message . . .*

'Lara.' I place one hand on to hers and she doesn't shake it away. Just stares at it, as if there's truth to be found in the puckered skin around my knuckles. 'What did you mean, before? Who's Gillian?'

Slowly, she raises her head, lets her eyes meet mine. And when they do, her expression is distant, like she's barely seeing me at all. 'You wouldn't understand.'

I lean towards her. 'What wouldn't I understand? What message?'

'I . . .' she begins, and I wait, not wanting to push her, and she opens her mouth again, but instead of saying anything she lets out a choked shriek, leaps to her feet and runs past me. I turn to see

Poppy being led towards us by another high-vis-jacketed member of staff, and jump to my feet as well, by which time my sister already has Poppy in her arms, is screaming at her and embracing her and crying, all at once. Poppy looks a little bewildered, and starts crying too, and I find I also have tears in my eyes, but I wipe them away, and go to thank the official.

'We found her in the tunnel,' he explains.

I remember the sign we saw on the way into the playground – the secret entrance Poppy opted not to take at the time. 'Of course . . . we didn't think . . . Thank you so much, thank you—'

'All part of the job,' the man says, and I thank him again, and apologise, before tapping my sister on the shoulder and suggesting maybe it's time for us to leave.

LARA

That message will always haunt me. As I sit in the back of Jackie's car, clutching Poppy's hand while Mum tells us about Chatsworth House, I know this to be true. I know it in the same way a felled forest knows the absence of trees.

I thought I'd done the right thing, emailing Olivia about Gareth and Gillian. It was a couple of years back, and I felt I had to write, that I wouldn't be able to live with myself if I didn't. And it wasn't as if I didn't take precautions: I went to a library in Birmingham, over a hundred miles away from our flat in London, and used an anonymous account.

Perhaps my real mistake was to go back and check. Perhaps, if I'd just sent the email and then abandoned the account completely, I wouldn't now have this gnawing anxiety at the back of my throat; a sense of impending doom. But I had to make sure it had been delivered successfully, that my warning had got through. And so I'd returned to Birmingham, to the library, and logged into the account again. Where the message had been waiting for me.

You fucking bitch, it said. *One day I will find you and your daughter. And I will make you pay.*

HANNAH

I give Cassie a lift back to Grove Cottage. Hers isn't the company I'd choose, but at least there are no tears or screaming. We talk politely for a while about Chatsworth, Singapore and holidays abroad, before the conversation takes a more difficult turn. 'Why was your sister so upset?' she asks. 'In the car park?'

Lara made me promise not to tell the others what had happened with Poppy. 'It will only worry Mum,' she said as we walked back to meet them. Which was true. 'And, actually,' she continued, 'Poppy was completely fine – it was me who overreacted.' Which was also true. But still I had my doubts, because even if Poppy was okay, the incident was one more mark against Lara's mental health.

And yet she was insistent. 'Please, Hannah,' she said. 'It's just because I've lowered my meds, and I'm a bit all over the place, but I'll stabilise soon. And it will be easier to do that if Mum isn't fussing – you know what she can be like.'

A third truth. I nodded. 'Okay.'

'Thank you, thank you!' The gratitude in her voice made it seem almost worth it. A glimmer of light in our troubled relationship. One that I don't want to extinguish by saying the wrong thing to Cassie now. 'I think she's just a bit overtired,' I choose to say.

'Oh.' Cassie pauses, turning to look at the green fields flashing past the car window. 'Can I ask you something?'

'Sure.'

'What's the deal with her and Max?'

I'm pleased to have a reason to keep my eyes on the road. I ask what she means.

'Max talks about her all the time,' she says.

'Really?' I change gears to keep my hands busy.

'And he looks at her like . . . well, she's very pretty, isn't she?'

'Uh-huh—'

'So, I guess it seems like . . . maybe . . . they have a romantic history. Max says they don't, but sometimes I wonder if he's being entirely truthful with me—'

'You don't need to worry on that front.' I study the satnav to see which road to take at the roundabout.

'No?'

'No. Lara's never been interested in Max. Not in that way.'

There's a long silence, and it's only after I've come off the roundabout that I realise what I've implied through omission. 'I mean . . .' I begin, but I'm not sure how to make it better. The silence grows thicker. 'It's always been platonic between them,' I say. 'And it always will be.'

I can feel Cassie's gaze upon me, so intense it almost itches. 'How can you be sure?'

There's no easy response to this. If I were being truthful, I'd say Lara's never looked at Max with a scorching heat in her eyes; has never made him a mixtape, or dressed up for him, or chosen to spend hours by his side when there's been a viable alternative. Has never followed him around, or come to life when he's entered a room. But how can I say any of this without explaining he's done the opposite?

It starts to rain, and I turn on the windscreen wipers. 'Lara's not really in a relationship place at the moment,' I say, thinking about how she acted in the playground earlier. How she shouted at me in the garden yesterday simply for showing Poppy my phone.

'But that's when it happens.' Cassie's voice is stiff. 'It's always when people aren't looking for love that it finds them.'

Love? Perhaps Cassie is more perceptive than I'd realised. Although she clearly isn't aware of Lara's history. Without giving too much away, I try to explain about my sister's leukaemia and transplant; how she finally became well, only for Dad to die of a heart attack. How her time in France was difficult, and she's had some trouble with anxiety since returning.

'Yes, Max mentioned that,' Cassie says. 'That she's suffered from panic attacks and weird things can set her off. Like being freezing cold, or the smell of mountain pines.'

This is news to me and, not for the first time, I'm hurt by the confidences shared between Max and my sister. Confidences to which I'm not privy. There's a burning sensation in my stomach as I turn the wheel, as I mumble 'Mmm-hmm', not wanting to admit to being out of the loop.

'It must be difficult,' Cassie goes on, her voice smooth and full of false concern, and suddenly I can't bear this conversation any longer.

'Do you mind if we talk about something a bit cheerier?' I say and then, before she has time to object, 'It sounds like things are going really well between you and Max.'

'Why, what have you heard?' Her tone is curious, with perhaps a shade of suspicion.

'Oh . . . just . . . a little bird told me there could be an important announcement sometime soon?'

'Who said—'

'I can't disclose my sources.' Now I wish I weren't driving, because I'd like to scrutinise Cassie's face more closely. See whether she looks surprised, or smug, or horrified. I sneak a quick glance to my left and notice a faint smile. Dammit. If Jackie is right, and Max is going to propose this week, it looks like he'll get a positive answer.

'Interesting,' Cassie says, turning to look out of the window, where the rain is now falling harder.

That's one word for it, I think, before cranking the wipers up, and deciding I need to speak with Max.

We drive the rest of the way in silence.

Pride and Piggy Bliss

It's been a busy twenty-four hours since I last posted, during which I've visited the famous **Chatsworth estate**, *home to the Duke and Duchess of Devonshire, and enjoyed a meal fit for a duchess, courtesy of a talented young chef whom I'm lucky enough to call my friend . . .*

So, Chatsworth first. I've included some photos here of the majestic house, constructed in 1555, and of the beautiful gardens, which were overhauled by Joseph Paxton in the 1800s, to incorporate the immense Emperor Fountain and the Arboretum. Given all this grandeur, it's hardly surprising that Chatsworth House was used as a stand-in for Pemberley, the home of Austen's handsome, enigmatic Mr Darcy, when filming Pride and Prejudice in 2005. The film featured not just Chatsworth's exterior but also some of its famous interiors, including the Painted Hall and the Sculpture Gallery. A perfect backdrop for all that pent-up romance and desire . . .

But I didn't see either of these on my trip, because instead of visiting all the grown-up stuff, I embraced my cool inner auntie and went to the farmyard and adventure playground! My niece loved the goats and tractor, and I loved the gorgeous Old Spot pigs, and both of us loved the playground, which was so fun and whimsically designed, like something from a Tolkien story, with wooden towers and walkways – a full write-up, with entry details and useful tips for making the most of your day, is included **here** *...*

And now on to the meal. Although 'meal' is a bit of a misnomer, because it was more of a banquet, really, with ten incredible courses, all autumn-themed and making the most of sumptuous seasonal produce, including roasted woodcock with truffled celeriac, and venison with wild mushrooms (see photos below). This culinary magic was created by my incredibly talented childhood friend Max Thompson, who works as a chef at **Le Petit Jardin**, *a fabulous neighbourhood restaurant in the heart of London's theatre district (which has a* **special offer on pre-theatre meals** *until the end of October). If you ever get a chance to check it out, you really must – I feel extremely privileged to have been treated to my own chef's table for the night!*

Tomorrow will bring more culinary adventures, but focused on one particular product – the

Bakewell tart. This delicious creation is made using sweet shortcrust pastry, frangipane and jam, and is different from a Bakewell pudding, which has a puff pastry exterior and a soft custard topping. Tomorrow I'll be visiting some of Bakewell's finest eateries, to enjoy their takes on the famous tart, which I'll rate according to crispness of pastry, tastiness of filling, quality of extras, and overall presentation. I'll share my winners tomorrow, along with my plans for some physical activities later in the week, to counteract all this gluttony!

And that's it for tonight. The weather wasn't amazing today (although at least the rain held off until we'd finished at the playground), but we've got a great forecast for tomorrow, so fingers crossed it stays that way . . .

The first chance I get to speak with Max comes after dinner, when everyone disperses. Lara and Poppy head to bed, Mum and Jackie settle down on the sofa with a bottle of wine, and Cassie takes a bath. But then, while I'm washing up, Max disappears too, and Mum and Jackie don't know where he's gone.

Looking around, I see my sister's perfume bottle sitting on the edge of the bookshelf. Opening it, I dab a little on to my wrist and breathe in its scent: a clean, peppery smell. Unmistakably Lara. I place the bottle into my washbag for safekeeping. Then I head into the corridor and tap on Max's bedroom door. No response. I try again, softly call his name. Still nothing. I think about returning to the kitchen, but something sends me in the opposite direction, to Lara's room at the end of the corridor. As I approach I can hear muted voices, so I creep closer; realise it's Max and my sister whispering inside. Unusually for them, they seem to be having some sort of disagreement. I hear Max say, 'I'm really not sure it's a good idea,' and my sister reply, 'Please. I need to know.'

I press my ear to the door.

'If we try to contact him, we just risk stirring things up,' Max says.

'But I'm not suggesting we contact him, I'm suggesting we contact Olivia.'

Olivia. My sister mentioned a Gillian earlier, and now an Olivia. Who are these women, and why have I never heard of them before? *Perhaps I should ask Cassie*, I think bitterly, *seeing as she seems to know more about my sister than I do.*

There's a long pause before Max speaks again. 'I'm not sure. What if he—'

'You can ring her at the office. The Grenoble office. Olivia Williamson.'

Grenoble. Near the Alps. Almost certainly something to do with Poppy's father. I don't remember exactly which ski resort Lara was at, but it can't have been too far from Grenoble.

'I'm really not—'

'Please, Max.'

'I'm sorry. I want to help, I really do. But it's been years, and I genuinely think—'

But I never find out what Max genuinely thinks, because at that moment I hear the bathroom lock being pulled back and I run away down the corridor towards the kitchen as Cassie appears in a kimono. 'Hi,' I say, too breathlessly.

'Hi Hannah. Are you okay?'

'Me? Yes! Why? Do I not look it?'

'You look a little flustered.'

‘Flustered? No, not at all; I just need to use the bathroom.’ *For God’s sake.*

She raises her eyebrows. ‘Okay, well, it’s all yours.’

I’m about to thank her when Lara’s bedroom door opens and Max steps out. The temperature drops a couple of degrees as Cassie sees where he’s come from. ‘I was just . . .’ he begins, making everything so much worse with his apologetic tone. ‘Lara needed—’

‘I don’t give a shit what she needed,’ Cassie hisses, before turning on her heel and storming into their room.

‘Cass!’ Max calls. He runs down the corridor and I can’t help but notice the way his body moves: the sway of his chest beneath his sweater; the strong, flexing muscles in his legs.

And then he is gone too, and I remain outside the bathroom, alone.

MONDAY

LARA

I can't sleep. Poppy is in bed with me again, and I have to restrain myself from running my hands across her face, from squeezing her into wakefulness.

I need to find out where Gareth is, what he's doing. But Max is refusing to help me. He says it's been four years; that, if Gareth were going to come for me and Poppy, he'd have done it by now. But Max never saw the message. *One day I will find you and your daughter. And I will make you pay.*

And it's not as if I'm proposing to contact Gareth directly. I won't even type his name into a search engine, let alone try to call him, or seek him out in person. All I want is for Max to ring Olivia. The two of them have never met, aren't aware of each other's existence, so there's no danger to be had in a quick conversation. And it would hugely help my state of mind if I could find out what Gareth is doing, what he's up to.

I get out of bed to check the windows. They're all shut, but the expanse of dark glass is discomfiting, and I half expect to see a face pressed up against the panes. My heart thumps as I redraw the curtains and return to the safety of the bed.

Why won't Max help me? Perhaps it's churlish even to ponder the question, given everything he's done for me in the past, and I'm grateful for all of it, I really am. And maybe he's even right to refuse my request, because perhaps I'm just being paranoid, and should let sleeping dogs lie. Perhaps my fears are simply a result of my reduced medication, or my earlier scare with Poppy, and I need to ignore them, move past them.

But what if I can't? What if I'm beginning to spiral, and the only way to halt the process is to find out where Gareth is? To learn for certain he's no longer a threat?

Yet how to do this without putting Poppy or myself in danger? Dad is dead, and Max won't help, but there's one other person who's come through for me before, and might just do so again. In fact, the more I think about it, the more I convince myself it's the right course of action.

I need to ring Steve.

HANNAH

In the early hours of the morning, when the others are safely ensconced in their rooms, I take out my laptop and run a search for *Olivia Williamson Grenoble Gillian*. I click into any results which look promising, unsure what I'm looking for but discounting the elderly woman from California who is sharing her European holiday snaps, and the schoolgirl with an Instagram account devoted to eating fondue. I end up with three possible Olivia Williamsons (none including the word 'Gillian'): a twenty-something snowboarder, a woman who works as a photographer in France, and a woman who works at a Grenoble travel agency. There are contact details for each: a Twitter account for the snowboarder, and telephone numbers for the photographer and travel agent. I look at the Twitter account first; the profile picture shows a woman wearing a white snowsuit, helmet and goggles, spinning in the air. The posts are almost all of this woman performing tricks, with occasional clips of other snowboarders or skiers. I scrutinise any footage that includes a man, even though I don't know what Gareth looks like, and the men's faces and hair are hidden by sunglasses and helmets. Their clothing, meanwhile, is variations on a theme: technical jackets and salopettes, chunky boots and gloves. Nothing noteworthy.

I save the telephone numbers for the photographer and travel agent, to ring at a more civilised hour, put my laptop to one side and re-plump my pillows. I'm thinking about visiting the bathroom when I hear footsteps in the hall.

I quickly spritz myself with Lara's perfume, undo the second button on my pyjama top, and pick up a philosophy book I found on the bookshelf. Then I recline against the pillows and position the book across my knees.

My efforts are rewarded when Max pads into the kitchen a few seconds later. He's dressed identically to last night: navy pyjamas on his bottom half, and nothing above. He stops when he sees my bedside light is on. 'You're still up?' He speaks softly.

'Afraid so – the jet lag has really got to me. Or maybe this book is just too riveting.' I let out what I hope sounds like a self-deprecating laugh.

'What are you reading?'

'Just something I found on the bookshelf.' I turn to its cover, already regretting my decision to pick something so pretentious. '*An Introduction to Philosophical Thought*.'

'Heavy stuff.' He comes into the living room and takes the book. 'Socrates, Descartes, Wittgenstein. Crikey. But I suppose I shouldn't be surprised – you've always been smart.'

My skin glows warm at his words, and a memory resurfaces of helping him with his GCSE English assignment one wintry weekend afternoon. The two of us sat close together at the breakfast bar in the kitchen, thighs almost touching, looking through passages from *Lord of the Flies*. I explained the conch represented democracy, and its breaking meant the end of civilised rule. He jotted notes before going to make us both drinks: a cup of tea for him and an espresso for me, not because I liked it, but because I liked the way it made me look – older, sophisticated, an intellectual. We tapped our drinks together and said 'cheers', laughing at the contrast between his large mug and my teeny-tiny cup. Not thinking about my sister for once, despite the fact he'd originally come over to see her.

'Lara was the smart one,' I say now, without knowing why I'm saying it. Whether it's because it's too weird not to acknowledge the dynamics of our former trio, or I'm testing him.

'She was incredibly smart,' he agrees. '*Is* incredibly smart.'

I tell myself it wasn't a test.

He sits down on the end of the bed and flicks further through the book, before reading out a passage. '*Happiness is not an ideal of reason but of imagination.* According to Kant, anyway. Does that mean we only imagine ourselves to be happy?'

'I'm not sure.' I shuffle down the bed and kneel up to read over his shoulder. I imagine what it would feel like to move forward a couple of centimetres, to press myself against his back. To map his vertebra through the touch of my body.

But simply imagining it doesn't make me happy.

'It says here that people often sacrifice long-term happiness for short-term pleasures.' He trails his finger across the page as he speaks.

'I can believe it.'

'That the more we try to pursue happiness, the further away from it we'll get.'

Maybe that's my problem, I think, as I breathe in Max's proximity. That I'm always pursuing something – validation from a magazine editor, the perfect relationship with my family, the perfect relationship full stop – instead of just being.

Except, isn't striving to accept the status quo a pursuit in itself? And wouldn't true abandonment of pursuance mean a person should just . . . act? My lips hover by the back of Max's neck. 'Do you believe that?' I ask.

'Not really,' he says, turning to face me. 'I think pursuing happiness makes me happy.'

What does he mean by such a statement? With him this close to me, I don't dare to ask; I simply take in the bones of his jaw and its constellations of stubble. His brown eyes striated with hazel, umber, chestnut. The tiny red capillaries that traverse his corneas. The jumbled hairs of his eyebrows. His eyes, again, staring into mine.

He jerks backwards, scrambles to his feet, and heads into the kitchen, where he switches on a light and starts looking in cupboards. I want to ask if he's hungry, but find my throat is dry, and reach for my water bottle instead.

'Granola,' he mutters, his back to me, and I'm unsure if I'm meant to respond. I watch as he searches through the cereals for the granola, and opens the fridge to get milk. He pours both into a bowl and begins to eat, and tonight the sound feels too loud, too intimate, in the silence of what isn't being said.

So I break it. 'Who's Olivia?'

He looks towards me. Stops chewing.

'I heard you talking about her earlier,' I say. 'With Lara.'

He looks back at his bowl, his face unreadable.

'And I don't mean to pry but . . . I just wondered what you were talking about, because I'm a bit worried about the way Lara's acting, and I thought if I could understand . . . what's troubling her . . .'

'I'm sorry, Hannah.' His voice is stiff. 'But it's not my place to say.'

'But what if . . . not saying . . . could ultimately make things worse for her?'

He scrapes at his bowl with his spoon, becomes focused on one spot within it. 'It's a risk I'll have to take. I can't betray her confidence.'

'And what about Cassie?'

He looks up sharply. 'What about her?'

'How does she feel about you keeping secrets for my sister?'

A flash of anger crosses his face, and I wonder if I've pushed things too far. But then his shoulders slump, and he sighs. 'She doesn't like the fact I'm close to Lara. Even though I've assured her time and time again that nothing's ever happened between us.'

'But surely you can see why she might feel threatened? If you're having all these clandestine conversations—'

'We're not having "all these clandestine conversations". I had one entirely innocent chat with her, at her request—'

'But that's enough to invoke jealousy, right?'

'Apparently so.' He sighs again, turns and puts his bowl into the dishwasher. 'Cassie's really upset about it. She says if I'm serious about her, and not Lara, then I need to prove it to her this week.'

'And how does she propose you do that?' It's a poor choice of words, but at least I don't put any emphasis on the word 'propose'.

'If only I knew.' I'm relieved at his lack of certainty. And then a little ashamed, because he sounds tired and unhappy; a man with many burdens to bear. It occurs to me that perhaps he is so busy supporting others, and trying to juggle their needs, that he's not taking sufficient care of himself. 'And Max?'

'Yes.'

'I'm here for you. If you ever need to chat or . . . anything.'

'Thanks. I appreciate it.' And with that, he switches off the overhead light and leaves the room.

LARA

I lie awake, thinking about Gareth. About the fact I moved in with him just three weeks after we started having sex. It made sense at the time, given we were spending every spare minute together. And given he lived alone, in a beautiful chalet at the edge of the village, whereas I lived in a shared dorm. Prior to moving in, I'd go over to his as soon as I finished a shift at the hotel, and head back only minutes before the next one, so it wasn't as if anything really changed; the only difference was that my few belongings now resided at his.

It was thrilling initially, like I was a proper grown-up for the first time. Living with my boyfriend, with no one else to tell us what to do. We could eat what we wanted; play music loudly in the middle of the night; and fuck, of course, wherever and whenever the fancy took us. And it often did: there was cunnilingus in the kitchen and blowjobs in the bathroom; doggy-style in the doorways and cowgirl on the couch. There was sex outside too, in the trees that lay at the bottom of a blue run, and in a dip near a quiet chairlift. I was late to work a few times because I was too busy coming to go, and Steve, my boss at the hotel, got annoyed, but I made up for it by being super-friendly and helpful to all the guests. I smiled as I brought out their starters and mains, as I offered them more wine, as I ran from table to table delivering bread, clearing plates and offering advice on the best ski runs in the region.

During this period, I tried not to let myself think about home. Occasionally my mind would wander there – to thoughts of Mum lying alone in her and Dad's king-size bed, or my sister trying to keep Dad's vegetable garden under control – but I quickly redirected it to a less painful place. There was no trace of my family in the Alps; the snowy mountains were essentially clean sheets – a place to lay down new tracks, and forget the old. And while I sometimes felt guilty for not making contact, I justified it by telling myself they were better off without me. That Hannah had always been resentful of the space I took up and could now live more expansively, could find herself without my being in the way. And as for Mum, well, she had enough on her plate without worrying about me too.

The problem was, the longer my silence became, the harder it was to justify. But also – the harder it was to undo. It's easy to find something to say to a person you converse with daily, but when you haven't spoken for months, the words can be elusive. Particularly when they are important words; words that can make a difference. And thus a few missed calls turned into many, and a brief silence turned into a lengthy one, and I blocked it all out by doubling down on distractions. Working, skiing, drinking, fucking, and not necessarily in that order. In fact, the working and skiing started getting squeezed out by the drinking and fucking, or at least the boundaries became blurred, such that I had silly, avoidable falls on the pistes, and tested the patience of my co-workers at the hotel. I turned up to shifts late, and sometimes drunk – one evening, I dropped a platter of snails because I could barely see straight, and splattered garlic butter over the chairs. Steve gave me a warning for that, but he gave me another chance too, saying he knew my dad had died recently. 'I know it must be hard for you,' he said. 'But

I'm running a business here, not a charity, and you need to get your shit together.'

For a couple of days, I did better, spending less time with Gareth and alcohol, focusing on being an exemplary employee. But then, one afternoon, I received a message from Hannah which cut me to the core. Mum wouldn't stop crying, she said, and she didn't know what to do.

I didn't know what to do either. But when Gareth appeared at the hotel that night with cocaine and a bottle of red, I slunk off with him into a guest bedroom and had crazed sex on the balcony, looking out at the lights of the piste bashers below.

And then I was fired.

HANNAH

I didn't drink much last night but morning still hits hard. It's Mum and Jackie who come into the living room first, talking loudly about going to Bakewell later until they remember I'm on the sofa bed, at which point they whisper loudly instead. My limbs are heavy as I sit up, my conscience heavier when I think of Max beside me in the middle of the night. The physical pull of him. *Nothing happened*, I tell myself. And yet, if I'm completely honest, I know it was his willpower, not mine, which stopped us from going any further. His loyalty as a boyfriend. A loyalty which simultaneously irks me and makes me like him all the more.

I check my phone. It's Monday today, a working day. But there's still nothing from the magazine editor. I guess it's early. Chris has sent a message saying he misses me.

'I'm going to ring Chris from the garden,' I announce to the room. I slide from the bed, still in my pyjamas, and open the blinds.

'Good idea,' Mum says. 'It's shaping up to be a gorgeous day.'

She's right: with the blinds open, the morning sun streams through the glass, suffusing the room with warmth and light. Casting a gentle glow across the oilcloth on the table and the marbled worktop in the kitchen. Meanwhile, beyond the grass of the garden, the bracken is sparkling with dew, and the golds and russets of the leaves have been deepened by the sun's rays. Even the cliffs seem less austere than yesterday, perhaps because the sky behind them is such a vivid blue, streaked only by the lightest traces of cloud.

I head outside, enjoying the dampness of the grass under my bare feet and the heat of the sun upon my arms. I sit down at the picnic table, stretch my legs out across the bench, and video-call Chris.

He answers with his camera off, but I can hear the smile in his voice. As well as the rustling of fabric. 'How's it going?' he asks.

'Okay,' I say, wiggling my toes in the warmth. 'A few minor stresses. Are you going to switch your camera on?'

'It depends if your family are there. I don't want to scare them.'

I hope Chris isn't fishing for compliments. He can be a bit sensitive about the way he looks sometimes, saying he is happier behind the camera than in front of it. I think it's because of his mother; he once told me she always criticises his appearance, and praises his brother's. An issue I can identify with, but not necessarily support him on – there's only so much sibling-induced insecurity one person can take. 'I'm on my own, in the garden. Why would you scare—'

His camera comes on to reveal his naked, near-hairless chest, and his grinning face atop it. 'I was just getting changed when you called.'

I smile. 'Good timing on my part.'

'I'm glad you think so. So what are the stresses?'

I hesitate. I've made a point of not telling Chris much about my family to date, partly because it's nice to be admired on my own terms for once, rather than in relation to Lara, and partly because I don't want to bore him. But I briefly outline the issues now. How perpetually on edge my sister seems, and how annoyed she is with everything I do. How freaked out she was when Poppy disappeared yesterday for all of a couple of minutes.

'No offence, but your sister sounds like she can be hard work,' Chris says.

'She really can,' I agree. 'But what's even more frustrating is how everyone else dances around her, trying to keep her happy.' I don't mention the conversation I overheard last night, in which Max seemed reluctant to do Lara's bidding. Looking into the kitchen, I can see Mum and Jackie drinking tea at the table, and Cassie opening the freezer. No sign of Max or my sister.

'Family reunions are always fraught,' Chris says. 'I think it's because everyone regresses to how they used to act together, even if they're thirty years older and supposedly wiser.'

'Maybe you're right.' It does sometimes feel like we're trapped in our teenage roles: Lara centre stage and emotionally fragile, Max the adoring, dependable audience, and me waving wildly from the wings. But our infant selves were different: a happy, boisterous trio, clambering on rocks, having water fights and shouting with glee and indignation. 'It's just . . . she used to be so much more . . . *alive.*'

'I guess some people aren't cut out for motherhood.'

His words surprise me in their harshness. Particularly coming from a man about a woman. From a childless man about a single mother. And perhaps he realises this, or sees it in my expression, because he scrambles to make amends. 'Sorry, I just mean . . . not everyone thrives on being a parent. It's cracked up to be this huge thing, this amazing thing, and I'm sure it is for many people, but for others it can all be too much.'

'Maybe,' I say, unsure whether I want to complain more about Lara, or defend her. Or whether I should probe into the delicate subject of his own mother instead. But ultimately I chicken out of all three. 'How's your day been?' I ask.

'Not too bad.' He tells me about a story he's covering for work, and the restaurant he's going to tonight. I try to focus on what he's saying, but my mind is still centred on Lara, particularly as Poppy has just entered the kitchen. I watch her sit at the head of the table, feet dangling high above the floor while Mum fetches some bread and jam. It's only the two of them in the kitchen now; still no sign of Lara. It's unusual for Lara and Poppy to be apart, and it occurs to me that perhaps it's not healthy to live quite so much in each other's pockets, and perhaps that's why Lara reacted in such an extreme manner in the playground yesterday. But what do I know? As everyone keeps telling me, I don't have children.

Chris is saying he needs to iron a shirt, so we say goodbye, and I feel a brief pang at not being able to kiss him. But then I return my gaze to the house and notice a face at the attic window. The reflected sun on the glass makes it impossible to see who it is, but I'm fairly certain they're staring right at me. I raise my hand in a semi-wave.

Seconds later, the face has gone.

LARA

Bakewell is a pretty town, with lots of little shops and cafés, and a river with an arched bridge across it. But we've only been out of the car for about five minutes when Mum and Jackie announce they have a surprise. Turning down a side street, they lead me and Hannah to a beauty salon, where they've booked me (but not Hannah) in for a treatment. 'It's on us,' they keep saying, even as I insist I don't need it, and one of them should enjoy it instead. Jackie tells me that everyone needs to relax occasionally, and Mum says they'll look after Poppy, and they practically manhandle me into the place, despite my protestations. When I say I can't leave Poppy, they give each other a look, saying she'll be fine, and then they go, Hannah promising Poppy an ice cream, and I try to accept it – to tell myself it's a kind gesture and might even be good for me.

I'm escorted to a sofa, next to a water cooler with chunks of fruit floating in it like dead rats in a puddle, and a woman hands me a clipboard. 'Do help yourself to a drink,' she says. 'There's green tea, chamomile tea or fruit-infused water. And if you could just hand your form to your therapist once you're done . . .'

I nod and turn back to the clipboard. Most of the questions on the form are straightforward: *Are you receiving dialysis treatment? Are you, or could you be, pregnant?* But a few are trickier. When it comes to the question *On a scale of 1–10, how stressed are you?* I circle 8, only to want to take it back when I see the next question: *If you answered 7 or more to the above, please outline the main cause of your stress.* I stare at the paper for a few seconds, wondering what would happen if I were to write *I can't move past the past*; whether the doctors in white coats would come rushing out. Ultimately, however, I opt for a simple answer that won't set any alarm bells ringing. *Work, childcare, family responsibilities.*

A petite woman in a white tunic arrives and introduces herself as my 'therapist for the afternoon' (although her name badge says *Anne*). She takes my form and escorts me down a corridor into a small room which has a sweet and woody scent. Like pine trees, I realise with a flutter of panic. I tell myself to calm down, to focus on the soft music emanating from speakers in the corner. Anne passes me a robe and paper knickers, before pulling a curtain between us and inviting me to undress and climb on to the bed.

It's been years since I've been naked around anyone other than Poppy, so even with the curtain in place, I feel deeply self-conscious as I strip down to my underwear. My fingers fumble as I take off my bra, the hooks tricky to unlatch, and I look around for hidden cameras. I move on to my lower half, peeling down my pants and replacing them with the paper knickers, which are far too large, ballooning around my abdomen like some sort of comedy parachute. Then I climb on to the bed and, lying face down, arrange the sheet to cover as much of my body as possible.

'Are you ready in there?' Anne asks and I tell her I am, although it's a lie, because as soon as she opens the curtain I stiffen, and the touch of her hands on my shoulders makes me flinch.

'You're carrying a lot of tension,' she whispers. 'Try to relax.'

I tell myself it's fine, that Anne massages people all the time and won't be disgusted by my bony body. But I don't like the fact that there's only a small hole in the bed through which to breathe, nor that the gentle music seems to be overlaid by the sound of snow falling. It makes me think of the balcony at Gareth's chalet, looking out across the glittering pistes. *No, don't think of that.* I need to turn my mind elsewhere, to inhale deeply, but Anne is pressing down harder now, which makes my lungs feel like they're being compressed, and the pine smell seems stronger, like I've been transported to the forested slopes of the Alps, and my breath is becoming shallower, the snow is falling harder, there's too little oxygen—

I sit up, clutching my throat, and lurch from the bed to the floor.

'Are you all right?' asks Anne, no longer whispering.

'The music,' I say. 'What—'

'It's our "Sounds of the Mountains" playlist,' she says, concern etched upon her face. 'For our Mountain Relaxation Experience. But we can change it—'

'No need,' I say, pulling my trousers on over the paper knickers and my top over my bare chest.

'I'm sorry it's not to your taste.' She consults her notes. 'You were originally booked in for our Jungle Relaxation Experience, but someone rang to change it just this morning. Shall we change it back?'

'No,' I say, pushing my feet into my shoes, on top of my balled-up socks. 'Sorry to waste your time.'

And I run from the room.

HANNAH

Leaving Lara at the spa feels like a minor miracle. Not just because I wasn't expecting her to stay, but because the mood lightens almost instantly, all of us joking and smiling and practically skipping along the streets of Bakewell, eating ice cream and enjoying the sunshine. Max and Cassie have gone to see some friends with a new baby in Sheffield, and while I was initially disappointed Max wasn't coming with us, I have to admit it's a relief right now not to be thinking about my appearance, or how witty I'm not being. We wander into a gift shop, where Jackie buys a wool blanket for herself, and I buy Poppy a squishy sheep she immediately cuddles.

Then we carry on to Granby Road, the site of Bakewell's weekly market. Mum and Jackie sniff at some handmade soaps which smell overwhelmingly of lavender, while Poppy and I find a baking stall, which reminds me of my cupcake-baking promise. I tell her she can pick three types of decoration, and she reacts by bouncing with excitement, sifting through what's on offer and holding something up every couple of seconds to proclaim how amazing it is. 'Gold icing!' she exclaims. 'Roses! Sprinkles!'

While I wait for her to decide, I check my emails (still nothing from the editor) and look at the nearby clothing stall. After a quick browse, I treat myself to a T-shirt in a pretty cornflower hue, much like the one Lara wore the other night. My skin isn't as pale as hers, but the colour should bring out my eyes. I'm just returning to Poppy when the Connect app goes off in my bag. I extract my phone and notice Poppy staring. 'Have you chosen your decorations yet?' I ask.

But she won't be distracted that easily. 'Are you doing the pictures? For your boyfriend?'

She's too smart. I nod.

'Can I take them?'

'No, sorry. Your mum wouldn't like that.'

'But I won't look at anything on your phone, or play with it. I just want to take the pictures. I've never used a camera before.' She looks at me beseechingly. 'Pleeeease. Pretty please. Pretty please with sprinkles on top! Pretty, pretty—'

'Oh, go on then.' No doubt I'll pay for this later. 'But just taking the photos, okay? Nothing else.'

She squeals with joy and hugs me.

'And you can't be in the photos either, so you'll have to hold the camera out to your side.'

'How do I do it?'

I bend down to show her how my phone works, and where she has to press, conscious that my two minutes are quickly running down. 'Can you get a photo of me in front of this stall?' I say. 'And then hold it out, like this' – I move her arm to one side – 'to get the market in the background.' She takes the photos and I check them, see that she's captured my legs and chest but cut me off at the neck. I explain she needs to tilt the camera up and she tries again, slightly more successfully, in that my face is now in shot. The rear camera image shows a woman walking through the market with a Labrador. Not great, but they'll have to do.

Seconds after I send them, Chris's pictures come through, and I'm careful to shield my phone from Poppy in case they're unsuitable. Yet he has also opted for more wholesome images today:

a plate full of sushi and a room full of diners. I show them to Poppy, but she has lost interest and returned to the decorations.

Looks tasty, I write.

Not as tasty as you, comes the reply.

I'm with Poppy, I type quickly, feeling myself blush. I want to be wanted, but seeing it in writing makes me cringe. *Are you having a good night out?*

So-so, he messages. *Good food. Middling company. Bad beer.*

I post a laughing emoji. *Lol. Who are you there with?*

Just a couple of friends. Do you want to chat?

No, I'm about to do my Tart Crawl.

OMG send me pictures!!

Behave. I don't want to sound like a prude. *My BAKEWELL Tart Crawl.*

Spoilsport.

How late will you be out? Poppy picks up a jar of red sprinkles and starts to shake it. *I should go*, I write. *Shall I call you after?*

I think I'm nearly done tbh. Speak tomorrow?

'Auntie Hannah!' calls Poppy. 'I've chosen.'

Sounds good, I write. *Miss you.*

Miss you too.

I smile as I put my phone back in my bag and go to buy cake decorations. Poppy has chosen gold icing, pink roses and silver balls, none of which are Halloween themed, so I add some black icing, pumpkin toppers and rice paper ghosts. Not long after, Mum and Jackie reappear with a bag of soap, and then the four of us wander round the market together until it's time for me to leave.

I walk up the road to the triangle at the centre of town, where I sit down on a bench with an unobstructed view of my surroundings. Taking out my phone, I check Twitter to see if the twenty-something snowboarder Olivia has followed me. She hasn't. So then I ring the photographer Olivia, and a man answers. 'Hello?'

I inhale sharply – could this be him? Gareth? The man on the phone has a French accent and I've always imagined Gareth to be British, but I don't think Lara has ever confirmed either way. He could be French, or Italian, or Swiss, although 'Gareth' doesn't sound very continental. I only have a moment to decide what to do.

I ask for Olivia Williamson.

'She's not here right now,' he says. 'Can I help?'

Can he? I bite my lip as I try to decide what to say. 'No, I'll try again later.' My hand is sweaty around the phone. I thank him and hang up.

Sitting on the bench, I rub my hand on my jeans and watch as people and traffic pass me by. Wondering if I should have asked a question, or left a message. Wondering if trying to track down Olivia when I know nothing about her is a fool's errand. But then, if Max already knows who she is, I don't see why I shouldn't.

I pick up my phone again and ring the third Olivia, the travel agent one. This time a female voice answers, says something in French.

'Er . . . do you speak English?'

'Yes, of course, good morning, Alpine Retreats Travel, how can I help you?' The switch of language is so fluid that I feel embarrassed at my own lack of linguistic ability.

'Er . . . is Olivia Williamson there, please?'

'Speaking.'

I take a full breath. 'Sorry, this might sound a bit odd, but do you know a snowboarder named Gareth?'

'I think you might have the wrong number. This is a travel age—'

'I'm trying to find someone,' I break in. 'He's a snowboarder called Gareth, who knows an Olivia Williamson in Grenoble.'

'I am sorry, I cannot help you.'

Cannot or will not? Her voice is smooth, giving nothing away. 'There's nobody in your office called Gareth?' I try. 'Or one of your clients? I know you can't give out personal information about your clients but if you could just say if the name rings—'

'I cannot help you,' she says again, more firmly this time. 'I am sorry. Goodbye.' She hangs up.

Dammit. I stare at the ground, at the sandy-coloured pavement tiles which border the kerb.

Then I look up and around. Locate The Cup and Sorcerer and make my way towards it.

It's time to eat some tarts.

LARA

I stand on the bridge, looking out at the river beyond, slick and shining, almost still. A willow tree is draped across the water to my left, and more trees line the riverbank to my right. It's a bucolic scene, at odds with the traffic behind me: lines of cars grunting and belching fumes as they cross the bridge. I watch two women walking with a little girl between them, and almost duck down, thinking for a second that it's Mum, Jackie and Poppy. But the women are too young and the girl is too old. I look at my watch again. Only half an hour until I'm supposed to finish at the beauty salon. I practise smiling, saying how relaxing the treatment was, because obviously I can't say what really happened – that I had a panic attack on the massage table and ran away.

I remember walking with Dad along the riverbank here, many years ago. We fed the ducks, laughing as they swarmed our feet and poked at my wellies for scraps. I wasn't any good at tearing the bread, ended up giving them hunks as opposed to Dad's neat crumbs, so most of the ducks stayed by me, fighting for the pieces I dropped, sometimes making me startle, then giggle, with their flapping and squawking. If they became too aggressive Dad would lift me on to his shoulders. I felt unassailable up there, like the world was mine for the taking.

Sometimes I wonder how different life could be if Dad hadn't died. If I might have stayed in England instead of fleeing to France. If I might have avoided entering into a toxic relationship, or at least been better equipped to escape it. Sometimes I scare myself by thinking how lucky I was to get away; how many pieces of chance had to come together. If Max had been less caring, or Steve less vigilant, I would probably still be stuck in Gareth's chalet.

The room in the spa really brought it all back. That sense of suffocation, of not knowing which way was up. I thought I'd made progress – that I'd left the worst of the fear behind – but it turns out my memory is a traitor, hanging on to the pain and biding its time to wound me afresh. I lean more heavily on the parapet, the heat of the sun pressing down upon my skin, my breasts hanging loose, and wonder how it's come to this. How, at the age of twenty-six, I'm standing on a bridge wearing paper knickers and no bra and wondering where it all went wrong.

The only certainty: I need to do something about it.

HANNAH

The first seven stops on the tart crawl go well, although the eating becomes less enjoyable as I grow full. I've made my task more complex than it needs to be, by rating each tart according to five criteria, but I'll only list the winners on my blog, as I don't believe in naming and shaming bad performers. Mum doesn't agree with this approach – she says if you're not prepared to give negative reviews, there's no point being a reviewer – but I think her stance is old-fashioned. Churlish, even. Because what's wrong with praising good businesses and not castigating struggling ones? There's enough negativity in the world already.

But so far none of the tarts have been bad anyway. Most have been presented in slices but one came as an entire miniature tart, set on a handmade plate. Beautiful. I had to stick to my two-spoon rule, to leave room for the remainder of my tastings, but I made sure to tell the waitress just how delicious and beautiful it was, so the chef wouldn't be offended by my leftovers.

I only wish Max could be here too. We'd make a good team: him brimming with knowledge about the texture of pastry, the evenness of a tart's finish, the sweetness of its frangipane; and me, the amateur enthusiast, able to describe its mouthfeel in a relatable way. I wonder how he and Cassie are getting on in Sheffield. She was bad-tempered with him this morning, no doubt still brooding over his whispered discussion in Lara's room yesterday. He, on the other hand, was practically falling over himself to appease her: making her coffee and poached eggs, and nodding and smiling at everything she said. It's maddening that she doesn't seem to realise how lucky she is. That while she's gallivanting with him in Sheffield, I'm sitting on my own, scribbling in a notepad about almonds and jam. Writing about mouthfeel instead of experiencing it properly.

After leaving my seventh tasting, and needing a reprieve, I head into a quiet side street and try the photographer Olivia again. This time a woman answers. 'Hello?' Her accent is English, her tone friendly.

'Oh, hi,' I say. 'Is Olivia Williamson there, please?'

'Speaking.'

'Oh, great, great.' I pause, looking at the outdoor clothing shop beside me, its window a montage of lurid jackets and backpacks. Then I take the plunge. 'Sorry, this might sound a bit odd, but do you know a snowboarder named Gareth?'

'Who is this?' All the friendliness in her voice has gone.

'Um, he gave me some snowboarding lessons a while back, and I wanted to get in touch—'

'And he gave you *my* number? The number I use for work?'

'Um . . .' My body is thrumming with adrenaline at the realisation that she seems to know Gareth. That I might finally be getting somewhere in learning about my sister's past. I pace around in circles on the pavement, trying to expel my nervousness through my feet. 'No, sorry, but I've lost the number he gave me and—'

'So how did you find mine?'

'I . . . er . . . I remember him saying something, about an Olivia—'

'You've got a fucking cheek.'

The venom in her voice is startling. 'I'm sorry,' I say, my circles on the ground becoming smaller, tighter, until I'm practically spinning on the spot. 'I think there might have been a misunderstanding. You took photographs for Gareth, right?'

'That's about the only thing we haven't done together.'

Oh. Is Olivia his girlfriend? Or someone who's had a fling with him in the past? Either way, things don't seem too great between them now. 'I'm sorry,' I say. 'I didn't know you two had a history.'

'A history? He's a fucking dickhead—'

'Right—'

'And also, unfortunately, my fucking husband.'

LARA

Still standing on the bridge, I dig my old Nokia from my bag and scroll to the number of Le Bellevue. The hotel where I worked in France for nearly two months, until I was fired. I call before I can lose courage, and when a receptionist answers I ask, in English, for Steve. Hoping against hope that he still runs the place and is willing to talk to me.

'Certainly.' A rush of relief. 'Who is calling, please?'

I hesitate. I trust Steve but don't want to give my name to strangers who might know Gareth. 'Just tell him it's the woman who dropped the snails,' I say.

There is a pause. 'One moment, please.'

Tinny music plays as the seconds pass – surely too many seconds – and it takes all my willpower to stay on the line. But finally someone picks up. 'So?' he says, with a small chuckle. Definitely Steve. 'The woman who dropped the snails?'

'Yes.'

'Well, well.' An intake of breath. 'It's been a long time. You were one of the best waitresses I've ever had here until . . . well . . . How are things?'

We exchange pleasantries for a while – me telling him about Poppy, that she's four years old and at preschool now, and him telling me about the hotel – and it's weirdly good to hear his voice.

I feel a sudden rush of guilt that I haven't ever properly thanked him. 'I'm sorry I haven't rung before,' I say, my words coming out too quickly. 'I'm so grateful to you, for everything you did, and I should have told you before, should have—'

'Stop,' he says. 'Please. You don't owe me anything.'

'But I do. You helped me, even after I behaved terribly—'

'It wasn't you that behaved terribly. It was that man. I hope you're well clear of him.'

'Actually, that's why I'm ringing.'

There's a long pause, and when Steve speaks again, his voice is stiff. 'I see.'

'I mean . . . I'm not back with him or anything, but I'm worried he might come after us . . .'

'Has he threatened you?' Steve sounds angry now.

'No. Well, yes, but a couple of years ago.' I explain how I emailed Olivia when I found out on Instagram that she was pregnant. How I told her what had happened with me and Gareth and Gillian, because I felt I needed to warn her. And how, not long after, I'd received that awful response. *One day I will find you and your daughter. And I will make you pay.*

'What an arsehole,' Steve says. 'If I see him again, I'll kick his head in.'

'I don't want you to get dragged into this.' The idea of Steve getting hurt or into trouble, because of me, is unbearable. 'If you see him in the village, please don't mention any of this, or confront him, or anything—'

'You're safe on that front – he sold his chalet a while back.'

'He what?' Small spots appear at the side of my vision, and I grab hold of the parapet.

'He left. And good riddance too. There's a nice couple living in the chalet now, who run a ski touring outfit – they come into the hotel occasionally—'

'But where did he go?'

'Who, your ex? Who cares?'

'*I* do. I need to know where he is.'

'It's been a long time, Lara.' Steve's voice grows gentle. 'You're free of him now.'

'But you know what he's like.' My heart is racing. 'And he threatened me!'

'Two years ago, you said. I think it's been long enough now that you don't need to worry.'

I swallow hard, larger spots dancing across my vision; everything feeling darker, closer. 'When it comes to Gareth, I always need to worry. When did the chalet get sold?'

'I can't remember exactly – it's not like he and I were on speaking terms. But maybe nine months ago?'

'And you haven't seen him since?'

'No.'

Shit shit shit shit shit. If Gareth left the ski resort nine months ago, then he could be anywhere. I swivel round on the spot, watching the cars cross the bridge, peering in at the faces of the drivers and passengers. He could be anywhere at all.

And he could be coming for me and Poppy.

HANNAH

Gareth is a married man. A married man whose wife is not my sister. This potentially explains a lot: why she's not in touch with him, why she won't speak of him, why she becomes so prickly whenever I bring him up. And I wonder if he was in fact married to Olivia when Lara met him, and wouldn't leave her; if Lara's refusal to let him into Poppy's life is a direct reprisal for his rejection. Or whether he doesn't even know about Poppy. I can absolutely believe my sister is proud enough to struggle by on her own instead of risking humiliation.

Or perhaps she is ashamed. Not wanting to admit she had an affair with a married man, and thus choosing to claim it was a one-night stand. A narrative which paints her as careless, but nothing worse.

Unsure what to do with this newfound information, I lean my head against the shop window.

'I take it you're one of his hussies?' Olivia's voice is so acerbic that I straighten up again.

'No—' I begin, but she cuts across me.

'I'm not a fool. I know what he gets up to. Picking up girls, showing off with his stupid snowboarding tricks, making out like they have a special connection.'

'It's not—'

'But if he's giving out my number, just to rub it in my face, that's a new fucking low, even for him.'

I trace one foot across a crack in the pavement. 'I don't—'

'Oh, look, I don't even fucking care anymore. I know about Lara, you know. And Gillian. So another affair hardly comes as a surprise to me.'

She knows about Gillian. The woman my sister mentioned at the playground. So presumably Gareth had an affair with Gillian too, but lied about it? It seems odd that my sister was so gullible; if he slept with her while married to someone else, can she really have been surprised when he proceeded to cheat on her as well?

'I'm sick of his twisted shit,' Olivia continues. 'We're in the process of getting a divorce, and this conversation only makes me more convinced it's the right thing to do. Tell him that from me—'

'I'm not with him,' I say, noticing that one of the coats costs £199.99, and that my hand is shaking. 'I'm trying to find—'

'And also tell him if he gives my number out to anyone else, I'll walk away with every last penny.'

'Wait—' I say, but she's already hung up, and I'm left staring at my phone screen. At the contact name I entered last night. *Olivia2.* I contemplate changing it to something more relevant: *Ex of Lara's ex*, perhaps. Or *Separated (?) wife of Poppy's dad.*

But then I think again of the vitriol in Olivia's voice. Of the rage that fuelled her every word. And I think about my sister's extreme reluctance to discuss even the smallest element of her time in France, and her meltdown in the adventure playground. *Gillian, oh my God*, she'd said.

I can't decide whether to tell her what I've learned. She's clearly not in the best mental state at the moment, and discovering that I know the truth about Gareth – that he's a serial adulterer in the middle of a divorce, that she and Poppy are not in any way special or important to him – might just push her over the edge. Unlike me, Lara has spent her whole life being at the centre of things, so she probably hasn't developed the requisite toughness to deal with existence at the periphery. Or, at least, with the humiliation of others knowing she resides there.

But, at the same time, there's a part of me that wants to tell her. A nasty little voice at the back of my head urging me to speak. *So now you know how it feels*, it wants to say. *To be forever in second place. To be useless.*

I silence it, dig deep to find my better self. Instead of dredging up the past, I should simply support my sister in moving on. In finding someone better.

I delete Olivia's number and head off for my next tasting.

The Queen of Tarts

Drum roll please . . . it's the moment you've been waiting for! After tasting nine Bakewell tarts and judging them on five criteria, the scores are in. And the highly deserving winner is **The Bakewell Bakehouse**, *which served up a totally delicious, utterly beautiful tart with a jug of freshly made custard on the side. For those interested in the detail, more information on the top five tarts can be found* **here** *– congratulations to all involved!*

In addition to eating too much pastry today, I've also enjoyed wandering through Bakewell's streets and shops (in gorgeous sunshine, no less!) and browsing its weekly market, which is held in the town every Monday. Mum bought some pretty handmade soaps from a small family business called **Bath&Bubbles**, *while I went big* *on cake decorations, so my niece and I can do some Halloween baking later in the week. But the market also sells flowers, jewellery, food and lots of lovely gifts – photos below, including the two I took when my* **Connect app** *went off – see if you can pick them out! I've enjoyed using the app so far; I found the time pressure a bit stressful at first, but I've since learned to relax into it, to accept it's about connection, not polish or perfection. My OH and I have certainly had a good laugh at our efforts!*

And while we're on the subject of having a good laugh, I've been looking through the bookshelf at Grove Cottage and have made the mistake of trying to read a primer on philosophy, which has sent my head reeling! There's a section on Immanuel Kant, a German philosopher from the 1700s, who apparently believed reason is the source of morality, and humans should act according to the laws they give themselves. But I don't understand this – does it mean each individual should act according to their own set of laws and, if so, what if one person's set of laws contradicts another's? With stealing, say, or adultery: is it 'moral' if all parties are content, but immoral if one objects? And, if the latter, why does one person's reasoning and morality trump another's? It seems to me that, throughout history, trumping has indeed taken place, and has done so along gendered lines, which is why the word 'tart' is not just shorthand for a pastry snack, but is also used to denigrate a woman who acts on sexual desire.

Well, time to reclaim such slurs, I say. So this blog is dedicated to Bakewell tarts, in each and every form!

LARA

I'm sitting in a café with Poppy, Mum and Jackie, and I feel sick. Jackie keeps offering me cake, but I couldn't eat anything right now. Not after learning that Gareth is out there, somewhere, potentially intent on revenge. I squeeze Poppy to me, but she pulls away – Mum has bought her a hot chocolate and she wants to dip her spoon into the whipped cream and marshmallows.

Breathe deeply, I tell myself. It's been four years since I left France, and two since I sent that email, so Steve is almost certainly right that the moment of danger has passed. Indeed, nothing material has changed: just because Gareth's chalet has been sold doesn't mean he's after me and Poppy. Likewise, if he and Olivia still owned it, that wouldn't mean he isn't. The only thing that *has* changed is that I've cut down on my pills, and started having those awful dreams about Hannah. Which is probably just a natural part of the healing process, of my brain trying to work through old fears and emotions.

'So how was the spa treatment?' asks Jackie.

'Great. Thank you.' I sound like a child who's been told to thank their friend's parents for having them over.

'I'm delighted you enjoyed it,' Mum grins over her teacup. 'Your skin looks beautiful.'

'Really?'

'I think you look taller,' Jackie agrees. 'Perhaps your massage loosened some tight muscles.'

'Perhaps,' I say, forcing a smile, not wanting to admit that I'm probably sitting differently because of the paper knickers, which rub in all the wrong places. And that if my skin looks better, it's only because I've been out in the sun for the last half hour.

Gareth often used to compliment my skin. In fact, he complimented almost everything about me – not just my breasts and legs, but less obvious candidates too: the tips of my elbows and the cleft above my hips, the mole on my forearm and small scar on my left thumb. I'd never felt so cherished, nor so *seen*; it was as if I'd only been viewed through a screen before, and the screen had finally dropped away to reveal my living, breathing flesh. After being fired from the hotel, this sensation became even stronger – when Gareth wasn't working, or travelling for work, the two of us spent all our time fucking and drinking, or lying together in sweaty sheets, whispering sweet nothings. He was a generous man, prone to lofty declarations of affection and grand gestures. Like when I mentioned I was partial to a particular wine sold in the mini-mart and he bought up their whole stock, using the bottles to spell out 'I LOVE YOU' across the chalet floor. Or when he commissioned a local ice sculptor to carve a likeness of me skiing, which he placed on the chalet balcony, preserved for several days and nights by the stinging cold of the Alpine winter. Or when I made an offhand remark about my tatty ski jacket and he went straight out and bought me a new one, smiling with approval as I zipped it up and proceeded to dance around in the snow.

And now that same smile resides upon my daughter's face: the same wide mouth; the same narrow lips, tilting up on the left. Both totally perfect and a reminder that nothing can ever be perfect again. Because he promised that he loved me, that he'd look after me, that life would be good as long as we were together.

But his promises were just like that ice sculpture on the balcony. Showy, pretty and entirely transient.

A facade that melted into glittering shards.

HANNAH

The tastings are over and my blog written but, walking back to the car park, I can't stop thinking about my phone call with Olivia. I'd always thought everyone placed my sister on a pedestal, but now I've learned that, to one man at least, she was dispensable, and not some mythical Holy Grail to be forever pursued.

But perhaps even more surprising is my changed view of Lara herself. Of her ability – or rather, inability – to make sound decisions. And the implications of this are huge, because if her judgement is poor, then her views should no longer hold so much sway for me. Should no longer cut so deep.

I still remember her words as if they were spoken yesterday. When neither Dad nor Mum were stem cell matches for Lara, they suggested I might want to get tested, stressing that it was my decision, of course, but that the gift of health was the most profound thing I could give my sister, and that siblings were the most probable matches. The attention was intoxicating, and I went along to the blood test with the air of a righteous fighter; bore the pain of the needle with all the stoicism of a martyr throwing herself upon her sword. Assumed the glory before it had been earned.

And then: the news, two weeks later, that I wasn't a match after all. That I'd failed this most important, life-giving test. I sat hunched over in one of the kitchen chairs, waiting for my parents to tell me it wasn't my fault, but they were too busy comforting Lara. So I went upstairs, and it was there, on the landing, that I heard them. Mum saying she was oh-so-sorry, and my sister's tear-choked response. *It's useless. Hannah is useless.*

I ran back down the stairs, breath heaving, and straight into the garden, where I burrowed my way into the shrubbery, branches scratching at my face until they drew blood. I sat in the dirt, hidden from view, for what felt like hours, tasting the tang of my cut lip and watching my tears drip on to the dry earth and leaves.

And then, when nobody came to find me, I clambered back out.

And nothing was the same again.

LARA

Sitting around the table at dinner, everyone waxes lyrical about their day. Everyone except me, that is. I try to sound enthusiastic when the subject of my visit to the spa comes up, but can't muster the energy to convince. Mum's shepherd's pie sticks in my throat: the meat too fatty, the potato impossibly thick and cloying, and it's all I can do to swallow a few mouthfuls. Poppy, on the other hand, eats hers in a matter of minutes and immediately requests seconds, much to Mum's delight. 'Good girl,' she says, dolloping a ladle of minced lamb and potato on to her plate. 'It's so important to eat well.' And then she glances at me, just briefly, but long enough for me to get the message. *You need to eat more.* Her expression similar to when I was young and too sick to keep food down: smiling, but with frustration not far from the surface. *You need to at least try.* And I get that it comes from a place of concern, but such concern brings pressure, which only makes swallowing more difficult.

'So,' Jackie says briskly, 'Helen and I were thinking that tomorrow would be a good day to head over to Mam Tor.' She turns to Cassie. 'You might not know this, but Mam Tor is a beautiful hill in the High Peak, where Robert proposed to Helen many years ago.'

'Really?' asks Cassie politely.

'Yes.' Mum's voice is wistful and, even though Cassie doesn't request it, she starts to tell the story of her and Dad's engagement, which I must have heard at least fifty times before. How he'd planned for a romantic betrothal at the summit of Mam Tor – a picnic with champagne, roses, the works – but how, in the event, it poured with rain, and they ended up sheltering in the lee of a fence. Mum was chilly, the sandwiches soggy and, worst of all, Dad's hands were so slippery and numb that he fumbled the ring and dropped it; had to scrabble around in the shale before emerging, sheepish, with the diamond-topped gold band and asking the all-important question while his thumb was bleeding. But then – and this has always been Mum's favourite part of the story – as he slid the ring on to her finger, the sun broke through the clouds in a burst of glorious yellow-white which filtered down to touch the land around them. Like a blessing from above. Illuminating their way back along the ridge, with the appropriately named Hope Valley below them while, to the north, the long line of Kinder Scout lay under still-dark skies.

'It sounds lovely,' says Cassie, her eyes shining.

'Yes,' says Mum, with a quivering smile. 'It was perfect.'

'Perfect for Helen and Robert,' says Jackie, patting the still-sparkling diamond on Mum's left hand. 'But perhaps not to everyone's taste? The rain and walking and everything. I imagine some people might prefer something a little more . . . urbane?' She is far too obvious in looking at Cassie. 'A fancy hotel, perhaps, or a restaurant with champagne?'

'We do have quite a few proposals in the restaurant,' replies Cassie thoughtfully. 'But I think a proposal somewhere rural, and beautiful – somewhere a bit wild – would be romantic too.'

'Interesting.' Jackie looks pointedly at Max. He stands up with his plate in his hand. 'Is everyone done?'

There are murmurs of assent from around the table, followed by another silence. Hannah gets up to help Max with the clearing. 'So are we just going to Mam Tor?' she asks. 'Or are we going to visit one of the caverns as well?'

I get a tingling feeling at the back of my throat.

'That could be fun,' Jackie says, looking at Mum, and the tingling becomes more acute. Because even though I haven't been to the caverns for years, I know they're full of dark rocks, just like the ones in my dreams about Hannah.

I take a deep breath. *Don't think about Gareth. Like Steve said, it's been over two years since that message.*

'It could,' Mum agrees.

Cassie looks vaguely horrified, and I wonder if she can rescue the situation. 'Caves?'

'There are several of them round Castleton,' explains Jackie. 'But don't worry, they're designed for tourists, with safe, well-lit passages – nothing to worry about. They're quite astonishing actually: all these ancient chambers, and that rare mineral that you only find in the Peak District – what's it called?'

'Blue John,' Hannah and Max say simultaneously. And then, while Poppy is asking me if she can watch cartoons before bed, Max adds, 'I'd be up for a trip to the caverns – I loved them as a kid. They're great, Cass, honestly—'

'I don't know.' Cassie stares at her hands. 'I don't want to crawl through holes or anything.'

Poppy tugs on my arm and repeats her question, and I tell her to wait a moment. Meanwhile, Max starts to laugh. 'You don't have to crawl! As Mum says, it's all been designed for tourists to walk through. From what I can remember, there's about a million steps—'

'Because you go so deep down.' I look at Cassie as I say this, hoping it might alarm her enough to suggest we go somewhere different. 'You go down and down, and down some more. It's like something out of a Jules Verne novel . . .'

As the conversation turns to *Journey to the Centre of the Earth*, and from there to Icelandic volcanoes, I kick myself for side-tracking the conversation away from Cassie's fears. And now I've lost the chance to alter our plans for tomorrow. Because, after I tell Poppy it's time for bed, Mum says she's going to get an early night too, so she can be full of energy for a walk up Mam Tor tomorrow.

And for a trip to the caverns first.

HANNAH

Dinner has been hard work tonight, very much 'The Max and Cassie Show'. Whatever Max has said to her today seems to have worked, because she's all smiles and chat this evening, in sharp contrast to her grumpiness this morning. We've had to endure endless details of their trip to Sheffield; of how gorgeous their friend's baby was and how he kept smiling at Cassie, and then we've had to endure all of Mum's compliments – 'You sound like a natural!' – and Jackie's probing into Cassie's thoughts on having children. Cassie smiled and said nothing, but that only seemed to make Jackie more determined to quiz her, and soon we were on to questions about marriage proposals, and whether they should take place in an urban or rural setting, as if these things are entirely binary. Cassie did express some views on this front – some guff about the romance of a proposal in the wilderness – but Max clammed up entirely, and I couldn't tell whether this was a good or bad sign. Whether he became awkward because he is planning to propose to her, or because he isn't.

I suppose some things are binary, after all.

Now, as Max and I stack the dishwasher, I try to gauge his state of mind. He was quick to praise Cassie earlier, to say how good she was with their friend's baby, but when we go for the same slot on the lower shelf, his arm brushes mine. He lets it linger for a moment before moving away, and his eyes do the same, touching upon me for just a fraction too long. I've gone for a no-make-up look tonight, and maybe it's having an effect. 'Sorry,' he says, as my breath catches in my throat, and I say sorry back, because I am, although not for brushing against him. I'm sorry that he has a girlfriend, and I a boyfriend, and that even if we didn't, any chance of romance would be quashed by my having a sister whose beauty renders me plain. Whose dramas – and constant need to be saved – make me pedestrian.

And yet now I know an important truth: Lara's judgement is poor. Terrible, even. Because how else could she have shacked up with a married man when Max is right here, unmarried, and when he clearly still adores her?

'I think the dishwasher needs setting off,' he says. 'Can you pass me a tablet?'

I take a tablet from the packet under the sink and, as I pass it across, my fingers graze his palm. I can't tell whether desire is making me clumsy, or whether I'm just hyperaware of my touch in his presence. Do my fingers normally graze a person's hand when I pass them a dishwasher tablet?

Poppy runs over to say goodnight, and I kneel on the kitchen floor to hug her, pulling her close. When we've finished the Bed Bugs routine, she turns to Max. 'Goodnight,' she says, her voice a little formal.

'Goodnight, Poppy!' He leans down towards her, holding out his arms. 'Can I have a hug too?'

She considers for a second, before shaking her head and running to my sister. 'Sorry,' Lara says. 'She can be a bit funny with men sometimes.'

'That's okay,' Max says, although I can tell from his face that it isn't, not entirely.

And then there's Poppy to consider. Surely it's not healthy for her to be 'a bit funny with men'? But then how could she be otherwise, when her dad is a douchebag and there are no male relatives in her life? No father, no brothers, no uncles. No grandfathers.

If only she could have known Dad. He would have taught her that men aren't to be feared, that they can be kind and funny and gentle.

But he's gone.

I look at Mum, who is gazing at her wedding ring, and listen to Lara bolting and re-bolting the door in the hall.

And wonder if it will ever stop feeling like our family died with him.

LARA

Tonight, when I finally fall asleep, I have another of my terrible dreams. I see the sky first: an eerie expanse of orange. Then my sister: her eyes open but unseeing and her hair flung around her head, Medusa-like. My vision tracks lower, to her neck, and lower still, and I know what I'll find but can't look away.

The blood. So much blood. The redness of it is violent, shocking against the islands of white fabric, and at its worst across her chest, where the shirt sticks to her skin in a wrinkled wetness. The buttons are red too, discernible only from their raised surfaces.

And then there's the rock she's lying on, and the way her limbs are twisted. I try to see the rock's edges, and what exists beyond, but my vision sticks to this gruesome tableau and won't yield any context; nothing beyond the strange orange sky. Almost as if someone's lifted an image of my sister, warped in this awful way, and planted it into my brain without its original backdrop.

I need more, I tell myself. *There must be more. Does this happen inside a cavern?* I attempt to turn my head, but it's frozen, immobile. My mind starts to writhe in its bodily prison, and the dream recedes. *Not yet. Not yet!* I will it back, but it's slipping away and I can't reach out to grab it, can't do anything but watch as I'm pulled towards wakefulness.

But then, just before my eyes open, I see something. At the very edge of my vision, withdrawing so fast it's but a snapshot: a flash of silver. Long, sharp, and coated in blood.

A knife.

HANNAH

Poppy and Lara are first to bed, but the rest of us aren't far behind. I think we're all tired of being around one another, or possibly just exhausted from pounding pavements. And, in my case, eating too much pastry.

Whatever the cause, it's a relief to be alone. I'd planned to read for at least half an hour but my eyes start to close after ten minutes, so I switch off the bedside light and burrow under the duvet. In a matter of seconds, I'm drifting into sleep.

A noise. Soft steps at the fringe of my consciousness. I'm too tired to wake up, wonder if I'm dreaming, but it's still there, the sound of feet moving about. Then the sound of something closing – a drawer? A cupboard?

I force my eyes open. 'Max?'

No reply, but the sense of a presence. Of the shadows not meeting where they should. I strain my eyes to decipher the darkness. 'Max?' I say again. 'Poppy?'

Reaching for my phone on the bedside table, I see it's 11.31. Is someone sleepwalking? The glare of the screen leaves a blot of light at the front of my vision, making it even harder to see. 'Hello?' I try to keep my voice strong, to sound confident. 'Hello?'

Swallowing hard, I reach for the light switch and flick it on, wondering if a face will loom out of the blackness beside me. But there's no one there, nor in the kitchen beyond. I get out of bed to be certain; search behind the kitchen worktop. Switch on the hall light and check the front door, which is still locked, with the chain pulled across. Scan the corridor past the bedrooms for any signs of disturbance.

Perhaps it's just the jet lag playing tricks on me. I rub my eyes, turn and head back to bed. There's a rush of relief as I climb under the covers and turn the light off.

But it takes an age for my heart to stop thumping. And even longer to fall back to sleep.

TUESDAY

LARA

We're here, at the Blue John Cavern, and I'm forcing myself to stay calm. We're standing by the entrance, all seven of us, waiting for our guide, and my instinct is to drag Hannah and Poppy away. Mum and Jackie are having an involved discussion about art, something about British landscape painters, while Hannah is speaking into her phone, oblivious to the semi-shouting around her. She's smiling and twirling a strand of hair around her finger, so I presume she's talking to Chris. I move towards her, pulling Poppy with me. If we have to go on this accursed tour, then I'm sticking right by both of them.

At least I've already dealt with the knife.

'Mummy, when are we going in?'

'Soon, little one.'

'I'm hungry.'

Mum breaks off from her conversation with Jackie – which has somehow moved on to the rewilding of a Scottish estate – to tell us she has an apple in her bag. 'It's fine,' I say. 'She's only just had breakfast. But thank you.'

'I'm hungry!'

'You'll be fine. We're having a picnic later.'

'But—'

'Look, we're going in.' Luckily, the movement distracts her, and I position myself behind Hannah as she hangs up and heads to the cave entrance. Our guide is at the front, along with Max and Cassie and four strangers joining our tour, while Poppy is trailing behind me, and Mum and Jackie bring up the rear. It's as good an arrangement as I could hope for, and yet, as we head into the caves, I can't shake a sense of foreboding. The steps down are steep and narrow, with damp walls hemming us in on either side. *Breathe*, I tell myself. *Long, slow breaths. And don't think about Gareth.* I can't afford a repeat of what happened at the spa yesterday. I feel briefly better when the passage opens up into a wider, higher area, with some old mining machinery on display, but soon we're off down more steps, and the walls close in again. The air becomes cold and dank, and the stone around us wet to the touch.

When the steps finally end, and we enter a huge cavern, my mind returns to last night's dream. To the knife I saw just before waking. *But no one would ever want to stab Hannah*, I tell myself. She's the type of person who avoids confrontation and aims to please, not someone who invokes violence.

While the four strangers in our group examine the seams of Blue John in the walls, I examine *them*, on the lookout for a twitching, murderous eye. But they seem innocent enough; genuinely engrossed in what they're looking at.

'Lara.' Max has sidled up to me, leaving Cassie on the far side of the cavern. 'Can I talk to you for a moment?'

'Of course. Is everything all right?' His expression is earnest, thoughtful, like he's dwelling on a difficult maths problem.

'Everything's fine. I'm just . . .' He looks down at his hands, twists his fingers together. 'I wanted to seek your advice on something. If that's okay?'

'Of course,' I say again. 'Although I should warn you that I'm hardly a great source of wisdom.' My mind flashes back to Gareth's chalet, to the balcony looking out to the pistes far below.

Max gives a nervous laugh, and his words topple out. 'You know loads . . . you always have . . . and what I'm wondering is . . . if you like someone a lot but you're not sure if they like you . . . at least not as much, or in the same way, and you want to know if they ever might . . . should you ask them?'

I look across to Cassie, who is chatting with the guide, and then to my sister and Poppy, who are gazing up at the cavern's ceiling. 'I don't know,' I admit. 'In the past, I would have said yes, but now I think people should tread carefully. Should be kind and gently appreciative of one another, not rush into anything. Bide their time to see how they really feel. Otherwise . . . it can result in a horrible mess.'

He nods sadly. 'Maybe you're right. Maybe gentle appreciation is the way to go. And biding one's time.' His voice is downbeat.

'Hey, but what do I know?' I try to smile. 'I'm a woman of darkness, destined only to see the awful things in life.'

He swings his head towards me. 'Why do you say that?'

'Oh, no reason.' I look away. 'I've just not been sleeping very well, that's all.'

'How come?' He steps a little closer, concern in his voice. 'Are you having bad dreams again? Like you did when we left France?'

I'd forgotten I told him about those dreams. My mind was all over the place when I fled the Alps, barely cognisant of where we were going, let alone what I said.

'You are, aren't you?' He speaks more softly. 'Are they the same as before? That you're suffocating?'

I shake my head.

'Then what?'

I consider denying everything, but Max is watching me so closely that I feel compelled to be honest. I outline what I've been seeing – Hannah, lying injured on a rock – although I'm careful to downplay the severity of it, and don't mention the blood or the knife.

'You mustn't read too much into dreams.' He touches one hand to mine briefly. 'We all have agency over what happens. And Hannah's a sensible person.'

'Yes.' But on this occasion even Max can't reassure me. As I look across the cavern, I see Cassie staring coldly in our direction. 'I should go to Poppy,' I say.

Without waiting for an answer, I walk away, to the guardrail at the far side of the cavern where Poppy's pointing at the blue threads running through the rock. And there, instead of looking up, I look down.

Where there is nothing but a black abyss.

HANNAH

The Blue John Cavern is mesmerising and otherworldly, so different from the green, verdant land above. After walking down 245 steps in total, we pass through a canyon where grey rock rises on either side, clutched in wet fingers of calcite. And then, as we go deeper into the hillside, the rock begins to shine with curtains of flowstone: weird snow-like drapes formed by deposits of dissolved minerals. Taking us to a chamber where we can see the famous Blue John itself, striated through the limestone in shining bands of indigo, grey and white. Thick at the centre with thinner strands ribboning around, like a bird's-eye view of a river and its tributaries. Poppy is as enchanted as I am, or possibly even more so. 'That's really old!' she says, when the guide tells us that the Blue John was formed millions of years ago. 'That's older than the oldest person in the world!'

'A lot, lot older,' I tell her.

'It's even older than William the Conker!'

'Conqueror. Yes, a lot older than him too.'

We carry on like this for a while – Poppy mentioning something old, and me saying the Blue John is even older (apart from when she says 'the universe!' and I have to explain the Blue John couldn't exist if there were no universe for it to exist in) – until Lara appears silently beside us. I try to make conversation but she seems preoccupied, so I give up, and soon it's time to make our way back to the surface. Going up the steps is a lot harder than going down, and conversation gives way to heavy breathing. Jackie makes a few comments about how unfit she is, and Mum makes a reference to some run they did years ago, but then even they fall silent, and we carry on climbing, the world reduced to darkness, breath and dripping water. We ascend until the air becomes warmer and drier and we are eventually ejected, dazzled and disoriented, into the daylight. Jackie throws herself on to a grassy knoll and sits there, puffing, while Max stretches his arms above his head, his jacket rising to expose a band of skin. I try not to look too obviously in his direction, to concentrate instead on Poppy, who is spinning around in circles until Lara tells her not to.

My phone pings and I squint at its screen, realising that, while underground, I missed my daily alert from the Connect app. There's a notification with a sad face, telling me I didn't send my photos in the allotted two minutes. *Sorry not to CONNECT today*, I message Chris, adding a winking emoji. *I didn't have any reception.*

A reply comes almost immediately. *No reception, in this day and age? OMG how is that possible? Have you been under a rock?*

I send a laughing emoji, along with a promise to stay above ground tomorrow.

Once everyone has adjusted, Jackie and I go to the toilets, while the others head to the café and gift shop. We are washing our hands when Mum comes bursting in and seizes Jackie's shoulders. 'He's looking at the rings!'

'What?' Jackie fiddles with the soap dispenser. 'Does this thing actually contain any soap?'

'The rings!' Mum bounces up and down on the balls of her feet. 'In the gift shop! Max!'

I swallow hard as Jackie spins round to face Mum. 'You don't think . . . today?'

'Who knows? Maybe he's been inspired by my engagement story. And Cassie did say she thought a rural proposal would be romantic—'

'But today, now?'

'Why not? It would certainly be memorable. And there's something rather special about proposing with Blue John, don't you think? Given it's so rare, and the Peak District is the only place you can find it—'

'Some people reckon it might exist in China too,' I say, but Mum and Jackie ignore me, entering into a frenzied discussion about engagement rings and the price of platinum. About the setting of precious stones and some woman they know who lost the sapphire from her ring after twenty years of marriage.

'Which is hardly a good omen,' Jackie says, before shaking her head and grabbing hold of the sink. 'I think I might need to sit down.'

'Are you all right?' Mum reaches out to pat her shoulder.

'I'm fine. I just . . . I don't know what I think about all this.'

'About Max and Cassie?'

'Yes.'

'Why? She seems nice.'

'Ye-es.'

'No?'

'Oh, I don't know.' Jackie grips the sink harder. 'I suppose it's just . . . is she nice enough for Max?'

My thoughts exactly. I look into the mirror, attempt to smooth down my hair.

'You're bound to feel a bit nervous about the prospect,' Mum says. 'It's a big change, after all—'

'Yes—'

'But an exciting one. One which might result in grandchildren—'

Jackie smiles tentatively. 'I *would* like grandchildren—'

'But aren't they a bit young?' I break in. 'For marriage and children and all that?'

They both turn to look at me. 'I was married to your dad by their age,' Mum says, incredulous. 'And your sister had Poppy even younger.'

Precisely, I want to say. *Think how well that worked out.* But it feels too mean, so I pick my next words carefully. 'Poppy is amazing, but it can't be easy for Lara, can it? Being a single parent? And I wonder if maybe, if she'd waited—'

'Your sister's situation has nothing to do with her age.' Jackie's voice is terse. 'Her ex is . . . Well, anyway, it's not the same.'

I look at her jaw, working its way up and down, and wonder what she was going to say. That Lara's ex is a cheat, a philanderer? A man who doesn't want to be involved in his daughter's life?

'No, of course it's not the same,' says Mum, rubbing her hand across Jackie's upper back. 'Shall we go and get you a cup of tea?'

'Yes, let's do that. And maybe a slice of cake, if they sell it? I think I'm going to need all the energy I can muster—'

'Tea and cake it is,' Mum cajoles, opening the door and ushering Jackie through. 'Maybe it will warm us up a bit – my feet are freezing after traipsing through that cavern.'

As they begin a debate on walking boots versus trainers, I follow behind and let my own thoughts wander. To Max, sitting on my bed in the early hours, a palpable heat between us. To the way he blushed when I walked past him in a towel. To our hands touching when we stacked the dishwasher. Surely these aren't the actions of a man who's about to get engaged to someone else? And how about his undying devotion to Lara?

Lara and Cassie are at a table in the café, drinking water and coffee, respectively. There's a small glass of milk on the table too, but Poppy is running around the room instead of drinking it, her arms outstretched like a plane. 'Sit down,' Lara says to her now, and then, when she nearly collides into a queuing couple, 'I told you to SIT DOWN!'

Poppy sits for about two seconds, before she sees us approaching and jumps up again. 'Granny! They have poppy cake here!'

'The best sort of cake,' Mum replies, as Lara clarifies that it's lemon and poppyseed. 'I might have to buy a slice. Now, you go and sit down with Mummy.'

Poppy sits down again, beaming, as Mum, Jackie and I get into the line for drinks. I lose myself in my own thoughts while the two of them talk, but break off when I realise they're giving each other funny looks, and glancing at the café doorway.

I follow their gaze to see Max standing there, staring at Lara and Cassie.

But it's his right hand which really draws my attention. Because it's holding a small jewellery box, which he slips into his pocket before entering the room.

LARA

There are many steps leading to the summit of Mam Tor, and I think about Dad – and try not to think about Gareth – with nearly every one. Now that Hannah is safely out of the caverns and I can breathe properly again, the world has a surreal quality to it, almost like I'm communing with the past. As I trudge up the hill from the small car park at its base, there's a connection between my feet and the ancient ground below. Looking at the stillness that comes over Mum, and the quiet, steady way she walks, I can tell she feels it too. And I hope it brings her comfort.

The five-year anniversary of Dad's death was only a couple of weeks ago. I dropped Poppy off early with the childminder that day and took the train up to Cambridge, where Mum met me and drove us to the graveyard. It was pouring with rain, so we stood in our cagoules, rain tracking down our noses. Dad's headstone looked too shiny next to the weathered ones beside it, and my eyes stung as I studied its inscription. *Robert Skelton, much-loved husband to Helen, and father to Lara and Hannah.* No mention of being a grandfather.

I think that's one of the things I most regret: that he never lived to know Poppy. She reminds me of him sometimes, particularly when she sings – her lips make an 'O' in the exact same way his did, and her eyes are full of the same merriment. He would have been so good with her; would have loved taking her around his garden, showing her how to rake the soil level. How to earth up the potatoes and stake the peas. His vegetable beds have been overrun with weeds since he died, not because Mum doesn't know how to look after them, but because she can't bring herself to do so. I once suggested she employ a gardener but she said that would be worse, because then she'd have to eat the vegetables, and each mouthful would be a reminder of everything she's lost.

Continuing up the steps, Poppy complains of being tired and I try to channel Dad's patience – to remember that I too once had small legs and an even smaller tolerance for walking uphill. I tell her to look out, instead of down; to marvel at the fact that the entirety of Hope Valley used to be underwater, beneath a warm, shallow sea. When that doesn't work, I tell her how Mam Tor is known as 'the Shivering Mountain' because of the landslides which still occur here, and which have led the once-smooth road below to be buckled into disuse. And when she continues to complain, I pick her up and carry her, annoyed at myself for capitulating to her grumpiness, but desperate for a few moments' peace.

A fort was apparently built here three thousand years ago, which makes perfect sense – we can see out for miles. Sometimes I wonder if that's what Poppy and I need: a residence with commanding views across a great sweep of countryside. Somewhere with ample warning of any approaching threat. Except, if we lived in such a place and danger came to our door, what would we actually do?

Perhaps it's best to stick to our nondescript flat in its nondescript area of London. A place where we are anonymous, part of a seething unknown.

A place where we can't see out, but where we are, ourselves, hard to see.

A place where it's possible to be entirely lost.

HANNAH

I watch Max as we climb Mam Tor, looking for any signs of nervousness. When he was a teenager, he used to bite his lip when anxious: a nibble with his top teeth, as if he were tugging at a piece of loose skin. But right now there's no nibbling; he's simply striding up the steps, pausing to admire the view occasionally, or to point something out to Cassie.

She, on the other hand, is constantly tugging at the hem of her coat, trying to draw it lower. When Max shows her the brickworks in the valley, she launches into a strange spiel about Rome and laying foundations, to which he just smiles brightly, before she flushes and skips ahead. She was acting oddly in the café too: repeatedly stirring her coffee instead of drinking it, and tapping on the table with her pretty nails. Which makes me wonder if she also saw the jewellery box in Max's hand.

And then I think of Max and Mum talking secretively in the garden a couple of days ago, and it occurs to me that maybe this was the reason. Given Mum's own engagement story, it would make sense, were Max planning to propose on Mam Tor, to check she was okay with the idea.

I watch Mum now, uncharacteristically quiet as she walks, before turning my gaze to Lara, who is marching up the hillside with a grim expression. I remember running up these steps together when we were very young, plotting to put a whoopee cushion under the picnic blanket, and wish we could recapture even a fraction of that camaraderie. Or some of the wild pleasure of rushing up here with Max a couple of years later, challenging each other to hop and jump backwards.

What happened to the three of us? How did we go from those laughing children to our current, unmoored selves? Did we grow wiser, or is the reverse actually true: did growing up mean we lost sight of what's important?

At the summit, Mum wants a photo, so Lara gets out her instant Polaroid (which is apparently the only camera allowed anywhere near her daughter). Cassie and Max take turns being the photographer, while the rest of us place our hands on the trig point and attempt to smile. Then it's on to the picnic, which involves bustling about with blankets and Thermos flasks before we can finally sit and eat. The sky is a mottled grey, but the air is dry and the wind gentle. I unzip my coat to enjoy the cooling breeze on my neck; take some selfies with my food, with the span of Hope Valley below.

I'm just finishing up, smoothing my sandwich wrapper on my thigh, when Max gets to his feet and clears his throat. 'If no one minds, I'd like to say a few words.' I ball my wrapper, squeeze it in my palm. *Surely not.* I look down at the ground, focus on a pebble, beige against the darker brown of the earth.

'It feels special for us to be here,' he says. 'It's a special place for both our families. A place we've come many times over the years.'

I kick at the pebble and watch it roll away from the dirt into the green sward beyond. Sensing Max's gaze upon me, I look up, only to see his eyes move to Jackie, who is blinking rapidly, as if to fight off tears, and from her to Mum, who is definitely crying, and then to Lara, who isn't. She looks directly at him, and he at her, seemingly bewitched for a second, before snapping out of it and turning to his girlfriend. 'Cass,' he says, and I breathe in sharply, because I can't believe he's going to propose to her right now, right here, in the very spot where my parents got engaged. 'I'm not always great at saying how I feel, but I thought this was a good opportunity to let you know how much I appreciate you.'

'Appreciate' seems a bad choice of word for a betrothal. He should be saying he loves her, that he's crazy for her, that she makes him complete. I try to gauge what Cassie is thinking, but her face gives nothing away.

'Thanks for putting up with me,' Max goes on, and he gets a slight smile from Cassie for that. 'I know I can be hard work sometimes, and I know you'd have preferred a holiday in the Med. So, to make up for it, I've got you a little something . . .' He reaches into his pocket and pulls out the box—

I look away, put my nails in my mouth and try not to chew.

There is a pause, during which I focus on the valley below. On Winnats Pass, carved out steeply between the rocks, and the small villages of Castleton and Hope.

'Thank you.' Her voice, when it comes, is oddly flat. 'They're beautiful.'

'I'm glad you like them. The colours in the Blue John seemed interesting, unusual.'

'Ye-es.' It's only as Cassie says this, drawing the word out into two syllables, that the incongruous plural hits me. *They're beautiful. I'm glad you like them.* I look up.

The first thing I notice is Mum, scratching furiously at the back of her neck, and Jackie sitting awkwardly beyond her. Poppy asks what to do with her apple core and Jackie takes it from her wordlessly, stuffing it inside her bag without even looking. Max turns in their direction and then back to Cassie, who shuts the jewellery box with a tight click.

'Are there any biscuits?' Poppy asks.

'What's wrong?' Max says to Cassie.

'Nothing's wrong.' She busies herself with the zips on her coat, places the box in her inside pocket. 'But I can't very well wear earrings on a mountaintop, can I?'

Earrings. Not a ring. My breath rushes out of me all at once.

'Are there any biscuits?' Poppy asks again.

Cassie gets to her feet. 'I think I'll head back to the car. I'm feeling a bit chilly.'

Max takes off his coat. 'Here. Have my jacket.'

'No. I'm fine.'

'Go on.' Max steps towards her, proffering his coat. 'If you're cold.'

'I'm *fine.*'

'Are there any biscuits?'

Jackie stands up. 'We can all go back—'

'No.' Cassie forces a smile. 'You stay here and finish your picnic.'

'But we're nearly done—'

'No. Really. Take your time. Please. I fancy a stroll on my own.'

Doubt crosses Jackie's face. 'Are you sure?'

'Yes, definitely.'

Throughout this exchange, Max has remained standing, his coat hanging limply from his hand. Now, as Cassie walks away, his face slackens and his shoulders slump, as if he's a little boy again.

'What are you doing?' Jackie practically hisses at him. 'Go after her!'

'But she said she wanted to be alone—'

'That doesn't mean she actually does! Honestly, have I not taught you anything?'

Max's hand drops, his coat brushing the ground, and I want to go to him, to tell him I hate it too – these stupid games people play – but he is already setting off. He walks slowly at first, and then faster, breaking into a jog.

'My God.' Jackie sinks on to the picnic blanket. 'What was he thinking? Or was he just *not* thinking? Are you all right, Helen?'

Mum's face is pale, and there are tears in her eyes. 'I'm sorry,' she says. 'It's just . . . it brought it all back . . . Robert . . . and . . . I'm sorry—'

'I'm the one who should be sorry.' Jackie takes Mum in her arms, her poncho rustling. 'My son is an idiot!'

I want to tell her not to call him that; to point out she didn't even want him to propose. But instead I look down at my phone and see, with a lurch, that the magazine editor has finally replied. I open her email with sweaty fingers, my heart beating too hard in my chest.

Thank you so much for bringing your blog to my attention, she has written. *However, while there is much to admire, I'm afraid I don't love it enough to take it forward at the current time.*

In other words, it's a no.

LARA

If the evening continues in this vein, I'll have to take Poppy to bed even earlier than usual. Everyone around us is drinking, but not in a sociable, convivial manner; instead, the atmosphere is silent, oppressive. Mum and Jackie are on the sofa, drinking wine, barely turning the pages of their books, and Hannah is doing much the same, except at the dining table, with a laptop. Max, meanwhile, is standing alone in the kitchen, downing shots of whisky and glaring at the bottle. When Poppy runs over to ask what he's up to, he gives a one-word answer – 'Drinking' – before turning to pour another measure.

'Leave Max alone, sweetheart,' I tell her.

'My tummy's empty,' she says in response.

'I guess it's nearly dinner time.' I hope Mum will jump up to get started on prep or at least tell us what we're supposed to be eating. But nobody says a word, and I'm forced to ask directly. 'Mum?'

'Yes?'

'Would you like me to make dinner?'

'Oh, dinner.' She wafts a hand in the air as if it's a nebulous concept. 'Jackie and I thought maybe we should wait for Cassie to get back before we cook anything.'

'But how long is she going to be?' We'd only just returned from Mam Tor earlier when Cassie said she was heading out again. She didn't say where, or for how long; she simply changed her clothes, grabbed her bag, and left. Max didn't try to stop her.

Mum looks at Max now, and then at Jackie, before returning her attention to me. 'Are you hungry?'

'Poppy is.'

Her eyes soften. 'Oh yes, Poppy! Sorry, I wasn't thinking; I'll make her something—'

'I can do it.' I'm in the kitchen before Mum is halfway off the sofa. 'What can she have?'

As Mum starts to reel off the options, I pass Max to get to the cupboards and he turns, his eyes full of pain and regret. Much like his expression five years ago, when I told him I was heading to France. Now, as then, I ask if he's okay. But this time, instead of replying, he picks up his whisky bottle and heads into the garden.

I stare at the space he's left behind, and the space behind that: the empty slot in the wooden block, where his chef's knife used to reside.

And then I take out a pan, to cook some pesto pasta.

HANNAH

Downs and Ups

If life is all about ups and downs, then I've lived a full life today! I've gone deep underground and also to the summit of a hill; have stared both into the dark recesses of the Earth's underbelly and out across a vast expanse of its surface . . .

To start with the 'down', we visited the **Blue John Cavern** this morning, which is an extensive network of limestone tunnels and caves containing fossilised remains of ocean creatures and bands of the very famous, very beautiful (and very rare) mineral Blue John. To see all of this, you walk down 245 (!) steps, to go deep into the Peak District's lower, secret reaches, where it feels almost as if you've entered another world completely. My niece couldn't get her head round the age of it all, and I felt much the same, because geological timescales are too long to make any sense to the human brain. To think that the Blue John was laid down millions of years ago, and that where we were walking was once an ocean, made me feel so tiny and insignificant . . .

. . . which in turn got me to thinking about what's expected of us in life; how the idea of marriage and children is inescapable for many, either because we want to follow that path, or because we want to break away from it. And similarly, we're encouraged to find a career that we're passionate about; that brings us enrichment in all senses. But how about if you don't know what you want? Or if the path you seek is barred to you? What then? Do you work to overcome the barrier or look for something different?

Perhaps I'm just over-deliberating because my other visit of the day was to the place my parents got engaged: a moment which led to them enjoying over twenty years of marriage. Their betrothal took place at the summit of **Mam Tor**, or Mother Hill, which is 517 metres high and has amazing views out across Hope Valley and Edale. A really beautiful spot, and an easy walk too, with a clear, unchallenging path all the way from the **car park** to the summit.

If only navigating life were so simple . . .

The mood in Grove Cottage tonight is downbeat, to say the least. Lara and Poppy have gone to bed, Mum and Jackie aren't saying much, Cassie isn't here, and Max is in the garden. I keep thinking about that email from the magazine editor. *I'm afraid I don't love it enough to take it forward at the current time.* I'd really thought this might be it – my breakthrough; the moment when my family finally understood what I'm capable of – but it's another bloody rejection. Which means perhaps it's time to accept it may never happen for me. That I am, as Lara rightly said in her bedroom all those years ago, useless.

I've been trying to comfort myself by reading online tales of successful bloggers who received countless rejections before their big break. And by looking at discussion forums where others share their experience of knockbacks, and how to deal with them. But their suggestions aren't helpful. *Take a walk* – done that already. *Spend some time with your family or partner* – doing that too, and it's not going so well. I suppose I could ring Chris, but he doesn't know about the magazine, so it'd be hard to explain why I'm feeling down. In fact, the more I think about it, the more I realise Chris and I don't do 'down' together, or indeed any emotion that goes beyond 'a little subdued'. I've spent the majority of our relationship being the glossy, fun version of myself that I want to be, always up for new experiences and a laugh. As if, by looking pretty in enough photos, having enough sex, and ticking off sufficient exciting destinations, I can overcome my weaknesses and model myself anew.

And what is the point? If it isn't benefiting me, then who the hell am I pretending for?

I get up from the table and go into the kitchen, asking if anyone would like something to eat. Mum says she isn't hungry, although she wouldn't mind my opening another bottle of wine if I'm in the kitchen anyway, while Jackie heads outside to talk to Max. She leaves the double doors to the garden open so, as I grab a bottle and corkscrew, I can't help but overhear their conversation.

'You shouldn't have let her go out,' Jackie says.

'She's a grown woman.' Max's voice is slurred. 'She can make her own decisions.'

'Right, but it'd be nice for her to know you care. That you understand—'

'But I don't understand! I haven't done anything wrong—'

'Not deliberately, no. But surely you can see she feels hurt and disappointed. Maybe a little embarrassed too—'

'I gave her some earrings, for Christ's sake! Not syphilis!'

It's fortunate that Poppy has already gone to bed. I look around the room nonetheless, see Mum staring studiously at her book.

'Don't be so cloth-headed!' Jackie's voice is rising. 'You and Cassie have been together for two years, and you presented her with a *jewellery* box. Of course she thought it was a proposal. We all did—'

'Then that's your issue, not mine—'

'It was the exact same spot where Helen and Robert got engaged!'

'Right, so you've conflated the two things.' From where I'm standing, the only part of Max I can see is his arm, moving up and down as he talks. 'But like I say: that's your issue, not mine. I was just trying to be kind, to show Cassie I appreciate her, and that I know this isn't her ideal holiday—'

'Because I'm here?'

'What?'

'Never mind.'

'You can't say something like that without explaining what you mean.' There's anger in Max's voice now, amid the slurring.

Jackie sighs. 'I sometimes . . . I suppose . . . well, sometimes I feel Cassie doesn't like me very much.'

'What the hell?'

'It's just . . .' There's a long pause, and I take the opportunity to top up my glass and Mum's, before sitting back down at the dining table in front of my laptop. Jackie's voice becomes more tentative. 'The two of you have never come on holiday with me before—'

'We're on holiday with you now! And look how well that's working out—'

'That's not fair! I had nothing to do with what happened today. I wasn't the one who raised Cassie's hopes—'

'Look, what do you want from me, Mum?' The whisky bottle is back in Max's hand. 'One moment you're saying poor Cassie, that I should have proposed, and the next you're saying she doesn't like you—'

'I'm not saying you *should* have proposed. I'm saying she thought you were going to.'

'And I'm saying that's on her, not me. I've never said I wanted to get married—'

'You don't?'

There's another long pause. I take a gulp of wine, my ears straining in case I miss Max's response. When it eventually comes, he speaks quietly. 'I don't know. Maybe. Or maybe I've been put off the idea by my mother, who has always told me marriage is a patriarchal, anti-feminist institution.'

This gets a small chuckle from Jackie. 'Your mother sounds like a very sensible woman.'

Max grunts.

'Look, I may have said those things in the past, but I don't want you to feel you *can't* get married—'

'I don't—'

'Or be put off marriage because of what happened with me and your father—'

'I'm not . . .'

It occurs to me that my heart is beating faster than usual, and I place one hand on my chest.

'There's nothing inherently wrong with marriage, whatever I might have said in the past. So long as the two people entering into it do so as equals, and the man doesn't ask the woman's father for *permission*. And of course it doesn't have to be a man and woman anymore, which is a good thing. For the institution of marriage, I mean.'

'Okay, Mum.'

'How about I take that whisky inside now?' I recognise this tone of Jackie's, because I've heard it many times. A tone which brooks no arguments.

'I'm still drinking it—'

'But don't you think you've had enough?'

'Says the woman who's nursing her tenth glass of wine—'

'It's not my tenth!'

'Eleventh, then?'

'No, but seriously, Max, I'm worried.'

'About my whisky drinking?'

'A little. And about Cassie being out there, somewhere, alone . . .'

'She'll be fine,' Max says. 'She always is.'

As if on cue, the front door opens, and Mum coughs a couple of times. 'Cassie! Hello!' She says it extra loudly, presumably for Max and Jackie's benefit. And, sure enough, all goes quiet in the garden.

'Evening, Helen.' Cassie's voice is clipped, precise.

'Would you like some food?'

'No thank you. I'm going to get a drink and call it a night.'

'Fair enough.' As Cassie starts clanking around in the kitchen, I can hear some whispering from outside, but can't make out what's being said. 'Have you been somewhere nice?' Mum asks.

'Uh-huh.' Cassie doesn't even try to sound convincing. 'Goodnight, Helen.'

'Goodnight. Oh, would you mind locking up and pulling the chain across? Lara asked me to ask you . . .'

Of course she did. Lara's obsessive about locks these days, always checking and rechecking. Doors, windows, car doors, even when we're *inside* the car. Now, I hear the clatter of the chain being fastened, and Cassie's footsteps disappearing down the hall.

A few minutes later, Max comes in from outside. His gait is unsteady, his body lurching as he walks. 'Cassie. Wait up!' He hurries into the hall. 'CASSIE!'

'Don't wake Poppy!' Mum calls, but he gives no indication of having heard. There's a loud thud as a door shuts.

Shortly after, Mum and Jackie head to bed too.

And then all is silent.

LARA

Poppy falls asleep quickly tonight, and I'm not far behind her. But it's an uneasy sleep – not plagued by dreams, for once, but fitful and wired, my thoughts unable to switch off. And cold too – so very, very cold. I snuggle closer to Poppy and pull the duvet tighter until I realise it's my feet that are suffering. They're freezing, in fact; a burning sensation pulsing across my soles. I wriggle my toes to try to warm them, but something hard brushes against my ankle and I sit up, suddenly very awake.

I look around. Poppy is still asleep and I can't see anyone else in the room. I crawl forward, pull back the end of the duvet and notice what looks like a stain on the sheet, as if Poppy's had an accident. I sniff it – not urine – and touch my fingers lightly to its surface. It's damp, and cold. What the hell? I look to the ceiling, wondering if there's a leak. It's too dark to see properly, but I can't hear or feel any dripping. And besides, if it is a leak, why did I brush against something hard?

I pull the duvet back further and notice a few small cube-shaped objects, each no more than about three centimetres across. Some sort of game of Poppy's? I pick one up and am startled by the stinging coldness of it; try to drop it but find it's partially stuck to my palm.

At which point I realise. It's ice.

HANNAH

The air in the kitchen seems sour, or perhaps that's just the residue of wine at the back of my throat. I put a stopper in the bottle I've been drinking, return it to the fridge and reach for the Baileys instead. It tastes good: sweet and creamy, if a little warm; I take the last couple of ice cubes from the freezer and swill them round my glass before taking another mouthful. Better. My head is beginning to pitch from my liquid dinner, so I eat a bag of crisps. As I'm chomping, Max walks into the living room. He makes no acknowledgement of my presence, simply heads out to the garden beyond. I watch as he sits on the picnic bench, then leans forward on to the table, resting his head in his hands.

I want to go out to him, to take him in my arms. *I'm the only one who understands you. Can't you see? I'd treat you far better than Cassie or Lara ever could.*

Refilling my glass, and taking another swig, I head over to my case and swap my current top for my new cornflower-blue T-shirt, which I layer with a cardigan. I tie my hair back into a messy bun and dab some of Lara's perfume on my neck. Then, armed with both glass and bottle of Baileys, I head outside. It's already dark, one of those velvety autumn evenings when the sky is swollen with cloud and summer breathes its dying gasps. I look up at the canopy above me, at the fat leaves swaying in the breeze, before taking a seat on the picnic bench beside Max.

He looks up. 'Hello.'

'Hello.' My lips feel thicker than usual. 'I thought you'd gone to bed?'

'Cassie's gone to bed. But she doesn't want me there.'

I pause a fraction too long. 'I'm sorry.'

'Yeah, well.' He looks at the bottle in my hand. 'Baileys, huh?'

'Would you like some?'

'Why not?'

Before I can suggest he fetches a glass, he takes the bottle, tips it to his lips, and drinks. Then he passes the bottle to me. I'm about to point out I have a glass, and like drinking it cold, when I think *what the hell* and put the bottle to my mouth. Our lips are touching by proxy, I realise, as I gulp the sweet liquid and pass it back.

'I've just remembered I fucking hate Baileys,' he says.

I laugh. 'There's other drinks inside.'

'Yes, but the key word there is "inside". When I want to stay *outside*. Enjoy the view.'

'It's too dark and cloudy to see much.' I look towards Curbar Edge, but can't see anything of its cliffs or rocky promontories. Some of the nearby trees are visible, but only as ghostly slivers of silver.

'I can see enough.'

I feel his gaze upon me before I turn to confirm the fact, my skin hot with a sensory knowledge that somehow outpaces my brain. I look at him, but only fleetingly. I have imagined this moment so many times, too many times, and can't compute what it means for the imaginary to become real.

'Do you want to go for a walk?' I find myself saying.

LARA

Why is there ice in my bed? My mind starts to whirl, thinking about that night on the balcony at Gareth's flat, and my breath begins to quicken. How could it have got here? It can't be Poppy – I would have noticed – and it wasn't me, so who the hell was it? And when did they put it here? The ice isn't fully melted, so it can't have been that long ago, which means – *oh my God* – what if they came in while we were sleeping? *Breathe*, I tell myself. *Think of a rational explanation*. It's probably just an unfunny prank by someone in the cottage; they've all been drinking too much tonight.

But what if it's someone from outside?

I jump from the bed and hurry to the window, checking the latches are closed. Then I run into the hallway and check the front door – that's closed too, and bolted. My breath is becoming ragged, and I feel light-headed, wondering if perhaps I've imagined the whole thing. But looking at my hand, I can see a patch of red skin where I picked up the ice.

We need a plan of action, so I return to the bedroom, shake Poppy awake. She is tired and groggy, confused as to what's happening. 'You need to practise going somewhere safe,' I say urgently. 'Which means we're going to the attic.' I pull her upright and she lets out a wail, wriggles from my grasp and lies down again.

'Poppy,' I say. 'This is important.'

'I'm tired.'

I feel a stab of guilt for disturbing her sleep, and wonder if I'm being overdramatic, if I should let this wait until morning. But how much guiltier would I feel if we didn't prepare, and something terrible happened? Someone has already been into our room. So I sit her up again, to another wail of protest.

'Come on,' I say. 'Upstairs.'

There is further complaining as I drag her upstairs, and tell her to climb into the wooden dresser. 'Imagine it's a den,' I say, over and over, until eventually she clambers inside.

'Well done – that was great.' I reach in to give her hair a ruffle. 'But if you ever have to do this for real, you need to be quieter; as quiet as you can possibly be.'

'As quiet as a mouse?' She pokes her head out between the dresser doors, more awake now.

'Exactly. And you need to make yourself as small as a mouse too, so you can pull these doors fully shut.'

She lowers her body to the floor of the dresser. 'Like this?'

'Exactly. Well done. Now pull the door shut, so I can't see you.'

Her hand hooks around the edge of the door, but she struggles to shut it without trapping her fingers. 'I can't do it!'

I pull the door open. 'Look. *Here.*' A strip of wood runs across the inside of the door. 'You can get your fingers round this. Go on, give it another try.'

She does so again, then a third time, finally succeeding in pulling it shut. 'Brilliant,' I say. 'You're a superstar. So remember: this is where you go if you need to hide.'

'Why will I need to hide?'

'I don't think you will. But we're practising, just in case.'

'Just in case what?'

'Just in case someone bad comes.' I don't use any names.

‘Like who?’ Her voice sounds muffled from inside the dresser, so I pull it open. I explain it’s a bit like keeping a fire extinguisher on the wall; you don’t know if there will ever be a fire, or where such a fire might come from, but it’s important to be prepared all the same.

‘Is a fire going to come?’

‘No, no.’ I’m making this too complicated. I sit cross-legged on the floor and take her on to my lap. ‘Tell you what. If I think you need to hide, I’ll say “Den Time” to you. Okay?’

She nods.

‘Good girl.’ We run through the logistics a few more times, until I’m happy she understands, at which point I let her return to the bedroom. I place a towel across the wet patch on the mattress, and a pile of Poppy’s toys by the door, so we’ll hear if anyone attempts to get in.

And then it’s time to sleep again.

Or at least try to.

HANNAH

Max and I get up from the bench and walk away from the house, across the grass. Max stumbles and grabs my arm to right himself. 'Sorry.'

'That's okay.' But he doesn't let go, and we carry on walking in silence, until the ground transitions from grass to bracken. 'How far are we going?'

'I don't know. How far do you want to go?'

I'm not sure if he means it suggestively, or if it only becomes suggestive after the fact, but suddenly we are stationary in the bracken and facing one another, his hand tighter around my arm. It is darker here, outside of our daily lives. Barely real at all as our lips touch, as I taste the Baileys upon his tongue. As he kisses my neck, telling me how good I smell.

'We should stop,' I say, or at least I mean to, but the pressure of his body against mine destroys any verbal ability I once possessed. He traces my spine and I can't quite believe that this is happening – this is happening! – and I tell myself to just enjoy the moment, and I am, but still my brain insists on a running commentary on the mechanics of the event: how his hands are on my chest, while my hands have reached his waist and sweep lower.

He pulls away. 'We shouldn't be doing this.'

I shake my head. He's right, but he can't be the one to break it off. He's supposed to be overwhelmed with lust, unable to resist me. I reach for the button on his trousers.

He pushes my hand away but only half-heartedly, which I take as encouragement to continue. I undo his flies and tug at his trousers.

'We really shouldn't,' he mumbles again. 'I mean . . .'

To stop him from saying what he means, I pull down his pants, kneel on the ground and take his penis in my mouth. 'Oh my God,' he says. I move my head, feeling the scratch of bracken in my hair, and he murmurs something unintelligible, before groaning. A rush of endorphins surges through me at the effect I'm having on him; at the power I possess, even if my knees are wet and my jaw is beginning to ache. I bring in my right hand and he groans more loudly – *good* – and I carry on, trying to build up a rhythm, trying to adjust my grip and suction according to the noises he is making. I can't quite believe what we're doing; at one point, I break my rhythm to look up and see Max's beautiful, familiar face, his eyes closed in pleasure, and I feel another rush that, after all these years, we are finally doing this; that the intimacy is real, and I'll never be just the kid sister again.

As I accelerate the pace, I wonder how everything will be between us, after – whether he'll be awkward and try to pretend it never happened, or whether the scales will fall from his eyes, and he'll realise how good we could be together. And then Chris's face flashes into my mind, but I shove the image away, and as I do so Max grabs the back of my head, to push himself deeper, and I almost lose my balance, have to splay my fingers across the ground to keep myself upright, and my jaw is really aching now, but he must be close, he must be close—

And then he comes, and a single word leaves his lips.

Lara.

WEDNESDAY

LARA

Poppy has gone back to sleep but I am struggling – my mind is still racing after everything that's happened. I look at the clock and see it's gone midnight. Which means it's now officially Mum's birthday.

I used to be brilliant at family birthdays. I was the person who, when my health allowed, baked elaborate cakes and made special breakfasts; who sourced gifts with an individual touch. Like the time I found Dad an early edition of Coleridge's poetry, or the time I typed up all of Mum's favourite recipes and had them printed and bound. I think it was because each birthday seemed precious – another milestone I'd successfully reached.

But my birthday brilliance ended when Dad died. And when the date of his birthday came round in February, while I was in France, I was ridden with disgust at what I'd become. After Gareth left the chalet to teach his snowboarding class, I drank two glasses of wine with breakfast, grateful for the way it blunted the edges of the day. My fingers crept to my phone, to Mum's contact details, but I couldn't bring myself to call, so I had another glass of wine to give me courage. But still I couldn't do it. I had a message from Jackie, reminding me what day it was – as if I could forget! – and I wondered if there was some gesture I could make, to show Mum and Hannah I was thinking of them, to show them I was sorry for not being there and, more importantly, that I was sorry for *not having been there*. That I knew my lack of contact over the past few months was inexcusable.

But no gesture seemed big enough. I was ashamed that I'd left them, that I'd run away to work in France and not even succeeded on that front, that I'd been fired and was doing nothing constructive with my days. That I was wasting the life they had worked so hard to give me. I thought about my teenage years – Dad, driving me to and from hospital appointments; Mum bringing me cold grapes and dry crackers to nibble on in bed – and the guilt was so acute that I doubled over, my abdomen cramping in pain.

There seemed to be only one way to relieve my discomfort, and that was to have another drink. I finished the first bottle of wine and opened a second, and the knowledge that I was medicating with alcohol brought on a new wave of shame, which necessitated drinking even more. A terrible, self-reinforcing cycle.

By the time Gareth returned, I was lying on the sofa, watching television without really seeing it, the constituent parts of my brain looping and whirling around each other like children in a maypole dance. The cramping in my abdomen had gone away but my stomach was queasy and my skin felt too hot. I mumbled incoherently at Gareth as he helped me to bed, before crashing out into darkness.

In the middle of the night I woke again, sick and in pain, and lurched to the bathroom. On my way there I heard Gareth whispering more of his sweet nothings. But it wasn't until the next morning – when I thanked him for helping me in the bathroom, and he said he hadn't – that I realised.

Maybe he hadn't been whispering them to me.

HANNAH

Alone, in bed, I clutch my legs to my chest and squeeze as hard as I can, trying to block out what has just happened, to lessen the humiliation. That whole time, in the bracken, he was thinking of Lara. She barely even gives him the time of day whereas I was there, on my goddamn knees, sucking him off, practically dislocating my jaw for him, and still it's *her* he thinks of.

He did at least have the grace to apologise after, but it was a clumsy apology – a stumbling collection of words that didn't quite go together; lots of *sorry* and *I shouldn't . . . I didn't . . .* and *it's not how it seems*, without explaining how it wasn't. I could barely stand to listen, but didn't want to give him the satisfaction of thinking I cared, so I said, 'No big deal – it was just a blow job,' and started walking back to the house, but he ran after me and began a whole spiel about not being a bad person and how he hoped I could forgive him, and I wanted to shout in his face that I could still taste his semen, so maybe he could do me the decency of shutting the fuck up, but instead I just said 'uh-huh' and walked faster, and soon we were saying goodnight and I clambered into bed without even bothering to undress.

I'm still clothed now, my jeans rough against my fingertips, damp at the knees. I should get into my pyjamas, but I don't want to move, don't want to disturb the duvet which is swaddled around me. Guilt needles at the underside of my skin, and all I can think is: *Why? What was it even for?* Perhaps I should leave Grove Cottage right now, at this very moment. I could stuff my things into my case and drive into the night, head to the airport and check in to one of those large, featureless hotels where no one would know, or judge, me; where I could eat bland food, watch meaningless films and pretend I don't exist.

But it's Mum's birthday tomorrow. Today, in fact. The whole reason I came to this bloody place. I bury my face in the pillow, where I can smell my stale breath. If only I could rewind to earlier this evening, when Mum and Jackie went to bed. I could go to bed too, leave the Baileys well alone, stay silent when Max came blundering back from whatever happened with Cassie. Pretend to be asleep. If I'd done that, I'd still possess some self-esteem, and would probably now *actually* be asleep, instead of lying here smothered by my own respirations.

I'm an idiot, a grade-A prize-winning fantasist. And if I was delusional about Max, then perhaps I'm delusional about everything else too. About my blog rising from the quagmire of online content, or Chris and I making a good couple. About Mum being proud of me, or our family functioning without Dad.

And certainly, definitely, about ever being close to Lara again.

LARA

Poppy sleeps later than usual this morning, probably because she's tired from being woken last night. In the light of a new day, my actions seem overblown and rather foolish. It was only ice in the bed, not a knife or a gun. Probably one of the others got drunk and came into the wrong room by mistake, maybe tripped over and spilled a gin and tonic or something.

The rest of the house is still quiet when Poppy wakes and we head to the kitchen. The other bedroom doors are shut, and the living room dark, with only a weak grey light filtering through the blinds. When my eyes adjust, I'm annoyed to find empty bottles and glasses scattered across the dining table, and food packaging strewn on the worktop. Peering at the sofa bed, I see the huddled, unmoving form of my sister, and for a second I panic she's hurt until I see the rise and fall of her chest, at which point my fear returns to irritation. I start getting Poppy's breakfast ready.

'Good morning!' Jackie appears in a fluffy robe and slippers and yanks open the blinds, flooding the room with light. 'It's the big day at last! The great 5-0!' Hannah turns her face into her pillow. 'Your mum's still asleep, so I want to get started on the decorations – can you girls give me a hand?'

The last thing I feel like doing is hanging decorations, but I guess I should show willing. 'Of course,' I say, as Jackie pulls packets from a cupboard.

'Balloons!' Poppy runs over to grab them. She waves a bag in front of my sister. 'Will you blow them up with me, Auntie Hannah?'

'Not right now, sorry. I'm not feeling too good.'

'Have you got a bug?'

'Maybe.'

'Mummy!' Poppy runs back to me. 'Auntie Hannah's got a bug.'

'Has she?' I say wryly, looking at the bottles and glasses on the table.

'Do you think she'll be okay for Granny's birthday?'

'I'm sure she'll be fine, little one. Now, look, why don't you sit at the clean end of the table to eat your breakfast, while I start clearing up?'

As I gather the empty bottles and biscuit wrappers, I look at my sister, hoping she'll tell me to stop tidying her mess, or at least get up and help. But she takes one glance in my direction, her face pale, before turning over on the mattress with her hands clasped to her head. I make a point of knocking the bottles together harder than necessary and rustling the wrappers. After throwing them in the bin, I shut its soft-close lid as loudly as I can.

Jackie observes Hannah still buried in her bed. 'Oh dear,' she says. 'Seems like someone's not feeling too well.'

'Auntie Hannah's got a bug,' Poppy explains.

'Has she now?' Jackie raises an eyebrow. 'That's unfortunate timing. Perhaps she should go and sleep it off in your room, and we can get Max and Cassie up to help instead.'

'Is that all right, Lara?' Hannah doesn't meet my gaze. 'If I go and use your bed?'

I load the glasses into the dishwasher with force. 'You'll need to move Poppy's books off it.' *And that wet towel.*

'That's fine.' She stands up, leaning on the side table for support, and I realise that she's still in last night's clothes. *For God's sake.*

Jackie notices too, and makes a point of unfurling some birthday bunting as Hannah trudges past. 'Can you knock for Max and Cassie on your way?'

My sister stops dead, her face even paler than before. 'I wouldn't want to wake them.'

'Oh, it's late enough that they won't mind. Besides, it's Helen's birthday!' Jackie examines the flags in her hands. 'How can these be tangled already? They're brand new!'

'But I really don't think I should be the one to knock. I mean, perhaps it'd be better if Lara, or Poppy—'

'Jesus, Hannah!' My temper gets the better of me. 'Are you incapable of doing *anything* this morning?'

She stares at me with the strangest look in her eyes, like I'm a grotesque insect she can't quite bring herself to squash. 'Not all of us can be as perfect as you, Lara,' she says, her voice icier than I've ever heard it.

And then she runs from the room. Seconds later, there's no knock.

Just the sound of a door slamming.

HANNAH

I spend most of the morning in a guilty half-sleep in Lara's bed, with *Hoarse Horse* jabbing into my arm and Moo Moo watching me reprovingly. I know some more water and paracetamol would help but I can't quite bring myself to get up and fetch them. My head is too delicate for the angry energy within it and my throat is dry, barely able to swallow. It doesn't help that I can hear festive noises from elsewhere: music and laughter and the occasional shriek from Poppy. I can't stop thinking about Max calling out my sister's name in the dark, and console myself by remembering that Lara had an affair with a married man, who proceeded to cheat on her. So it's hardly as if she's God's gift to men. But thinking this way makes me feel even guiltier, like I'm polluting my own conscience, and I can almost sense Mum's disappointment in me from the other side of the house. It's bad enough that I'm sleeping off a hangover on her birthday, let alone taking comfort in my sister's misfortune.

And then my phone pings on the bedside table. *Morning gorgeous! Are you free to chat?* I stare at the screen for a few seconds, letting my eyes blur until the message becomes illegible, wondering if I should write back equally cheerfully, pretending nothing has happened. Or if I should break up with Chris straightaway.

I continue to stare at the screen, my finger inching towards the dial button but not quite pressing it. Perhaps it doesn't make sense to break up with him simply because I'm feeling guilty. Or at least, not to do so from another country, while I'm hungover and can barely form sentences. I need to explain some things to him in person. Like how I've realised our relationship looks good from certain angles but has little substance to it, much like the reflection of a mountain in the water. That we have no knowledge of each other's greatest fears or moral outlook; no sense of what drives us or underpins us; no inkling of what the other stands for. We are essentially just false mirrors, shining back what the other wants to see.

Morning, I type back. *Probably best if I don't chat right now – I feel terrible.* Not a lie.

Sorry to hear that, comes the instant response, and my guilt clenches tighter. *What's up?*

Self-inflicted I'm afraid. Baileys, to be precise.

Ouch. How's your mum feel about turning 50?

I haven't seen her yet. Typing is almost worse than speaking, although at least I don't have to worry about the tone of my voice. *I should go and say happy birthday. How are you?*

Bored. I've been working all morning. Are you sure you don't want to chat?

Later, I write.

Speak later then, he messages back. *And send some birthday photos!!*

Will do, I write.

But as I return my phone to the bedside table, I realise I no longer feel like taking photos, or even writing my blog.

I just want to stay in bed and never see anyone again.

Not Taking Things in my Stride

Sorry – it's only a short one today. Partly because my mum is celebrating being fifty years young, so the day is a whirlwind of decorations, Bucks Fizz and festivities! And partly because, if I'm entirely honest, I'm not feeling very inspired to write. Which might seem a strange thing to say on my mum's birthday, but I think we're all prone to building things up so much that when they finally happen, it can feel like an anti-climax. I'm not sure exactly what I was expecting, and in many ways it's been really lovely – Mum has said how special it is to have us all with her, we've gone for a beautiful walk, and she's loved her presents (including a jasmine candle from **Dianthus**, a **Nantucket Interiors** silver photo frame and some **Embruns** perfume) – but I think it's important to be honest with my readers, and the fact of the matter is I'm struggling a bit today, despite all the loveliness.

So perhaps you'll forgive me for providing just a brief overview of where we walked earlier. We went to **Robin Hood's Stride**, a rock-strewn hill near the village of Elton – perfect for scrambling on, provided you're not hungover (which, unfortunately, I was). It's called Robin Hood's Stride because legend has it that the famous outlaw leapt between two pillars of rock there. Just round the corner is **Cratcliffe Tor**, where you can find the **Hermit's Cave**, a hollow in the rocks which used to be home to a religious recluse, back in the 1500s. The identity of the hermit is unknown, but you can still see the crucifix which he carved into the stone, and a ledge which might once have been his bed.

I'm afraid that's it from me today: sorry for the brevity and downbeat tone – I'm definitely identifying more with the hermit than Robin Hood at the moment! But we're about to eat some birthday cake and in a couple of hours we're off for Mum's birthday dinner at **The Shot**, so maybe all that food will cheer me up! And then I can start taking life in my stride once again . . .

LARA

Hannah has been off with me all day. There was that angry remark in the kitchen earlier and she's been avoiding me ever since: keeping her distance on our walk and now turning her back to me at the dining table. I would put it down to her hangover, except she's currently chatting perfectly happily to Jackie, congratulating her on her baking skills. So it must be something I've done. Although goodness knows what. It's true that Hannah and I haven't been close for years, and that she still resents me for going to France after Dad died, but none of that has changed since yesterday.

So maybe it's something to do with Chris? She's been checking her phone even more than usual today, and a couple of times I've seen her shaking her head too, as if she doesn't like what she's reading. But that has nothing to do with me. In fact, if I had my way, none of us would look at our phones at all.

I prod at my slice of cake with my fork, feeling a little nauseated by the quantity of chocolate and thick sludgy icing.

'What do you think of Jackie's creation?' Mum asks me.

'Delicious,' I say, eating a small forkful to validate my response. It sticks in my throat, so I follow it up with a gulp of tea.

'Isn't it?' Mum watches me a little too closely. And then she addresses the table at large. 'I don't suppose anyone has seen an earring, have they? Shaped like a teardrop? I'd like to wear them tonight but one's gone missing. I swear I left it in my jewellery box . . .'

Apparently Mum isn't the only person who's lost something. Jackie has misplaced a silk handkerchief, Max's aftershave has gone missing, Cassie can't find her black and gold hair clip and Hannah has lost a bracelet. And then Hannah mentions her white shirt. She says it disappeared from her case on the day we arrived and Mum asks if she's sure she brought it with her. When Hannah says yes, Mum asks where she last saw it. 'My *case*,' says Hannah, irritably.

'But are you *sure*?' asks Mum.

'Are you sure you left your earring in your jewellery box?'

'No need to get snarky, I'm just trying to help. And yes, I'm sure, because my other earring is still there.'

Hannah rolls her eyes, but fortunately Mum doesn't notice because she's returned her attention to her plate. Cassie is looking at her plate too, but as I watch, she lifts her head and stares at me with a strange, defiant expression. Almost like she knows the truth about the shirt. I turn away, ask if anyone's seen my perfume, which has also been missing for the last couple of days.

'Goodness, we're a fine lot, aren't we?' Jackie laughs. 'Has anyone *not* lost anything? This cottage is turning into the Bermuda Triangle!'

'Also,' I say. 'While we're on the topic of strange happenings . . . Did anyone accidentally spill their drink in my bed last night?'

'What!' Jackie laughs again. 'No, I had a few glasses of wine, but I wasn't *that* drunk.'

'Anyone else?' I glance around the table, but nobody seems to be owning up to it, or even looking sheepish, like they were drunk enough for it to be a possibility. Although perhaps I can see a tinge of guilt on my sister's face . . .

'What happened?' Mum asked. 'Did you see someone come in?'

'No.'

'Then why do you think—'

'There was ice,' I say. 'In my bed.'

'What do you mean?' Mum is wearing a concerned expression now, her eyebrows drawn together and her hand fluttering at her neck.

'Exactly what I said. I woke up because my feet were cold, and when I pulled the duvet back, I found pieces of ice on the mattress.'

'You're sure it was ice?'

'Yes.'

'And you didn't put it there?'

I clutch my fork harder. 'Why would I put ice in my own bed?'

'Poppy, then?'

'No – I would have noticed.'

'Well, that's very . . . *peculiar.*' Mum looks at Jackie, who looks back at her, and I get the distinct sense they don't believe me. That they think I've made the whole thing up, or somehow misinterpreted events.

But I know what I saw; what I felt. Or at least I'm pretty certain I do.

It's Jackie who attempts to break the tension. 'Strange things always happen when lots of people spend time in close proximity! Do you remember, Helen, when we had that girls' weekend and all of our periods were synchronised!'

'Mum, please,' Max says. He's been a bit off today too – not actively avoiding me, like Hannah, but definitely more surly than normal.

'Anyway, hopefully everything will settle down soon,' Jackie goes on. 'And we'll find everything by the end of the week!'

The end of the week can't come quickly enough, in my opinion. I hated being at Robin Hood's Stride earlier, because there were too many rocks like the ones from my dreams about Hannah. But nothing untoward happened, thank God, and now it's Wednesday afternoon, which means there isn't long to go. We've only got to make it to Saturday morning.

Sixty-six more hours of shredded nerves. And then this whole ordeal will be over.

HANNAH

The Shot lives up to expectations in terms of appearance – the decor is opulent, with dark, textured wallpaper, large modern artworks and velvet banquettes – and my figure-hugging orange dress complements it perfectly, providing a pop of colour against the moody backdrop. Unusually for me, however, I'm struggling to care. I take several selfies, but my heart isn't in it, and I have to actively force myself to photograph other aesthetically pleasing elements: a painting of a wolf in a top hat, a hand-woven slogan cushion, the gin cocktails which Jackie insists on ordering. I take around thirty photos before slumping back and closing my eyes, letting the sounds of eating and talking wash over me.

'Bread, Hannah?' I open my eyes again to see Jackie proffering a large platter of breads, butters and oils. I take a photo of the platter before randomly picking a slice and dumping it on my plate.

'You might want to actually eat it,' Jackie suggests, winking. 'It's delicious, and might help with the sore head? Or, alternatively, get going with one of these.' She taps at my glass. 'Hair of the dog and all that.'

I force myself to laugh and take a sip of the cocktail – which, surprisingly, does seem to help. The gin has been mixed with some sort of fruit syrup and the soda water feels rejuvenating, its bubbles popping against the roof of my mouth. I can barely taste the alcohol.

Jackie taps her fork against her glass to get the table's attention. 'I'd like to make a toast. To Helen, the most wonderful friend, mother and grandmother, whom I was lucky enough to meet all those years ago, on the corner table in Miss Riding's class. And who today is turning fifty years young! We love you, Helen, and are so glad you're in our lives. So here's to another fifty. To Helen!'

'To Mum!' I say, and clink my glass with each person in turn, including Lara and Max, although I'm careful to avoid eye contact. I've been trying to keep away from them all day, which hasn't been easy: during our picnic lunch earlier, Max plonked himself down next to me, saying we needed to talk. I responded by standing up to photograph our surroundings, focusing hard on the slabs of lichen-dotted rock and the muddy grassland, on the spindled trunks of silver birch trees and the sprawl of evergreen forest beyond. On everything that wasn't Max. And then I sat back down, on the far side of our group, next to Mum.

I've been avoiding Chris too. Which is less forgivable. I was going to ring him when the Connect alert came through at Robin Hood's Stride, but I couldn't face it, couldn't face *him*, not when Max was loitering nearby. So I just sent my photos – one of me with the rocks behind, my face largely in shadow, and the other of a drystone wall – and then a message, saying I wasn't up to speaking after all.

But we didn't talk for long yesterday either, he wrote back. *A more suspicious man might think you're trying to avoid me . . .*

Without any tonal inflection, it was hard to judge his sentiment. Whether he was just making a joke or was actually suspicious, and trying to hide it beneath a veneer of humour. The three dots of the ellipsis capable of communicating playfulness or threat. But it was his next message that drew me up short. *You still haven't shared any photos of your family. Just lots of you and the countryside. And that chef guy!*

I stared at my screen, heart pounding in my throat. Did he know? That wasn't possible, surely; he was still in Singapore, more than seven thousand miles away. And yet that exclamation mark niggled. Another ambivalent symbol, so often conveying comedy.

But also a warning.

I look at my phone now, return to the conversation in question. Trawl through Chris's words and punctuation, and my subsequent reply. *It's because of the food! I just can't resist.*

That reminds me of a line in Measure for Measure, he wrote back.

Oh? I hate it when he quotes Shakespeare at me; he read History at university, not English, yet somehow seems to know more famous sayings than I do. But I simply replied: *What line? I never studied M4M.*

It's like Angelo says, he continued. *'It's one thing to be tempted, Escalus.'*

?

'Another thing to fall.'

LARA

The restaurant isn't a good choice for Poppy. Nor me, for that matter: the food is rich and decadent – lots of red meat and thick, shiny sauces – and the gin cocktails Jackie orders are too strong. I sip at mine, to show willing, but the alcohol burns at the back of my throat. Poppy, meanwhile, only manages a couple of mouthfuls of her 'Sweeter Rabbit' meal: she likes the way the dish is presented, but not the idea of actually eating rabbit, because it makes her think of Benjy the preschool bunny. I tell her to eat the rest of her food, but she says the sweet potato is 'disgusting' and she doesn't like the 'weird black spots' (pepper) on her carrots, so ultimately I just feed her lots of bread, which I know is poor parenting, but I don't have the mental bandwidth to deal with a meltdown.

I do my best to act merry, for Mum's sake; to plaster a smile on to my face at regular intervals, but the restaurant makes me uncomfortable, and not just because the food is rich. The dining room itself is too crowded, too dark, the sort of place where someone could hide in plain sight. I find myself surveying the other tables for a glimpse of a familiar face, and a small shiver runs through me.

'Are you cold?' Jackie asks, and before I can say no she takes the cashmere shawl from her shoulders and places it over mine. I try to return it but she pushes it back, saying she insists. Saying she has more natural padding than me. She laughs uproariously at this, taking a large bite of sticky toffee pudding, and Mum laughs too, flopping back against the banquette.

'I think I might be defeated,' she says with a contented smile.

'There's still some chocolates to come,' Jackie reminds her.

'No!' Mum clutches her stomach. 'I knew I shouldn't have eaten such a big slice of cake this afternoon!'

As the two of them start discussing birthday cakes, millefeuilles, and past holidays in Brittany, I scan the room again, taking in the group of laughing men in one corner and the multi-generational party near the entrance, before looking back at my dining companions. Jackie is trying to feed Mum a spoonful of sticky toffee pudding and Mum is shaking her head, laughing. Hannah is photographing the dessert menu. Max is helping Poppy make origami with a napkin. And Cassie is picking an unused sharp knife off the table.

Wait, Cassie is—

I blink once, twice, unable to believe what I'm seeing.

Cassie puts the knife into her handbag, and clicks the clasp shut.

HANNAH

It's a relief to be back at Grove Cottage, saying our goodnights. With Mum's birthday over, it feels like the familial duties are done. If it weren't for the fact I have a flight booked for Saturday, I think I'd leave tomorrow, or even now. Although would being in Singapore be any better? The thought of returning to Chris early – the thought of returning to Chris *at all* – makes my insides curl like the edges of waterlogged paper. Because surely he'll be able to tell what I've done as soon as he sees me, the guilt marked indelibly upon my body.

I should break up with him right now, aided by the gin and wine in my bloodstream. Except what sort of coward ends a relationship over the phone?

Lara and Poppy have gone to bed, Cassie too, and I'm hoping Mum, Jackie and Max won't be far behind; they've already said their goodnights but are still hanging around the living room. Max and Cassie have barely spoken all day, which makes me wonder if Max is waiting for her to fall asleep before going to bed himself. A scenario which might once have gladdened me, but which now feels sad, and pointless, like all of us are reaching out to the wrong people. Like we're each destined to want what we can't have – or worse, that we don't even know what we want, and are simply flotsam in a turbulent, rising sea.

Mum and Jackie start whispering to one another and giggling. I stare at them, puzzled at what there is to laugh about. Perhaps I stare too hard, because Mum gets to her feet. 'Let's go, Jacks,' she says.

'Night, kids. Don't stay up too late!' Jackie waves as they leave the room, and I set about the process of preparing my bed: sofa cushions off, bar up and out, sheet reattached, cushions replaced. I am halfway through when I feel a tap on my shoulder. 'Hannah?'

I don't want to turn, don't want to see him watching me with his entreating expression. *Make me feel better about making you feel bad.* So I focus instead on securing the sheet over the corners of the mattress. 'I'm about to go to bed,' I tell him.

'Please. Can we just go for a walk or something?'

'A walk?' I turn now, see that he's fiddling with the back of the armchair, squeezing its fabric between his finger and thumb.

'Yes. I really need to speak with you, and I'd rather do it outside, given . . .' He trails off, and for a moment I'm furious, because he doesn't deserve anything more from me, not even a distanced walk in the dark, but at the same time I want to know what he has to say for himself. How he can justify his behaviour. And at least going outside means I won't have to look at his face, or watch his hands pick at the furniture.

'Fine,' I say. 'A quick walk.'

'Great.' He runs his hand down the side of the armchair. 'Thank you. I appreciate it.'

We put our shoes on in silence and step out into the night. The air is colder than I expected, much colder than when we left the restaurant, and I wrap my arms around myself. He walks slightly faster than me, just a couple of steps ahead, until he reaches the tree line and pauses, as if remembering what happened when we came here last night.

I look up at the sky. The stars are out in force: a great sweep of them, flung across the darkness like an arc of spilled salt.

'I'm sorry,' he says.

'What for?'

'For last night.'

'What about it?' I don't want to make this easy for him.

'For . . . I can't bear for you to think . . . I shouldn't have . . .'

'What?'

'Look,' he says – and I do, but he's just nudging at the bracken with his foot – 'I think you're an amazing woman—'

'For fuck's sake.' I turn to go.

'Wait.' He grabs my arm. 'If things were different . . .'

'Do you mean if you weren't Cassie's boyfriend, or if you weren't in love with my sister?' My boldness surprises me. I look him straight in the eye.

'Both. Neither. I mean, I'm not in love with . . . Look, I'm not in a great place right now . . . I don't really know what I want, or even what I feel—'

'I'm not sure I can help you with that.' I try to throw his hand off my arm, but he doesn't let go.

'I think Cassie and I are splitting up.'

'And I'm supposed to care?'

'No, I just—'

'Fuck you, Max.' And I slap him across the cheek – a firm, resounding slap that hurts my hand.

'I don't think—' he begins, but I slap him again, and suddenly we're kissing: hard, angry kisses, like pellets to the lips. He bunches my hair in his hand, pushes me back against a tree and presses the length of his body against mine. I pull up his shirt and rake my nails down his skin, wondering if I'll draw blood, hoping I do, and then he steps back, gathers the hem of my dress and hitches it above my waist, and in a matter of seconds we're having sex.

Bark scratches my back, and my neck is jolted with the force of him. But I want the pain, I need the pain, because the physical sensations crowd out the mental ones, and as long as we're doing this, I can't think about anything else. I'm free from my past and future, existing only in the scratching and pounding.

I try to let it all go – the guilt and shame, the inadequacy and resentment.

And I scream out into the starry, starry darkness.

LARA

Poppy falls asleep almost immediately after getting into bed, exhausted from the day's excitement. I'm tired too, but my brain won't switch off. I keep thinking about Cassie stashing the knife in her bag. I took her aside after the meal, when we were waiting for our taxis, and she simply denied all knowledge, said she didn't know what I was talking about. 'But I *saw* you,' I insisted, to which she shrugged, said we'd all been drinking, and then I started to doubt myself, because I wasn't used to alcohol and my head *did* feel strange. By the time I decided I hadn't imagined it, she was already squeezed into the taxi next to Mum, so what could I do? Short of leaping on her and pulling the knife from her bag, there was no way to make her tell the truth.

But why did she take it? Only two nights ago, I dreamed of a knife lying beside Hannah's bloodied body. But why would Cassie want to hurt my sister?

Poppy makes a groaning sound and rolls over in the bed. Her skin looks flushed, so I touch a hand to her forehead. She feels hot, and I can only hope she's not coming down with a virus.

Come to think of it, I feel hot too, although maybe that's just the alcohol. Or it could be the start of another panic attack. *Shit.* I stand up and head to the window, open it and stick my head outside.

The night air is bitterly cold, laced with the winter to come, and I start to shiver almost immediately. The cold feels good, though – an antidote to my hot, quivery breath. I remain there until my lungs regulate, before climbing back into bed, soaking up the warmth of my daughter beside me.

I don't know how much later it is when I hear the sounds. A creaking, a padding. I assume I'm asleep until lucidity kicks in and I realise the creaks are coming from the toys behind the door, the padding from someone's feet upon the carpet.

I open my eyes and survey the room.

There's a figure standing in the corner.

Fear ices my veins, sets my heart racing. The toys behind the door weren't enough; I should have hidden a weapon beneath the mattress. Now Poppy and I are an easy target. Adrenaline surges wildly as I try to think of an escape plan. Perhaps if I could grab something heavy, smash it over the intruder's head?

Poppy's *Big Book of Fairy Tales* is lying on the floor, just a couple of metres from the bed. If I can just reach out, hook my fingers around it—

'Lara?'

The voice from the corner is familiar – female, with well-rounded edges – and my pulse starts to subside.

'Cassie!' I sit up, pull the book into my lap. 'What the hell are you doing here?'

'Mummy?' says Poppy, sitting up too.

'It's okay, go back to sleep,' I whisper, wrapping an arm around her shoulders and lowering her to the mattress. She blinks a couple of times before closing her eyes again.

'I'm sorry,' says Cassie, who is now close to the bed, a strange, spectral form in the darkness. 'I didn't think you were in here . . .'

'It's *my* bedroom.' My whispers are taut with anger. 'What's your excuse?'

'I just . . . I woke up, and Max wasn't in our room.'

'So you assumed he was in mine?'

'Yes.' She takes a step back. 'I'm sorry. It's just . . . there were these noises . . .'

'What sort of noises?'

'They were . . .' She falters. 'Kind of breathy, I suppose . . .'

'You came into my room because someone was *breathing* loudly?' It's just as well for Cassie that I haven't stashed a weapon under my mattress.

'It wasn't just *breathing*. It was more . . . um . . . it was louder than that, and there was this weird light; sort of an orange gl—'

'What did you say?' The fear is back, vice-like around my chest.

'I said, "It wasn't just breathing—"'

'No, the other thing. About the light?'

'Just that there was this glow, from the window. Wait, your window's open—'

'What?'

'There.' She walks to the edge of the room, and I see that the window is indeed partly open. Did I fail to shut it properly earlier, when I thought I might be having another panic attack? I press my face into my hands, disturbed that my brain seems even more muddied than usual. 'Where was the orange glow?' I ask.

'Why is your window open? Has someone been through it?'

'The window doesn't matter! Where was the orange glow?'

Cassie stares at me for a couple of seconds. 'I thought it was spilling from your room into the garden, but now I'm wondering whether it actually came from outside—'

'Let's go.' I get up.

'What?'

'Let's go outside.' I pull on my dressing gown and trainers, and shut and latch the window.

'I'm in my night things—'

'So am I. It doesn't matter.' I pick up the heavy book again.

'What are you doing?' Cassie asks.

'Arming myself.' I head towards the door.

'Why?'

'Just in case.'

'In case what?'

At that moment there's a scream from the garden – a sound which sparks through me like an electric shock. 'What was that!' says Cassie, but I say nothing, just sprint down the corridor to the living room. 'Wait!' shouts Cassie, but I don't, I keep running, out of the double doors and into the garden. And then I see it: an orange glow near the picnic table. There's a smell of burning too.

'Stay there!' I whisper, holding one hand out to stop Cassie coming any nearer.

She hovers by the double doors, a look of scared confusion on her face. 'What—' she begins.

'Just stay there!' I creep towards the picnic table. As I do, I hear the breathy sounds she mentioned and raise the book above my head.

And then I hear a loud, familiar laugh, followed by an equally familiar high-pitched giggle. Which makes no sense, because if my sister is being attacked, why would Mum and Jackie be *laughing*? I tiptoe closer, my head spinning as I wonder if this is some sort of macabre ritual, or whether I might in fact be asleep, or losing my mind completely, at which point I see Mum and Jackie huddled together, focused on something at their centre.

Only that something isn't Hannah, or a body of any sort.

It's a spliff.

HANNAH

When it's over, Max pulls up his trousers and looks away from me, and I'm left with a horrible dark feeling, like the mind-hole that comes after an extreme drinking session. *What have I done?* It feels sordid to be half-naked among the trees together, not making eye contact, like we've just performed a shameful act that must never be spoken of again.

Which in a way, I guess, we have. Because there's Chris to think of, and Cassie, not to mention Mum and Jackie and Lara. If they could see us right now – me hoicking up my knickers in the undergrowth and Max refastening his flies – they would be disgusted, appalled. And, if I'm honest, I wouldn't blame them. I had always imagined sex with Max would be profound – that our shared history would lend a new, deeper dimension to the act – but this feels all wrong.

If only he would look at me. If only he would say it meant something.

I pull down my dress and try to clear my thoughts, wondering if I should lean over and kiss him, or walk away. 'I'm going to . . .' I begin, because those three words don't close down my options, but before I can say anything further Max puts a finger to his lips.

'What is it?'

'There's people talking,' he whispers. 'Over near the house.'

He's right: there's a murmur of voices nearby, although I can't make out what they're saying. 'Do you think they heard us?'

'I don't know.' He smooths out his shirt. 'Perhaps we should go back separately.'

More creeping around. I didn't expect us to walk back hand in hand, but surely we could at least walk *alongside* one another, rather than sneaking singly through the trees . . .

Stop being so ridiculous, I command myself. He's still officially with Cassie, so of course he must split up with her before he can be seen meandering in the moonlight with me. Although even as I'm thinking this, it occurs to me that perhaps he's not worried what Cassie thinks.

Perhaps he's worried about Lara.

'It's Mum,' Max whispers, and he's right again, because Jackie's laugh is unmistakable, carrying loud and clear through the trees. 'I'll go first,' he says. 'Try to get her inside.' He heads off without checking to see if I'm okay with his plan – if I'm okay, full stop – and I want to shout at him for leaving me, for using me, except perhaps I needed to feel this way: wrung out and empty.

I lie on a rock, and look up. I wish I'd paid more attention to Dad's astronomy lessons over the years; to which band of stars is Orion's Belt, and which constellation the Plough. For millennia, people have used the night skies to guide them, but I am clueless as to which way I am facing, or what my next steps should be.

Yet perhaps I should forget all that for now, because sometimes living is just about the moment, right? Just breathing and existing, taking it all in.

Just lying on a rock and gazing at the infinite space above.

LARA

'What the hell are you doing, Mum?' I march over to where she's standing, head bowed as she sucks on the spliff in her right hand. She straightens up, her eyes temporarily widening as she sees me, before creasing as she dissolves into giggles and passes the spliff to Jackie. 'Caught in the act!' she declares.

'Are you smoking *marijuana*?' I ask.

She nods, like a naughty schoolgirl, and giggles some more.

'And very good it is too!' says Jackie, taking a long draw before proffering the spliff to me.

I bat it away. 'What were you both thinking?'

'It's my fiftieth birthday!' says Mum. 'Best not to think!'

'But Poppy's in the house. And you've brought *drugs*—'

'Pot is hardly *drugs*. And it's my birthday—'

Jackie roars with laughter. 'You can't argue with that.'

'I absolutely can.' I can't believe the two of them could be so irresponsible, smoking illegal substances near Poppy. And where the hell did they get it from in the first place? Has a *drug dealer* been to the house?

'What was that screaming?' I try to keep my words level, but there's a tension forming in my shoulders, rising into my neck, taking up residence behind my teeth.

'What screaming?' Jackie offers the spliff to me again. 'Go on, Lara, you should really have some. It will help you relax.'

'I don't want to bloody relax! I just want the adults in my vicinity to act responsibly!'

Jackie peers around me. 'How about you, Cassie?'

Cassie shakes her head. 'There *was* a scream,' she says.

'I don't think we've been screaming,' laughs Jackie. 'Have we been screaming, Helen?'

'No.' Mum shakes her head over-vigorously. 'We've been quiet as mice!' And then she starts to giggle again.

'Quiet as noisy mice!' Jackie cackles.

'Mice who have found cheese!' says Mum, giggling so hard she can barely enunciate her words.

'For God's sake.' I need to leave before I say something I'll regret. 'Perhaps the two of you can keep it down from now on. Some of us are trying to sleep.'

'Sorry.'

'Sorry!'

I'm about to start back towards the house when I notice Cassie stiffen. Turning, I see Max emerge from the trees.

'Where have you been?' Cassie looks slowly between him and me.

'For a walk.' Max speaks haltingly. 'I didn't realise you were up.'

'Where?'

'Just around.' He gestures to a branch above him.

'Why?'

'Do I need a reason?'

'You didn't tell me you were going out.'

'You were asleep. Or, at least, I thought you were.'

There is a sense of accusation in the air, mingling with that awful, choking marijuana smell, and I really want to leave, to climb back into bed with Poppy. But I have to check something first. 'Did you hear any screaming, Max? When you were on your walk?

'Screaming?' His tone is quizzical but he doesn't meet my eye.

'Yes, screaming.' Something about this situation feels off; something more than the drugs and giggling fifty-year-olds. It occurs to me that all the adults are out here, bar one. And that Max is shifting from foot to foot. 'Have you seen my sister?'

'Um.' Max looks at the sky. 'I remember Hannah being on the sofa, and then I headed out, and I think she said she was off to bed – yes, she did. So she must be asleep now.' He turns to the side. 'Have you seen what Mum and Helen—'

'She's not asleep,' I say, recalling my passage through the living room.

'How do you know?' says Max, but I don't wait around for him to work it out; instead, I start to run again, but through the trees this time, cursing that I don't have a torch.

'Hannah!' I call. 'Hannah, are you there?' I push through low-hanging branches, stumble over fat roots, the rot of dead leaves squelching around my bare feet. *The Big Book of Fairy Tales* is cumbersome in my arms and I consider dumping it in the dirt, but I might need it, so on I go, the hems of my pyjamas growing heavy with the dew. 'Hannah!' I call again.

And then, entering the bracken, I see her, lying on a slab of rock, and I cry out, sink on to my knees. It's happened, she's been killed and I'm too late to save her. A wailing sound emanates from deep inside me and I beat at my chest, claw at my face, wish I could tear my entire useless self apart.

Until I feel a hand on my shoulder. 'Lara,' comes a voice. 'Hey, Lara, it's okay.'

And I glance up to see my sister, standing behind me, looking deeply concerned but also very much alive.

HANNAH

'Lara.' I crouch down on the ground beside her. 'What is it? What's happened?'

'I can't. I just . . .' She makes fists of her hands and presses them against her eyes. 'I'm fine.'

'You're not fine.' A few seconds ago, she was scratching at her face in a frenzy, like she was trying to peel away her very skin, and the noise she made – that noise! It made me think of a war cry, piercing and terrifying, but also sadder than that, shot through with the ragged dissonance of grief. 'But that's okay,' I soothe. 'It's okay not to be okay.' I'm aware I sound like a mental health ad, but have no idea what else to say, how to comfort her when there's something so clearly wrong. When she's out here in the middle of the night in just her dressing gown, with a book of fairy tales beside her in the mud, like she wants to fix her problems with magic. I could try to hug her, but I don't think she'd appreciate it; she's already removed her hands from her face to wrap her arms around her knees, and is sitting in a ball, head buried in her legs. So I pat her gently on the back. 'Talk to me.'

'You don't want to know,' she mutters.

'I do.'

'You'll just get annoyed—'

'I won't—'

'You'll say I'm making stuff up, trying to put myself at the centre of things . . .'

'Try me.' The wind coming down from Curbar Edge is glacial, and I want to suggest we go inside, cradle mugs of hot tea as we talk, but I'm worried that delaying our conversation will mean we don't converse at all. So I run my hands across my goose-pimpled arms, and wait.

'I thought you were dead.'

'What!' I half laugh, half splutter at this pronouncement. 'You thought I was . . . *why?*'

'Because I heard a scream, and then I saw you, on that rock—'

It's a good job she's still looking at her knees and not my face, because I can feel heat rushing into my cheeks. *She heard me screaming.* 'But I was just lying down, looking at the stars,' I say. 'I was thinking about the constellations.'

There's a pause, and her breathing evens out. Her next words are unexpected. 'Do you remember that poem Dad liked so much? The one about looking to the heavens?'

I nod. '"The Presence of Love". Coleridge.'

'*And in Life's noisiest hour, / There whispers still the ceaseless Love of Thee.*' She recites it quietly, and my chest tightens at the memory of Dad saying these same words to us, normally when we were tired from walking, and he was trying to get us to admire the view. '*You lie in all my many Thoughts, like Light, / Like the fair light of Dawn, or summer Eve / On rippling Stream, or cloud-reflecting Lake.*' I join in for the last two lines, my lips barely moving. '*And looking to the Heaven, that bends above you, / How oft! I bless the Lot, that made me Love you.*'

There's another pause, a longer one, during which we look at each other and away again. My heart beats in my throat and I wipe my eyes, trying to imagine what Dad would do if he were here. He would seek to comfort us, but would also be practical and level-headed, searching for solutions. And I should try to emulate that. I think how I might have reacted had the situation been reversed. If I'd heard Lara screaming and come outside to find her lying on a rock. I might have been momentarily worried, sure, but I'd have gone a lot closer to her, had a really good look at her, before concluding she was *dead*.

'So why did you . . .' I'm not sure how to phrase my question. 'Why were you so sure I—'

'Because of my dreams, all right?'

'Oh—'

'The ones I told you about, when you were at the airport—'

'I remember.' I think back to our conversation that day, how annoyed I was at all her dramatic talk of blood and rocks. 'But the thing is,' I say now. 'Just because you've had dreams about me dying, doesn't mean I will.'

'But they're so vivid. And persistent. Like they mean something . . .'

'Perhaps they do. Only not about the future.' I feel as if tonight's events have made me see the world more clearly. 'Maybe they just mean you're still pissed off with me.'

'What? Why?'

I take a deep breath. Can I really do this? I look out towards Curbar Edge, and the darkness makes me brave. 'For not saving you.'

There is a long silence and, when Lara speaks again, her voice is small, directed at her knees. 'I needed you.'

'I know. But you have to remember I did try. It wasn't my fault I wasn't a match.'

'What are you talking about?' She is sitting up straighter now, frowning, and I stare at her, wondering how she can feign ignorance of something so wounding. Something that divided my childhood into a 'before' and 'after'.

'When I wasn't a match for your stem cell transplant,' I say, my words coming out in a rush. 'I felt so bad about it, that I couldn't save you, but then I heard you in the bedroom, with Mum. Saying I was useless.'

She's blinking at me rapidly, 'What? I didn't say that.'

'You did. I remember it clearly.' I turn away so she can't see the tears in my eyes. 'You said, "It's useless. Hannah is useless."'

'No, I said, "Hannah – it's useless." Because I felt so bad that you'd gone through all of that – the doctors, the stress, the blood test – for nothing.'

My head suddenly feels hot, like it can't quite process what it's hearing. Could it be true? That all this time I've been divided from my sister by the unrealised existence of a single letter 't' and its accompanying apostrophe? 'Is' and 'it's' do sound very similar (particularly from behind a closed door) so it's plausible, but at the same time preposterous. Because surely I couldn't have let such a tiny thing come between us. And if I have, then it's the most unthinkable waste. All those years of resentment; all those precious sisterly moments that could have been but weren't.

'I was so cross with the world,' Lara goes on. 'That you and Mum and Dad were sacrificing so much for me, and yet we were no further forward. But I was never cross with you.'

What she's saying . . . I both desperately want and don't want it to be true. 'But how about what you said a moment ago?' I point out. 'That you needed me?'

'That was something else.' Her voice has hardened. 'Nothing to do with my transplant.'

'So what was it?'

She pauses, knots her hands together. 'I rang you from France, when I needed you. But you didn't come to the phone.'

This is news to me; the only time I can remember her calling was late one night, when I was at a house party. Some drunken woman picked up my phone and brought it to me, but when I answered, the line went dead.

'I only received one phone call from you the whole time you were in France,' I say, puzzled that this should be the thing she's bitter about. 'And there was no one there when I answered.'

'You didn't come fast enough.'

'I was at a party. If that's the time you mean?' I study her face for a clue, but her expression is inscrutable. 'It was the middle of the night, and we'd all been drinking. Surely you can't be mad at me for that?'

'But you didn't ring me back, or follow up my call. Even though I'd said it was urgent.'

'I'm sorry.' There's too much new information to take in here. 'I think possibly that message got lost in translation. Or in tequila . . .' She doesn't smile. 'And I didn't ring back because I assumed it was an accidental pocket dial. It wasn't like you were calling me on a regular basis . . .'

'But that's why you should have realised!' Her fingertips are white because she's squeezing them together so tightly, or maybe because of the cold. 'The fact that I didn't normally ring, that we weren't really talking; surely that should have made you realise it was an emergency . . .'

The fear and anguish in her voice is scaring me a little. 'What happened, Lara?' I ask. 'Why was it such an emergency?'

She shakes her head, her voice tight. 'It doesn't matter.'

'But it clearly does matter.' I take her hand in mine. 'Look, I'm sorry. For not realising. For not being there for you. For all our misunderstandings. But you can tell me now.'

She shakes her head again. 'Best to leave it in the past.'

'I'm not sure that's true.' If there's one thing I'm learning this week, it's that trying to leave difficult things behind creates more problems than acknowledging their presence. Because you'll bring them with you either way. 'I think from now on we should try to speak as honestly and openly as we can. Especially given we appear to have . . . got things wrong about each other . . .'

She pulls away from me suddenly, stands up and begins to pace around. 'That's all very nice, Hannah, but right now I'm concerned about current dangers, not past ones. The things I've seen in my dreams.'

'So tell me,' I say. 'Tell me what you've seen.'

What follows doesn't make a whole lot of sense; she talks about rocks and strange lights, knives and blood, and I realise she must be in a worse state than I'd thought. I force myself to nod, to make little murmurs of acknowledgement, and when she's finished, I give her a gentle smile, saying I'm glad she's told me. That it must be tough to feel this way, and to let me know if I can do anything to help.

'You can stay away from rocks,' she says.

'Um . . .'

'Please, Hannah. If you want to help me, stay away from Curbar Edge and Froggatt Edge, from Baslow Edge, from all the edges.'

I almost laugh at the ridiculousness of her request but manage to stop myself. If this is what it takes . . . 'Okay,' I agree.

'Really?'

'Yes. But only if you do something for me.'

'What?'

'I want you to promise to go back to the doctor.'

She stops her pacing and stares at me. 'You think I'm crazy—'

'No,' I say quickly. 'I don't think you're crazy. But I do think you're suffering. And I think you might want to increase your medication again.'

'You think I need more pills—'

'I think it might help,' I say carefully. 'Or maybe talking therapy or . . . I don't know . . . I'm not an expert.'

Her mouth straightens into a stubborn line. 'I've seen too many doctors in my life.'

'Please, Lara,' I say. 'For me. If I stay away from rocks for you, will you go to the doctor for me?'

She looks away for a few seconds, towards Curbar Edge, and I wonder if I've pushed things too far. But then she turns and nods. 'Fine,' she says. 'You've got yourself a deal.'

THURSDAY

LARA

I wake up with a terrible headache: a pulsing pain directly behind my eyes. And then memories of last night's events come surging back, making the pain ten times worse. The powerlessness I felt when Cassie crept into my room, and the utter, debilitating horror when I found Hannah on that rock in the garden. The panic and then the relief when I learned she wasn't hurt. The gulp of embarrassment now at my wild overreaction.

And then there was our discussion. I can't believe that all this time, all these years, she's been under the illusion I thought *she* was useless. When actually I've been nothing but grateful for everything she and Mum and Dad did for me growing up; for everything they sacrificed. I knew Hannah resented me for taking up so much airspace, but I had no idea the resentment burned so deep, nor that it pivoted around a single moment – discovering she wasn't a match. Although, thinking back on when we grew apart, it makes perfect sense. I'd just been too preoccupied with the national donor register – and the eventual match we found there – to notice.

Which brings me on to the phone call I made to her from France, the one she'd thought was an accident. I'd always pictured her sitting stubbornly in a corner, refusing to come to the phone, whereas the image she painted last night was one of chaotic merrymaking, in which my urgent message got lost, or at least scrambled.

Is it possible I've misunderstood Hannah in the exact same way she's misunderstood me? That we were each too quick to judge the other, to be hurt by a mirage of indifference and contempt? And, if so, is it too late to unpick our mistakes and start again?

I'm not sure, but at least we're taking tentative steps in the right direction. She's agreed to stay away from rocks for me, and I've agreed to return to the doctor for her. And I'll stick to this if it keeps her safe. Even though I'd prefer never to set foot in a medical establishment again, and can't see how any good can come from it. Because either I hold back on talking about my dreams, or I don't, and if the former, there's not much point going in the first place. But if the latter, then what if I'm deemed to be psychologically disturbed, maybe even dangerous? What if they separate me from Poppy?

My head is still pounding, making me think of the hangover I had the morning after Dad's birthday, in the Alps, when I realised Gareth might be cheating on me. The problem was I had no way to know for sure, merely a drunken memory of him whispering to someone else. He had been whispering about love, I remembered that much, but had he said something else about missing their lips, their body, or had I imagined that part? And where had he been whispering from? In my inebriated state I'd assumed he was in the bathroom too, but perhaps he was actually in the hall. In which case his loving murmurs definitely hadn't been aimed at me.

When I asked him about it, he looked concerned. 'I think your drinking's getting out of hand. I wasn't talking to anyone else last night.'

'But I'm sure I heard you . . .'

'Lara.' He placed a hand on my shoulder. 'You started drinking at breakfast. By the time I got home you could barely walk, let alone make sense of what was going on around you. So I think you might be imagining things . . .'

Remembering this, my head hurts even more. Why can I never understand a situation until it's too late? Gareth's lies then, and Cassie's lies now – because, whatever she claims, she *did* take a knife from the restaurant last night.

I go into the en-suite bathroom to find some painkillers, which I swallow with a large glass of water. I need to get my act together.

By the time I return to the bedroom, Poppy has woken up. I quiz her on our emergency drill – what to do if I say 'Den Time' – and she answers correctly, so I let her read her book instead of making her go and hide. We should probably practise again, but she's currently quiet and happy, and there's a risk of putting her off the attic if I'm too draconian about it.

A few minutes later she announces she's hungry, so we head along the corridor to breakfast. I explain Auntie Hannah had a late night, so we'll need to tiptoe in without disturbing her. Poppy nods and makes a point of walking quietly, raising her arms and legs like a deranged marionette, only for us to find all the lights on, the bed packed away, and Hannah standing by the coffee machine. 'Good morning!' She seems twitchy, like she's drunk too much caffeine. Which maybe she has. 'Would you like some coffee?'

'No thank you.' I sit down on one of the dining chairs. 'I've got a headache.'

'Oh no! Bet you're feeling better than Mum and Jackie though. Can you believe they were smoking—'

'Not now,' I say, inclining my head towards Poppy.

She cringes a little. 'Of course. Sorry.'

'No worries.' Things feel different between me and Hannah today: kinder, but also more awkward.

'So . . .' I sense she feels the shift too, because she clears her throat a couple of times. 'I was thinking of going for a bike ride. The trail—'

'Ooh, biking!' says Poppy. 'Can I come?'

'Auntie Hannah was talking,' I say quickly, not wanting to cut my sister off.

'No, it's fine, I . . .' She rubs the back of her neck. 'The trail is probably a little stony in places, but it's very safe . . .'

'It sounds like a good plan,' I tell her. Because, compared to some of the alternatives I've heard Mum bandying about – The Roaches, Stanage Edge, Higger Tor – it actually does. Obviously, I'd feel happier if Hannah left the Peak District altogether, but if she's going to stick around, cycling on a traffic-free trail is a decent option.

'Great, great,' she says, obviously relieved. 'Would you like some coffee? Sorry, I already asked you that.'

'Can I go biking too?' Poppy asks, bouncing around.

'I'm not sure.' I press my hands to my temples, try to massage away the pain.

'Lara?' My sister comes over to me.

'I'm okay,' I say. 'It's just a headache.'

Glancing back at Poppy, who is pulling wooden spoons from a drawer, Hannah drops her voice to a whisper. 'I could take her if you like. Let you get some rest.'

I'm about to decline when Cassie enters the room, fully dressed.

'Good morning!' Hannah says to her, too loudly.

'Morning.' Cassie's tone is curt. She takes a gluten-free bar from the cupboard and pockets it, making me think again of the knife from the restaurant. 'I'm off to Sheffield,' she announces. 'I'll eat lunch there.'

‘Okay. Bye!’ says Hannah, as Cassie leaves the room, and I mutter goodbye too, but my mind is turning over the fact Cassie’s heading out.

‘You know what,’ I say. ‘Maybe I will stay here, try to shift this headache. So if you’re happy to take Poppy, that would be much appreciated. Thank you.’

My sister raises an eyebrow. ‘Okay. I mean . . . great. So . . .’

If she’s trying to say anything else, I don’t get to hear it, because Poppy comes running over and gives me a giant hug. ‘I love you, Mummy!’

‘I love you too,’ I murmur into her hair. ‘I love you more than anything.’

But even as I’m saying it, I’m thinking of Gareth’s lies in the mountains. And of the fact that, just a couple of weeks after I discovered he might be cheating on me, I discovered something else too.

I was pregnant.

HANNAH

Riding the Monsal Trail is a welcome distraction, speeding along in the fresh air with beautiful views and no need to worry about traffic or navigation. It's simply a case of pointing our bikes along the trail and pedalling, and I can hear Poppy squeal with delight from the seat behind me, just like I used to on the back of Dad's bike all those years ago. When we reach the first tunnel, she grows even more excited, and the two of us whoop as we pass through the darkness, laughing as our voices echo back to us.

In another echo of the past, Max is cycling behind me, but on an adult bike instead of his childhood BMX, and with both hands firmly on the handlebars. I wish he'd stayed behind at the cottage, but Mum and Jackie wanted him to come, to keep an eye on me and Poppy. A duty he's taking too seriously: whatever speed I go, fast or slow, he maintains the same distance between us – far enough that we don't have to speak, but near enough that he'd see instantly if we skidded or fell. Watchful to the nth degree. Maybe it's a way of assuaging his guilt.

The events of last night don't seem real. Max and I having sex. Lara and I talking frankly, to find we didn't resent each other as much as we'd thought. That we'd suffered from a catalogue of misunderstandings.

I don't know whether to be elated or depressed by it all.

'Hannah!' Max calls as we exit the tunnel. 'Wait up!'

I turn to see him gesturing to the side of the trail. 'One minute!' I shout back, a heat flickering through me as I wonder what he might want.

I brake by a grassy embankment and Poppy asks why we're stopping. 'I'm not quite sure. Max wants to.' We watch as he draws up alongside, and Poppy repeats her question.

'I just thought we should wait for your gran and my mum.' He slings his bike on to the ground and throws his helmet down beside it.

'They could be a while.' I've heard about Mum and Jackie's exploits last night, and although they took place uncomfortably close to where Max and I were having sex, the idea of the two fifty-year-old women smoking pot in the garden is undeniably comic. As is the fact that, when I finally went back inside, they were working their way through all the crackers and cheese and laughing like crazy. They've been rather more subdued this morning – sipping hot drinks while wearing dark sunglasses – but insisted on joining our outing nonetheless. The poor man at the hire shop had to bring out three different bikes before Jackie found one she could cope with, and even then had to suffer through jokes about her 'getting her leg over'.

'Indeed,' Max says. And then, to Poppy, 'Shall we get you out of that seat? Give you a chance to run around?'

She agrees, and as Max deftly unbuckles and lifts her down, I try not to watch his hands. Try not to think about what they were doing in the garden last night.

'I need to speak with your Auntie Hannah,' Max says to Poppy. 'Are you all right to stay here a moment?'

'We can't leave her alone,' I whisper. My mouth feels dry.

'We won't go far. Just out of earshot. Over there, perhaps?' He points to a line of trees. 'We'll still be able to see her.'

'Okay.' I look at Poppy, who is spinning the back wheel of Max's bike, watching the spokes become a blur of grey. 'Tell you what.' I pull out my phone and flick to an audio app I downloaded recently, which came with a bunch of free books. I click on *Alice in Wonderland* and listen as the narrator begins. *Alice was beginning to get very tired of sitting by her sister on the bank, and of having nothing to do*. Perfect.

'Here you are.' I pass Poppy my phone, explaining how to pause and rewind the story, and make her promise not to look at anything else. 'Max and I will be just over there.' I point to the trees. 'Don't go anywhere. We'll be back very soon.'

She sits down, cross-legged, holding my phone in her small, chubby fingers. As Max and I walk away, I look back, wondering if this is a terrible idea, if Lara will find out what I've done and never forgive me. And just when we're starting to talk to one another again! But I reassure myself that Poppy's only listening to a story, which is not so different from having a book read to her.

Besides, I can't *not* listen to what Max has to say. Particularly when he might be rethinking things after last night's events. I know I am. The fact I was willing to act like that makes me realise I need to change my life; to work out who I want to be when I'm not trying to impress someone else.

And that should start with breaking up with Chris.

Max stops and turns to face me. 'I just wanted to apologise—'

'You don't need to apologise—'

'Please. Let me say this. I've behaved abominably: to you, to Cassie—'

'I've been just as bad—'

'And I don't think anything should happen between us again.'

It's the abruptness of his words which gets me, the finality of them. I turn to look at Poppy so he can't see the tears already threatening. 'Of course,' I say. 'I wasn't expecting it to.'

'No, of course.' He drops his head for a moment. 'I didn't mean to sound presumptuous.'

'The timing's bad,' I say. 'But if you ever wanted to get away from everything, you could always come and visit me . . . in Singapore . . .'

He leaves my words hanging for a few seconds before replying. 'That's kind of you.' And the careful, hesitant way he says it makes it indisputably clear he won't be coming. That he'll never like me in that way. The pressure builds behind my eyes, and I keep my focus on Poppy, who hasn't moved from her spot by the bikes. 'So are you and Cassie . . . ?'

'It's over. Not officially, yet, but things haven't been right since Mam Tor. Because it turns out she wants to formalise things between us and isn't willing to wait. She says there's no point staying together if I'm not sure about the prospect of marriage and kids with her . . .'

'And you're not?' I turn back to see him shrug. A loose shake of the shoulders, just like when he was a boy. The ripple across time makes my chest ache.

'I don't know.' He draws a deep breath. 'Part of me thinks it would be amazing, but another part wants to run a mile. And surely you shouldn't commit unless you know, right?'

'I don't know.'

'I think maybe some of my behaviour over the last couple of nights has been about reacting against what's expected of me, testing out my feelings . . .'

The idea I've been a guinea pig for his emotions makes me want to hurl. And perhaps he realises this, because he reaches a hand to my cheek, strokes along my cheekbone, just as the tears begin to fall. 'I'm so sorry, that came out all wrong. You're special to me, and what happened between us . . .'

I knock his hand away. 'It was no big deal.'

'Well, it meant something to me. We've spent so much of our lives together, and I hope we'll always—'

'Are we done here?' Our conversation has become intolerable. 'We should get going—'

'Not like this,' he says. 'Not when I've upset you—'

'I'm fine.' I start to walk off but he grabs my hand, brings me back towards him. 'Please don't cry.' He strokes my cheek again, before kissing me clumsily on the lips. I feel my body begin to respond, and pull away.

'Please,' he murmurs. 'I feel terrible for upsetting you.'

'I'm fine.'

'No, you're not, and I'm sorry, I'm an idiot . . .'

I wipe my face dry with my free hand and look pointedly at my other hand, still held in his. 'This isn't about you,' I say.

'It isn't?'

'No.' *Yes. Maybe.*

'Then what?'

'I don't know.' I stare at his hand, with its rough, hairy knuckles. 'Maybe it's about the stupid decisions I've made, and the unrealistic ambitions I've harboured. Maybe it's because I haven't achieved anything of note, and probably never will. Maybe it's because I've realised it's all pointless and I should just *stop trying*.'

There's a long pause. 'That's pretty bleak,' Max says eventually.

'Yeah, well, so is life.' My heart is beating fast and, ironically, I feel more at the centre of my own existence than I've ever been. Like I'm an actor in the spotlight, and the rest of the stage has fallen dark around me.

'Is there anything I can do to make things better?'

'You could give me my hand back—'

'Sorry.' He loosens his grip and I snatch my hand away, sink it into my pocket. 'So are you okay?' he asks. 'Are *we* okay?'

'Hunky-dory.' I don't think I've ever used that expression before, and once again I get the weird sense of being on stage, of delivering lines. I need to say something to lighten the mood, to show just how okay I am. 'Perhaps we could take a leaf out of our mothers' book,' I say. 'By *smoking* the leaf.'

He lets out a half-laugh. 'I'm not sure I'll get a chance to pick up any more. My mate's mate was in Sheffield earlier in the week, when your mum wanted some, but said he was heading to London for the weekend.'

It takes me a while to realise what he means but, when I do, it makes an awful sense. Max was the supplier of the cannabis. The conversation I saw between him and Mum in the garden: that's all it was. Nothing to do with proposing to Cassie, or anything involving me or Lara; it was simply about getting high.

As I walk back to Poppy and the bikes, it seems entirely apposite. Because, as everyone knows, what goes up must come down.

And sometimes, when something comes down hard enough, it crashes and burns, sending everything around it into flames.

LARA

Everyone has left and the house is quiet. I stay in bed for a few minutes after the cars have pulled out of the driveway, wanting to make sure they've definitely gone. My head is no longer hurting quite so violently, which makes it easier to get up, slip on my dressing gown and head into the corridor. I pause by Cassie and Max's room. I can hear a faint droning from outside the house, maybe someone mowing a lawn, and a slight rumbling from inside – the heating? – but no voices or footsteps. I look in the kitchen to be doubly sure, and then go to the front door, where I check the lock and pull the chain across.

I return down the corridor and open the door to Max and Cassie's room. It's surprisingly tidy: a couple of magazines lie on one of the bedside tables, but the top of the chest of drawers is clear, as is the floor, aside from a few pairs of shoes lined up under the radiator and a wheelie case in the corner. I search the bedside tables and find nothing of note; just some cleanser and a small pile of coins and receipts. The wardrobe is equally unrevealing: jumpers, shirts and dresses. I turn to the chest. The top drawer contains men's underpants and socks, while the second has the female equivalent: bras and knickers, socks and tights. It feels wrong to sift through another person's underwear, but I'm careful to ignore the details, pushing any fabric aside to look for the gleam of a knife's blade, or the smooth shine of its handle.

Finding neither, I head back to my room and lie down again. I consider trying to get some more sleep, but by mind is restless, plagued by thoughts of Cassie. Of why she took the knife, and what she's done with it. And, worse, what she might yet *do* with it. I thought I'd made things safer by hiding Max's chef's knife (and I've been lucky that he hasn't cooked for the last couple of days, so hasn't noticed its absence), but with another knife entering the mix, I feel like I'm losing control.

I should have insisted Poppy practise hiding again this morning. Given the ongoing – or perhaps increasing – danger we're facing, it's unforgivable that I didn't. I tried to justify my inaction through a desire not to put her off, but that's a feeble way to parent a child. As her guardian, my job is to keep her safe, not pander to her preferences. To tell her very clearly what she needs to do, without allowing room for negotiation. Or, if I'm incapable of that, to at least seek creative solutions; look for ways to make the attic more exciting.

I remember how much she loved it the first time we went up there. How she called it a 'secret den'. And perhaps that's the answer: to make the dresser as den-like as possible. I get out of bed, grab a couple of blankets and several of Poppy's books, and climb the spiral stairs.

But when I reach the last step, I notice something on the attic floor. A strange glancing of the light, as if a tiny flame has been lit. Dropping the blankets and books, I go to investigate. And what I find is not a flame at all, but rather a teardrop of shimmering silver, catching the sun's rays from the window above.

Mum's missing earring.

HANNAH

I barely speak for the rest of the bike ride; I just pedal, pedal, pedal, wanting my heart to pump and my muscles to burn; wanting my body to scream so my mind doesn't have to. The scenery passes in a blur: the trees, the bridges, the grassy embankments. And Poppy's chatter is similarly indistinct – words which register on an individual basis but don't quite compute as sentences. My lack of responsiveness doesn't seem to bother her, however, because she keeps talking, and when we finally return to the hire shop, she's grinning wildly. Mum and Jackie turned back before us so are already on the café terrace, drinking tea. They make space for Poppy between them. 'Where's Max?' Jackie asks, her sunglasses slid partway down her nose, and I shrug, even though I know exactly where he is, because he insisted on following me and Poppy even more closely after our tortuous conversation, like a dog who doesn't understand he's not wanted and keeps lolloping along out of some sort of misplaced loyalty, or because he feels guilty for shitting all over the carpet. So I'm well aware that Max is currently chatting to the hire shop man about the virtues of fork shocks versus frame shocks, although this makes no sense to me in either specific or general terms, because what the fuck is a fork shock and how can he be dwelling on such matters after everything that's happened?

But Jackie is still looking at me, scrutinising me, so I tell her he wasn't far behind us.

'Are you going to get yourself a cup of tea?' Mum asks.

'No, I think I'd like to head back.'

'Coffee then? I'll come with you.' She stands up and walks towards the café, and I'm left wondering if my words aren't coming out right. How 'I'd like to head back' has translated into 'I'd like a coffee'. But Mum's opening the door now, beckoning me over, and when I approach, she pulls me into the drinks queue, saying she wants to speak to me.

My first thought is: she knows. She must have overheard the conversation between me and Max earlier. Except, as she smiles nervously, I realise that's impossible, because she and Jackie arrived on their bikes long after our conversation had finished.

So maybe this is actually about Lara. I think of my sister in the bracken last night, clawing at herself and sobbing, convinced I was dead. Her disproportionate fury when I showed my phone to Poppy earlier this week and her overreaction in the adventure playground. Thank God she's agreed to see a doctor again.

'It's about your blog,' Mum says, and I stare at her, because this wasn't what I was expecting at all.

'What about it?' I think back through my recent posts, wondering if I accidentally included something rude. Or whether Mum wants to reiterate that blogging isn't a viable career option. I brace myself for her criticism and start formulating possible ripostes. *No offence, but you're a bit old to understand the online world.* Or: *There's more potential in it than you think.* Or: *It'd be nice if you occasionally had some faith in me.*

'I read your blog from yesterday,' she says.

I cast my mind back to what I wrote. An overview of her birthday celebrations and Robin Hood's Stride. Nothing rude.

'It saddened me.' She turns her lips down to emphasise her point.

'Why?'

'Because you seemed upset. Not to mention hungover. And it was my birthday.'

I don't know what to take from this; whether she's genuinely concerned for my feelings, or simply annoyed I felt them on her birthday. We reach the front of the queue and the woman behind the counter asks what I want. I consider making a quip – 'good looks, better brains, even better follower numbers' – but ultimately just ask for a skinny latte. And then I consider making a quip about that – because surely I should just drink black coffee if I want to be skinny? – but thinking of skinniness returns my mind to Lara, which, in turn, makes me think about Max, and I'm so tired of it all, so very, very tired, that I don't say anything. I just pay for my drink and lean against the wall.

'I'm fine,' I tell Mum now.

'You didn't sound it,' she says. 'In your blog. You said you were struggling.'

'Oh.' I cast my eyes to the ground. 'I guess I just feel . . . I don't know . . . that I'm somehow . . . lacking, I suppose . . .'

'Goodness.' Mum's sturdy walking shoes appear beside my trainers. 'What on earth do you mean by that?'

'Just . . . I don't know . . . I sometimes feel no one cares about me all that much.'

'What nonsense!'

'It's not nonsense.' I hate that tears are pricking at my eyes. 'All our lives, everyone's been more drawn to Lara than me, more sympathetic towards her, more admiring. Has given her more attention—'

'For goodness' sake, is that what this is about?' Mum's voice is sharp, and when I look up, her jaw is rigid. 'You're feeling sorry for yourself because your sister got attention when she had leukaemia? Because she's bringing up Poppy without an ounce of help from the man who fathered her? Do you actually want those same things for yourself?'

'It's not about wanting those things, it's—'

'Then maybe you should be careful what you say.' Mum's voice is starting to crack. 'Because your father and I did our best—'

'I know you did—'

'And I don't think it's fair for you to make it sound like we didn't care—'

'That's not what I'm saying!'

'Because why would I even ask about your blog if I didn't care—'

'I'm not saying that—'

'One skinny latte!'

'I know I'm not perfect' – Mum has started to cry – 'but it's not fair to say I don't care, when I've spent my entire adult life caring for you and your sister; when I've given up any chance of a career in order to look after you—'

'And I'm grateful for that—'

'No, you're not.' She picks up the takeaway coffee cup from the counter and presses it into my hands. 'You haven't got a clue what it's like: worrying about everyone else all the time, putting your own needs behind those of the rest of your family for years, for decades! And then for your husband to *die*, leaving you trying to hold the family together on your own; forcing you to put on a brave face to celebrate the little things in life, like your fiftieth birthday, only to discover that one of your daughters is unable to enjoy it because she's too busy being jealous of your other daughter, for being sick, for being troubled—'

'That's not how it is, *at all*,' I try to say, but I'm crying as well now, and my voice is choked by sobs. 'I'm worried about Lara too, I've persuaded her to see a doctor, and I didn't *not* enjoy your birthday, I was just feeling a little down, and trying to be honest about it, because I'm so sick of everyone concealing everything all the time, of not saying what they mean—'

'You want me to say what I mean?' Mum's eyes are flashing and I can only nod, numbly, as snot slithers towards my mouth. 'Fine. I'll say what I mean, and I'll say it in just two words. Grow up.'

And with that she marches out of the café, back to the table where Jackie and Poppy – and now Max – are waiting. Well, let them wait. If they think I'm childish, then childish I will be. It was Mum who forced me to buy a coffee in the first place, so she can damn well sit in the cold while I drink it.

I take a swig from my cardboard cup and yelp as the liquid scalds my lip.

LARA

As soon as I've found the earring, I find other things too. Jackie's silk handkerchief, which is fanned out across the desk, and the knife from the restaurant, which is lying on top of the bookshelf. My sister's silver bracelet, looped around the window clasp, and Cassie's hair clip and a bottle of men's aftershave, pressed in among the old books.

None of these items were here before, so I can only assume this is Cassie's work. If she stole the knife, it stands to reason that she stole the other items too. But why? And why go to the trouble of taking them, only to dump them in this dusty old attic? Not only is it odd, it's downright *irresponsible*, because she must know that Poppy sometimes comes up here. The knife was on top of the bookshelf, but Poppy could have reached it if she'd stood on the chair. And the aftershave is in a glass bottle, so it could easily have been broken.

There's a loud thud at the window and I flinch, jump up. Peering through the glass, I see a bird lying on its back in the garden, legs twitching.

A second dying bird. Really? It's only been a few days since Max dispatched the one on Curbar Edge, and now there's another in its final throes, quivering in the grass just a few metres below.

Despite the pervasive nature of my dreams, I'm not a superstitious person. I believe in what I *see*, not in aphorisms and old tales. Black cats don't bother me, nor cracked mirrors or the number thirteen.

But looking at the bird outside, struggling through its last, shallow breaths, it's hard not to feel a little unnerved. Not to reach the seemingly inevitable conclusion.

Death is coming.

HANNAH

As I drive back to Grove Cottage, I play music loudly and swear at other drivers on the road. Max, Mum, Jackie and Poppy are travelling in Mum's car, which is a blessed relief, as I don't think I could deal with their judgement right now. Or worse, their pity: my tears are coming thick and fast, and I couldn't stand for anyone to be sympathetic. To see my ugly, snivelling face and ask what is wrong, or to sit there, full of false concern, while I attempt to tell them.

Nobody loves me. Not really, not fully and wholeheartedly. Not like Dad used to. Whatever people claim, we are not born equal, and we certainly don't live equal lives. Lara will always be more adored than me because she is beautiful and magnetic and tragic, whereas I am just dull. Plain in both appearance and personality; a grey squirrel to her red one. The existence of the red squirrels might be fragile, but that just makes everyone love them more, doesn't it? People are drawn to them, go on holiday to see them, feel some sort of magic in their presence. Whereas grey squirrels are considered overabundant and greedy, a plague on the planet's resources. But it's not their fault they were born grey, nor that they're better adapted for survival, and people would do well to remember that.

Back at Grove Cottage, I park under the horse chestnut tree and blow my nose. Entering the house, I head straight for the bathroom, hoping for a chance to splash some cold water on my face before seeing anyone, but am only halfway along the corridor when Poppy appears from her room. 'Mummy's found the things!'

I stare at her, confused, until she grabs my hand and pulls me into the dining room, where Mum, Lara, Jackie and Max are gathered round one end of the long table, peering at an array of objects.

'Are you sure Poppy didn't put them there?' Max asks.

'I'm sure,' Lara says. 'It's not the kind of thing she'd do. Besides, I found the *knife*, from the restaurant, which I saw Cassie take.'

'But why would anyone . . . ?' Max is staring down at the table and I follow his gaze to a knife with a wooden handle. Just beside it is one of Mum's teardrop earrings, Jackie's silk handkerchief, a bottle of aftershave, Cassie's hair clip and my silver bracelet – the one with the heart charm.

'What's happening?' I ask.

'Poppy, I told you to go and play in our room,' Lara says.

'But—'

'Go. Now.'

Poppy looks like she's about to protest again but then, perhaps recognising the seriousness in her mother's voice, she turns and leaves.

'What's happening?' I ask for a second time.

'Your sister found these things in the attic,' Mum explains.

'What? How did my bracelet get into the attic?'

'How did any of it?' Mum picks up her earring and cradles it in her palm. 'I haven't even been up there.'

'It's very strange,' says Jackie, glancing round the room as if it might be haunted.

Mum turns to me. 'You didn't put them there, did you?'

'Of course not!' I pat at the skin under my eyes. 'Why would I?'

'I don't know.' She sighs. 'But then I don't know why anyone would.'

'Maybe it was some kind of practical joke?'

'Not a very funny one.' Jackie folds her arms across her chest. 'But if none of us put the things up there, then I suppose it must have been Cassie.'

'I very much doubt it,' Max says. 'I mean, she doesn't love my aftershave, but hiding it in the attic seems a little extreme. And as for taking your things and putting them up there – there's no way she'd do that.'

'But I saw her with the knife,' my sister protests.

'Why did Cassie have a knife?' I ask, but no one pays me any notice. Max is looking at Lara, and Jackie is looking at Max.

'Well, can you at least ring her and ask?' Jackie says to him.

'No.'

Jackie's cheeks redden. 'We need to understand what's going on here.'

'I understand that,' he replies. 'But Cassie's not responding to any of my calls or messages.'

I feel a stab of hurt at this, because it suggests he's been trying to contact her all morning. That his thoughts were with her when we were cycling together, and maybe even when we were talking. Remembering his words – *I don't think anything should happen between us again* – my stomach clenches.

'Oh, for goodness' sake!' says Jackie. 'I'll ring her myself!' She picks up her handbag and marches into the garden. For a moment, it looks like Max is going to run after her, but then he shakes his head and sits down.

There's a long, awkward silence. Letting my gaze traverse the room, I notice my open case, down by the bookshelf. 'Lara,' I say. 'Did you find my shirt in the attic too?'

She looks away, to Jackie standing in the garden, phone pressed to her ear. 'No, I didn't see it.'

'Are you sure? It's been missing since Saturday. My white one.'

'I didn't see it,' she says again.

'Are you sure?'

'I know what I saw—'

'But could it have been somewhere else? In one of the cupboards or—'

'I searched the whole room. But feel free to take a look yourself.' There's something odd about the way she's talking, her voice leaden and monotone. I recall the way she acted in the bracken last night and wonder if I was too quick to be reassured by our subsequent conversation. If maybe she's more unwell than I thought.

Jackie comes back into the house, her mouth set in a grim line.

'Is everything all right?' Mum asks.

'Not really.' Jackie looks at the table.

'Why, what did Cassie say?'

'She said she hadn't taken anything.'

'But then how does that explain it? All of our stuff, in the attic?'

'It doesn't. Cassie thinks . . .' Jackie trails off.

'What?' Mum presses.

'It doesn't matter.'

'You've got to say,' Max insists. 'Did she blame it on me?'

'No.' Jackie flattens out her handkerchief, smoothing its creases with her palm. 'No, this is one thing she doesn't think you're guilty of.'

'So what did she say?'

Jackie throws her hands in the air. 'Look, I'm not saying I agree with her. But she reckons Lara took the things herself.'

LARA

It takes me a moment to realise what Jackie has said. And when I do, a fist of anger forms in the centre of my chest. How dare Cassie make my family doubt me! How dare she make me doubt *myself*. I refuse to be gaslighted again, by Gareth or Cassie or anyone. 'It's not true,' I say.

'Of course it's not true,' says Jackie, laying a hand upon my shoulder.

'But why would Cassie say such a thing?' Mum looks briefly in my direction, then back to Jackie. 'Did you ask her?'

Jackie nods.

'And?'

Now Jackie looks deeply uncomfortable. She removes her hand from my shoulder and clasps her hands together. 'I don't know . . . I think she maybe . . .' She trails off again.

'What exactly did she say?' Mum asks firmly.

'She said . . .' Jackie glances at me. 'She said she thinks Lara isn't well. That she's – and I should stress that I don't agree with her on this – delusional.'

'What utter nonsense!' Mum is indignant. 'It sounds like Cassie is the delusional one. Because why on earth would Lara want to take our things? And then give them back to us? It doesn't make any sense!'

It certainly doesn't. Cassie and I aren't close, but there's never been any hostility between us. I think back over our past conversations, trying to remember any occasions where I acted oddly, or said something to give her cause for concern, but nothing comes to mind. Nothing at all.

And now, despite my best efforts, a seed of doubt *is* taking up residence. Is it possible that I just don't remember, that I'm blocking out events from my past, due to trauma or fear? That I did indeed take the earring and all the other belongings up to the attic, and my mind has erased the act? That I'm merely imagining what took place in the restaurant last night?

Except I *saw* Cassie put the knife in her bag; I know I did. And I also know that *she* came into *my* bedroom last night, not the other way around. I tell the others this now, explaining how Cassie claimed to have heard strange noises; how she'd automatically assumed Max was in my room when he wasn't in hers.

Max looks up sharply, and Hannah grips the edge of the table, her fingers pressed into the oilcloth. But neither of them says anything; instead, it's Mum who speaks. 'Gracious! What odd behaviour! Do you think we should call the police?'

'No,' both Max and I say together. 'Cassie isn't dangerous,' Max goes on. 'She's just . . . upset. We both know things are over between the two of us; that's all it is.'

'I'm not so sure.' Mum puts her earring back on the table. 'Upset would be shouting at you, or walking out on you, not stealing things and then pretending Lara's done it. Nor going into Lara's room in the middle of the night . . .'

'And I think maybe she came into my room the night before too,' I say, as it suddenly occurs to me. 'Put ice cubes in my bed.'

Mum and Jackie give each other a look, and I get a strange sense that time is slowing down. Mum turns to me, her voice gentle. 'Why would she do that?'

'I don't know,' I say. 'Why would she do any of it?'

'It just seems very . . .' As Mum searches for words, the slowing sensation grows stronger. Like I'm somehow stuck in a pocket of time. 'You don't think it's possible you've got the wrong end of the stick?'

'You don't believe me,' I say.

'It's not that we don't believe you,' Mum clarifies. 'It's just that you've been under so much stress, and stress can take a toll . . .'

'You think I've gone mad—'

'No, not at all. It's just that your medication . . . you've been easing off . . . and maybe . . .'

'You *do* think I've gone mad!' I sink on to a dining chair and place my head between my knees. Shutting my eyes, I focus all my energy on keeping it together.

'No, Lara, that's not what I'm saying.' But the soft, careful tone of her voice suggests otherwise, and I sense her exchanging another worried glance with Jackie.

An awkward silence follows.

'Maybe Cassie is jealous.' It's the first thing Hannah has said in a long while, and I sit up to look at her. She's trembling, and there are indentations in the oilcloth in front of her – small, overlapping crescent moons where her fingernails have dug in. 'Maybe she's doing all this weird stuff because she's pissed off, because she suspects Max of cheating on her, and wants to exact her revenge—'

'Hannah.' Mum's voice grows stern. 'I know you're annoyed about our argument earlier, but I think it's best if you keep out of this, instead of indulging in wild theories—'

'For God's sake!' My sister presses her palm into the oilcloth, near the crescent moons. 'It's always the same spiel, isn't it? *Grow up, Hannah; keep out if it, Hannah; never complain, Hannah . . .*'

Mum narrows her eyes. 'Now is not the time for your histrionics—'

'Histrionics! Is that really all you think I'm capable of? Does it never occur to you that I might have something useful to bring to the discussion?'

'Well, go on then!' says Mum bitterly. 'Why don't you tell us whatever it is that's so important, so relevant to this situation with Cassie and your sister that it can't wait until later—'

'Fine!' Hannah pauses dramatically, and I suddenly get a terrible feeling, a sense that, if she utters even a single word more, events will spiral beyond redemption.

'Maybe we all need to take a moment—' I begin, but my sister cuts across me.

'Cassie was justified in suspecting Max of cheating,' she says. 'Because he did.'

I look at Max, who is staring at her. He gives the slightest shake of his head, almost imperceptible.

'Only it wasn't with Lara.' She stares back at him, defiance blazing in her eyes. 'He had sex with me.'

HANNAH

As soon as I say it, I want to take it back. There's an element of satisfaction in shocking everyone, but the change in Max's face is terrifying. His jaw tightens, his lips flatten and his eyes become cold. 'What are you doing?' His voice is quiet but filled with a barely suppressed rage, and I realise that anything which remained between us – any vestige of intimacy, any possibility of possibility – has been destroyed.

'Is it true?' Mum looks horrified.

Perhaps if I laughed now, claimed it was all a ridiculous joke, I could rescue the situation. Or maybe it would only make things worse. Besides, it *did* happen. I look at Lara, expecting her to be angry, maybe even a little jealous.

Yet her expression is not one of ire or envy, but fear. She glances between me and Max with wide, tremulous eyes, and I don't know if it's just because she's so thin, but I swear I can see a vein pulsing in her neck.

Max nods, looks away from me towards the table. 'I'm sorry.' I can't tell who he's apologising to.

'What were you thinking?' This is Jackie.

'I've fucked up.'

This hurts. Even if it's true.

'You can say that again.'

Mum slumps down on to one of the dining chairs. 'What are we going to do?'

'Max needs to talk to Cassie,' says Jackie. 'In person.'

'Can you not decide on a course of action for me, please,' says Max. 'I'm an adult—'

'You're not acting like it—'

'I'm an *adult*,' Max says again, 'and I'll deal with this how I see fit.'

His dealing with it seems to involve trying to catch Lara's eye, but her gaze is darting around too rapidly to notice. I will him to look in my direction, to prove he doesn't hate me. But he keeps looking at her.

There's a queasiness to my stomach, a sense of wrongdoing, even if its nature isn't clear. Whether I've wronged others or been wronged myself, or whether the two are in fact tangled up together. Bile rises in my throat and I try to swallow but begin to cough, and Max turns to me with such hatred in his eyes that I can't bear it, I'm going to be sick, and I dash to the double doors, clutching my stomach with one hand while pulling at the doors with the other. I run into the garden, just making it to a pile of leaves before my chest heaves and white-yellow drool drips from my tongue, and I retch again, my stomach convulsing, but still there's no vomit, just viscous liquid dripping on to the ground. Desperate to purge myself, I cough and spit, but when I don't expel anything substantial I sit back on my haunches and suck at the air, trying to find a place of equilibrium. I stay in that position for a few minutes, gradually steadying my breath, the wind bitter against my skin. I look into the house but no one is looking back, so I get to my feet and walk through the trees. I walk to where grass meets bracken, garden meets hillside, past meets present, but instead of stopping, I keep going, navigating the divots in the earth and the tall, scratching bracken, and sweating as I start to climb steeply, towards the might of Curbar Edge. The lack of a path makes the going difficult, but in some ways that's good, because my heart pumps hard and the cold air scours my lungs. Rain begins to fall, making the terrain treacherous, and when I slip on to my hands and knees, I can't bring myself to get up again. I lie down on my front and press my face to the earth. It occurs to me that it might be best for everyone if I were to stay here, buried in the bracken – only, my queasiness has been replaced by hunger, and I don't think bracken is good to eat. In fact, I think it might be poisonous. Flipping over, I see that the sun, visible through a gap in the rainclouds, is already past its peak, which means I should be eating lunch right now, not lying here like a rotting cadaver.

If it's already afternoon in the UK, it will be evening in Singapore. So not only should I be eating lunch, I should also have heard from Chris. Or at least received an alert from the Connect app. I open it now to find two photos from him: one of a glass of beer, and one of a ceiling fan. How did I miss these earlier? There's something about this that makes me deeply uneasy.

And then I realise what it is. Something which should have been obvious, because I even wrote about it in my blog . . . *you don't get to see the other person's photos unless you share yours.* But I haven't shared any photos with Chris today. Have I?

With damp fingers, I scroll across to see, and when I do it's like my stomach drops out of my body. Two photos have been shared from my phone, and neither was taken by me. The first is a close-up of Poppy's face, with the Monsal Trail in the background – Lara will kill me if she realises that not only have I let Poppy take and share a photo, I've let her take and share a *selfie* – but the second picture is worse; much, much worse. It shows me and Max standing by some trees.

And we're kissing.

LARA

This is a disaster. Hannah ran off outside a few minutes ago and nobody has followed her. Jackie is too busy berating Max, and Max is too busy sitting at the table with his head in his hands. I stare at him, unable to believe what he's done. That he's slept with Hannah, my little sister, a person I thought he wanted to protect as much as I do. Mum, meanwhile, is pacing around, saying Hannah needs some time alone to reflect on her actions. Which might be true, except what if she's now in danger? By revealing she slept with Max, she's provided others with a reason to hate her. Cassie, obviously, but maybe also Max himself. Whenever he lifts his head, he has this wild look in his eyes, like an animal that's been backed into a corner. *I thought I knew you*, I intone to myself. *I thought you were one of the good guys.*

The garden is now empty. 'Where did Hannah go?' I ask.

'Through the trees,' Mum says icily.

'Towards the rocks?'

'It looked like it.'

A twist of fear, then, deep inside my gut. 'We should go after her.'

'No, she'll come back soon enough.'

'But what she said . . .' I want to explain about my dreams, that this recent sequence of events makes them more likely. And she's heading towards the *rocks* . . .

'She just wants to create drama.' Mum looks at Max, who is threading his fingers through his hair. 'And she's succeeded. My goal this week was simply for us to be together, to enjoy each other's company, but apparently that was too much to ask—'

'Let's not forget it takes two to tango,' says Jackie, who is now standing by the table, drumming her fingers against the teapot. 'It's Max's fault just as much as it is Hannah's. If not more so. He was here with his *girlfriend*, for goodness' sake, and he's older, so he really should know better—'

'I can hear you, you know,' Max says. 'I've already admitted I've messed up—'

'*Massively* messed up—'

'Massively messed up, yes, but I'll fix it.'

'And how exactly will you do that?' Jackie's voice increases in pitch. 'How are you going to smooth things over with Cassie, make things better with Hannah? And how are you going to make things up to Helen, whose birthday—'

'There's no need to worry about me,' Mum says, still pacing.

'Yes, there is! I raised him to be respectful to women, not treat them like objects—'

'For God's sake!' Max slams his hands down on to the table, and the sudden violence of it makes me jump. 'I *do* respect women, and I don't treat them like objects! It shouldn't have happened, but it did, and now—'

'Stop it! Stop trying to justify your behav—'

'I'm not trying to justify it; I'm just saying that it's happened and your screaming about it doesn't help any—'

'I'm not screaming! I'm—'

'Yes, you are! Just listen to yourself! You're screeching like a full-on banshee—'

'How dare you!' Jackie's face is puce. 'I brought you up to be better than this.'

Mum pulls out a chair. 'Shall we have another cuppa?' she tries.

'Better than what, exactly?' Max asks.

'Better than a man who throws around misogynist slurs!' Jackie shouts. 'Better than a man who cheats! Better than your bloody father!'

'How dare you bring him into this! Fucking hell!' Max pushes his chair back so hard it falls over, and while I'm scrabbling on the floor to pick it up he leaves the room.

Jackie lets out a guttural roar and flings a mug at the sideboard. It shatters with a loud crack, sending pieces of pottery flying across the sisal mat. 'Jacks,' Mum says, extending a hand, but Jackie just shakes her head and runs from the room. Turning to me, Mum says, 'I should . . .' and then she goes too, and I'm left in the dining room, alone.

With no clue what to do next.

HANNAH

The rest of the day passes in a blur of anxiety, self-recrimination and attempted contact with Chris. I try ringing him, but he doesn't pick up, and my many messages go unanswered too. They range from a simple *Hi are you there?* to a long, convoluted missive about absence – how it makes the heart grow fonder but the flesh grow weaker. I have no idea what I'll say if Chris does get in touch, but trying to contact him feels important, necessary even, so I carry on, over and over, like one of those demented monkeys with a cymbal. *Crash, crash, crash.* I keep checking my phone, to see whether he's read my messages and isn't replying, or isn't reading them at all. So far it seems the latter is true, which is entirely out of character; Chris always has his phone with him, always looks at his messages the instant they come through. But then, he did receive a photo of another man kissing me (it's Sod's Law that Poppy took her photo just as Max was making his clumsy apology) so perhaps it's not surprising he's acting differently. When I think about it, I feel sick. What the hell must Chris have thought? Did he imagine the whole scene was engineered to be as cruel and hurtful as possible, or that I made a foolish error and was caught? That it was a casual nothing of a kiss or something I'd actively sought? And which is better?

It's not like I can talk to anyone about what happened. Since I returned to Grove Cottage earlier, Mum has given me the cold shoulder, and even Jackie has been distant. Lara, meanwhile, has reverted to her usual brittle self, and Max was out all afternoon and went straight to his room upon returning. I envy him that room; I could really use some privacy right now. Preferably a soundproofed, padded cell, where I could fling myself to the floor and scream.

I make up the sofa bed for the night, before checking my phone. Nothing. I change into my pyjamas and check again. Still nothing. I brush my teeth and check for a third time.

Before switching off the light, I write one final message to Chris. *Goodnight.* And then, a couple of minutes later, a final, final message. *I'm sorry.*

It's only as I'm falling asleep I realise I haven't updated my blog.

LARA

By the time Poppy and I go to bed, nothing has been resolved. Hannah and Max have both returned safely to the cottage, but no one is talking about what happened between them, or addressing any of the other elephants in the room: Cassie's whereabouts, for one, or who hid the objects in the attic. No one has questioned my reliability again either, but I've felt Mum and Jackie thinking it. And the more this thinking-but-not-saying has gone on, the worse the tension has become, until the atmosphere in the cottage is akin to Gareth's chalet, where even breathing in the wrong direction could get me into trouble.

Everything changed when I found out I was pregnant. I had thought Gareth might be freaked out by the news – we were both young, after all, and hadn't been together long – but I hadn't expected him to be actively hostile. He asked how I could have been so stupid, and when I pointed out it was an accident – an accident in which he'd played an equal part – he became even angrier, accusing me of ensnaring him, of trying to pin him down and take his money.

I was frightened by the sudden change in his demeanour; by the way his eyes took on a mean, calculating quality, and the new vehemence in his words. He was just scared, I told myself, and it would pass soon enough.

But it didn't. The day after I'd told him the news, he came storming into the chalet after his morning's teaching, asking if I'd successfully killed the baby yet with my 'overconsumption of wine'.

'I'm not drinking anymore,' I said. 'Not now I know . . .'

'I see.' He shook his coat free of snow and threw it over a chair. 'So you're willing to be a rambling alcoholic mess for me, but not for a few cells in your sodding uterus?'

The vitriol in his words was breathtaking. I sat down on the sofa, ran my hands across the leather in an attempt to stay calm. 'Surely it's a good thing that I want to turn over a new leaf? That I don't want to cause any harm to our baby?'

'Our baby? *Our* baby?' His voice was building in volume. 'There's no "our" about it – you've brought this on yourself.'

I stared at him in shock. 'How can you—'

'It's because you found out about Olivia, isn't it?'

'Wha—'

'And you were pissed off and wanted to get the upper hand?'

'What the hell are you talking about?' But even as I asked the question, a chill ran through me, remembering his whispers in the hallway.

'Oh, don't act all innocent. It's obvious from the timing – you find out about Olivia, and then a few weeks later you're up the duff—'

'Who's Olivia?' My voice was trembling.

'Either that, or you're really fucking stupid.'

'Who's Olivia!' I asked again, but shouting now. And perhaps I was finally loud enough to get his attention, because he came and stood beside me, lowered his face to my level.

'She's my wife.'

As Poppy drifts easily into sleep, I think back over the afternoon: how tense both Mum and Jackie were, barely talking even to one another, and how, once Hannah returned, she did nothing but look at her phone. And how, later on, when I begged Max not to be angry with Hannah for disclosing what had happened, he thumped the wall and bellowed, 'Everything's gone to shit!' before turning to me and saying, 'You must hate me.' To which I didn't respond; just watched as he shook his head and walked away.

Perhaps I was wrong to assume any danger to my family would come from Gareth. I still believe he poses a risk to me and Poppy, but I don't think he's a threat to my sister.

The statistics are clear: women are most likely to be attacked by someone they know. And that doesn't preclude people they've known all their lives, even if they were once small, harmless boys.

Because small, harmless boys grow into men. Even the seemingly nice ones.

FRIDAY

HANNAH

I sleep fitfully, dreaming of derelict houses and long empty roads. At one point I dream I'm underwater, in an ocean of such breadth that it's the size which scares me more than the lack of oxygen; the unknowable scale of it. When I wake up, my breath is coming in short, sharp bursts, like I've just broken free from the water for real, and it brings back a memory which is so old that I'm not sure if I've genuinely remembered it, or merely remembered its retelling. In the memory, I'm three or four, not yet able to swim, but splashing about in a rubber ring in a backyard swimming pool. The sun is bright on the water, and the ring is decorated with ducks, or is it seagulls? Birds, anyway, encircling me as I kick and float, as I look up at the sky and see there are no clouds whatsoever, just a sheet of brilliant blue.

But then, somehow, the ring has gone, and the sheet of blue slips out of reach. I try to yell but my mouth fills with water and everything around me is muffled, as if sound itself has been sucked from existence. I'm alone, totally alone, and fear I might stay this way forever until out of the void comes a flash of orange – Lara's goggles, and she returns me to the noisy world above. I cough and cry in her arms and Dad races over to take me.

Thinking of this now, I find myself crying again. *Pull yourself together*, I say as my pillow grows damp and the snot bubbles up in my nose. *You're an adult woman, not a drowning toddler.* But, instead of dimming, the memory only strengthens, hovering luminous in the night. Producing a desire so strong it startles me. A desire to get up, walk down the corridor, and climb into bed with my sister. To hold her in my arms until we see that blue sky again.

But I cross my legs to prevent myself from moving. Because, if I've learned one thing this week, it's this. Desire only gets you into trouble.

LARA

The orange light, the rock, the blood are back. My sister with unseeing eyes, and limbs at odd angles. All of it is in sharper focus than it's ever been, such that I can see the downy hairs above Hannah's lip and the grooves of her fingernails, lacquered with blood. *What can I do?* I try to ask her. *How can I stop this?* But there's no sound in what I see; just the image itself.

The knife is present again, more obvious than before, lying at my sister's side. I can't identify details, other than that it's long, with a thick blade. I wish I could see the handle, see if it's wooden or metal; a forensic expert could probably tell from the way the blood pools on its surface. But a forensic expert would also be able to pick up the knife and examine it, would be able to physically poke around the crime scene, instead of just watching on, powerless.

Except, if sight is my strength, maybe I can broaden what I see. Maybe I can zoom out from this terrible montage to its periphery, where clues might reside. I try to move my eyes to the edge of the slab of rock: in one direction, then another, but my focal point stays stubbornly fixed. So I attempt to turn my head, but of course I'm asleep, which means my body doesn't want to comply, or perhaps it does, as I experience some motion, although I realise too late that I'm waking myself, because the image starts to slip away altogether and I can't bring it back. It narrows into the distance and I could cry at my stupidity, except I can't cry, I can't do anything but watch as it slides out of range and my hands are left empty.

Wait, my hands – what? I never normally see myself in my dreams; they take place outside my physical being. And yet, these are definitely my hands: small, pale, with a scar on my left thumb from where I trapped it in a door aged eight.

But it's not my left thumb which is the problem now. It's my right hand, which sits apart from my left, suspended in a hook-like position and shockingly red.

Covered in blood.

HANNAH

The first thing I do upon waking is check my phone, but there's nothing at all from Chris: no missed calls, no messages, not even an angry voicemail telling me to fuck off and die. He hasn't read my messages either – I keep checking the colour of the WhatsApp ticks, under a variety of different lights, but they stay resolutely grey.

Jackie and Mum come into the kitchen for breakfast, disapproval making their speech overly courteous. *Good morning. Have you had breakfast? Did you sleep well?* The last question a trap, because to reply 'yes' would seem insensitive, but 'no' would be childish. So I just say 'okay'. They eat their toast at the opposite end of the table from me, which is surely as childish as anything I've done, and read yesterday's newspapers, mentioning points of interest to one another. A new restaurant here, an outbreak of violence there. I know better than to try to engage; instead, I eat a bowl of cereal and check my phone. Some readers of my blog have left kind comments following Wednesday's post, saying they hope I feel happier soon, that looking after one's mental health is vital and they're grateful to me for being honest about my struggles. Although another person has written, *You've got far worse coming to you, you stupid self-centred slag*, which doesn't help my mental health at all.

Poppy and Lara enter the room, and Poppy rushes towards me, wraps her arms around my legs and tells me a story about her teddies. Lara pours her a glass of milk while Mum and Jackie discuss options for the day's outing. They settle on Baslow and Curbar Edge, and I say I won't be joining them.

Mum purses her lips. 'It would be nice for us all to be together. Given it's our last day here.'

'Sorry.' I glance across to the bookshelf, where the items from the attic remain in a pile. Seeing Max's aftershave brings back memories of the other night. The rich heat of his body against mine. 'I think it's best for everyone if I don't go.'

Jackie starts to object on Mum's behalf, but then, surprisingly, Lara speaks up in my defence. 'Hannah's right,' she says. 'If Max is coming on the walk, that is?'

'Max *will* be coming,' says Jackie, emphatically.

'Then she's right not to,' says Lara. 'Because I think they both need a bit of time apart, after yesterday, to just . . .' She doesn't finish her sentence.

Jackie looks sceptical. 'I don't know. Surely it will be more healing for everyone if we just get on with it, spend time in each other's company?'

'I wouldn't waste your breath, Jacks,' Mum says. 'This seems to be how the younger generation deal with difficult things – they shut themselves away.'

It's a strange thing to say, when I'm the one who puts my life out there on my blog, who tries to express my mental state honestly, who told the truth about what happened with Max, but I'm not going to start arguing now. When Jackie asks what I'll do instead, I say I'm thinking of going to Higger Tor. We often went there as children, and I'd like to locate the tunnel that Lara and I used to crawl through. A place where I can literally burrow into the past.

'No!' Lara says. She seems extra twitchy; her gaze is on me but she can't keep it there, flitting instead between my face and the window. 'Remember what we agreed the other night? In the garden?'

Don't go near any rocks. Of course. I slowly incline my head.

'What did you agree?' Mum asks.

'It doesn't matter,' I say quickly.

'If it doesn't matter, then you can come on the walk with the rest of us.' Jackie sounds fierce, and when Lara says no again, her shoulders rise. 'I don't think it should be beyond any of us to go for a walk together.'

'But . . .' Lara begins. 'But . . .' And then she looks at Poppy and her face becomes animated. 'Hannah and Poppy will have to stay behind.'

'Because of what you discussed in the garden?' Mum says, her voice weary.

'No.' Lara pulls herself up straight. 'Because they're going to make cupcakes.'

LARA

As I walk along the stony path on Baslow Edge, it's like I'm in a fugue state – neither fully awake nor quite asleep – my feet moving automatically as I follow Jackie and Mum, with Max somewhere off to the side. He walks in silence too, and our mothers compensate by talking extra loudly, about the perpetual challenges of the Peak District weather (an unexpected bout of rain meant it was after midday by the time we finally left the house). Neither mentions what happened between Max and Hannah, the unresolved mystery of the objects in the attic, or where Cassie has disappeared to, even though these subjects must be uppermost in everyone's mind. It's as if we've silently agreed not to discuss them; as if doing so might light a touchpaper and cause everything to explode.

Have I done the right thing in leaving Poppy and Hannah at Grove Cottage? I just wanted to stop my sister from coming here, or to the rocks of Higger Tor. To keep her away from Max – whom I don't feel I know anymore; who may as well be a stranger – and, most importantly of all, to keep her away from me. It doesn't make sense that I'll hurt her, but that's what my dream showed. The blood on my hand. The knife by Hannah's limp body. It doesn't seem right, it *can't* be right, but equally there are several events from the past few days that don't stack up. All those items going missing before turning up in the attic, and the ice in my bed. I don't like to think about any of it too hard, in case I uncover a part of my memory I don't want to find.

But I'm not mad, I tell myself. *I'm not, I'm not, I'm not.*

Still, Poppy and Hannah will be safer at the cottage. I asked Hannah to bolt the front door and told her about the emergency drill Poppy and I had practised. I told her that if anything seemed unusual or worrying, she simply had to say the words 'Den Time' and Poppy would run and hide in the dresser upstairs.

Mum and Jackie stop by the Eagle Stone, a huge standalone boulder which Hannah and I used to try to climb. 'I won't be long,' says Jackie. 'If you loop gradually round, then hopefully you'll be close by the road when I come back up.'

'Where are you going, Mum?' Max's voice sounds alien over the hum of the wind.

'Just back to the house. I need my hat and gloves – I underestimated how cold it would be. Too much wind chill! Does anyone else want anything?'

Mum says something about a loaf and a Thermos and Jackie nods and begins to walk off. 'Oh!' It suddenly occurs to me. 'Can you make sure Hannah bolts the door again once you've left?'

But Jackie's already some distance away and, although she raises her hand, I've no idea if she's heard me, or is just waving goodbye.

HANNAH

I didn't realise making cupcakes with a four-year-old would be so messy. I had expected buttery fingers, maybe a bit of rogue flour, but the reality is something else altogether. There's a cracked egg lying in a gloop on the worktop and flour *everywhere*: in my hair, on my T-shirt, all the way down Poppy's dress and tights, and on every surface within a metre's radius of the mixing bowl. As I survey the devastation, there's a beep on my phone. The Connect app.

'One minute,' I say to Poppy, as I scan desperately around. 'Well, two minutes, strictly speaking.' I have no idea what to send to Chris, or if he'll respond, but I have to take advantage of this opportunity to make contact. To express *something*. While I'm thinking, Poppy traces a finger through the flour on her dress.

'That's it!' I say. 'Thank you, Poppy!'

She looks up, confused, but I don't have time to explain. Instead, I scoop the flour together on the worktop and drag my index finger through it, to form letters. The tail of the 'y' is a little short, but my handiwork is legible nonetheless. *Sorry*. I think about adding *Can you forgive me?* but there's not enough time, nor enough flour, so I simply take a photo, check it and the corresponding rear image (the ceiling: boring, but not problematic) and press send.

The seconds that follow seem bloated, interminable, as I wait to see if he'll reply. It's like that old children's game with a daisy, where you pull off one petal at a time, chanting *He loves me, he loves me not*, except here it's seconds rather than petals, and there's nothing cute or charming about it; in fact, I think I might be sick in the cupcake tray. When a notification flashes up on my screen, my mouth becomes so dry that I take a swig of water directly from the tap. Then I press on the notification, readying myself for anger or melancholy; for extreme emotion encapsulated in two images.

But what I see is quite different. The first photo shows an oil painting in a black frame, with damask wallpaper behind. The painting depicts a naked, muscular man lying face down on the lap of a woman who is naked from the breasts up, and swathed in crimson satin below. I zoom in to look more closely. Is the woman supposed to be me? And is the man meant to be Max, or Chris himself? Neither Chris nor Max has a beard, but the man in the painting does: a brown curly one to match his brown curly hair. There are two more people in the painting, another man and woman, both fully dressed. The second man is hovering above the naked man's ear, cutting his hair, while the second woman is holding a candle to illuminate the scene. So is that what this is actually about – illumination? Cutting away the hair that obscures a man's eyes, so he can finally see the truth?

I turn to the other photo. A portion of a man's arm is visible, and I'm pretty certain it belongs to Chris, because I recognise the shirt he's wearing: a blue-and-grey checked one, cross-hatched by purple lines. It's the first time all week he's featured any part of himself in his photos, which makes me wonder if he's now too angry to bother crafting his pictures carefully, or if this is some sort of intentional statement. Behind him are two people facing away, looking at another painting. So he's in an art gallery? I can't see much of the other painting, just half of a naked woman with a cherub clutching her thigh. So maybe the nakedness is the point here, something about women and sin? Or maybe he's just trying to make me feel stupid for not understanding, and there's not a point to it at all.

'Auntie Hannah? Can we do some more baking?'

'Yes. Sorry.' I put my phone down and resolve to ignore it for the time being, to do my best to give Poppy my undivided attention. After all, it's not her fault that two relationships have imploded here in the space of a week. Nor that our family bonds are too frayed to cope with the fallout. 'But I don't think we can continue on the worktop. It's too high for you, and we're making too much mess. Ideally we'd do our mixing on the floor but . . .' I look at the cream herringbone tiles, shiny and pristine. Then I look at the dining table and have an idea. 'Hang on.' I remove the oilcloth from the table, carry it to the kitchen and spread it out across the floor. 'There we are. Wipe-clean.'

Fifteen minutes later, the cupcakes are in the oven, and Poppy is cross-legged on the oilcloth, licking a wooden spoon. When I ask if she wants to help get the icing ready, she says nothing, just keeps licking, and it occurs to me that this is probably the most sugar she's ever had in one go.

The doorbell rings and I jump up, worried Lara has returned to admonish me. But it's Jackie. 'Thanks,' she says as I unfasten the chain to let her in. 'I've just come back to get a few bits, and then I'll be off again.'

'Sure.'

She looks at me for a couple of seconds, before heading to the kitchen. 'How are the cupcakes going – oh!' She takes in the cracked egg and scattered flour, the sticky utensils and bowls, the child smeared in cake mix.

'I haven't cleared up yet,' I say.

'So I see.' She picks her way around the oilcloth to the kettle. 'Goodness, doesn't the dining table seem bare now? Such a giant slab of stone! A little funereal, if you ask me.'

'I imagine the owners are going for more of an architectural vibe.' I unwrap the icing sugar and fetch a sieve. 'Pops, can you give me a hand?' As Poppy starts to scatter icing sugar in all directions, and occasionally in the bowl, I sense Jackie watching us from behind. But when I look at her she turns away, pours water into a flask. Then she opens a cupboard and rustles around inside. 'Poppy,' she says, her face hidden by the cupboard door. 'Would you mind playing in your bedroom for a couple of minutes, to let me and your Auntie Hannah have a chat?'

I stiffen, both at the unexpected request and the flat tone in which Jackie delivers it. She's clearly still annoyed about what happened between me and Max. When Poppy sets off for her bedroom with sugary hands, I suggest the garden instead. 'Just stay where I can see you,' I say as I open the double doors. She runs to the trees and starts hurling handfuls of leaves in the air, trying to catch them as they descend back to earth. When I turn round, Jackie is holding a knife.

'I hope you don't find this unfair.' She jabs the knife in my direction.

'Um . . .' I don't know what to make of this, so I stay still, watching her.

'I think you should make a greater effort,' she goes on. 'For your Mum's sake.'

I look at the light glancing off the knife's serrated blade. 'Perhaps you should put that down.'

'What?' She follows my line of sight. 'I need to cut some slices of the date and walnut loaf. You know, the one your Mum and I bought yesterday.'

I shake my head.

'No? Anyway . . .' She looks down at the worktop, and I see that there is indeed a cake there: an unappetising, turd-like oblong. 'As I was saying . . .' She proceeds to cut the cake into thick, uneven slices. 'I don't mean to interfere, but Helen's really quite upset, what with everything that's happened.' She goes on to tell me how hard the last five years have been for Mum and how, while she's much stronger now, she needs the family to knit together. That she hates all the arguments and resentments; hates the feeling that her daughters are at odds. I nod and make understanding noises, say I'll do my best to patch things up, and this seems to satisfy Jackie, because she puts down the knife and starts to wrap the slices of cake in greaseproof paper.

Poppy is crouched beside the picnic table, poking at something on the ground. It's the same spot the two of us were in a few days ago, back when we looked at the photos of Chris's underwear. Before I was so stupid with Max. Which makes me think of the photos I've just been sent.

I show them to Jackie and she recognises the painting straightaway. 'It's extremely famous,' she says. '*Samson and Delilah*.'

'From the Bible?'

'That's right. Samson had superhuman strength, and a secret: that his power stemmed from his long hair. But he made the mistake of telling Delilah, and she told the Philistines, who then cut his hair and captured him – see, here they are, coming in.' She points to a corner of the painting, where soldiers lurk in the doorway.

'In which case . . .' I'm trying to process this, to understand how such a painting relates to me and Chris. 'Are the main themes—'

'It's a painting about betrayal,' Jackie says, and all at once it becomes horribly clear. 'Because he shouldn't have trusted her.'

'I see.'

'Why are you asking about it?'

'Just interested.' I shrug. 'I don't suppose you know which art gallery it's in?'

'The National Gallery,' she says instantly. 'In the Rubens room. One of my favourites.'

There's a prickling sensation in my leg, like the precursor to a cramp. 'The National Gallery of Singapore?' I ask hopefully.

She laughs. 'No! I've never been to Singapore. *Our* national gallery.'

'As in—'

'The UK's, yes. If you want to visit that painting, you're in luck. Because it's in London.'

'I see,' I say again. But I don't, not really. Because if Chris is standing in front of the painting, and the painting is in the UK, then . . .

Chris must be in the UK too.

LARA

After Jackie has gone, Mum, Max and I walk to Wellington's Monument, before turning and retracing our steps. The intention is to meet Jackie at the road, before heading across to Curbar Edge, so we try to walk slowly – to string out the short distance for as long as possible – but the lack of conversation makes this difficult and we find ourselves back at the road too quickly. At which point we hover at the edge of the car park, waiting for Jackie to reappear, blowing on our hands and jogging on the spot in a bid to stay warm. Mum makes a few attempts at small talk which go nowhere, and it's almost a relief when Max's phone rings. 'It's Cassie,' he tells us, before walking away to take the call.

And then it's just Mum and me. She asks about timings for tomorrow, and I explain that Poppy and I are planning to leave straight after breakfast. We discuss routes for a while: whether it's better to go down the M1 the whole way or branch off on to the A14 near Rugby. But the jollity in her voice is forced, and she's watching Max the whole time, pacing up and down past the same four cars, his mouth moving urgently. 'What do you think they're saying?' she asks eventually, when she's unable to sustain the traffic chat any longer.

'I don't know.' From here, it's impossible to tell whether Max is angry or contrite. He is agitated, certainly – one arm angled up towards his ear, the other coiled at his side – but without being able to hear the conversation, I can't gauge what's happening. Whether he's confessing to having sex with Hannah and begging Cassie's forgiveness, or whether the relationship is ending without culpability being assigned. Not that the two are mutually exclusive, of course: if Max is anything like Gareth, he could be confessing what happened with Hannah and *blaming* Cassie, or assigning culpability but somehow keeping the relationship going.

Certainly, Gareth stuck to the line that I'd become pregnant because of Olivia. That it was the perfect means of both seeking revenge on him and winning one over on her. And the more I protested I hadn't known, the more incensed he became, until somehow I started feeling like the culprit, even though he was the one who had cheated and lied. It transpired that he and Olivia had been together for four years, and married for two; that he spent summers with her in Grenoble, and winters in the mountains, and that she came from a rich family, who had bankrolled the chalet. 'You must have realised a snowboarding instructor's salary can't pay for a chalet like this,' he said, like that was my fault too.

With hindsight it's obvious I should have left him, should have told him where to shove his marriage and deflected blame and got the hell out of there. But I kept hoping he'd come round, kept remembering the early days when he'd listened to me so kindly, so thoughtfully, and wondered if maybe this new angry phase was just that – a phase. He was obviously wrong to have had a relationship with me while married to someone else, but perhaps his guilt over that was translating into anger, and he would eventually come to his senses and leave her – start a new life with me and the baby. Go back to how he used to be, but on a more honest, solid footing.

And besides, if I left him, where would I go? I had abandoned my mother and sister in their time of need, so couldn't very well go crawling back. The very idea of it – of returning, pregnant, when I was supposed to be making something of myself, when I was supposed to be validating their years of love and attention – was enough to make me shrivel up inside with hot, acrid shame. I had failed them utterly. And, worse still, I had failed Dad. I had taken all his sacrifices, all the life he'd never lived, and made a mockery of it.

And now I was paying the price.

HANNAH

Maybe it's just a photo of the painting, I tell myself, as Poppy and I dollop icing on to not-quite-cooled cupcakes. Chris can't be at the National Gallery in London, because he's in Singapore, on the opposite side of the world. Where he *lives*. But when I look again at the rear camera image – at the arm in a blue-and-grey checked shirt— I'm convinced it's him.

Yet this makes no sense – why would he come all this way without saying? If he's too angry to talk to me, surely he's also too angry to see me? I suppose it's possible he's come for some other reason, for a work assignment or family visit, but it seems unlikely.

I tip the ghost and pumpkin decorations into bowls for Poppy. She asks about the roses and silver balls, so I fetch those too. While she starts sprinkling, I create cobwebs by icing concentric circles on to the cupcakes and using a toothpick to pull strands of them together. I'm pleased with the overall effect and realise I'm almost enjoying myself, despite the chaos in my life. Who would have thought decorating cupcakes with a four-year-old could be so calming?

Next, it's time for some photos of our handiwork. I take them in two batches: one of all the cupcakes – including those piled so densely with roses, pumpkins, ghosts and silver balls that they're barely discernible as food – and one of the Halloween-themed creations. I place the latter in the centre of the dining table for their starring moment. There's too much light so I draw the blinds, but then it's *too* dark – the cupcakes coming out as amorphous blobs, even with a flash. I compromise by opening half the blinds, which leads to patchy exposures. I need something to filter the light uniformly, so I grab hold of my bedsheet, before catching sight of my orange dress. The perfect Halloween colour. Sure enough, after rigging it up, an amber glow is cast across the cupcakes, which makes for some fabulously atmospheric photos. I feel a welcome return of desire to write a blog post, starring these photos, along with the revelation that baking with a four-year-old can be therapeutic. But first I need to clean up.

This is rather less therapeutic. In fact, it's sufficiently awful to kill my earlier Zen state completely. It takes an age to wash all the utensils and bowls (how did we use this many bowls?), and even longer to clean the worktop and dining room matting. The oilcloth on the kitchen floor needs washing but is too large for the sink, so I hose it down in the garden and hang it over the picnic table to dry. Returning inside, the room feels too hot, too stuffy, so I leave the double doors ajar.

And then it's time to clean myself and Poppy. She won't countenance a shower, so I take her for a bath, help her to undress while the tub is filling. I search for clean clothes similar to those Lara put her in this morning, but can't find another pair of tights. Perhaps leggings will do? As I continue to search – through small jumpers and even smaller socks – I come across an incongruous item of clothing at the back of the wardrobe. Its collar is bent and its fabric riven with creases. Yet even in this state, there's no mistaking what it is.

My white shirt.

LARA

Sometimes I wonder if I actually went mad years ago. If the leukaemia drugs did something terrible to the wiring of my brain, leading me to dream those long, lonely months in Gareth's chalet, when my body was growing but my world was shrinking. I didn't ski or drink anymore, or see anyone – most of the people I knew had left at Easter anyway – so there was nothing to do except wander round Gareth's chalet, looking out at the mountains through smeared glass. I read a lot too; Gareth didn't own many books, but I read the few he did, along with old magazines and the backs of cereal packets. Anything that could divert me from my own existence, and the thickening inside me.

But then, one morning, the books were gone. I asked Gareth where they were.

'I've given them to a more deserving home.'

'What do you mean?'

'You don't deserve nice things.' His mouth twisted into a leer. 'I mean, have you seen the state of yourself? It's nine in the morning and you're still in your dressing gown. Your hair's a mess, you've put on a ton of weight, and you contribute absolutely nothing to this household. Why should I let you have books just so you can sit around on your lardy arse all day doing fuck all?'

By this stage, we were rarely sleeping together, and I felt weirdly awful about this, like it was the only barometer of my worth. Like maybe all the other stuff would be resolved if only I could be attractive again. But there seemed no way to bring this about: where once I had been svelte, I was now swollen, and patches of my hair had begun to fall out – if I ran a hand across my scalp, my fingers would alight on ovals of smooth skin, which I prodded at, trying to impress clarity upon my soupy brain. I had stopped looking in the mirror, because I didn't like what I saw, and lived in pyjamas and old stretchy thermals because my other clothes no longer fit. 'You disgust me,' Gareth said on a regular basis, and I didn't refute these remarks, or even note their cruelty, because I disgusted myself even more.

He didn't leave Olivia; in fact, he started disappearing off to Grenoble to see her, openly and brazenly. He told me he needed to keep the marriage going if he was going to support a baby, and forbade me from leaving the house while he was away. Said he'd rigged up cameras to make sure I didn't. Said it was for my own good, because I clearly couldn't be trusted on my own. Said that if I deviated from the rules, I'd be punished.

And I accepted all this, because I was terrified and ashamed, and didn't see him for what he truly was. It sickens me to think how grateful I was for occasional scraps of his attention, for a rare kind word. Once I made a beef stew that he said was 'quite nice', and I was so pleased that I made it again a few nights later, and then a few nights after that. I only ate a little stew myself, but it gave me vicarious pleasure to see him tucking in with such relish, using a piece of bread to mop up the sauce.

Except, the third time I cooked it, he didn't eat it with relish or, indeed, at all. Instead, he frowned at the bowl I placed in front of him, as if it had personally offended him. 'Is this the only dish you know how to cook?'

'No . . . but I thought you liked it . . .'

He ran one hand across his forehead, then examined his fingers. 'That's funny,' he said. 'I thought I must have "total fucking mug" written on me, but I can't see any ink.'

'Er . . . ah . . .' My body felt hot, my abdomen fluttering.

'Do I have "total fucking mug" written on my forehead?' He was looking directly at me now, his eyes full of loathing.

'No.'

'Interesting. So has somebody come to the house and ripped out all my taste buds?'

'No.'

'Then perhaps you can explain to me why you insist on repeatedly feeding me the same old slop?'

'I . . . er . . .' The flutters were getting stronger. 'I can cook something else if you'd prefer?'

'Don't fucking bother.' With a sudden movement he swiped his bowl from the table, sending food everywhere: chunks of potato and lumps of beef; thick gravy soaking into the carpet. I lowered myself to the floor to begin clearing up.

'God, you're pathetic,' said Gareth. And then he picked his way across the mess, and said he was going out for dinner.

'I told her. Lara . . .' It takes me a while to realise Max is talking to me, and I do my best to refocus on my current surroundings: the car park at Curbar Gap, with Max beside me, and Mum a few metres beyond. 'I told Cassie about Hannah. I wasn't going to, I was going to wait and tell her in person, but then it sort of came out.'

'What?'

'I told Cassie what happened with Hannah. I felt I owed her the truth.'

'What?' Part of me is still in the mountains, and I'm struggling to come back. But when I do, it's with a jab of fear. My sister is at risk. Much more so now that Cassie knows what she did. 'And?'

'And what?' Max looks confused.

'How did she take it?'

'Better than I expected.'

'Really?' I can't help thinking that Cassie must hate my sister now. And that Hannah is alone, with Poppy, at Grove Cottage. 'We should go back,' I say. 'As soon as your mum returns with the car.'

'Why? Are you cold?'

I shake my head. 'I'm just worried about Hannah. Do you think Cassie will confront her about . . . what happened?'

'I very much doubt it. Cassie's much angrier with me than her. Which is how it should be, I know. I'm angry with myself too, for spoiling everything . . .' He looks searchingly at my face, then away again. 'Can you forgive me?'

'Give me some time, Max,' I say. But what I don't add is: *It depends what's going to happen.*

HANNAH

So Lara *was* responsible. I'd been so certain it was Cassie who'd taken our things and hidden them in the attic; that Lara was telling the truth when she said it had nothing to do with her. Or maybe I'd just hoped that was the case, because the alternative – that my sister took our things for no reason and lied about it – is terrifying. It suggests a level of mental instability far beyond anything I'd imagined, because either her lying was deliberate, which seems borderline psychotic, or else she genuinely believes her version of events, which is perhaps worse.

Poppy and I are now washed and redressed and, as I watch her play with her toy animals, I think how unfair it is that she has an absent, philandering father *and* an unwell mother. In a fair world, disadvantages would be parcelled out equally, but in reality they're often lumped together, crushing some individuals while others are allowed to skate along, unhindered. Which makes me wonder if perhaps I need to do more for Poppy and Lara, if perhaps it's not enough to take my sister's word that she'll see a doctor. Perhaps, instead, I should sit down with her this afternoon and watch as she *books* a doctor's appointment, or drive her to a surgery and refuse to go anywhere until she's inside a consultation room.

I'm debating this when I hear a thud from the far side of the house. Did I forget to re-latch the chain after Jackie left? If so, Lara will be too angry to make an appointment, let alone get into a car with me. 'Hello?' I call out, my tone apologetic in case it's her.

But no one replies. 'Hello?' I call again.

Still nothing. But now I can hear footsteps coming down the hall, and fear ticks inside me. 'Poppy,' I say, my voice quiet but authoritative. 'It's Den Time.'

She pouts. 'I don't like Den Time.'

'I know, but it's important.' The footsteps are coming closer, and while it's almost certainly no one sinister, the fact they haven't replied to my greetings makes me uneasy. 'Go on, up you go.'

'I don't want to.'

'I'm afraid you have to.' I consider trying to forcibly carry her upstairs, but what if she screams, or runs down again? And then I have an idea. 'You can take my phone,' I whisper. 'Go through my photos as much as you want.'

Her face brightens. 'Really?'

'Yes. So long as you're super quiet.' I turn my phone on to silent, unlock it, and hand it over.

'Thank you, Auntie Hannah!'

'Off you go.'

This time there's no protest; she scampers up the stairs and out of view. I listen for the footsteps again, but they seem to have paused. Do I need a weapon? Some means of defence in case this person wishes me, or Poppy, harm? Or should I hide too?

I'm being absurd. We're in a cottage in the middle of the countryside. It will just be Jackie, back again for more of her turd cake, her hearing obscured by a hat. Or Mum, too busy thinking about what to make for dinner to listen to what's going on around her. No one dangerous.

I walk to the bedroom door, open it, and step out into the hall.

LARA

Gareth was increasingly absent as my pregnancy progressed, which meant no one bore witness to my existence. I spent my days cleaning cupboards and dusting empty shelves, imagining alien worlds where caterpillars proliferated and butterflies danced under pale skies. I watched the snow recede from the mountains as summer took up residence, and the sun beat in through the windows so heavily that I abandoned pyjamas and lived in my underwear, wandering around empty rooms which were perpetually cast in bleached white light, like a fever dream. Gareth left notes for me on pieces of A5 paper that yellowed in the sun, giving them the appearance of ancient documents. Certainly, they had a whiff of Old Testament stricture about them: *Don't eat more than 100g of carbohydrates per day. Don't go out. Don't speak to other people.*

I followed these commandments because I no longer knew how to do otherwise. And because of the cameras. I'd once wondered if they were an empty threat and had left the chalet when Gareth was away; had meandered around the village in circles, thinking that there couldn't be any problem with just doing this, with trying to get my head straight. Looking at Le Bellevue, the hotel where I'd worked, a question mark arose in my mind, but I couldn't quite pin down the question, let alone the answer, and soon I'd wandered on past it, watching the gondola carry late-summer passengers high into the mountains.

But that night I learned the cameras were very real. I was fast asleep when Gareth came in and pulled me from the bed, dragged me down the hallway and through the living room. I was too tired to understand what was happening, but the next thing I knew I was outside, on the balcony, with the door locked behind me. I could see Gareth sitting on the sofa inside the chalet and I called to him, banged on the door to get his attention, but he didn't let me in. Didn't even look up. It might have been late summer, but the night air was bitter in the mountains, and I was only wearing a thin nightie. My feet, meanwhile, were bare, and the concrete underfoot was painfully cold, searing my soles and permeating into my lower legs, before ascending into my thighs and pelvis, causing the baby to kick. I called to Gareth again, began to pummel on the door, and finally he stood up and I thought he was going to show some mercy, to let me in, but instead he turned his back and went to bed.

I spent the entire night outside, on that balcony, cradling my arms around my belly. And those long, cold hours ripped me apart, tossed out what little confidence and autonomy I still possessed and reknitted only guilt and regret. So when Gareth opened the door and asked if I'd learned my lesson, I merely nodded. And when he told me he was going to Grenoble for a fortnight, and I wasn't to leave the chalet, I nodded again.

And I would have adhered to his order except one evening a week later, as I was cleaning my teeth, I felt a warm gush of liquid between my legs. I stood staring at my feet for at least two minutes – wondering which part of me had prolapsed and grateful that it had done so on the bathroom tiles, which were a lot easier to clean than the carpet – before I realised it must be amniotic fluid. That the baby was on its way. I rang Gareth but he didn't pick up. At which point I had no choice but to break his rules: to put on a dressing gown and boots, slip my phone into my pocket, and step out into the night. But where to go? I stood in the village square, hopelessly casting around before I found my answer. The hotel. I walked to it and pushed open its heavy wooden doors. The face behind the reception desk wary as I stepped inside. 'Can I help you?'

'I need Steve.'

Back in the present, as Max walks across the car park to Mum, I remember Steve coming down the stairs, taking one look at me and whisking me into his car outside. And as Max and Mum make small talk, I remember the long, dark journey to the hospital, when my insides squeezed interminably as we traversed hairpin bend after hairpin bend, like everything in the world was too tight and sharp to bear.

And then, as Mum explains to Max where we're going for the rest of our walk, I remember entering a brightly lit ward and screaming.

And how, nearly twenty-four hours later, baby Gillian was finally born.

HANNAH

'Hello?' I'm not going to be scared or silly about this; I'm just going to find the person who's come into the house and have a chat with them. Put my mind at rest. But they're not in the hall, so I walk down the corridor to the kitchen; if it's Mum or Jackie, they'll almost certainly be making a cup of tea. My heart beats a little faster than usual as I turn the corner, but I ignore it and look around. There's nobody by the kettle, but in the dining room maybe? Or the living room? No and no.

I return the way I've come, opening the door to each room in turn along the corridor. Bedroom one, the bathroom, bedroom two. And it's in the last of these that I find a figure kneeling over a suitcase, shoving objects inside.

Cassie.

She looks up when I enter, her eyes narrowed. 'Why are you in my room?'

'I'm sorry,' I stammer. 'I heard someone come in and I . . .'

She doesn't say anything, just fixes me with a penetrating stare.

'I called hello, but there wasn't a reply, so I thought maybe it was an intruder, or . . . or . . .'

'Or maybe I just didn't want to speak to you.'

'Or that.' I stand by the door as she continues to fill her case, balling items of clothing with a barely disguised fury. Perhaps she's angry to have been accused of stealing when it was actually Lara all along. Or, even worse, she's found out about me and Max. I dig my fingers into my palm. I don't want to be thought of as the type of person who sleeps with another woman's boyfriend. No, scrap that: I don't want to *be* the type of person who sleeps with another woman's boyfriend. 'How was your time in Sheffield?' I ask.

'Fuck off.'

So she *does* know. I wonder if I can do anything to appease her, whether I should come straight out and apologise, or whether that might antagonise her further. Perhaps if I tell her it was all a mistake – that I understand that now? That the two of us shouldn't be in contention with one another, because we were never really in the running for Max's affections in the first place? But instead I say, 'Are you leaving?'

'Yes.' She zips up her case and pushes past me to the door. 'You can have Max to yourself, just like you wanted.'

Her hatred feels abrasive, like pieces of grit in my socks. She marches down the hall, and I hobble after her into the kitchen. 'I'm sorry,' I say. 'It's not like that.'

She takes her gluten-free snacks from the cupboard and shoves them into her case. Then she marches into the living room, where she picks up a couple of books. My dress is still hanging over the window but, if she notices, she doesn't comment.

'I'm sorry,' I say again. 'I didn't mean for any of this to happen.'

The books won't fit; she has to lay her case flat on the floor and rearrange its contents to get them in.

'I shouldn't have done it,' I continue.

She gives no indication of having heard me, simply re-zips her case and stands up.

'I know it was unforgivable.'

She takes her coat from the back of an armchair and slings it over her case.

'If it's any consolation, he's not at all interested in me.'

'He must be a little interested in you.' Her voice is bitter.

'No, he isn't. He doesn't want anything more to do with me. Not like that, anyway. He's made it clear he regrets the whole thing . . .' My voice cracks slightly.

She wheels round, eyes flashing. 'Please don't tell me you want me to feel sorry for you?'

'No! God, no. I'm just explaining. I've fucked up. He's fucked up. We both—'

'Yes, I get it. There's been a lot of fucking.' She takes a couple of steps before spotting the items on the bookshelf. My bracelet and Max's aftershave. Mum's earring and the knife. She looks them over slowly and then turns, sees me watching.

'I'm sorry about those too,' I say.

'What about them?'

Where to start? I take a deep breath. 'Lara claims she found them in the attic, and I thought maybe you'd put them there because you were pissed off, and I said as much to Max and Jackie and Mum, but only as a theory, because it was all so strange, but I realise now that I was wrong, that it was Lara all along, and I'm sorry.' I force myself to stop talking.

'What made you change your mind?' Cassie is watching me carefully.

'Because I just found *this*' – I tug at the white shirt I'm wearing – 'in Lara's room. She'd hidden it at the back of the wardrobe, behind Poppy's clothes.'

Cassie frowns for a second, then turns back to her case. 'You lot really *are* all bloody nuts,' she mutters.

'What did you say?' I ask, even though I heard.

'I said "you're all bloody nuts"!' She's speaking more loudly now, and there's a jittery feeling in my belly. 'You, and Max, and your sister – you're all fucking certifiable! Your Mum and Jackie too—'

'That's not true.'

'Really? Consider the evidence. Your mum cries at the drop of a hat, you and Max are supposedly like brother and sister and yet you *fuck* each other, and your sister, well, she's the most unhinged of all.'

'How dare you . . .' The jitters are intensifying.

'Oh, come on! You've said as much yourself—'

'I've said no such thing—'

'Really? Do you not remember our car journey, coming back from Chatsworth? When you told me how Lara's time in France had made her go completely gaga?'

'That's not what I said!' But the truth is I can't remember what I said. Not precisely, anyway. I recall saying that Lara's time in France had changed her, that she'd needed space to rebuild herself, but I was sympathetic towards her, and careful with the language I used, sensitive to the complexities of mental health. Wasn't I?

'She's insane,' Cassie goes on. 'She told Max she thought you were going to fall off a cliff or something.'

'She just worries about us, that's all.' My voice is weak. 'It's hardly a crime to love your family . . .'

'There's love, and then there's lunacy—'

'I think you need to leave now.' My teeth are knocking together, and I try to still them with my hand.

'Christ, you two are as bad as each other.' She grips the handle of her case.

'Please *leave*—'

'Don't worry, I'm going.' She wheels her case into the hall and I follow her, to make sure she actually is. But as she reaches the front door, she stops. 'You were right, by the way. About me taking that stuff.'

'What!'

'Not the shirt, but the rest of it. I thought you'd know because you saw me from the garden that time, when I was scoping out the attic.'

The face at the window. I can feel my jaw hanging open. 'What?' I say again. 'But . . . why?'

'Because I *did* think Max was having an affair with your sister, and I was so pissed off that I wanted him to realise how unhinged she is . . .'

I stare at her.

'It was clear that something was going on with somebody – I'm not a complete fool – and I swear I saw Max with Lara on Tuesday night, walking off into the trees.'

Tuesday night: after Max and Cassie's argument on Mam Tor. The night I'd worn my plain blue T-shirt and styled my hair like Lara's. Worn her perfume too.

The terrible realisation: *this is my fault.*

'I put the ice in her bed as well,' Cassie goes on, 'and changed her spa treatment to the mountain one, and she properly spun out over it all, just like I hoped she would. It didn't take much to reveal her true colours! But it turns out *you* were the one sleeping with Max, and your sister was able to demonstrate how unhinged she is all by herself!' Cassie laughs – a caustic grating sound. 'Although maybe she just hid that shirt of yours because it's so large and ugly.'

I don't know how to respond; just continue to stare as she heads to her car and climbs into the driver's seat. Before she starts the engine, she makes one last remark. 'You do realise,' she says, 'that all these dreams your sister has? All this stuff that she "foresees"?' She draws air quotes around the final word.

'What about it?'

'It's just shit of your family's own making. A self-fulfilling fucking prophecy.'

LARA

'She's here!' Mum waves us over to the edge of the car park as Jackie finally pulls in. I hurry over to Jackie's car and request that we please go back to Grove Cottage immediately.

She smiles and tells me not to worry. 'Hannah and Poppy are having a wonderful time. A *messy* time, but wonderful, nonetheless. There's no need for you to go back, I promise.'

'I'd rather we did.'

'You might change your mind if you saw the kitchen!' she laughs. 'Look, come down with us to watch the climbers and have some cake first. And then, if you're still worried, we can go back straight after, I promise.'

Mum and Max join in with the reassurances, and I let myself be persuaded, bringing up the rear of our group as we walk along Curbar Edge and down a winding, wooded track to the foot of the cliffs. As Jackie hands out refreshments, we sit on a boulder and watch the climbers. They're remarkably agile, balancing on the merest pinpoints of rock before launching themselves to equally precarious footholds above. Using cracks in the rock as leverage for their fingertips, and stretching their limbs into impossible positions, seemingly unaffected by the gravity which pulls the rest of us to the ground.

It was immediately after giving birth that I finally understood: I had to leave Gareth. I'd lost sight of myself in the preceding months – had been sapped of all self-esteem by his twisted, controlling behaviour – but now, with Gillian in my arms, everything became clear. She was so tiny and vulnerable, but also so perfectly new, uncorrupted by the evils of the world.

And I'd do anything to keep it that way.

I was exhausted from my labour, sore and spent, but love and protectiveness were surging through me. I'd considered telling Steve everything, but instead had sent him back to the hotel, with reassurances that I was fine. That I had family who could be contacted. And it wasn't a lie, except, sitting in the hospital bed, watching Gillian nap in the crib beside me, I didn't know if I could be the one to contact them.

But what choice did I have? Picking my bag off the floor, I reached for my phone. Unable to find it, I unpacked the bag's contents, item by item, and the more methodically I searched, the worse I began to feel. A slow, dawning nausea; a sick realisation.

I'd lost my phone.

I got up from the bed and rifled through the sheets, checked the floor and Gillian's crib with a pulsing, frenetic energy, and then started to look around: anywhere, everywhere. A midwife asked if I was okay, and I told her I'd lost my phone, that I must have dropped it somewhere on my journey from chalet to hotel to hospital, and that I desperately needed to ring my family. She took pity on me, handing me some coins and telling me there was a payphone in the corridor, and I was instantly off, running as fast as I could in my torn, bleeding state, pushing Gillian in the wheeled crib in front of me, until I was in front of the phone, picking up the receiver. But whom to call?

There was only one person whose number I knew off by heart.

My sister.

I dialled and held the receiver to my ear, listened as the phone rang once, twice, three times. On the fourth ring someone picked up. 'Hello?' An unfamiliar voice, with music and laughter in the background.

'Is Hannah there?'

'Er . . . she's somewhere around, I think.'

'Can you get her for me?' I didn't have time for niceties.

'Hang on . . .'

'It's important!' I said, but the other end went quiet, and all I could hear was background music and muffled discussion. I squeezed the receiver in one hand, touching the other to my daughter's soft, rounded cheek. And then the voice returned. 'She's coming shortly.'

My skin began to prickle. 'Tell her I need her right now! Tell her it's urgent! Tell her I'm in trouble.'

'Okay, okay, I'll tell her.' More muffled discussion. 'She'll be here in just a minute.'

I waited, but as one moment lapsed into another, I had my second terrible realisation. My sister wasn't coming. *I need you, Hannah,* I mumbled under my breath. *Please. Whatever's happened in our past, please help me now.*

But still no one came to the phone and I became aware of another sound. Footsteps.

I turned just in time to see Gareth strolling up the corridor, the cruellest of smiles upon his face.

HANNAH

I stand on the doorstep and watch as Cassie manoeuvres her car out of the driveway. My body is still shaking, my brain whirling from her confession that she *did* try to frame my sister. From the fact she successfully convinced me Lara might be losing the plot. And from the fact none of it explains why I found my white shirt stuffed at the back of Lara's wardrobe, among Poppy's clothes.

Poppy. It's been too long; I must go and see her, make sure she's okay. I return inside as soon as the car disappears, but almost immediately hear the crunch of tyres on gravel once again, which makes my shaking worse. It's her – Cassie – coming back. I brace myself against the lintel, trembling with fury at the hateful things she said. My sister might be fragile – unstable, even – but at least she doesn't play cruel tricks to serve her own ends.

And my fury makes me realise I don't have to put up with Cassie's nastiness anymore. I can shut the front door and pull the chain across. I reach for the handle as her car rolls into the driveway.

Except it's a different car. A *taxi.*

It takes me a while to grasp the identity of its passenger. I can see they're not Cassie: they're too tall and broad, and their hair is too short. But it's not until they're almost at the front door that my brain makes the leap.

The person walking towards me is Chris.

LARA

The first couple of weeks back at the chalet were a blur. A blur of fluids – warm milk and tears, blood and sweaty sheets – and of time itself: wailing nights segueing into days where mornings disappeared and afternoons stretched into implausible entities, measured in feeds, naps and changes instead of minutes and hours.

On the day of Gillian's birth, Gareth had found me by asking around at the resort. He'd seen on the cameras that I'd left the chalet and had returned immediately, full of rage that I'd broken his rules for a second time. Once back, it hadn't taken him long to discover that a pregnant woman had gone into labour and been taken to the hospital in the valley. And once at the hospital, it hadn't taken him long to locate me, to slam the telephone receiver down and lead me back to the ward, declare himself to the midwives as the loving father who had oh-so-sadly missed the birth.

But there was nothing loving about keeping a woman and her child prisoner. Enclosed once more within the chalet's walls, with no phone and under the constant surveillance of Gareth and his cameras, I realised just how trapped I was. Because even if Gillian and I somehow managed to escape, where would we go? It wasn't as if a newborn baby could hitch lifts or sleep by the side of the road; we would need to take buses and trains, would need to find safe and warm places to stay, and I had next to no money to facilitate this.

But still I daydreamed of fleeing over the mountains – of trudging across glaciers and taking refuge in mountain huts. Of Gillian bedding down among climbers' ropes and crampons, mewling in the night as they began their early ascents. Of finally making it to a town where we could disappear into anonymity; where some kind person might take us in. I could do cleaning, or cooking, or childcare – look after someone else's children alongside my own.

Gillian changed rapidly, her skin morphing from livid red to pale coral, and her hair loosening and lightening. Her legs began to straighten, and she made tentative smiles. Her eyes, too, became more knowing, more observant of the world and her place within it. Perhaps picking up on the fact Gareth never held her and that, if she cried, he'd go to another room, or head out altogether.

One afternoon, however, he asked if he could take her. He walked towards us with his arms outstretched, and I was torn, because she deserved a shot at a father's love, but he wasn't just any father, and—

'Are you going to hand her over or what?' He tried to prise her from me, but I didn't let go. Looking back, I don't know whether I could sense what was coming, or if it was my reluctance that angered him. But I'll never forget what happened next. Gareth yanked her from me and she started to cry.

'Why in God's name are you making that noise? You're as bad as your mother – ungrateful.' And he shook her. 'Stop crying.'

'Don't shake her!' I was pulling at him, Gillian was wailing, and my abdomen pulsed with a deep, primeval pain.

'I'm her father and I'll shake her if I damn well want to.'

'No! You'll hurt her!' I kept tugging at his arms, trying to free her, but Gareth pushed me away. And then he raised her above his head, her neck unsupported.

'Put her down! You'll hurt her! Give her back!' The pain in my abdomen was worsening and I think I must have been screaming, because Gillian was crying at full throttle now, or maybe she was crying so hard because I was screaming – the fear and noise were inseparable. Gillian and I operating as entangled particles: simultaneously together and apart.

And perhaps that's what really angered Gareth: that Gillian and I had a bond that didn't include him, that didn't need him, that didn't centre around him in any way. He went to the balcony and lifted Gillian, held her out across the void below.

'No!' I wept, tugging at his shirt, yelling at him, begging him not to drop her, saying I'd do anything, anything, so long as he didn't let go, and then suddenly, miraculously, she was back in my arms and I collapsed to the ground, hunched over her, sobbing.

'You're pathetic.' I didn't look up, but his voice was close. 'Grovelling and snivelling and useless. Just like your stupid baby. I should wash my hands of both of you. But I'm a generous man, so I'll let you stay. For now.'

Gillian clawed for my breast, and I felt a rush of wetness from my nipple.

'I'm going to Grenoble.' He was whispering now, his breath hot in my ear. 'But just remember. If you ever do anything to piss me off, I'll kill her.'

After that, the horror of my predicament – and the myriad ways in which I was failing my daughter – made proper sleep impossible. My existence took on a twilit, treacly quality, where movement was difficult and nothing was in focus. When I did fall into a semi-slumber, it was plagued by nightmares of being swept up in an avalanche and buried alive. Suffocated by tightly packed snow. I was waiting, always waiting, for something bad to happen.

And then the opposite: a minor miracle. I was alone in the chalet with Gillian one evening, trying to soothe her by walking around in circles and singing half-remembered nursery rhymes, when the doorbell rang. 'Shh, shh, shh,' I whispered as Gillian started to cry harder, cradling her to my chest as I pulled back the latch, scared as to what might lie beyond. Expecting to see Gareth on the doorstep, telling me I'd failed a test and would now be punished.

But it wasn't Gareth.

It was Max.

◆ ◆ ◆

I look at Max now, eating cake, before turning to see a figure striding along the path. At first I assume it's an energetic walker but, as they come closer, I realise they're headed directly for us. And then they start to become recognisable: a woman, young, with long legs and long hair, wearing a cropped jacket and an expression of righteous fury.

Cassie.

Max goes to meet her, and the rest of us try not to listen as she lambasts him for cheating on her, for dragging her to the Peak District when she wanted to go to Italy, for never listening to her or trying to understand. I clutch the Thermos flask while she tells him she's taking the car, and the cat. Jackie continues to eat her cake, but each mouthful takes longer to chew than its predecessor.

'You won't see me again.' Cassie's voice has increased further in volume, and I realise she's addressing us. Mum and I make awkward noises of acknowledgement while Jackie drops the remainder of her cake in the bracken. 'I'm sorry it's ended like this,' she says. 'I wish—'

'Have this conversation with your son instead of me,' Cassie snaps. She turns to face Max. 'I hope it was worth it.'

'It . . . er . . .' He shakes his head.

'Because you clearly don't mean all that much to her. She's got another guy round there right now, you know. Is probably shagging him as we speak.'

Dread envelops me, dense and cold, pressing in upon my skin. As Jackie asks what she means, I consider grabbing her keys and sprinting back up the path to her car. But then I look down the hill to Grove Cottage.

And begin to run.

HANNAH

I freeze in the doorway, stare as the taxi manoeuvres out of the drive and Chris approaches. He's wearing a bright yellow fleece I've never seen before.

'Hello,' he says, giving me a kiss on the cheek.

'What are you doing here?' There's a ringing in my ears, a sense of dislocation.

'That's not quite the greeting I was hoping for.'

'No . . . I . . . sorry . . .' I kiss him on the cheek in return, noting the bristles on his skin. He clearly hasn't shaved for a couple of days. 'I just wasn't expecting . . .'

'Can I come in?' He gestures at the hall behind me.

'Yes, of course . . . sorry.' I stand to one side to let him pass, my mind reeling. He shouldn't be here, it makes no sense that he's here, and the way he's acting – smiling, apparently happy to see me – is so unexpected that I wonder if I'm dreaming. Is it possible he doesn't know about me and Max? That the photo of us kissing never got through to him? I feel a spike of relief at the possibility, which is almost immediately quashed by the memory of the photo he sent this morning – *a painting about betrayal.*

'Which way am I going?' he asks, and I point him weakly in the direction of the kitchen.

'Coffee?' I hope he can't hear the tremor in my voice.

'Yes please. Well, this is quite something, isn't it?' He looks at the closed blinds and my orange dress hanging between them.

'Mmm-hmm.' I'm glad to have the distraction of making coffee, to concentrate on refilling the water in the machine.

'I think you undersold the place.'

'Mmm?' I check there are sufficient coffee beans in the grinder but, in my peripheral vision, I can see him walk to the window and peer out behind the blind.

'You never told me the view was this impressive.'

'Didn't I?'

'No. But then you haven't told me much. I suppose you've been busy.'

Was there something in the way he said 'busy'? A hint of hardness, of knowing? I take a mug from the cupboard, press the button to start the brewing. 'You still haven't explained why you're here.' I make sure to face away from him. 'Not that I'm not pleased to see you, but—'

'Can't a man surprise his girlfriend from time to time?'

His girlfriend. That's not how I thought he'd be referring to me after everything that's happened. 'There's surprises and then there's *surprises*,' I say. 'Appearing in the Peak District when I thought you were in Singapore is definitely the latter.'

'Some might say it's romantic. Missing your girlfriend so much you fly halfway across the world to see her.'

'But I'm flying back tomorrow—'

'Which makes it all the more romantic, surely? A literal flying visit.'

'I guess . . .' I take his coffee to him, holding it in both hands to keep myself from spilling it. 'But you could have stayed for the week, if you were going to come all this way. Then you'd have had time to meet everyone properly . . .' *And events might have panned out very differently.*

'You don't seem very pleased to see me.'

'No, I am! I'm just . . . in shock . . .'

'Right.' There's a long pause as Chris wanders round, running his hands across the surfaces. The warm wood of the bookshelf and smooth stone of the dining table. 'Where is everyone else?'

'Out for a walk.'

'All of them?'

'Yes, except . . .' I'm about to mention Poppy when for some reason I stop myself. Maybe Lara's doom-mongering has finally got to me.

'Except?'

This is crazy. I can't keep Poppy's presence a secret when she's up in the attic, playing on my phone. And what will Chris say when she eventually grows bored and comes downstairs? But even as I think this, I find myself saying, 'Cassie. Max's girlfriend. She left just as you were arriving.'

'Oh.' He raises his eyebrows. 'Why did she leave?'

'She and Max have split up.' I try to keep my voice as neutral as possible, walk back into the kitchen to busy myself with clearing the sides.

'How sad.' There it is again, that note of hardness. 'What caused the break-up?'

Now there's a new hollowness in the room, or perhaps inside my head. I give a strangled laugh. 'Who knows? Something to do with different expectations around the future, I think.' It's not entirely untrue.

'Oh? How so?'

I give a small shrug of my shoulders. 'She wanted to get married, and he . . .' I pause, unsure what to say next.

'Don't stop there.' Chris smiles but his teeth seem larger than usual.

'I'm not sure what I was going to say.'

'You were just telling me about Max. About what he wanted.'

I take a step back, knock into the dishwasher. 'I don't know—'

'Oh, but I think you do.' Still smiling with his too-big teeth, he steps towards me. 'So, go on, Hannah. What did Max *want*?'

There's no mistaking it this time: his emphasis on the word 'want', the threat in his voice. He knows, he must do, how could he not? If Poppy weren't here, I'd leave immediately; drive away and deal with all this later, from the safety of a warm hotel room. But she's upstairs, with my phone, which means it can't wait. 'Did you send me a photo from the National Gallery?' I ask.

'I did take some photos in the National Gallery,' he says, moving closer. 'And I had them developed as a gift for you—'

'A gift?'

'—but then I was travelling up here when my Connect app went off. So I sent you some pictures of the photos.'

'Why?'

'Why what?'

'Why the National Gallery? Why that painting?'

'It seemed appropriate.'

'Oh.' My attempt at nonchalance is poor, the quiver in my voice too obvious. 'How so?'

'Because it's of Samson and Delilah.' He's looking straight at me now, no longer smiling. 'And you know their story, right?'

'I vaguely remember it.'

'Only vaguely? Then let me refresh your memory. Samson was a strong man, a good man, a man who fought for what was right.' He comes so close that I can feel his breath in my hair. 'His one flaw was to trust Delilah, to think she cared for him, when actually . . .'

As he trails off, I realise Jackie was right. Air is rushing through my body now, making me unsteady, like I might keel over at the slightest touch. 'When actually?'

He takes a large swig of coffee before replying. 'She was a treacherous fucking bitch.'

LARA

It's a long time since I've run like this, at full tilt, arms pumping and chest burning. Normally the steep, uneven hillside would give me pause, but the thought of a man coming to the house unexpectedly, when my sister and Poppy are alone, drives me forward without hesitation. Hopefully Hannah won't let him in, will keep the chain pulled firmly across the door. Except she lets everyone in. She's too open, too trusting, too willing to share her life with others.

I should have asked Cassie about the man's appearance. What car he drove. Although I'm not sure any answer could have reassured me.

The bracken scratches my hands, spikes my legs through my tracksuit bottoms. From a purely physical perspective, it's a relief to get to the bottom of the hill and enter the garden of Grove Cottage. But from a mental perspective it's terrifying. I suppose it's possible the man was just delivering something and has already gone. Yet even as I think this, I know it isn't true.

When I finally left Gareth, I did so in Max's car, with Gillian strapped to my front. We drove for hours, not stopping until we reached northern France, where Max checked us into a small auberge. A place from which he sorted our paperwork, while I sat on the bed feeding Gillian, fearful that Gareth might appear at any moment. Max told me I didn't need to worry – that Gareth hadn't followed us and there was no way we could be tracked – but he didn't know Gareth like I did. Didn't know about his cameras and commandments, his relish for control and punishment.

It was a combination of good luck, kindness and persistence that had led Max to me. Steve had found my phone in the hotel a few weeks after I'd given birth, and had powered it on, but was unable to unlock it. But then, while it was still in his hand, Max had rung, and he'd answered. At which point the two men ascertained that I'd never contacted my family or gone back to the UK, and started to fear the worst. Max came straight to France, and Steve did some investigative work to locate me, and we struck it lucky that Gareth wasn't in when Max finally came to my door.

They rescued me. Rescued us. And pacing up and down in that auberge in northern France, I realised it was time to start over. To register my daughter as a new person, with no record of a father.

I didn't have long to decide on a name. But looking from the window, I could see a memorial to fallen soldiers. To those who had shown courage in the face of horror.

And so she became Poppy.

Approaching the rear of Grove Cottage through the trees, I see the blinds are down, and the double doors ajar. *Why has my sister left the doors open?* As I step into the dining room, my pulse hammers so hard I think I might be having a heart attack. And then all my dread and angst crystallises into the scene in front of me. The long dining table, with its exposed stone surface. The shaft of orange light filtering down from above. Hannah wearing the white shirt I thought I had successfully hidden.

And in the kitchen, looming over her: a man. His hair is shorter and darker than I remember and the beard is gone, but his face remains the same. That same tilt of the eyebrows and that same horrid, tunnelling gaze; that same cruel mouth. And that same too-bright yellow fleece.

Gareth.

HANNAH

I don't know how long Chris and I have been standing here: too close, and yet so far apart. The crudeness of his language was shocking, his use of the word 'bitch', but the way he spat the words even more so, because Chris has always been courteous and measured. Even when I've seen him riled, he's managed to stay civil, like the time we went out for dinner and my chicken wasn't cooked properly, on which occasion Chris very politely informed the waiter (and then the manager) that we were leaving and wouldn't be paying, and stuck calmly to this line even as they argued that it was impossible, saying he was very happy to take the matter up with Food Standards.

But here, now, he's a different man. Still calm but seemingly full of disgust, like my very presence might make him sick. When I tried to apologise, saying I was sorry for what had happened with Max (without specifying what *had* happened), he stood silently, watching me, making me gabble on and on – that it was stupid, that it didn't mean anything, that I seriously regretted it – until eventually I asked if he was ever going to respond. At which point he said, 'I don't want to waste my breath. You have no idea what a tedious, irrelevant little slut you are.' Which drew me up so short that I haven't said anything since; have simply stood here, breathing in his contempt.

But now there's someone else in the room and we both turn to see Lara, standing by the double doors. The expression on her face is one of unadulterated terror. 'This is Chris,' I mumble, but she says nothing, just keeps staring at us like we're corpses raised from the dead.

'Hannah.' Her voice is more incisive than I've ever heard it. 'Take Poppy and get out of here.'

'What . . . I don't . . .' I begin, but before I can form my question, Chris is speaking.

'So she *is* here,' he says, his eyes not leaving Lara. 'Hannah told me she wasn't.'

'What?' Lara looks across to me.

'Poppy's fine,' I assure her, but this doesn't seem the right thing to say, because Chris starts to laugh.

'Who knew you were such a conniving little liar! Where is she?'

'Don't tell him, Hannah. Just take her. *Please*.' There's true desperation in my sister's voice now, a depth of feeling I don't understand but can't ignore. I nod and turn to go, only for Chris to grab my arm and yank me back towards him. 'Get off me!' I shout.

'I don't think so.' His grip is tight. 'If you're fetching my daughter, I'm coming too. And I'm taking her as far away from here as possible.'

'What the hell are you talking about? She's not your daugh—' And then I stop, my entire body going numb as I take in my sister's panic and Chris's mocking smile. 'Oh fuck.'

'That's right,' he says. 'I knew even your pea brain could work it out eventually. Your sweet little niece – my *daughter* – is actually called Gillian. Your sister took her from me, hid her from me, changed her name and embarked on living a lie away from me. But the thing is, two can play that game. Lara might be capable of flying under the radar, but the rest of her family isn't, and all the details in your blog were extremely helpful in leading me to her.'

'No.' I'm shaking harder now, because this isn't true, it can't be true; it can't all be a lie. Chris, my relationship with him, the identity he provided: it's inconceivable that it was just a ruse to find my sister. Chris and I slept together, laughed together, explored Singapore together. We wandered along the harbour at sunset, holding hands and kissing as the container ships headed out into the South China Sea.

'Oh yes. I identified early on that you might be her sister, but I had to spend some time with you to confirm it. And all it took was a trip to Singapore and a false identity and then it was a piece of piss to ingratiate myself into your life. You were surprisingly shit at telling me about your family, but I knew, if you were Lara's sister, you'd lead me to Gillian eventually. And sure enough, you were dumb enough to send me a photo of her yesterday and, even though she's older, I could tell it was her.' He smiles at Lara. 'She has my eyes, doesn't she?'

This isn't real; it can't be happening. Although I remember the bitter conversation in Bakewell, Olivia telling me she knew about Lara *and Gillian*. I'd been so quick to assume Gillian was another notch on Gareth's bedpost that I didn't stop to consider she could be his daughter.

'But . . .' My brain is working overtime to process what I'm hearing. Poppy *did* take a photo of herself on my phone yesterday, and she *did* accidentally send it to Chris. To *Gareth*. 'The photo . . .' I say. 'Poppy . . . I thought . . . Max . . .' I'm not making any sense. But it's hard to be coherent when you're forced to re-evaluate everything you thought you knew. My first meeting with Chris – with *Gareth* – in the Kaleidoscope Bar. That strange feeling of familiarity I had, which I wrongly attributed to attraction. When, in fact, he has Poppy's eyes. 'That's why,' I said. 'I didn't realise, how could . . .'

But Lara isn't listening to me. 'You don't even want Poppy,' she says to Gareth.

'Gillian—'

'You don't even want her. You just want to hurt me.'

'And you deserve to be hurt. *You* sent that email to Olivia, telling her about us. Telling her about Gillian. Because you're a spiteful fucking bitch—'

'I told her because I thought she needed to know.' My sister's voice is quiet. 'Because I found out from Instagram she was pregnant and I worried that . . . what happened with me and you, and Gillian . . . would happen with her too.'

'What, that I would look after her? Keep a roof over her head, and food on the table?'

'You were abusive and you know it.'

'You only got what you deserved—'

'No, Gareth, I didn't.' My sister's voice is stronger now, and her eyes are full of fire. 'Nobody deserves to be treated the way you treated me. And no child ever deserves to be shaken.'

I can't believe what I'm hearing. I'd assumed Gareth was a low-life – a cheat, a philanderer – but not that he was abusive. *Not that he hurt his own child.* I make another effort to break free, but he redoubles his grip and steps towards Lara, dragging me with him, his expression twisted with hate.

'You're an ungrateful bitch, and you always have been. It wasn't enough to take one child away, you had to make sure I couldn't have *any* children. Olivia and I separated after you sent that email, you know—'

'Good—'

'And now we're getting divorced and she's trying to bleed me dry.'

My sister bites her lip, and I realise this might be news to her. Because I never told her what I learned that day in Bakewell: that

Gareth and Olivia were no longer together; that she detested him; that she didn't know where he'd gone. If I'd said something, maybe things would be different: maybe Gareth wouldn't be here, in Grove Cottage, threatening to take Poppy away. I was so busy trying not to damage my sister that I didn't realise her anxiety might be proportionate. That staying silent could ultimately hurt her more.

'So that's why you've come after me now.' Lara lets out a bitter laugh. 'Olivia's turned off the money taps and you want to use Poppy as a bargaining chip with the courts—'

'I want what is mine. It's payback time. I've had enough of entitled bitches trying to destroy my life—'

'You're not taking Poppy,' I say, my voice suddenly loud.

He turns to me with a look of such condescension that I can't see how I ever considered him attractive. 'I think you'll find I am.'

'No.' I look across at Lara, and when our eyes connect, I know we're having the same thought. That we will do anything to protect Poppy. *Anything.* The knowledge of our unity brings me resolve. 'You won't find her, because she's having Den Time.' I look at Lara to make sure she's understood. She gives a tiny nod.

Gareth sighs. 'You're extremely tedious, Hannah, do you know that?' He releases my arm. 'Because I *am* going to take my daughter today, and it can happen one of two ways. Either you bring me to her voluntarily, or I force you.'

'No.'

He sighs again. 'Have it your way. I'm sure your followers will enjoy seeing that photo you sent me of your tits. It might even win you a few new ones.'

'No.' A wave of dizziness hits me. 'You wouldn't . . .'

'Oh, I absolutely would,' he replies, with a sneering smile. He starts to scroll through his phone, and I stare at this man I thought I knew, while the world spins in previously unimaginable directions.

I turn, try to get my bearings, and notice that Lara has gone into the living room. That she's picking up the knife from the bookshelf. That she's approaching us with the knife in her hand. She catches my eye as she comes closer, her arm raised above her head.

Launching herself at Gareth, she shouts, 'Run, Hannah! Get Poppy!' and I hesitate for a split second, watching the shock dawn on his face—

And then I run.

LARA

I'm willing to kill him. I hadn't realised before – I thought I wasn't capable, and the risks too high – but now it's simple. He's a threat to my family and needs to be removed. I might go to prison, might lose custody of Poppy, but Hannah, Mum and Jackie will look after her. She will be safe.

And he's even more dangerous than I'd realised. To pursue my sister, to pretend to be a caring boyfriend, simply to get close to me. To go to such lengths to find a daughter he never wanted, simply to exact revenge upon me for escaping, and for telling Olivia the truth. He's a sadist, justifying his cruel acts through a warped belief that he's perpetually wronged by others.

As I pick up the knife and run towards him, I don't feel fear, or regret, just a lucid kind of necessity. The aim is to immobilise him with a stab to the leg, but if I end up severing an artery, so be it. I yell at Hannah to get Poppy and hurl myself at Gareth. Plunge the knife into his thigh.

Except it never makes contact. Instead, my wrist is grabbed in a vice-like grip and I realise Gareth is holding me, using my hand to point the knife back at my own chest. He chuckles as I squirm and desperately try to change the knife's direction, sweat beading on my skin. 'Well, that was exceedingly foolish,' he says. 'What do you think a court is going to say about a mother who tries to stab her own child's father? Who do you think might be awarded custody in that situation?'

Every inch of me courses with hatred. It's like an electricity in my body, sparking and fizzing. 'You're a twisted piece of shit!'

'That's not very amiable.' He holds me tighter. 'Drop the knife.'

'No.'

'Drop the knife!'

'No!'

'You do realise, now you've tried to stab me, anything I do will count as self-defence?' He moves the knife closer to my chest: closer, closer, until its tip touches my coat. Growling with frustration, I have no choice but to let go.

'See, that wasn't so hard, was it?' Still holding me with one arm, he uses the other to toss the knife away. I watch as it lands by the double doors; try to think how I might reach it.

And then something crashes into my head with such force that I'm blinded, and stagger forward.

Before everything fades to black.

HANNAH

I can hear my breath as I run – the terrified rasps of an animal in danger. Along the corridor, through the bedroom, to the spiral staircase. At the bottom of the steps I pause, torn between making a run for it with Poppy, or barricading the two of us in the attic and calling the police. Or returning to the kitchen, against my sister's wishes. I can't believe I've left her alone with *him*, with a knife, but then I can't believe any of it: that a man who seemed funny and kind should turn out to be a monster. But perhaps I'm leaping into full panic mode because I'm scared; perhaps, if I stop and think rationally, there might be a chance to settle this calmly, with lawyers instead of knives.

But what if there isn't?

I hide the staircase by pulling the curtain across from behind, which buys me some time. Perching on the lowest step, I think again of Gareth's face, of the disdain etched into his features, and the corresponding fear in Lara's. The urgency in her voice when she told me to get Poppy and flee. And I realise any harm to Poppy will hurt her far more than injury to herself. So I run up the stairs, across the wooden floor to the dresser. 'Poppy,' I whisper, opening the right-hand door to see her hunched over my phone, her face bathed in pale blue light.

'I found a game with dancing cows!' she says.

'Shh!' I put a finger to my lips. 'We have to be super quiet. But well done you; now, I need to take my phone—'

'But I haven't finished this lev—'

'Shh!' I say again. But it's only as I'm minimising the game and bringing up the dial screen that I realise my mistake in taking the phone so abruptly, because Poppy starts to cry and yell, something about wanting to get the red cow's hat, and I'm trying to shush her but also ringing 999, and trying to respond to what the operator is saying – 'Yes, police,' I say and then, thinking of my sister with the knife, 'maybe an ambulance too . . . We're in a cottage, in the Peak District . . .' and it occurs to me that I don't know our postcode, and I wonder if I can send a location pin, but before I've had a chance to work it out, there are footsteps on the stairs and Chris – Gareth – is upon me, seizing the phone from my hand, laughing that there was no point hiding the staircase because I'd shown it to him on the Connect app earlier this week. My heart is beating too fast, too loudly, and there's a sense of terrible inevitability as he opens the tiny round window and throws my phone outside. But I can't accept it, I refuse to believe our future is ordained, so I fling myself at his legs while he's still focused on the window and the unexpected force of it knocks him to the floor. At which point I see my opportunity and shove my full weight against him, sending him crashing down the staircase. I grab Poppy's hand and run down behind him, past him as he lies, dazed, on the bedroom carpet, and back into the hall, where I open the front door and scream at Poppy to run to my car, to wait for me there, and I just need to find my car keys and then—

'You fucking whore!' He comes out of nowhere, pinning my arms roughly behind my back. I try to squirm away but he's too strong, just holds me tighter, lowers his mouth to my ear so I can feel his hot breath on my neck. 'You'll pay for that, just like your sister.' He drags me through the kitchen, where Lara is lying – a cast-iron dish beside her and blood pooling around her head – and as he pulls me into the dining room I scream, sink my teeth into his arm and he bellows, swipes his arm up into my mouth such that I swear my teeth are knocked loose but I can't feel any pain, and then he's pushing me back on to the dining table and his hands are around my neck, squeezing—

This can't be happening, I tell myself, as I try to jerk my head, or kick him, or do anything to get free, but I can't move, and he's still squeezing, and I realise that I'm struggling to breathe, that my vision is fading, that my entire life is narrowing to a single point—

As I approach this singularity, I think of all the time I've wasted caring about things that don't matter. And then I think of the things that matter the most. Poppy's little face, looking at insects; Mum laughing over a cup of tea; Lara jumping with me in the ferns. Finally, I see Dad, striding over the moorland with his hand outstretched. 'Come with me, Hannah,' he says, in that warm deep voice I've missed so much.

And so I do.

LARA

My mouth tastes of metal and I'm lying on something hard. When I open my eyes, I'm confronted by the base of a fridge and, beyond that, crumbs of food and a few stray hairs on cream herringbone tiles. There's a greasy-looking mark beside me and I run my fingers through its sheen. Butter? I turn my head to one side and am overcome by a bolt of pain which makes me want to retch, so I lie still again and press my hand to the source of the pain, hold it there for a couple of seconds before bringing it back to my side.

It's covered with blood.

What the hell? I raise myself to my knees, keeping my head as still as possible, and become aware of a noise in the room beyond me. A choking, spluttering sound. Slowly, I crawl my way towards it, my arms trembling with each forward movement. I'm not far from the edge of a bank of kitchen units, so I crawl further and peer out, only to be pole-axed by another flash of pain. Jesus. I must have moved my head to the side too quickly. I stay where I am, panting as the sensation subsides, then gently, oh so gently, turn my head again. I can see a man's legs, encased in jeans and, above, a yellow fleece which hurts my eyes. There's something familiar about it, something familiar about all of this, including the woman's legs I've just noticed on the table, and the arm that's hanging over the side, clothed in a white shirt.

Hannah.

As soon as I remember her, I remember everything: Gareth's mocking grin, the knife pointed at my chest, the blow to my head, the blackness. And now, in front of me, is the terrible tableau I've foreseen so many times: slab of stone, white shirt, orange light. I need to stop Gareth, but how when I'm so weak, when any sudden movements overwhelm me? If I was useless at full strength, with a knife, what are my chances now?

Except. There's another knife, isn't there? The one I hid earlier this week, in the lowest kitchen drawer. Max's chef's knife. I'd assumed it would be the instrument used to hurt my sister, the instrument which would undo us all. But I was wrong.

I crawl backwards, feel my way to the drawer and prise it open. Then I creep one hand around inside, forcing myself to be careful even though I can still hear those awful gurgling noises. I want to call out to my sister – *I'm here, I love you, hold on* – but the only advantage I have is the element of surprise. I dig under the tea towels and aprons to find the tub, cursing myself for hiding the knife so thoroughly. But then I hadn't wanted Poppy to come across it, hadn't known I would need it to *protect* her. My fingers locate the hard plastic, but I can't take off the lid one-handed, so I pull the whole tub out of the drawer and set it on the kitchen floor. The gurgling sound is growing quieter, and I don't know if it's the horror of that – of what it might mean – or if my hands aren't working properly, but I still can't get the lid off, the seal is too tight, so I try with my teeth, but that only aggravates the pain in my head, and I could scream with the frustration of it all. *Keep it together, Lara.* I crawl back to the edge of the sideboard, pushing the Tupperware along the floor in front of me. Then, gripping it in my left hand, I begin the arduous process of standing up, pressing my right hand against the sideboard for support. My legs are weak, and as soon as I raise my head a wave of dizziness hits and I'm forced to pause, to let my vision stabilise before continuing up, inch by inch, thigh muscles burning. When I'm finally upright, I put the tub on the counter and survey the scene.

It seems too terrible to be real, like I'm trapped in a hellscape of my own making. Hannah's lying on the table, limbs flung to the side and eyes bulging as Gareth leans over her, crushing all the air from her throat. Exactly as I saw in my dreams, except *he*'s here, strangling her, and her shirt is glaringly white.

I try the tub again, hooking my fingernails under the lid for leverage, and this time it opens, and with a rush of relief I seize the knife. But the lid clatters to the floor, and as I step forward, Gareth starts to turn and I have no choice but to run towards him, the pain so intense that I'm retching, half-blinded, focused only on reaching the yellow of his fleece.

He just has time to notice me, to let out a yell of rage, as I thrust the knife between his shoulder blades. It slices easily through his clothing, through his skin, through whatever lies beneath, and I reel away, gripping on to the edge of the table as yellow turns to red. He hangs still in the air, his mouth contorted, the knife protruding from his back, before falling heavily on to my sister and rolling sideways, hitting the floor with a sickening thump.

My sister's shirt is no longer white. She is soaked in Gareth's blood and I am too, or maybe it's mine – my fingers are slickly wet. I need to check if Hannah's breathing, need to ring for medical help, but I don't have a phone and I'm done, I'm spent; there's nothing left.

So I slump on to the table and find my sister's hand. Hold it and let the rest of the world slip away.

THREE YEARS LATER

HANNAH

Poppy is tearing open presents at a rapid rate, squealing with delight at the gifts inside. She's just opened one from Jackie, a headband with *7 today* formed from big fluffy letters. 'Thanks, Auntie Jackie!' she says, placing it on her head immediately. 'It matches my badge!'

'You're welcome,' says Jackie, who is watching from the sofa with Mum. 'That's only a little something. There's another couple of presents from me too.'

As Poppy continues unwrapping, I look around the room. Max is watching on from Dad's old armchair and Lara is kneeling on the floor beside her daughter, helping her with difficult pieces of sticky tape. And standing by the window is Steve – the newest addition to our group. He and Lara have been dating for nearly two years now, and he seems like a genuinely good man: kind, dependable, practical. Although I still find myself watching him for signs of a hidden persona: eyes that conceal treachery, or a hand that stows hate.

If I'm honest – and I'm very much trying to be, having learned first-hand the damage wrought by misunderstandings and duplicity – I've struggled to trust men since the whole Chris–Gareth debacle. I often second-guess their motives or see red flags that aren't there. I've suffered from flashbacks too; I can be engaged in a totally ordinary task, like washing the dishes, or doing the laundry, when my breath becomes short and my vision narrows as I relive the sensation of hands around my neck. If this happens, I have to stop what I'm doing and ring my sister, breathe long and slow while she talks me out of my panic, reminding me in cool, soft tones that Gareth is no longer with us.

He was already dead when the ambulance arrived. They found him lying on the dining room floor, soaked in blood with the knife still in his back. Lara, meanwhile, was in a 'critical state', as a result of severe blood loss from her head wound, and I wasn't in a great way either – confused and scared, barely able to speak – although I don't remember this, nor the journey to hospital which followed. I've since learned that memory loss is common for victims of non-fatal strangulation, because of the oxygen deprivation involved. As are flashbacks, for that matter, with several victims going on to develop symptoms of PTSD.

I've had therapy to talk through what happened, to try to make sense of it. The worst part of the last three years was having to actively revisit the horror at Lara's trial, having to explain my fear when Gareth stormed up the stairs into the attic and threw my phone out of the window – how trapped I felt, how vulnerable and powerless, unable to defend myself or my four-year-old niece. I struggled to communicate with my therapist during the trial because I felt trapped all over again, and stupid too, so stupid, because how could I not have known that Chris was a charlatan, intent only on my family's destruction?

But I'm slowly beginning to accept it wasn't my fault, that some people are highly skilled at deceiving others. At playing on human nature and exploiting vulnerabilities. In my case, I was young and on my own in a foreign country and, following Dad's death, my ties to my family were relatively weak. Moreover, I believed I was inferior to Lara in every way – that she was more intelligent, more beautiful, more *loved* – and so for an attractive man to come along and admire me so completely on my own terms – to find me witty and clever and worship every inch of my body – well, it's not surprising I was drawn in. He threw out his hook with perfect timing and merciless accuracy.

Poppy is opening my present now: an art kit which comes in its own carrycase, with two layers of colouring pencils, felt tips and crayons. Her eyes grow wide as she sees it, and wider still when Lara opens the clasp to reveal its contents. 'It's amazing!' she gasps, and I try not to cry as she runs over to hug me. I've been getting better at crying less over the last few months, but my niece's continued ability to experience pure, all-encompassing joy, after everything that's happened, can still pierce my hardened heart.

Her recovery from our week in the Peak District was far smoother than mine. Which perhaps isn't surprising, given her age, although I like to think I deserve some credit for keeping her away from the horrors that lay in that kitchen. She waited outside by the car, as I had instructed, which means she never saw Lara with her head smashed in, nor me lying on the table, eyes bulging through lack of oxygen. And it also means she never saw her dead father, face down on the floor, bleeding into the sisal mat. She just saw the car, followed by Mum, Jackie and Max, who had returned after Lara ran off down the hill. And then she saw the ambulance which, in fact, forms her overriding memory of the day: when, nearly a year later, a teacher asked her to draw a countryside scene, she drew a grey cottage, with an ambulance driving towards it, and a pile of conkers on the doorstep.

One of the best aspects of being back in the UK is how much more I see Poppy: she comes over to mine every Wednesday night, while Lara's at her pharmacology class. We have dinner together and play, before she goes to sleep on an air mattress in my room. She can be a bit wild sometimes – charging around naked when she's supposed to be quietening down – but she's also hysterically funny.

I love her stories about the other children at school: how Tommy picks his nose when the teacher's back is turned and Beatrice thinks cheese is made from eggs. And I love the way her mind can segue so rapidly from the serious to the surreal – from climate change to the colours seen by seahorses, or from poverty in the favelas to a cartoon squirrel called Bertie.

I see much more of Lara now too. Ever since that terrible tumbleweed of revelations and violence in the Peak District, there's been a desire to make up for lost time. It hasn't been an entirely straightforward process – what with her guilt over my injuries and the need to unpick our miscommunication across the years – but we're getting there. We're at the family home in Cambridgeshire today, but at weekends I'll often make a roast for Lara and Poppy at my flat in London. Sometimes Mum visits too, to help with the cooking; we sing along to the radio together as we chop and stir, roast and baste. In between songs, she likes to ask how things are, and by 'things' I know she means my mental state, so I try to provide an upbeat summary of the latest developments, while not letting the vegetables boil dry. In turn, I ask about the dating app she and Jackie have recently joined, which seems to involve the two of them laughing wildly at a computer screen rather than going on any actual dates.

My sister leads us outside to the garden now, where Max's present for Poppy awaits. A shiny red BMX. My eyes water as my niece hollers with joy and leaps straight into the saddle, and I become properly teary when Steve runs forward to balance her. As the two of them set off across the lawn I realise that, for all my trust issues, I *do* trust Steve. I won't become complacent about it – I'll keep checking my instincts and checking them again – but he seems like the real deal. Unassuming and unflappable – a force for good in our family.

Certainly, there is a lot of love in this garden today. As Poppy pedals faster, shouting with glee, Lara walks across to me, takes my hand and squeezes it. I turn to her and smile through my tears.

I think we're going to be okay.

LARA

Poppy is beside herself with happiness to have her own bike at last, and is getting to grips with how to balance. Which feels like a metaphor for her life. Her attitude over the last three years has been nothing short of remarkable: the way she's been willing to ask questions, and to cry when upset, but to otherwise accept her lot. She's been matter-of-fact with her school friends about what happened to her dad, saying things like, 'He tried to hurt Mummy and Auntie Hannah, so they had to stop him.' And, in relation to the trial: 'The police had to ask lots of questions, because he was young when he died.' I keep waiting for the trauma of it all to start messing with her brain, and perhaps one day it will, but for now she seems largely unscathed, and for that I am truly grateful.

Jogging behind Poppy on her bike is Steve, our saviour in more ways than one. I was in no way looking for a relationship when he came back into our lives, but people say that's when it happens, when you're not looking, and certainly that's how it was for me. He'd decided not to renew his contract at Le Bellevue for the winter season and, upon returning to the UK, had rung me, only to discover I was in hospital with a serious head wound. He drove up to see me straightaway.

His first visit was on a wintry afternoon, when we conversed so easily that three hours elapsed without my noticing, the sky falling dark as we talked. When he came back the next day, we talked for even longer. And then, once I was out of hospital, we met for walks and low-key outings: to parks and museums, cafés and shops, our companionship so straightforward that I don't remember questioning it. I certainly didn't ponder if it was a good idea, or could lead to a relationship; weirdly, I didn't even think about the possibility of a relationship until one day, by the duck pond in the local park, I turned and kissed him and thought *of course*. And we've been together ever since. I've gone to see him at the hotel he now runs in Hampshire, and he's accompanied me to weddings and my trial, and it's been an unusual start to a relationship, for sure, but a surprisingly drama-free one. And that's not to say he's perfect – he often zones out of conversations that don't interest him and he has terrible taste in music, with a penchant for nineties boy bands – but after Gareth's scheming and controlling, being around him feels joyful and uncomplicated.

Although everything feels joyful and uncomplicated today. Watching Steve and Poppy wobble round the garden are Mum, Jackie and Max: three people who will always have my back. They were nothing but supportive in the period after Gareth's death, coming round to check on me with pre-cooked dinners and bags of books, taking Poppy off to the park so that I could rest, and undertaking practical jobs around the house, like fixing the lopsided door and unblocking the drain. Breathtakingly generous with their time, money and energy, and with their capacity for forgiveness. Never holding my past mistakes against me, even when I finally explained everything that happened in France. Mum cried her eyes out when I told her, said I should have 'said something earlier', but there was no anger in her words or demeanour, just desperate love and some too-tight hugs which earned her a ticking-off from the nurse.

I squeeze Hannah's hand now, note the tears still running down her cheeks. She assures me they're tears of happiness, but I can't entirely shake my concern. Ever since Gareth, she's been much more emotional, and there's a new wariness about her too: in the way she moves, and in the stiffness of her hand against mine. I'll always feel guilty for bringing his evil to her door. Yet, at the same time, I'm so proud of her, and thankful, because she stood up to him and protected Poppy at great cost to herself. She was – *is* – stronger than I'll ever be, and she's growing stronger all the time, filled with a new sense of purpose from shutting down her blog and taking a job with a domestic violence charity. She runs their social media campaigns so brilliantly, so powerfully, that I know she'll effect change; that she'll take the horror of what happened to us and use it to promote healing and reach a place of peace.

I just need to help her get there. 'Would you mind giving me a hand with the cake?'

She nods and we head into Mum's kitchen together, uncover Jackie's Victoria sponge. As Hannah transfers it on to a large chopping board, I fetch some candles and a box of matches. And then I calmly pick up a knife.

Since killing Gareth, I've enjoyed a blank, restful sleep, no longer troubled by horrific dreams about knives and blood. When I think back on the events in the Peak District, I sometimes wonder if they only came about because I was so fixated on what I'd 'seen' in my dreams. Certainly, it was my fault that Hannah was at Grove Cottage when Gareth arrived, instead of on a walk with the rest of us, and it was also my fault that he turned up in the first place. If I'd held back from sending that email to Olivia, or stayed away from Mum's birthday celebrations, or done a myriad of other things, he would have had no reason to be there that day.

There are smaller details too. Hannah's white shirt, which she wouldn't have worn that afternoon if I hadn't hidden it, and Max's chef's knife, which was only accessible because I secreted it in the kitchen drawer. And Hannah might never have thought to hang her dress across the window if I hadn't harped on about orange light all week.

And then there's the killing itself. If I hadn't dreamed of a knife, would I have even thought to plunge one deep into Gareth's back? Or would I have just lain on the floor as he strangled my sister?

Whatever the truth, I can only be relieved things worked out as they did. As Hannah and I return to the garden – me carrying the cake, and she sheltering the lit candles with scooped hands – I feel almost overwhelmingly lucky.

No longer can I tell what lies in store for us, what ups and downs might await. Or what bumps in the road we might ourselves create.

But I'm excited to find out.

ACKNOWLEDGEMENTS

Thanks to my agent, Sarah, who has supported me every step of the way in getting this, my second book, out into the world. Sarah, your writing suggestions are always spot-on, and I'm so grateful for the time you take to answer my questions and the help you provide in understanding and navigating the world of publishing. Likewise, a massive thank you to Vic and Hannah, for your superb editorial advice, your kindness and support, and for all the work you've done (and continue to do) to bring everything together so smoothly.

Also on the editorial side, a huge thank you to Victoria, who helped me to take my story to a whole new level, particularly in terms of bringing out the characters' emotions and making them more real on the page. Victoria, I thoroughly enjoyed, and learned so much from, working with you, and feel very lucky to have benefited from your expertise and insights.

I also feel lucky to have benefited from the expertise of the wider Lake Union and Amazon teams. Thank you once again, Gemma, for your eye for detail, and Swati for getting my work into a polished state. Thank you, Will, for the beautiful cover, and to Rebecca for overseeing the marketing and publicity for both *The Unforeseen* and my first book, *The Surfacing*. I am so impressed by, and grateful for, the data-driven and long-term approach to getting these stories into readers' hands.

I wrote the acknowledgements for my first novel before it was published and, as such, would like to take this opportunity to thank everyone who supported the novel (and me) over the publication period. Particular thanks are owed to Claire McGowan, the brilliant, million-selling author who took the time to provide a blurb – Claire, your generosity is very much appreciated. And to Elizabeth Knowelden, who did such an incredible job of narrating the audiobook, and Jonathan and the rest of the Brilliance Publishing team.

And unending thanks to my local book group, who know exactly when to ply me with reading material, and when to ply me with wine, and who threw a beautifully themed launch celebration for me. I am so touched by your kindness and grateful to have you as my friends. Similarly with the (mis-named) Cottage group – I love going away with you and your children each year, and will treasure all the photos of you and your pets with multiple copies of *The Surfacing* . . .

Ongoing thanks are owed to the Lucy Cavendish Fiction Prize organisers and fellow alumni – who are such a wonderfully talented and supportive community – and to my online writers' group, another fantastic and talented bunch. Thanks for all the writerly chat and workshopping, and long may it continue.

And, of course, thank you to all the readers! I am so grateful to anyone who has taken a chance on my books, and particularly those who have taken the time to rate or review them. Reading positive reviews is a real thrill, and reading less positive reviews is helpful in thinking about how I can improve; both make the world of difference.

Thank you to my dad, who must have walked every last inch of the Peak District, and has been invaluable in checking my Peak District references. Any factual errors are therefore his. (Only joking but, in all seriousness, Dad, thank you for raising us, and for doing so in such a beautiful area of the country).

And thanks to the rest of my family for putting up with my writerly ways, for championing my books in the wider world, and for all the love and laughter. To my husband: thank you for making this possible. And to my children: I'm glad you discovered the genius that is *Hamilton*, although your endless singing of it over the last year means it's perpetually in my brain. On which note: I'll try not to write like I'm running out of time. But please continue to blow us all away.

ABOUT THE AUTHOR

Photo © 2022 Lisa Jeffries Photography

Born in Washington DC and raised in Derbyshire and Oxfordshire in the UK, Claire studied at Cambridge University and LSE before working for many years as an economist. The quiet of lockdown provided an opportunity to rekindle her passion for creative writing. This is her second novel. Her first, *The Surfacing*, was published in 2025.

When not cold-water swimming or planning her next overseas adventure, Claire is partial to lots of coffee and a good cryptic crossword. She lives in Bedfordshire with her husband and two children.

Follow the Author on Amazon

If you enjoyed this book, follow Claire Ackroyd on Amazon to be notified when the author releases a new book!
To do this, please follow these instructions:

Desktop:

1) Search for the author's name on Amazon or in the Amazon App.
2) Click on the author's name to arrive on their Amazon page.
3) Click the 'Follow' button.

Mobile and Tablet:

1) Search for the author's name on Amazon or in the Amazon App.
2) Click on one of the author's books.
3) Click on the author's name to arrive on their Amazon page.
4) Click the 'Follow' button.

Kindle eReader and Kindle App:

If you enjoyed this book on a Kindle eReader or in the Kindle App, you will find the author 'Follow' button after the last page.